STEEL
Beauty
ALEX AND MAGNOLIA
BOOK ONE

ALSO BY GEORGIA CATES

BEAUTY FROM PAIN
BEAUTY FROM SURRENDER
BEAUTY FROM LOVE
STEEL BEAUTY
AMERICAN BEAUTY
BELOVED BEAUTY

DEAR AGONY

INDULGE

SWEET TORMENT
SWEET AGONY
SWEET MUSIC

THE SOUL ALWAYS REMEMBERS
THE SOUL NEVER FORGETS

BOHEMIAN GIRL
NEIGHBOR GIRL
INTERN GIRL

EIGHTY-ONE NIGHTS
BEAUTIFUL EVER AFTER

A NECESSARY SIN
THE NEXT SIN
ONE LAST SIN
ENDURANCE
UNINTENDED
REDEMPTION

WAITING FOR MY QUEEN

GOING UNDER
SHALLOW

BLOOD OF ANTEROS
BLOOD JEWEL
BLOOD DOLL

A BEAUTY SERIES NOVEL

Beauty STEEL

ALEX AND MAGNOLIA
BOOK ONE

GEORGIA CATES

www.georgiacates.com

Editing Services provided by Lisa Aurello

Cover Design by Swoony Cover Designs | swoonycoverdesigns@gmail.com

Special Edition Print ISBN: 978-1-948113-79-3

"I am half agony, half hope."
— *Jane Austen, Persuasion*

Chapter 1

Magnolia Steel

"FIRST OF ALL, I'M NOT LOOKING FOR A MAN. SO LET'S START there."

Joy—my coworker and hopeless romantic who fancies herself a matchmaker—leans back in her chair. She eyes me like I've said the most absurd thing she's ever heard. "Not looking for a man? Magnolia, that's like saying you don't want sunshine in your life."

I fold my arms across my chest. "Sunshine? Puh-lease. Men are not sunshine. They're more like passing clouds—here one minute, gone the next. Some of them are full-on thunderstorms, leaving nothing but chaos and destruction in their wake. Thanks, but I can live without that kind of *sunshine* in my life."

Joy takes out her phone and turns the screen toward me, displaying a picture. "My brother is perfect for you. He's tall, handsome, successful, and he has hair. Not just hair—*magnificent* hair. Do you realize how many men in this world are bald? Ethan is as rare as rocking-horse manure."

Not every woman's out here building a dream man from a checklist. Looks aren't everything—God knows some of the best-looking men have taught me the hardest lessons. Great hair won't hold you when you're falling apart. A sharp jawline doesn't make you feel safe. And charming smiles? Those fade fast when the truth comes out. Some of us have learned to want more. A man who listens. Who shows up. Who stays when it's hard, not just when it's easy.

"You compared your brother to manure."

"Fitting since he can be a little shit sometimes. But otherwise, he's great. You'd love him."

I glance at the photo. Ethan isn't fugly—in fact, he's good-looking —but he's a little too pretty. He looks like he spends more time on his hair than I spend on mine.

"Yeah, well, I'm sure Ethan is fantastic, as is his hair, but I'm not in the market for a man."

Violet jumps into the conversation with a smirk. "Unless he's Dak Prescott. In that case, she'd drop everything and start planning their football-themed wedding."

I let out a dreamy sigh. "I mean, why wouldn't I? The man is perfection wrapped in a football jersey. And let's be honest, I'd make the perfect Mrs. Prescott."

Joy laughs, undeterred. "Unless Dak shows up at the front desk asking for you, I'd say my brother still has a shot."

I shake my head though a smile tugs at my lips. "I'm happy biding my time until Dak realizes I'm his soulmate."

Joy raises a brow. "You know my brother's a private chef, right? He could cook gourmet dinners for you every night."

I stop in my tracks; the idea of perfectly prepared meals every day is tempting. A plate of something fresh—straight from the farmer's market—has a certain appeal.

"Just think of the roasted vegetables fresh from his private garden." Joy winks, aware of my weakness for anything fresh and unprocessed, clearly trying to use it to her advantage.

I click my tongue, smirking. "You sneaky little vegetable pusher."

Joy's lips curl into a devious smile. "Well, you are a vegetable harlot. All it takes is a good-looking carrot, and you're ready to commit."

I laugh. "Hey, I have standards. It's only the finest carrots for me."

Before Joy can come back with another reason I should drop everything and date her brother, Gabby's voice cuts through the office buzz, pulling everyone's attention toward her. "All right, everyone, conference room in five."

"Saved by the boss," I say to Violet, keeping my words between us as I stand up and grab my notebook.

Violet smirks and leans in closer. "Makes you wonder why Joy's so eager to play matchmaker for her brother if he's truly as rare as rocking-horse manure."

I grin, whispering back, "Probably because she only got the manure part right."

We file into the conference room where Gabby stands. "All right, let's settle in, everyone."

Elijah catches my eye from across the room, his grin wide. He leans back in his chair, tossing a wink my way. I give him a polite nod though my fingers tighten around the edge of my notebook. I focus elsewhere, pretending not to notice when his gaze lingers a little too long.

Gabby clears her throat, and the room gradually quiets. Her gaze sweeps over us, and she gives a small, proud smile. "As all of you know, Soul Sync started as a crazy idea in my living room and has grown into something bigger than I ever imagined. We didn't want to be just another matchmaking service. Our goal has always been to help people find meaningful connections, not swipe-right hookups."

I'm reminded of my passion for this job as Gabby speaks. Soul Sync isn't just my job; it's my home. I can't see myself doing this kind of work anywhere else.

"I know I've asked a lot from each of you along the way, but look at us now. Soul Sync is thriving, and that's thanks to your hard work and dedication."

She pauses, looking around the room, her eyes softening. "You've all helped build something truly special here—an elite service where we prioritize genuine, soul-deep partnerships over superficial nonsense. And trust me, that's rare these days."

Rare as rocking-horse manure.

Gabby continues, "We're not just matching people. We're changing people's lives, and that's because of you."

She's right. Finding something real in a world of shallow connections and fleeting encounters is like stumbling upon a rose among briars.

The irony isn't lost on me, though—working for a company dedicated to helping people find deep connections while I've only ever had fleeting, surface-level relationships myself.

The mood lightens as she cracks a grin. "And if I can survive launching a company fueled mostly by caffeine and blind optimism, I think we can handle whatever comes next."

A ripple of nods and smiles spreads through the room as her words sink in.

"Speaking of what comes next... as you all know, Soul Sync has been testing the waters internationally. We've received news that our beta test in Australia is successful. We've officially landed clients down under."

A round of applause erupts, and I clap along. Soul Sync's expansion to Australia is huge, and the excitement in the room is undeniable.

Gabby beams, waiting for the applause to die down. "This is a huge win for us, but the real challenge starts now—delivering our services on the other side of the world. We're talking about building a sister company from the ground up: designing entire matchmaking sets, coordinating events, and managing client experiences in a brand-new market."

She pauses, her gaze sweeping the room. "I need volunteers for a three-month assignment in Sydney. This is more than a job. It's an opportunity to help shape the future of Soul Sync. Please understand—you will be leaving home and living out of hotels while you're building something new from the ground up. Your responsibilities will include overseeing installations, working directly with clients, and ensuring that every detail runs smoothly. This is your chance to be part of something truly monumental."

I glance around, noticing the hesitant faces. This is a big ask—three months away from home, working in a high-pressure environment. But for me, it feels like exactly what I need. I love a challenge, and the thought of leading set designs in an entirely new market has my mind racing with possibilities. A new city, new people, a chance to prove myself and focus on my work—no distractions.

And no matchmaking or blind dates I didn't ask for.

But best of all? No constant feedback from Macy. She's excellent at what she does, but we always have to collaborate on set designs, which means compromises. I wonder what it would be like to have full creative control, to bring my ideas to life without running every decision by someone else. This Sydney assignment could be my chance to do precisely that.

Besides, Sydney? Who wouldn't jump at the chance to work there for three months?

Gabby continues, "I know some of you have families or commitments that might make this difficult, and that's completely understandable. We need people who are flexible and ready to take on the challenge."

Without hesitating, I raise my hand. "I'll go. The other set designers are married, and I'm single. This is the perfect opportunity for me."

Gabby smiles. "Thank you, Magnolia. I knew I could count on you."

From the corner of my eye, I catch Macy's reaction. Her lips press into a tight line, and she adjusts her posture, crossing her arms. The slight narrowing of her eyes is all I need to see to know that she's not thrilled about me stepping up for this. She's never liked it when I get a bit of the spotlight.

I feel Violet's eyes on me, and when I turn, she's smiling, her raised eyebrow saying it all—she's proud of me, maybe even a little impressed. The look says, *I knew you had it in you.*

I wish she could come too. Violet would be the perfect person to share this adventure with—her sharp wit and calm presence would make any high-pressure situation bearable. But it's not possible. Not with her mom battling cancer. Violet wouldn't leave her mom's side for anything, not even an opportunity like this. She's the kind of daughter who'd drop everything to be there for her family, and honestly, I admire her for it.

Elijah's hand shoots up next. "I'll go too. Magnolia and I work well together."

Great. Just what I need.

Elijah has been hovering around me for months, always finding excuses to stick close—offering to carry materials, hanging around after meetings, and dropping hints about grabbing dinner. It's obvious what he wants, but I'm not interested. Not in him, and certainly not like that. He tries too hard, always grinning like he's auditioning for a toothpaste commercial.

Don't get me wrong. Elijah's nice, but his persistence is smothering. I feel like I need a personal bubble to breathe around him.

Gabby nods. "Thank you, Elijah. Your skills will be a valuable addition to the team. We are going to need all the help we can get."

Sophie and Whitney, who handle client experience, raise their hands next.

They're both sharp, hardworking, and—like me—single. If anyone could make this trip productive and fun, it's them. We've always worked well together, and I'm already imagining the late-night brainstorming sessions turning into laughter-filled conversations over a bottle of wine. Or three. There's a sense of camaraderie among us, an unspoken understanding that we've got each other's backs.

Soul Sync has its pressures, but the women here—mostly—are a team. There's no cattiness, no competition—only support. I'm hopeful this assignment will be a career boost and a chance to make some unforgettable memories with Sophie and Whitney along the way.

Gabby's gaze settles on me. "Magnolia, you'll be leading the set designs, but would you consider also serving as a social coordinator with Rebecca's help? She'll be assisting remotely from the U.S. You would have her support, even from a distance."

This will definitely be different. Gabby can't send an entire team, so with a smaller crew, it's crucial for everyone to step up and take on multiple responsibilities—even those outside their comfort zones. I'm used to designing sets, not managing the social flow of events, but this is a huge opportunity, and flexibility is part of the deal. We'll all have to juggle roles we didn't necessarily sign up for if this is to succeed.

I nod. "I'd be happy to."

Rebecca leans forward with a reassuring smile. "Don't worry, Magnolia. I've got your back with the social coordination stuff. We'll make sure everything runs smoothly. Think of it as your chance to flex some new skills." She finishes with a wink.

Gabby smiles. "That's what I love to hear. It'll take some creative problem-solving, but I know we'll make it work."

A few more hands go up as Gabby thanks each new volunteer with her usual enthusiasm. The team is starting to take shape, and the room hums with excitement as others begin murmuring about the possibilities ahead.

The meeting wraps up with more applause, and as we head out, Violet nudges me with a smirk. "Elijah volunteering? Guess he's still convinced he's got a shot with you, huh?"

I cut my eyes toward Elijah and notice him looking pleased with himself. "Hell has a better shot at hosting a snowball-throwing convention."

Violet leans in, her words dropping to a whisper. "Maybe you should send him a fruit basket. Like a 'thanks, but no thanks' gesture."

Some men don't understand that when a woman says she's not

interested, she means it. They think persistence is romantic when it's really just fucking exhausting.

"With my luck, he'd think it was an invitation to a picnic. You know me, Vi. I'm not looking for romance with him or anyone else. Sydney is about work and furthering my career. So the dude needs to chase someone else's... *fruit basket.*"

Chapter 2

Magnolia Steel

WHAT A BEAUTIFUL SPACE THIS HAS TURNED OUT TO be. Comfortable velvet seating, carefully selected artwork, and fresh flowers come together to provide a mix of comfort and elegance. Soft lighting gives the dating suite a warm and inviting feel. A simple divider separates the two areas, ensuring privacy while allowing for easy movement throughout the room.

I aim to make my clients feel completely at ease when they walk in. I believe I've accomplished that.

Looking around, the thought crosses my mind: Even I might be able to fall in love in a place like this. A quiet laugh escapes me as I shake my head. Who am I kidding? Love and I don't mix—like oil and water, best kept at a safe distance.

With only an hour left until the clients arrive for their first date, there's still work to be done on the female side. Elijah has been hanging around, offering help with every detail. He means well, but his presence is beginning to wear thin.

"Do you need help with the finishing touches?" he asks for what feels like the hundredth time as he hovers too close to the mood board I worked on all week.

I inhale deeply. "Thanks, but I've got it."

He doesn't budge. "Are you sure? Looks like you're cutting it close. I could grab something for you or move a few things around."

Stay calm, cool, collected. "Elijah, I really appreciate it. You've done a fantastic job here—seriously—but I need to finish up without distractions."

And if you step on my mood board, I swear I'll use it as a weapon to beat you to death.

Stylishly, of course.

He backs off, blissfully unaware of how close he's come to meeting his demise. "All right, I'll leave you to it then."

Yes, please step aside and let me do what I do best.

The silence settles over the room, and I feel like I can breathe for the first time. The tension disappears the second he's out the door.

I take a moment to really look at the space I've created. It's everything I hoped it would be—warm, calm, inviting. With no distractions pulling me away, I can finally take it all in, and yeah... I think I've nailed it.

Due to the strict privacy policy, we don't get many personal details about clients at Soul Sync. I have no idea what this client likes explicitly, but I've tailored the room based on the information gathered during the client interview in the vetting procedure: simplicity, elegance, and nothing too overwhelming. It's all about using the psychology of design to create a calming and approachable space without being too distracting.

And for once, I didn't have to compromise my design with Macy. The space is entirely mine, and it shows. I love it.

I smooth the fabric of the throw on the armchair and glance around. Perfection... almost. Just a few more adjustments.

I'm almost finished when I hear the door open on the other side of the suite. Whitney's words drift through, carrying the polished professionalism she reserves for clients. She's talking to someone—a man. My stomach drops for a second—did Elijah sneak back in? But then I hear it—a deep, distinct Australian accent. Definitely not Elijah.

My pulse quickens as it hits me—the male client. Early. *Very* early. And Whitney has already escorted him into the men's side of the suite while I'm still here not quite ready to leave.

"Oh fuck-a-duck," I say under my breath.

Of course he's early—because why wouldn't he be, right, when I need everything to be flawless? I've poured so much into this project, perfecting every detail to create the ideal atmosphere for the client. Normally, I'm ready on time, early even, but this time? No chance. Elijah has been hovering nonstop like a human speed bump slowing me down at every step.

"Take a seat and make yourself comfortable. Can I bring you a drink while you settle in?" Whitney's voice is smoother than a politician's promise. The oh-so-polished way she speaks to clients feels worlds apart from the girl who'll chug a beer with me after work.

Tonight, we're definitely grabbing beers bigger than our clients' egos, if that's possible. It's a tradition at this point—work hard, celebrate harder.

"Water would be great, thanks," the client says, his deep Australian accent carrying through the divider.

"Would you care for sparkling or spring?"

"Sparkling, please."

Sparkling, of course. Heaven forbid, he drinks something as lowly as tap water. I bet he's never had water from a lime-green garden hose that's been baking in the sun all summer long—water so hot you could steep tea in it. He'd probably keel over on the spot.

Just as I'm deciding how I'll make a stealthy exit, Sophie slips into the room, closing the door softly behind her. Her eyes widen in apology, and she tiptoes toward me, speaking in a whisper.

"Magnolia, I'm so sorry." Her eyes dart in the direction where the client is on the other side of the divider. "The male client arrived early."

I sigh, rubbing my temples. "Why didn't Whitney seat him in the waiting room?"

She winces slightly, her lips pressing together in a sheepish, apologetic way. "He requested to wait in the suite instead. Said he wanted a moment to settle into his surroundings."

Clients who come to Soul Sync expect everything to be tailored perfectly to their needs. It's what they're paying for, after all. And we're here to give them exactly that.

"Is he nervous?" I whisper, still trying to figure out how to finish up this side of the suite and make my getaway.

Sophie nods. "Very. He's doing his best to play it cool, but I can tell."

"It's fine. Not your fault." I brush it off with a wave of my hand, glancing around the suite. "I need to make a few final changes before I go."

Sophie nods in understanding and quietly slips out, leaving me alone to finish up. I make the final adjustments—smoothing a pillow here, adjusting the throw there—my mind already plotting the quickest way to make my escape.

I glance around one last time. The suite looks exactly how I envisioned it.

I give the room one final approving look, telling myself it's time to get out before anything else happens. And that's when the unmistakable chime of my phone cuts through the silence as I'm about to make my exit.

Ohhh, fuck-a-doodle-doo!

I dash toward my phone, fumbling to hit the silence button, but it's too late. The alert has already echoed through the room. Meanwhile, this morning's French toast does a somersault in my stomach, teasing whether it'll decide to stay put or make a grand exit.

My ringer is usually off, but with today's workload, I turned it on in case someone from work needed to reach me.

And of course, it's Elijah. My annoyance with him bubbles up again.

Before I can even process how to move forward in a professional manner, I hear the client's deep voice on the other side of the divider. "Hello?"

Phone in hand, all I can do is freeze. There's no avoiding it now. "Uh... hello," I manage, hoping he can't hear the awkwardness in my voice.

Silence stretches between us for a moment. "Are you... my, uh, date?" His words stumble slightly, the uncertainty noticeable.

A soft gasp escapes me. "Oh, umm... clients who've been paired with potential mates are called Soul Sync matches. Not dates. But no, I'm not yours. I'm the set designer. I was putting the final touches on this side of the room."

"*Soul Sync matches,*" he parrots, sounding intrigued.

Odd. The term is used repeatedly in their contracts.

"So, you're the person who designed the room I'm in?"

I nod, then realize he can't see through the divider. Wow. My brain cells are really thriving today. "Yes, it was me."

I imagine him glancing around, taking in every detail of the room. "The design is really nice. It feels like you knew exactly what I would like."

Yes! I pump my fist in a victorious motion. A quiet exhale escapes me, and for the first time, a bit of tension eases. I never hear client feedback about what I do, so knowing he actually likes it is a relief. And I'll admit, a little flattering. "Thank you. I'm given a brief summary about the client—nothing identifying, of course—and I design the space based on that information."

"You're very talented."

"Thank you." A small flush of pride warms me as his compliment sinks in.

He clears his throat softly. "I arrived a little early. I thought it would give me a moment to adjust to my surroundings before I'm thrown into a conversation with a complete stranger on the other side of a wall."

His words throw me for a loop. I've never considered the

possibility before—the nerves, the uncertainty. People who can afford Soul Sync's services always struck me as the type brimming with confidence, the kind who walk into a room and own it. But maybe, despite their wealth and status, they need a moment to steady themselves, too.

"I completely understand needing a moment to settle in. Is there anything I can adjust in the space to help you feel more comfortable next time?"

"The room feels homey so keep everything as it is. It's comfortable."

A surge of satisfaction swells in my chest. "That's always my goal. The idea is to make you feel at ease so you can focus on the conversations you'll be having with your match."

This man showed up early to calm his nerves, and here I am, jabbering away. He's not going to find peace with me hanging around, disrupting the atmosphere. "I'll step out so you can relax."

"Actually, could you stay for a little while longer? Talking to you is helping me get over my jitters."

Gabby's reminder to embrace new roles echoes in my mind. If a little conversation helps ease his nerves, then it's part of my job to step up. "Of course, I can stay and chat for a bit."

A deep breath escapes him, followed by a soft "whew," as if he's been holding it in all along. "Thanks. I'm really grateful."

"You're quite welcome."

Unsure of what to say next, I wait for him to speak, hoping he'll take the lead.

"So, what's your name?"

Naturally, asking my name is the first question. It's a simple way to ease into conversation, but this isn't exactly a normal situation. "At Soul Sync, we have a strict privacy policy to protect both our clients and employees, so I'm not able to share that information about myself."

"Understandable." A beat passes. "You really don't know who I am, do you?"

"I don't. To me, you're Julius Caesar, your assigned alias."

His laughter comes easily, the sound warm and amused. "My alias is *Julius Caesar*? Seriously?"

Amusement tugs at the corner of my mouth. "All our matched clients are assigned the names of an iconic couple. The husband of Soul Sync's creator is a huge history buff. It's kind of a nod to him."

"That's hilarious," he says with a chuckle. "I guess my attorney forgot to mention that little detail."

"Well, now you know, *Caesar*. But it should've been mentioned multiple times in the contract you most assuredly read." A bit of concern crosses my mind—how did he miss such a detail? It's a standard part of the Soul Sync agreement.

He brushes it off with a laugh. "I'm sure it was. Guess I skimmed a little too fast. So, if I'm Julius Caesar, that must mean my Soul Sync match is—?"

It really is comical, Gabby's system of assigning aliases to clients. "You guessed it. Cleopatra."

"Makes sense. Keeping it all historically accurate."

"Cleopatra was never his wife, but their relationship was significant enough to shape history—and cause plenty of drama along the way. It's part of the quirky charm here at Soul Sync."

"I can't help but notice that you sound American."

"Guilty as charged."

"Did you relocate to Australia, or are you here temporarily?"

"Just here the next three months while on assignment with Soul Sync."

Three months for now, but what happens to our Australian sister branch after that? Will Gabby hire people locally in Australia? Will she rotate the team every few months? No, that doesn't make sense. It's too costly to keep sending people back and forth. Surely, she'll hire locally and establish a team here once we're fully settled.

"Are you enjoying your time in the *land down under?*" His deep voice carries a playful rhythm, almost singing the words in the unmistakable style of *Men at Work*, mimicking the famous song I'm quite familiar with.

A surprised grin spreads across my face at his humorous impersonation, and I let out a small laugh. Who knew this guy with the jitters had that in him?

"I'd love to say yes, but I haven't had much time to get out and explore. It's been a whirlwind of work since I got here."

"That's too bad. Sydney is an amazing city with so much to see and do."

My research on Sydney has been extensive, but there's nothing like hearing suggestions from a local. "What should I do when I actually find some time?"

"For starters, you should definitely check out our beaches— Bondi, Coogee, Manly. They have some of the best surfing in the world."

The thought of surfing makes me cringe, and my body still cries out in protest at the idea of trying that again. "I love a good beach day, but it's a no for me on the surfing. I'm absolutely terrible at it. I spent more time wiping out and swallowing saltwater than actually standing on the board."

He chuckles. "Sounds like you haven't had the best teacher. With the right guidance, I bet you'd be riding waves in no time."

"You wouldn't say that if you saw me in action. I wiped out so spectacularly that even the hungriest sharks skedaddled." The memory of it is forever scorched in my brain—an epic disaster on water.

He gives a thoughtful "hmph," like he's turning it over in his mind. "Well, even if you're not surfing, watching the pros is something else. But you don't need to surf to enjoy the beaches—the views alone are incredible. And if you're into nature, the Blue Mountains are a must. Great hiking, stunning scenery. Definitely worth it."

"My to-do list is getting longer."

"You can't skip the Sydney Opera House. It's one of those places you've got to see while you're here. If you can, catch a show. They've got way more than opera—there's theater, concerts, all kinds of performances happening year-round."

I have eclectic taste in music, but opera? That's never been on my radar. Growing up the way I did, it wasn't exactly part of the landscape. "I had no idea they offered so much variety. I'll have to check it out."

"And if you're feeling adventurous, there's climbing the Sydney Harbour Bridge. Not that I've ever done it myself. Or ever will."

I hold in a laugh, unsure how he might react if I let it slip. "Sounds like someone is afraid of heights."

"Extreme heights and I aren't exactly on friendly terms."

There's something surprisingly endearing about this man openly admitting his fear. Most men would keep something like that to themselves unless absolutely necessary.

"I've got to be honest with you, miss. I don't really understand how talking to someone with a wall between us is supposed to help me find a wife."

His hesitation is understandable. This isn't the normal way of meeting someone, and I can't blame him for feeling unsure about it. "It's different, for certain, but that's the point. A lot of the work has already been done for you—things like weeding out incompatibles. The wall helps keep your identity safe, especially if you're well-known. It encourages more honest conversations. There's no danger of sharing your darkest secret and then seeing it splattered all over the internet the next day."

"I suppose you're right." His voice softens, calmer now. "This setup makes me feel safe—like I can actually talk to a woman for the first time in a long time." His words take me by surprise, and I'm not entirely sure what he means. Safe? What's made him feel unsafe before? I don't want to brush past it, but it's not my place to push him to share something so personal.

Instead, I aim to keep things light. "Look at you, already so comfortable talking to me. I bet you're kicked back in that cozy big chair with your feet up on the ottoman right now."

He lets out a low hum of amusement. "Fair call."

"And you're finding it easy to talk to me, right?"

"Yeah, I must admit that you're very easy to talk to. Your voice is... soothing. And I like your accent very much."

The tension in my body eases as the conversation flows with little to no effort. "I like your accent as well."

"You're in Australia. Everyone here has my accent. It's nothing special."

"It's special to me."

"You don't sound like a typical American. I've only heard something similar to it once—my mate married an American girl from Nashville, and your accent reminds me of hers."

"Nashville is only a few hours' drive from where I grew up in Mississippi. But I live on the East Coast now, in Charleston."

The moment *Charleston* leaves my mouth, I realize I've crossed a line. I've told him where I live—far more information than I should've shared with a client.

Great job, Magnolia. Way to stay professional.

Worry crosses my mind. What if he's a weirdo? Or worse, some kind of stalker? My thoughts spin for a second before I push them away. No, he seems fine. Plus, he lives on the other side of the world. He's not going to travel across the globe to stalk me.

"You know, I'm not sure what I'm even going to say when my match gets here. I mean, how do you start a conversation with someone when you can't see them?"

A smirk tugs at my lips because this guy doesn't even notice how naturally he's been talking to me. He's giving himself far too little credit. "We're total strangers who can't see each other, yet here we are, chatting like it's second nature. Trust me, when you meet the one chosen for you, it'll be even easier. You'll have so much in common the conversation will flow without a hitch."

"You're really easy to talk to, but we're discussing general things. I'm not sure I'd know what to say when it gets more personal." He hesitates for a second. "Would you... maybe practice with me? You know, go over the kind of questions she might expect to discuss? Just to help me break the ice."

Embrace new roles. Do whatever it takes to make clients feel comfortable. Gabby's words play on repeat in my mind.

It's our job to help them, after all. And if this will ease his nerves... "I'd be happy to help with a practice run. Let's start with something simple. How old are you, Caesar?"

"I still can't get over being called Julius Caesar." His words come with a hint of amusement before softening into something more casual. "I'm thirty-two. How about you?"

Thirty-two. So close to my age. I wonder how someone so young can afford the elite services of Soul Sync.

"I just turned thirty."

He lets out a small hmph. "I thought you'd be older".

Feigning offense, with extra emphasis on each word, I say, *"You thought I'd be older?* Why's that?"

He lets out a quiet chuckle as if trying to cover it up. "You sound very wise and mature for thirty."

"Let's just say I've been through the school of hard knocks. Graduated with honors. Honestly, I could've taught a few classes there."

Wounds turn into scars and scars make you tough.

"What about your family? Parents, siblings?" he asks.

There are too many branches on my family tree for me to keep track of, let alone explain.

"I'm an only child... and also not. It's complicated. It would take a decade to explain, and even then, no one sane would understand."

"That sounds like an interesting tale." He doesn't push for more, and for that, I'm grateful.

"I come from a big family. Five siblings. Our parents are still married."

"Wow. You grew up with eight people in your household? That sounds... chaotic." And maybe even lovely under the right circumstances.

"It's extremely chaotic when four of the six kids are boys. Life at our house was never dull."

I smile at that, imagining the lively chaos. "Well, you already know what I do for work, but what about you? Are you able to tell me or would it give away too much?"

"I'm in the hotel industry. Family business. I'll spare you the dull details. Trust me, they're boring."

Considering he can afford Soul Sync's services, I have no doubt he's either a hotel heir or some kind of mogul.

Our conversation continues, easy and natural, like we didn't just meet. And I catch myself laughing more than I expected. There's something surprisingly comfortable about talking to him like this.

Our conversation flows effortlessly—more laughter, more shared stories. Time slips by, and I'm fairly certain I already know Julius Caesar better than I ever knew the last guy I dated. He's completely ready to meet his match, and honestly, the lucky woman who matched with him is going to adore him.

Finally, Sophie pokes her head in again, this time giving me the signal that the female client has arrived.

"Well, looks like it's time for me to go," I say, rising to my feet and straightening my clothes. "Your Soul Sync match is here."

"Oh," he says, a hint of hesitation coloring his words. "I enjoyed talking to you, *Charleston*. Thanks for sticking around and helping calm my nerves."

"I enjoyed our talk too."

"Thanks for the practice run. And hey, maybe I'll bump into you again," he says with a touch of humor.

It's unlikely, considering we don't know each other's names or what the other looks like. "Good luck with your match, Caesar. I'm sure it'll go well," I say, offering a final smile he can't see. Then, without looking back, I slip quietly out of the suite.

Just as I'm about to pull the door shut, his voice echoes behind me, "If you bump into Cleopatra out there, let her know Caesar is keeping the empire in order in here."

I bite down on my laughter, rolling my eyes as I walk down the hallway. Well, at least he has a sense of humor about all this.

Oh, Cleopatra, you're in for a real treat with this one.

Chapter 3

Alex Sebring

THE SKY SHIFTS TO SHADES OF LAVENDER AND ORANGE, THE SUN dipping toward the horizon in a slow, deliberate goodbye. Once, moments like this would have slipped past unnoticed, buried under the constant rush of practice schedules, game-day pressures, and the relentless pursuit of perfection. Back then, life was a blur of noise and motion, leaving no space for quiet reflection or something as simple as watching daylight fade into purple and gold. Now, with time stretching wide and unhurried, the stillness feels unfamiliar—like rediscovering a part of myself I didn't know I'd lost.

I take a slow sip of wine. As expected, it's excellent—Jack McLachlan's wine never misses. With vineyards across Australia and New Zealand, the man knows the grape. His bottles are top-tier, the kind that makes you pause and appreciate the moment.

Our dads have been friends for as long as I can remember, so Jack and I have always known each other. We weren't close growing up—him being ten years older and me just the kid tagging along. But that changed about five years ago. Maybe I'd finally grown up, or maybe Jack started seeing me as more than a kid. Either way, he's become one of the few people I can always count on.

Jack flips the shanks on the grill, the scent of rosemary and sizzling lamb filling the air. "How's the shiraz?"

"Excellent as always," I say before taking another sip.

He nods, satisfied, and turns back to the grill. "Glad you approve."

This is what life should feel like—good food, great wine, and even better company.

The McLachlan kids are splashing in the nearby pool, their laughter and shouting rising above the soft hum of music. Four of them—healthy and full of life.

The youngest, a five-year-old girl, paddles in the shallow end with floaties on her arms, squealing whenever one of the twins splashes her.

Sitting off to the side with her feet dipping in the water is the oldest—a girl who just turned nine. Her brown hair, the exact shade as Laurelyn's, clings to her face in damp strands. She hums softly along with the music playing in the background, lost in her own little world, her grin a replica of Jack's.

The twin boys, identical in every way, wrestle each other on a pool float, their boisterous energy sending waves in every direction.

And then there's Laurelyn. She's one of those people who makes you feel at ease the moment you're around her. And when she sings, it's something else entirely. Simply special.

Jack has what most people only dream of—a loving wife, great kids, a *genuinely* happy life, not just a show for others to admire. Watching them, I realize how much I want that too—a family of my own, a place to belong.

Jack once shared the story of how he and Laurelyn met, and it's stuck with me ever since. Their introduction was far from ordinary— messy, complicated, and nothing like a typical romance. It didn't follow any of the usual rules, but somehow, it worked. Against all odds, Jack found the person who is perfect for him.

And if that could work for them, then maybe my unconventional route isn't so crazy after all. If meeting through a matchmaking service can lead me to the kind of connection Jack and Laurelyn have, it'll all be worth it.

Jack's phone buzzes on the table between us, pulling me out of my thoughts. He glances down at the screen, raising a brow. "It's Chloe."

He wipes his hands on a towel, tossing it over his shoulder with a casual flick. "Sorry, mate. I've gotta take this one."

"All good here," I give him a nod. "Go on and take the call."

Chloe and I go way back. She's closer to my age, and we grew up together. She and Jack have their special sibling bond, but we always got on differently. No sparks, just good mates. Even when I was off playing rugby, we managed to stay in touch.

She's done a ripper job for herself. A few years back, she opened a restaurant. It took off quick smart, and now it's one of the top spots in Sydney. She made the leap from chef to restaurant owner look easy.

But that's the McLachlan family for you. Whatever they touch turns to gold. Jack's got his vineyards. Chloe's got her restaurants. Evan started out selling houses, only to build himself a booming property development business. Success is in their blood. If anyone's got grit, talent, and the drive to come out on top, it's the McLachlans.

From where I'm sitting, I overhear his side of the call. Jack, usually so calm and easygoing, speaks with a sharp edge that cuts through the evening air.

"Tell that bastard I'm taking my vineyard back," Jack says, pacing slowly near the grill.

There's a pause, the faint murmur of Chloe's voice coming through the receiver. Jack listens, jaw tight. "There's no way in hell he's keeping a McLachlan vineyard after what he did to you."

He keeps talking, his words measured and deliberate, but the simmering anger beneath is impossible to miss. I don't catch every word, but it's clear that whatever Ben did has Jack fuming.

The call goes on for a few minutes. When Jack finally hangs up, he tosses his phone on the table. "I guess you know Chloe filed for divorce from Ben."

"Yeah," I say, leaning back in my chair. "Sorry to hear it."

"I'm sorry for my sister's pain, but I'm not sorry to see him gone." Jack's lips set in a hard line. "I always knew he'd break her heart, but I didn't think she'd have to waste ten bloody years on him first."

I don't know the full story yet, but I've heard enough to know Ben did something bad—really bad. Neither Chloe nor Jack have shared the details, but knowing Ben, I can imagine. Whatever it was, Chloe deserves better.

Laurelyn steps onto the porch, wiping her hands on a tea towel. "The poor thing is struggling with the separation. She really loved Ben."

Jack shakes his head, his frustration evident. "I never liked him. Told her from the start he'd hurt her—it was only a matter of time."

Laurelyn gives him a look—the kind only a wife can get away with. "Yes, Jack Henry, we all know how you feel about Ben. You've been very clear about that from the beginning."

Jack doesn't flinch. "And I was right."

Laurelyn sighs, her face pinching with a mix of sadness and frustration. "Chloe's strong. She isn't okay right now, but she will be again one day. She needs time to mourn the loss of what she had with Ben."

Jack huffs a humorless laugh. "You mean what she *thought* she had with him. She never had anything real with that prick."

Laurelyn is right—Chloe will come out of this stronger, but it's going to take time. It always does.

Jack grabs the bottle of wine from the table and tops off my glass before filling his own. "So, mate, tell us about this Soul Sync thing. How'd the date go?"

"It was peculiar. The service assigns all clients an alias to keep things anonymous." A smirk pulls at my lips. "I'm Julius Caesar, and my match is Cleopatra."

Laurelyn arches a brow, amusement dancing in her words. "Caesar and Cleopatra? That's cute and creative."

"Apparently, the husband of the woman who started Soul Sync is really into history. All the clients get aliases inspired by iconic couples."

Jack prods the lamb shanks with the tongs, adjusting their position on the grill before glancing over at me. "And how was Cleopatra?"

"She talked a lot about herself—where she's traveled, how she stays in shape, her beauty routines. But she didn't seem too interested in hearing much about me."

Jack huffs a dry laugh. "Sounds like someone who's used to being the center of attention."

"Yeah, something like that." I shrug, a brief grin crossing my face before it fades. "Don't get me wrong—she sounds beautiful and clearly puts a lot of effort into it. But I have a Samoan mum. The women in my family don't obsess over beauty like that. They care, but it's not the focus of who they are."

Laurelyn gives me a knowing smile. "Doesn't sound like she'd fit in with Malie, your sisters, or the Samoan side of the family. You've been down that road before, Alex, and it didn't work out so well."

"Exactly." I lean back, take another drink, and let the wine sit on my tongue for a moment longer before swallowing. "But—"

Laurelyn catches on right away. "But?"

"There's another woman," I say, feeling a little foolish—and maybe a little guilty as well. She's not the one I'm supposed to be thinking about, but no matter how hard I try, I can't shake her from my mind.

Jack raises an eyebrow. "Another woman?"

"It's not like that," I say quickly, raising a hand. "Before the date with Cleopatra started, I ended up talking to one of Soul Sync's staff members—an American. She was setting up the room. There was a divider between us, so we couldn't see each other, and we started chatting. I was nervous and thought talking to her might help me settle down before meeting my match."

Laurelyn tilts her head, curiosity lighting up her expression. "And what's this mystery woman's name?"

"No clue. I only know she's from Charleston, so that's what I've been calling her. She's the set director—the one who designs the room for the date."

Jack's grin widens. "And you couldn't help chatting her up?"

"Something like that. The conversation flowed. No pressure, no pretense. She made me laugh, and for once, I didn't feel so uptight."

Laurelyn's smile softens. "Sounds as though you like her."

The truth settles in my gut. "Yeah. Honestly, I vibed more with Charleston than I did with my match."

Jack's grin turns sly like he's already a step ahead of me. "And I bet you've thought about her more than you have Cleopatra."

I haven't thought about Cleopatra once since the date ended. Not even a passing thought. It's Charleston who keeps popping into my head—her laugh, her voice, the way talking to her felt so easy. "Too true. I can't get Charleston out of my head. There was something about her... it felt comfortable."

Laurelyn glances at Jack, her brow furrowing in thought before looking back at me. "What if Soul Sync got it wrong? What if Cleopatra isn't the right match for you?"

I turn the idea over in my mind. "Cleopatra's the one they paired me with. That's how it works."

Laurelyn gives a small shrug. "Sometimes the best connections don't make sense on paper."

Jack grins. "Sounds like Charleston's the one worth chasing, mate. Maybe that's where your focus should be."

Their words settle deep, stirring thoughts I've been trying to ignore. But that conversation with Charleston wasn't just small talk. It sparked something real, something I can't shake. One thing is certain—whoever that woman is, she's got me thinking about things.

"All right, kiddos!" Laurelyn's voice carries across the patio, bright and buoyant. "Out of the pool. Time to eat!"

The kids scramble to the table, wrapped in brightly colored towels that cling to their wet skin. The heavy metal chairs screech against the patio floor as they clamber into their seats, dripping water everywhere.

"Here you go, champ," Jack says, sliding a plate toward one of the twins.

For the youngest, he cuts the shank into tiny bites, ruffling her wet curls as she grins up at him through a mouthful of bread.

Laurelyn trails behind Jack, placing forks and napkins within reach for the kids. "Try not to get dinner all over yourselves, yeah? We have a guest," she says, pushing wet hair away from the youngest's forehead.

Jack serves up another piece of lamb, passing it to Laurelyn without breaking stride. She nudges him with her elbow, a smile playing on her lips, and he answers with a quick wink—an unspoken language all their own between them. Theirs is a rhythm that's clearly second nature to them, the kind of coordination that comes only from years of loving and living alongside each other.

There's no fuss about manners tonight—just the easy comfort of family sharing a meal on the patio, surrounded by laughter, delicious lamb, and the tenacious scent of chlorine.

The hum of soft conversation and the clink of silverware settle around me. Jack's youngest kicks her legs under the table, her little feet not reaching the ground, while the twins exchange mischievous glances that hint at future trouble.

The kids' chatter overlaps, blending talk of school projects, a soccer game, and the twins' latest antics. It's noisy and chaotic, but it reminds me of my own childhood—messy and full of life. There's a warmth in it, something I've been missing. This easy rhythm, the simple joy of being together, the small gestures that say *we belong*— it's everything I want in my life, everything I'm missing out on.

For so long, life has been about chasing perfection—the next game, the next win, the next goal to conquer. But here, surrounded by the laughter of kids and the quiet ease of love, I wonder if family, connection, and belonging are what I've been running toward all along.

As the plates empty and the chatter fades, MJ, the oldest, leans forward with bright, excited eyes. "Mum, can I play the new song I learned for Uncle Alex? I've been practicing all week."

Laurelyn smiles at her daughter with that special kind of encouragement only a mother can give. "Of course you can, sweetheart. Go grab your guitar."

MJ bounces off her chair, still wrapped in her towel, and runs inside. Her excitement is infectious, and I smile as I watch her go.

Jack leans back, shooting me an easy grin. "She's been working on this one just for you, mate."

I chuckle softly, grateful to be included in moments like these.

MJ returns with her guitar, and the kids gather around, settling in to listen. Jack drapes an arm over the back of Laurelyn's chair, and she leans into him, their quiet affection as natural as breathing. She strums the first chords, her melody rising with surprising confidence that takes me by surprise. Music isn't a just a talent for this family—it's a part of who they are.

As I watch them, an ache stirs deep in my chest—a longing for something real. Not only a partner, but a life like this—messy, full of love, and beautifully imperfect.

Chapter 4

Alex Sebring

Soul Sync comes into view as I ease the car into a parking space, my heart drumming like it used to before a big match. Adrenaline buzzes through my veins, and my hands grip the wheel tighter than I'd like to admit. I roll my shoulders, trying to shake off the tension.

Thirty minutes early—intentional, not desperate. Or so I tell myself.

Okay, maybe a bit desperate.

I'm hoping my early arrival might leave room for a little luck. Hopefully another chance encounter with Charleston will satisfy the curiosity that's been gnawing at me all week.

Her Southern drawl has been on repeat in my head: *You'll do fine, Caesar.* I've played her voice over and over, as if it could somehow pull me back to that moment in the dating suite when I felt steady, grounded, and more myself than I have in a long time.

The entire drive here was spent rehearsing what I might say if we cross paths. Keep it casual? Compliment how she set up the room? Or maybe take a real chance and say something like *I've been thinking about you*—but not in a stalker-like way.

Yeah, smooth as sandpaper, mate.

A glance at my watch tells me I'm twenty-eight minutes early now. Not that I'm counting—but yeah, I'm bloody counting. Clients aren't supposed to hang around before or after their session. Rules are rules, but what's the harm in hoping for a small twist of fate?

Deep breath, mate. Play it cool.

The automatic doors swoosh open, welcoming me inside. The woman who showed me to the suite last week greets me with a polite smile. I return a quick nod, keeping my hands tucked firmly in my pockets, like that'll sell the idea that I belong here.

"Early again," I say, shifting my weight. "It helps to have a minute to settle in."

She offers a polished smile. "Of course, Mr. Caesar. We want our clients to feel completely at ease before each session."

I relax a bit, relieved she's not here to call me out for bending the rules.

I scan the lobby in search of anyone who might be Charleston, and my breath catches for a moment when I spot a woman with dark hair.

"Good evening, Mr. Caesar," she says, her voice cheerful as she offers a polite smile. "Welcome back to Soul Sync." Her accent is missing that unmistakable Mississippi lilt.

No sign of Charleston. Yet.

The letdown hits hard, heavy as a tackle to the ribs. She might not even be here today. This could all be wishful thinking on my part. It's stupid, really, coming early and hoping for a chance encounter that might never happen.

Still, I check the time again. Twenty-five minutes left. There's still time.

The client experience specialist returns with a practiced smile. "Your suite is ready, Mr. Caesar."

Mr. Caesar. Makes me sound like I should be leading a bloody legion into battle or wearing a laurel wreath. All I need now is a toga and a scroll to decree my greatness.

A twinge of disappointment hits. I force a nod and mutter a thank-you, though the words feel heavy on my tongue.

So, I guess that's it. No Charleston today.

I tell myself it's irrational to care this much. I'm here for Cleopatra—she's the match after all, which is the whole point of this process I paid far too much for, right? Yet the hollow ache of disappointment remains, as stubborn as ever.

Charleston's words replay in my head, uninvited, pulling me back to the moment we spoke. I can still hear her laughing through the divider—that easy, light sound that felt like a tether pulling me out of my spiral.

I shake my head, annoyed with myself. Focus, mate. Forget the American woman you talked to through a wall. Stick to the plan, Sebring.

The client experience specialist leads me down the hall, her heels clicking against the freshly polished floor. When we reach the suite, she turns and offers a smile so smooth it could sell sand to a bloke at Bondi. "Everything is all set, Mr. Caesar. I'll leave you to get comfortable."

She turns to go, and before I can think it through, my mouth acts without my brain's permission. "Is the set director here today?"

She freezes mid-step, glancing over her shoulder with a glimmer of surprise in her expression. "Is everything all right with the suite?"

I scramble for something to say, my mind racing. "Yeah, yeah—everything's fine. I was hoping to make a small request."

Her smile falters for a second, but she recovers quickly, professionalism sliding back into place. "Of course. I'll see if she's available to speak to you."

The suite feels smaller than I remember. I try to settle into the leather chair, but my nerves won't let me sit still. I shift, stand, pace the room, listen for footsteps in the hall or the other side of the dating suite.

The minutes crawl by, dragging my anticipation with them. Even if she's here, what if she's not interested in chatting with some bloke who can't get her out of his head?

I rub the back of my neck and force myself to sit. Deep breath, Alex. Keep it together. You're acting like a nervous schoolboy, not a grown man.

The door to the other side of the dating suite opens quietly, and the moment I hear her voice, my heart jumps to attention like it's just heard the starting whistle.

"Hello, Caesar. How are you?"

Her words come through smooth and warm, wrapped in that soft Southern drawl. It hits like a balm, settling the nerves simmering under the surface. There's something in her easy, honeyed cadence that makes everything around me fade just a bit.

I pause long enough to steady myself. "I'm good. Yeah, good."

There's a brief pause before she speaks again, her voice slightly slower, careful. "Is there something not to your liking? Your client experience specialist said you needed to speak to me about a change."

Every word I've rehearsed vanishes. "About that—" I feel like an idiot. "That's not exactly true."

There's a beat of silence. "If there's an issue with the suite—"

"No, no. The suite's perfect." I fumble to get the words out, wishing I sounded smoother. "I just... the truth is that I was hoping to talk to you again."

A brief silence follows, and for a moment, I wonder if I've overstepped.

"You wanted to talk to *me?*" The words come soft, edged with curiosity and a hint of caution.

"Yeah." Nerves buzz under my skin. "I said I had a request for the suite because I wasn't sure if it would be against company policy for staff to have a personal chat with a client."

She pauses, long enough to make me wonder if I've crossed a line. "I don't think there's a policy regarding that. To my knowledge, it's a non-issue."

"So we're good then?"

"I believe so."

Now that I'm calmer, I settle back into the chair. "You made things easier last time. Talking to you helped."

"Oh, what a lovely compliment. I enjoyed talking to you as well."

I've always been a confident guy, never one to stumble over my words, especially with women. But there's something about her that has me second-guessing everything I say, like I'm a teenager with sweaty palms and a crush. She's got me feeling a certain way. And as unsettling as it is, I kind of like it. That odd flutter is a reminder that not everything is predictable, and some things are still worth chasing.

"So Charleston... are you married?"

Her laughter is light, almost playful. "No, Caesar. I'm not married."

"Are you dating anyone?"

"Not at the moment... which is funny, right? I work for a matchmaking service, but I'm not in a relationship."

A smile tugs at my lips, and I'm glad she can't see me grinning like an idiot. "I don't know. Sounds like the classic case of the cobbler's kids having no shoes."

She laughs. "I figure the right relationship will come along when it's meant to. I guess I think it'll fall into my lap or something like that."

I pause for a moment, considering her words. "Yeah, I get that. Timing's everything, isn't it? Right person at the wrong time... well, that's just bad luck."

"It has to be the right person at the right time or it doesn't work."

"Now feels like the ideal time for me. I just have to find the right person." The words land heavier than I intended, so I clear my throat, hoping they don't sound as loaded as they feel.

I hear sounds from the other side of the divider—the faint murmur of whispers and unmistakable sound of someone coming and going from the other side of the dating suite.

Charleston clears her throat. "Cleopatra has arrived."

Oh bloody hell, she's early.

The announcement cuts through the easy rhythm of our conversation, sharp and sudden. I sit up straighter, the spell between us evaporating, and frustration rises in my chest. Of course, the moment had to end just as it was beginning. Timing, once again, working against me.

"It's time for me to step out. Have a good date."

"Thank you, Charleston."

"You're quite welcome, Caesar."

Think. Think. Think.

"Actually, umm... I thought of another place you have to check out while you're in Sydney. The Rabbit Hole. It's a speakeasy with an incredible whisky selection." I clear my throat, trying to sound casual. "It's a top spot. I'm going there tonight for a drink."

"I do enjoy a nice whisky." There's a flare of intrigue in her words, subtle but noticeable. It makes me wonder if she's more tempted by the idea of the speakeasy—or maybe by the thought of us both being there.

I lean in, a grin pulling at my lips. "You'd love the Rabbit Hole. It has a special kind of atmosphere—dark, a bit mysterious. You should definitely come."

She lets out a soft laugh. "Perhaps I'll pay the Rabbit Hole a visit."

Her words don't feel like a brush-off, but they're also not a confirmation that she'll come either—something in between, leaving me wondering.

"See you later," she says.

And then she's gone, leaving behind the echo of her voice—and the ache of something unfinished.

The soft click of the door signals Cleopatra's arrival. Her heels tap lightly against the floor as she takes a moment to settle in on the other side of the divider.

"Hi, Julius Caesar!"

The date with Cleopatra is everything I dreaded it might be. Polished, rehearsed, and utterly uninspiring. She talks about herself—

the Pilates classes, the raw vegan cleanse, the Bali trip—all in a stream of shallow anecdotes that leave no room for real connection. Every question I ask feels like a lifeline she ignores, pulling the conversation back to her achievements, her curated life.

It's unsettling how much she reminds me of Celeste. Even her voice has the same smooth, practiced lilt—except Celeste's had an edge to it, a sharpened sweetness meant to disarm before she cut you down.

I try to stay engaged, to focus on why I'm here, but my thoughts keep wandering. With Cleopatra, the words don't flow naturally. There's no rhythm, no spark. By the time she asks if I'm all right, I realize I've spent more time thinking about Charleston than I have about the woman sitting on the other side of the wall from me.

The date drags, every second stretched too thin, until I finally find an opening to interject. "Cleopatra, would you mind if I stepped out for a visit to the restroom?"

Cleopatra hums in acknowledgment, the sound light and indifferent. "Of course, go ahead."

She's probably already preparing to launch into another story about herself upon my return—something to do with her latest fitness routine or the skincare regimen she swears by.

Once I'm free of the suite, I pause, scanning the hallway. My heart kicks up a notch, foolishly hoping for a glimpse of Charleston. I know I'm crossing a line—one I shouldn't even be considering—but the pull is stronger than logic.

I glance left, then right. Nothing. Just the usual buzz of Soul Sync's staff moving about, familiar faces from before.

The client experience specialist spots me and approaches with a courteous smile. "Is everything all right, Mr. Caesar?"

I shove my hands in my pockets, playing it off. "Yeah, just, uh... looking for the restroom."

Her professional smile doesn't waver as she points toward a corridor down the hall. "Right this way."

"Thank you," I follow her, disappointment settling low in my gut.

Ridiculous. Here I am, paying an ungodly amount of money for this bespoke matchmaking experience, and I'm not even focused on the woman they matched me with. Cleopatra deserves better. Hell, I deserve better—better than getting caught up in someone I wasn't even meant to meet.

I splash cold water on my face in the restroom, leaning on the sink for a moment, forcing myself to breathe. I'm not being fair to Cleopatra. She paid for this experience too.

Focus, Alex. Give her a real chance. That's why you're here.

It's not her fault I've spent the entire evening comparing her to Charleston. And it's not Charleston's doing that she's still stuck in my head.

The guilt gnaws at me as I straighten up, dabbing water from my face with a paper towel. Get back in there. Do what you came here to do.

With one last glance down the hall—just in case—I head back toward the suite, determined to give this date the effort it deserves. Even if my heart isn't quite in it.

Cleopatra wraps up with the same polished farewell as last time, her words smooth and practiced like she's done this a hundred times before. "I enjoyed our time together, Caesar. I'm looking forward to the next date."

"Same here." Even as the words leave my mouth, they feel hollow, like an actor reciting a line from a script I didn't write. There's no spark, no sincerity behind them—just an obligation fulfilled. When her footsteps retreat through her side of the suite, the air feels lighter, less stifling.

The door clicks shut, and I find myself standing still for a beat longer than necessary. A pull at the back of my mind, dragging me toward the exit, hoping—no, praying—that fate will throw me a bone. Maybe I'll catch a glimpse of Charleston before I leave. Just one.

But there's nothing. No familiar drawl, no accidental meeting. Just the hum of Soul Sync's sleek, polished environment.

I stick around longer than I should, my gaze scanning every

passing figure, hoping against hope to see a new face. But no luck. Just the same old staff, moving in their usual rhythms.

It's irrational, I know that. But still, I can't seem to shake the feeling that I was meant to see her again.

"Maybe next time," I mutter under my breath, trying to convince myself.

The late afternoon air, cool and crisp, greets me as I step outside with the fading sun casting a golden glow over Sydney's skyline. I pause for a moment, taking it all in—the distant hum of traffic, the chatter of passing conversations, and the steady rhythm of a city that never slows down.

As I walk away from the building, each step feels heavier than the last, a pang settling deep in my chest. I know it's reckless, chasing a connection that wasn't supposed to happen. But real or not, planned or not, that connection feels like the only thing in this whole process that makes sense. And somehow, I know I'm not ready to let it go.

Sydney's skyline blurs as I walk to my vehicle, Charleston's voice echoing in my mind. And then the thought slips in uninvited, but I let it stay—how perfect it'd be if she showed up tonight at the Rabbit Hole.

Just the two of us, tucked away in a hidden speakeasy without rules or dividers. Just conversation and whisky.

Maybe, just maybe, she'll be there.

Chapter 5

Magnolia Steel

THERE'S SOMETHING SPECIAL ABOUT JULIUS CAESAR, AND HE lingers in my mind like a melody I can't shake. His words carry a warmth, edged with uncertainty, like he's piecing together a puzzle as he speaks. Thoughts of him keep slipping into my head at the worst times.

Clients aren't supposed to get under my skin like this. And yet, here I am—completely mesmerized.

I shouldn't be affected by a simple conversation. It was only small talk, nothing special. But somehow, it felt like... more. Not a struggle. Natural.

And today when he asked for me because he wanted to talk? I liked it. I liked it more than I should if I'm being honest.

You made things easier last time. Talking to you helped.

I've never thought of myself as the nurturing type. That's not who I am. I was raised by Robin and Charlene Steel—my mom and grandma. The Dysfunctional Duo. Neither of them was around much. When they were home, they had their own lives to manage—jobs, having a good time, sometimes other women's husbands. Scraped knees didn't get kisses, and bedtime stories were someone else's luxury. If I cried, I'd be more likely to hear *suck it up* than *it's gonna be okay*. I learned early in life that if I wanted to be comforted, I'd have to find it somewhere else. Or more often than not, simply do without.

But with Caesar, something has shifted. When I heard that he wanted to talk to me again because I made things easier for him, it stirred something I wasn't expecting. It made me feel needed even though I know better than to get caught up in it.

He's a client, and I'm here to do a job. That is the beginning and end of it.

My job is to make sure everything is perfect for his dates with Cleopatra. That's it. I can't get lost in conversations that shouldn't matter, and I sure can't feel something when he wants to talk to me.

Whitney and Sophie sit across from me in the break room, sipping iced coffees. The buzz of soft conversation hums around us, but my thoughts are stuck on Caesar.

"There's something really endearing about how nervous Julius Caesar gets before his sessions with Cleopatra. You can tell he's not used to feeling so out of his element," Sophie says.

Whitney tilts her head, considering. "Yeah, you don't see that very often with our clients. Most of them are all bravado and arrogance. Caesar is refreshing."

"Definitely unusual." Sophie taps her pen against her notebook. "He seems different."

Whitney nods. "Right. Our clients usually walk in and act like they own the place."

I glance between them, feeling very out of the loop. "I wouldn't know since I never deal directly with clients, but he seems pretty down-to-earth based on our conversations. At least, that's the impression I got."

Sophie leans in, a teasing grin on her face. "So what do you two talk about in there?"

I fiddle with the straw in my drink. "Just small talk. He says I help him relax."

Whitney raises a brow. "I can believe that. You're easy to talk to."

"Yeah," Sophie chimes in, flashing me a warm smile. "You have that way about you."

Curiosity claws at me. And while I know better, I can't help myself. "What does Caesar look like?" I blurt out.

Sophie's smile falters for a second. "You know I can't tell you that."

"I know," I mumble, feeling heat rise to my cheeks. But my gaze drifts to her laptop, the screen tilted enough that I could probably get a peek at his profile.

Sophie notices where I'm looking and snaps it shut. "Mag... nolia... Steel—"

"I wasn't going to look." The lie comes easy.

I was absolutely going to peek.

Whitney chuckles, shaking her head. "It's tempting, though, right? I mean, Caesar did ask for you specifically."

I've never struggled with self-control—not with clients, not with work—but there's something about this that's testing my limits in a way I can't explain. It's harder to ignore than I'd like to admit.

Sophie taps her pen one last time before snapping her notebook shut. "All right, enough work talk. How about we grab dinner and drinks?"

Whitney perks up. "I'm in."

For a brief second, I think about suggesting the Rabbit Hole, the speakeasy Julius Caesar mentioned. But the idea feels too risky after seeing their responses to my asking a simple question about him. If he were there, Whitney and Sophie would recognize him instantly even if I wouldn't. So I tuck the thought away, deciding that's a place I'll keep to myself.

I shrug, keeping it casual. "We could go to the restaurant in the hotel. Easy enough, and we won't have to go far."

Just as Whitney nods in agreement, Elijah's voice cuts in from behind us. "Dinner and drinks, huh? Mind if I tag along?"

Sophie's eyes light up, a little too eagerly. "Absolutely! The more, the merrier."

I bite back a groan, my enthusiasm for the evening deflating like a popped balloon. Of course Elijah invited himself. It's what he does.

"Go grab a table at the restaurant. We girls need to freshen up first, but we'll meet you there in a few," Whitney says.

Sophie practically vibrates with excitement, letting out a quiet squeal after he leaves.

I arch a brow at her. "What are you squawking about?"

Sophie leans in, her words dropping to a near-whisper. "I think I might have a thing for him."

I blink. "Seriously? Elijah?"

"What? He's cute." She gives a sheepish shrug.

Maybe it wouldn't be such a bad thing if Sophie and Elijah hit it off. It would steer Elijah's attention away from me. "There's nothing wrong with liking a coworker, Sophie. You should definitely go for it."

"Are you sure you don't mind?" Sophie asks, her voice a little hesitant.

Why would she ask me that? "No, not at all. Knock yourself out."

The workday ends with a mix of relief and anticipation as we leave the office behind. The walk back to the hotel is quick, filled with easy conversation about weekend plans and the excitement of exploring Sydney. By the time we reach our rooms, the promise of a relaxing evening has us ready to unwind.

After a quick change, Sophie, Whitney, and I step off the elevator, freshly dressed and ready for a night out. I've kept it simple with a casual blouse and jeans, but Sophie's ditched her usual ballerina flats for heels, her hair falling in soft waves over her shoulders. Even Whitney, ever practical, has swapped her blazer for an edgy leather jacket, giving off an easygoing cool vibe as we head toward the hotel restaurant.

Elijah is already waiting for us, leaned back in his chair at a table by the window. The moment we approach, he stands and gives a low whistle. "Well, look at you three. Talk about leveling up."

Sophie lights up at the compliment, her grin wide and unguarded as she twirls, giving him a full view. "You really think so?"

"Absolutely," Elijah says with a crooked smile.

His gaze lingers too long, but Sophie's eating it up. And his focus isn't on me so...

Sophie edges closer to Elijah. It's a move so subtle she probably doesn't even notice herself doing it. Happiness radiates off her, and I genuinely hope Elijah's interest in her is real. I can't help but hope he'll keep his focus on her—and not on me—from now on.

The conversation flows easily—small talk about how hard we're working to make Soul Sync Australia a success for Gabby, how none of us have fully adjusted to the new time zone, and how much we're all loving the hotel. The beds are fantastic, and we could definitely get used to this kind of luxury.

"So, what's the plan for the weekend? Any must-dos while we're here?" Elijah asks.

My list is ready to go. "I have a few ideas I think you all might like."

Whitney raises a brow with a smirk. "That's so Magnolia—already having Sydney mapped out before we even landed."

Growing up, I never traveled. While others were off seeing the world, I stayed in one place. My window to the world came through books and the occasional documentary as long as Robin or Charlene managed to pay the power bill on time. Research became my substitute for experience, a habit that stuck with me. So, yes, I'm the one who already has Sydney mapped out in my mind before ever setting foot there—because for me, research has always been the closest thing to exploring.

But now, for the first time, I get to keep a travel journal. Every quirky café, every sunset over the harbor, every memory worth preserving will go in its pages. I want to record it all, every sight and sound and feeling. I want to look back and remember not only what I saw, but how I felt seeing it for the first time.

I've waited so long for this—for a life I could step into rather than read about.

"Julius Caesar mentioned some things. He lives here so he knows all the cool places to visit."

Shock flashes across Elijah's face. "When did you talk to the client?"

Elijah's question doesn't sit well with me, like he's questioning my professionalism. Frankly, it grates on me. "We spoke last week and then again today."

"But you're the set director." Elijah's smile fades, tension creeping into his expression. "Can you do that?"

"There's no policy against it. If a client asks to speak with someone, there's nothing to prevent it," Whitney says.

His eyes widen. "He asked to speak to you?"

"Sure did," Whitney says.

I don't like that Elijah makes me feel like I have to defend myself, but here I am all the same. "Gabby told us we'd be taking on new roles here. I'm only doing what she asked."

Elijah frowns. "I don't think that's what she meant."

His words rub me the wrong way, but I push the irritation aside. "Back to the must-do list... Julius Caesar mentioned a few spots. Bondi, Coogee, and Manly beaches—he said they have some of the best surfing in the world."

Whitney perks up. "Surfing sounds fun. Would you give it another shot, Magnolia?"

"Not a chance. Surfing's strictly a spectator sport as far as I'm concerned, but I'd be happy to watch y'all."

"What else did Julius Caesar recommend?" Sophie asks.

"He said the Blue Mountains are a must—great hiking trails, stunning views, definitely worth a day trip."

Whitney takes out her phone. "That sounds incredible. Adding it to the list."

"And then there's the Sydney Opera House," I continue.

"Apparently, they have way more than opera. There's theater, concerts, all kinds of performances."

Sophie taps her chin thoughtfully. "I wonder if there'll be any good concerts while we're here."

Elijah raises a brow. "What else did he recommend?"

I throw in a casual shrug. "He mentioned climbing the Sydney Harbour Bridge."

Sophie's eyes widen. "That's a thing?"

"Apparently." A grin tugs at my lips. "But Julius Caesar said he's never done it... and never will."

Whitney laughs. "Smart man."

Elijah shoots me a sidelong glance. "You seem to have gotten a lot of recommendations out of *Julius Caesar*. How long did you talk to him?"

Is he still trying to make something out of this?

Whitney hums thoughtfully, changing the subject. "The coastal walk sounds good."

Sophie's face lights up. "Ooh, I'm so in!"

I knew Sophie and Whitney would be the perfect work friends for this trip. And I knew Elijah wouldn't be. "Great. We'll do the walk and the market tomorrow."

Elijah slouches in his seat, shooting me a look I pretend not to notice. "Guess Julius Caesar gave you our whole itinerary."

I shrug, taking a sip of my drink. "He lives here, so it's solid advice. I trust him more than Google."

"Let's make a toast." Whitney raises her glass. "Here's to making the most of Sydney for the next three months."

We lift our glasses in agreement. I lean back, letting the conversation flow around me, ignoring Elijah's obvious disapproval.

The warmth from the drinks thrums through my veins, smoothing out the edges of the long day. I'm not drunk—not even close—but there's a nice buzz settling in, making everything feel a little lighter.

Sophie stifles a yawn, and Whitney gives her a knowing look. "It's been a long week. I don't know about y'all, but I'm ready to call it a night."

Sophie nods, rubbing her eyes. "Yeah, I'm still not adjusted to this time zone."

I swirl the last sip of my drink, reluctant to end the night. "Y'all head up. I might stay for one more of these."

Whitney's gaze flickers toward Elijah, who's still nursing his whisky and looking way too comfortable. If I stay, he will too. He'd see it as an open invitation.

I force a smile. "Actually, you know what? I'll call it, too."

In the elevator, the conversation fades. When we reach our floor, Whitney, Sophie, Elijah, and I step out together, exchanging soft goodnights before heading to our separate rooms.

Inside my room, I kick off my shoes, unbuttoning my shirt halfway before pausing. My fingers hover over the buttons as an idea curls at the edges of my mind.

The Rabbit Hole.

I reach for my phone, typing in the name and watching as the location pops up on the map. It's only seven blocks from the hotel. Close enough to walk.

Excitement stirs, restless and tempting. What would it be like to be in the same room as Julius Caesar even if I don't know who he is? Just to feel that energy, that possibility?

My heart picks up speed at the thought. It would be exciting.

I glance at my reflection in the mirror, debating for a moment longer.

What am I thinking? Going out alone in a city I barely know to check out some speakeasy? And for what? To appease my curiosity about a guy who's already been matched with another woman. A client, no less. It's completely unprofessional. Irrational, even.

I should stay in, get some rest, and let it go.

But somehow, the thought doesn't sit right. It's more than curiosity. There's something about him that I can't quite shake.

I tilt my head, eyeing myself with a hint of a smirk. It's not like I came all the way to Sydney to play it safe. I deserve a little adventure.

The thought is ridiculous. I should stay, unwind, and get a good night's rest. Who knows what I'll run into out there?

But isn't that the point?

I sigh, weighing my options. One night out to see what this place is all about. Just a peek... then I'll come right back.

Oh, fuck it.

Before I can second-guess myself, I fasten the buttons on my shirt, leaving one extra undone. The deep V opens deeper, transforming my casual blouse into something a little sexier.

Grabbing my bag, I head toward the door, a flutter of anticipation building in my chest. If nothing else, tonight might be interesting.

Chapter 6

Alex Sebring

A SLOW JAZZ TUNE DRIFTS THROUGH THE AIR, WEAVING between the soft murmur of conversations and the occasional clink of glassware. Dim lighting glows from low-hanging chandeliers, the kind that casts enough shadow to blur edges and leave things undefined. The Rabbit Hole is the perfect place to be in public while remaining hidden.

I sit at a table tucked in a shadowed corner, whisky in hand, taking slow sips that burn enough to feel right. The bartender knows his stuff—smoky, smooth, with the perfect bite at the end. But even the best whisky can't stop the tightening of the knot winding in my gut.

She's on my mind.

I take another sip, feeling the burn settle in my chest as I admit the truth to myself—I baited her. I left that breadcrumb about coming here tonight, fully aware of what I was doing. I needed to know if she'd show, if there's any part of her that feels this pull as strongly as I do.

She's a professional, bound by rules and responsibilities. But if she walks through that door tonight... that would tell me everything I need to know, wouldn't it?

Maybe she won't show. Maybe she's not interested. Maybe I read too much into our conversations and saw a spark that wasn't really there at all.

Still, I can't shake the pull toward her. She's an itch I can't scratch, a thought that won't let me rest. It's irrational, I know. I signed up for this process to meet my match. Cleopatra is supposed to be the one. Not Charleston.

But the truth is, if Charleston shows up, I won't be able to walk away. And if she doesn't come... well, that's probably for the best.

My knee bounces under the table, a restless energy I can't shake. I glance at the entrance, hoping against reason that she'll walk through the door any second now. And I'll somehow recognize her.

The door creaks open, spilling a shaft of golden light across the dark floor, cutting through the shadows like a spotlight. A cool draft sweeps in, carrying the scents of leather and whisky. Then a woman, alone, steps inside. Her silhouette is framed by the exterior lighting before the door closes with a soft thud behind her.

The woman is unfamiliar, her face one that I haven't seen here before. It's certainly one I wouldn't forget. She pauses inside the doorway, letting her eyes adjust to the dim lighting. She's dressed simply—a green button-down blouse with rolled sleeves and dark jeans that hug her body just right.

Bloody hell, she looks good in those jeans.

There's a quiet confidence about her that turns heads without effort. Long brown hair falls in loose waves over her shoulders. Her gaze sweeps the room—brown eyes? Green? Maybe hazel? I can't tell.

And her face? God, she's stunning. Not just beautiful. She's breathtaking. The kind of beauty that sneaks up on you, leaving you off-balance.

I shift in my seat, feeling a sudden restlessness. Something about this woman pulls at me. She could be Charleston—or maybe not. Either way, I'm drawn to her.

She glances around the room, her gaze sweeping the space with quiet curiosity. There's a hint of hesitation in the way she moves, like she's not quite sure if she belongs.

I can't take my eyes off her.

The knot in my gut tightens as I watch her scan the bar, her brow furrowing slightly, like she's searching for something—or someone. Her gaze sweeps the room, and then, for a moment, her eyes meet mine. A spark of something unspoken passes between us before she looks away, breaking the connection.

She moves to the bar, leaning against it. The bartender approaches, and they exchange a few words. He nods, reaching for a bottle of Laphroaig, pouring the amber liquid into a crystal tumbler. With practiced precision, he produces an orange peel, twisting it to release its oils before dropping it into the glass. Then, with a quick flick of a lighter, he ignites a small wooden plank, letting the aromatic smoke curl over the rim of the glass before sliding it toward her. Her fingers wrap around the glass, her posture relaxed, but there's an air of focus about her that keeps my attention locked.

I try to concentrate on my whisky, but it's no use. My gaze keeps wandering back to her, catching the way she casually tosses her hair over her shoulder, almost like a habit, yet somehow deliberate. The way she tilts her head, scanning the room, studying people.

Our eyes meet again, long enough for my pulse to skip. Neither of us smiles, but there's something there—something electric, sharp, and impossible to ignore.

Dave, the bartender and a man I've known for years, catches my eye and gives a subtle nod, motioning me over. I drain the last sip of my whisky and rise from my seat, my heart kicking up a notch.

He gives me a knowing smirk before moving to the far end of the bar, away from where she's sitting. He leans in slightly, keeping his voice low. "I reckon the American woman you asked about just came in."

I feel my pulse jump. "The one in the green blouse?"

He nods, his eyes cutting toward her. "Yeah. Sounds like she's fresh off the plane. Yank, for sure."

I lean closer, the anticipation building. "Does she have a distinct accent? A drawl?"

His grin widens. "Oh yeah. Could charm a snake just by speaking, that one."

My chest tightens, excitement thrumming through me.

It's her. Gotta be.

I glance over, catching sight of her as she lifts her glass, taking a slow sip. For a moment, it feels like she's looking right through me— like she already knows exactly who I am.

A grin stretches across my face, unstoppable. I turn to Dave, nodding toward her drink. "Give me one of whatever she's having."

Dave chuckles, preparing the drink with an amused shake of his head. I take the glass and make my way back to my table, my pulse drumming a little harder with each step.

Our gazes meet again, and the corner of her mouth lifts, like she's in on some inside joke I haven't cracked yet. My stomach flips, and suddenly, I realize I'm grinning like a bloody idiot.

I take a long sip, then another, trying to quiet the nerves thrumming under my skin. Finally, I down the rest of the whisky, letting the burn settle in my chest.

Enough waiting. I can't sit here another second.

I start toward her. My heart pounds, but a grin tugs at my mouth, unstoppable now.

"Hello, *Charleston*."

She looks up, and damn if that smile doesn't hit me square in the chest.

"Hello, *Caesar*," she says, her words draped in that unmistakable Southern drawl.

It's her. I knew it.

The grin on my face stretches wider. I couldn't hide it if I tried, and I don't care to.

Without a word, she shifts slightly, nudging the barstool beside her with her foot—a clear, unspoken invitation to join her. I slide onto the seat, setting my glass down between us, my gaze locked on hers.

"I wondered if you'd come," I say, my eyes studying hers.

Her gaze dips for a moment, fingers tracing the rim of her glass in a slow, thoughtful circle. "I shouldn't have."

"I'm glad you did."

She lets out a small, shaky laugh, maybe more nerves than amusement. "This is incredibly unprofessional of me."

I lift my empty glass, and Dave gives me a nod. "To hell with professionalism. It's overrated."

Her lips twitch at that, but her eyes betray the hesitation she can't quite mask. "I could lose my job if anyone knew."

"Don't worry." I hold her gaze, steady, reassuring. "No one will know."

She glances down, adjusting the drink napkin with careful precision before looking back at me. "You've been matched with someone, and that match didn't come cheap."

"We might look like perfect mates on paper, but she's not the woman for me."

Her brow furrows, concern slipping through the cracks in her calm expression. "I hope I didn't say anything to make you feel that way."

I consider telling her everything—that talking to her felt natural while everything with Cleopatra felt wrong. But instead, I shake my head and offer a piece of the truth. "I knew Cleopatra and I weren't compatible within the first five minutes."

She studies my face, her eyes tracing over each feature like she's piecing together a familiar puzzle. "This is weird for me... putting your face with the voice."

I watch her closely, trying to read what she might think—if she's impressed, indifferent, or somewhere in between. But she gives nothing away, her gaze steady, unreadable.

Not all women are drawn to men like me. I'm a big bloke—broad shoulders, thick arms, the kind of build you get from years of tackling on a rugby field. Dark hair, dark eyes, and a five o'clock shadow that sticks around no matter how often I shave.

My tattoos speak louder than I do sometimes—black ink winding down my arms, across my chest, marking my heritage and parts of my life that words can't explain. And the scars... well, they're remnants from battles or challenges I didn't always win. They're souvenirs etched into my skin, reminders that life rarely goes easy on anyone.

I get it—I'm not everyone's cup of tea.

"You probably pictured some blond surfer." I gesture to myself with a smirk. "Not a half-Samoan guy straddling two very different cultures."

Her lips twitch, like she's holding back a smile, but she shakes her head. "I didn't have a picture in my mind."

But there's something in her eyes—a glint of approval, maybe even interest. Her gaze continues a beat longer than necessary, as if she's quietly sizing me up and maybe likes what she sees.

I nod, feeling a little relieved. "Yeah, same here. I couldn't picture you either."

She leans back, a teasing gleam in her eye as the corner of her mouth lifts. "Now that I see you... you look a bit like Roman Reigns, the wrestler."

A laugh escapes me, easy and unguarded. "You're not the first to say that."

Her grin widens, and damn if that smile doesn't hit me straight in the gut, stirring something I wasn't ready for.

"Well, you look like Kate Beckinsale."

She arches a brow, amusement sparking in her eyes. "I've heard that one a few times."

"It's true," I tell her, holding her gaze.

She tilts her head, pretending to weigh it. "I'll take that as a compliment."

I smile, letting it settle between us, slow and deliberate. "You should."

Dave slides a fresh whisky in front of me. I nod my thanks and turn my attention back to Charleston. "Have you had a chance to see any of Sydney yet?"

She shakes her head. "Not yet. But my coworkers and I have plans for tomorrow—a coastal walk, maybe the market afterward."

"Good choice. That walk's something else, especially at sunrise."

She glances at her watch and lets out a laugh. "Yeah, let's be real. Sunrise probably isn't happening."

"Fair enough. But when you're ready for that surfing lesson, you know who to call."

She laughs, shaking her head, her eyes bright with amusement. "That's a hard no. Once was enough."

I chuckle, raising my glass in feigned surrender. "All right, no pressure."

She smiles over the rim of her glass, her eyes dancing with a hint of mischief.

I lean in slightly, watching her carefully. "So you really don't know who I am?"

"Oh, I know exactly who you are. You're Julius Caesar."

I grin, giving her a teasing shake of my head. "So, no peeking at my file?"

She leans back, one brow lifting in exaggerated offense. "Nope. That would be completely against the rules. And grounds for termination. I happen to like my job, and I plan on keeping it."

I study her for a second, wondering if she's someone who sticks to the rules out of principle or if she's not interested enough to investigate me. Either way, there's a strange relief in knowing she's in the dark about who I really am.

The last woman in my life saw me as nothing more than an opportunity, using my celebrity status to her advantage. She twisted private moments to suit her needs, pulling me in until she'd taken everything she could.

I'm not about to let that happen again.

This whole setup—and the anonymity of it—takes me back to how Jack arranged things with Laurelyn at the start. He hid his identity, just as I'm doing now. And for the first time, I truly understand why he did it. There's a strange freedom in being known only for who you are in the moment without the burden of assumptions or reputation hanging over you.

And to have that with someone who isn't from Australia? Even better.

I lean forward, resting my forearms on the bar. "You know, you said something in our first conversation that has stuck with me."

Her brows lift slightly, curiosity lighting up her eyes. "Oh?"

"You mentioned you'd been through the school of hard knocks—graduated with honors and could've taught a few classes there."

She shakes her head, appearing embarrassed. "I'm sorry. I shouldn't have said that."

"You should never apologize for speaking your truth."

She looks down at the glass in front of her. "My childhood was a tragic comedy."

"How so? That is, if you're okay talking about it."

She shrugs, her expression softening. "I don't mind. Talking about it has been part of how I've made peace with it."

A wry smile curves her lips. "I was raised by two women—my mom, Robin, and my grandma, Charlene. They put the *fun* in dysfunctional. My mom had me when she was sixteen, and my grandma had my mom at sixteen. Both of them still kids themselves if we're being honest."

The math clicks into place. "Holy shit. Your grandmother was thirty-two, the same age I am now, when you were born?"

"Yep." She takes a sip, eyes twinkling with amusement as she watches my reaction. "Crazy, right?"

I blink, a little speechless.

She lets out a small laugh. "I'm sure it's a far cry from what you're used to."

I shake my head, absorbing the picture she's painting. "What was it like? Having a mom who was a kid herself?"

"Let's just say, Robin had some creative parenting techniques.

She thought Mountain Dew in my bottle was perfectly acceptable—which, as you can imagine, had me bouncing off the walls. And when I was too wired to sleep, Charlene would top off my milk with a splash of brandy to help me *settle down*."

What the actual fuck?

She shrugs. "I think Robin saw me as her little buddy rather than a daughter. I wasn't a kid she was responsible for—I was more like her sidekick, a playmate she could grow up with."

I lean back, letting that sink in. "A child raising a child."

She nods, her smile tinged with a sharper edge. "Exactly. Honestly, they showed me what to do in life by teaching me what *not* to do."

"I don't mean to judge people I don't know, but that doesn't sound like the best way to parent a child."

She waves me off with a laugh. "Oh, don't worry—I judge them all the time."

Leaning forward, she props her chin on her hand, an amused glint in her eye. "The first eighteen years of my life would make a successful sitcom."

I shake my head, wondering how she can find humor in it. "You left home at eighteen?"

"Oh, absolutely. When I got the chance to go to college, I didn't think twice." She pauses, her expression softening. "Someone I loved very much passed away and left me his estate. It was a bittersweet blessing... though my mom took the car for herself despite it being mine."

"Wait, your mom stole the car you inherited?"

"Yeah," she says with a small, humorless laugh. "That's exactly what she did."

She says it so matter-of-factly, but there's something deeper in her eyes. Perhaps pain?

"I decided that if she could live *with* it, I could live *without* it. So I used what was left of the inheritance to get out and start fresh. College was my escape. My chance to finally breathe and find myself.

It was the first time in my life I felt truly happy. That's also where I met Violet—my best friend. We both work at Soul Sync now. She stayed back in Charleston while I took this assignment in Sydney."

She's only spoken of her mother and grandmother. "What about your dad?"

She lets out a heavy sigh. "He was also sixteen when I was born... and mostly absent from my life."

I recall something odd she mentioned earlier. "You said you're not exactly an only child?"

A smirk tugs at her lips, but without any real humor. "Yeah, my dad has a slew of kids with a bunch of different baby mamas. It's very messy."

"And your mom?" I ask.

"No more kids after me. Robin knew she wasn't cut out for motherhood, and I thank God she had the sense to realize that early on. She made sure another kid never came along and disrupted her life."

The heaviness in her voice makes me think twice. Some things are better left unsaid, and I'm not about to push.

She takes a slow sip of her drink, her gaze drifting to some far-off point. "Whoever the man of the moment was, he always became my mom's whole world. Men are like shiny objects to her—once the sparkle fades, so does her interest. I figured that out pretty early on."

She shifts in her seat, a faint smile softening her expression as her words take on a thoughtful, almost wistful note. "I guess it runs in the family. My grandmother wasn't any less complicated than my mom. But I don't hold it against them. They each had their own trauma, and I've come to terms with that." She meets my gaze. "A long time ago, I decided I needed peace more than their expressions of regret."

There's a quiet wisdom in her words that surprises me. Her emotional intelligence—especially where her parents are concerned —is remarkable. She's learned to see their flaws, their mistakes, and the consequences of their past doings without letting any of it define her.

"Enough about me. What about you? What was your childhood like?"

Guilt tugs at me as I think about what she's shared. Compared to her stories, my childhood was a dream, filled with love, chaos, and laughter. It feels almost wrong to talk about it.

"I told you I've got five siblings, right? Three brothers and two sisters."

She nods, a soft smile touching her lips. "Yes, you told me."

"My parents are amazing. I grew up in two worlds. My dad's Swedish, and my tinā is Samoan. And trust me... those two cultures couldn't be more different."

Charleston tilts her head, intrigued. "Your *tinā?*"

"Tinā means mum in Samoan."

"How long has your dad lived in Australia?"

"Over forty years. I only got to experience the Swedish side of my heritage during visits to Sweden with him, meeting his family and seeing where he grew up."

She laughs, the sound light and genuine. "The closest thing I have to a cultural tradition is bad decisions, yard sales, and perfecting a potato-chip sandwich by the time I was seven."

I blink at her, stunned for a second. "I've never heard of a potato-chip sandwich."

Her grin widens, eyes sparkling with humor. "No one should ever hear of a potato-chip sandwich."

She yawns suddenly, covering her mouth with her hand. "Sorry."

I arch a brow, teasing, "Am I really that boring?"

Her laughter is soft. "Not at all. My body hasn't adjusted to the time zone yet."

I glance at my watch, noting the hour. "It's late, even for me. The Rabbit Hole will be closing soon."

I toss some money on the table, covering both our tabs plus a nice tip for Dave. I have to reward him for confirming Charleston's identity.

She frowns slightly. "I can't let you pay for my drinks."

"Too late. It's already done."

Her expression softens. "Well... thank you."

As she gathers her purse, I get up. "Can I drive you to wherever you're staying?"

She shakes her head. "Not necessary. My hotel is a short walk."

"Which one?"

"The Harbourview Grand."

I grin, and she narrows her eyes, catching on immediately.

"Your family owns it, don't they?"

I shrug, lifting a brow in silent confirmation.

We walk side by side toward the hotel, the quiet night disturbed only by the hum of passing cars and the distant roll of waves. Our conversation drifts easily from Sydney's weather to favorite movies and the places she hopes to see before her assignment ends.

Then, about half a block from the hotel, she slows, stopping and turning to face me. "I'm sorry. I can't risk being seen with you."

I nod, slipping my hands into my pockets. "I get it."

Honestly, I'm not too keen on being seen with her either—but for different reasons.

"So... are we really going to keep calling each other Charleston and Julius Caesar?" Truth be told, I like the game and mystery of it— it keeps things simple... or at least simpler than the alternative.

She nods, a thoughtful look glinting in her gaze. "Yeah... I think that's best."

"All right. I can roll with that." I'm in no rush to tell her I'm a former professional athlete. That's not a conversation I'm ready to have.

I glance toward the hotel entrance ahead, then back at her. "Goodnight, Charleston."

Her lips curve into that quiet, knowing smile I'm starting to crave. "Goodnight, Caesar."

I take a small step back, reluctant but knowing it's time to leave. "I hope we get to talk again next week."

She doesn't say yes or no. Just smiles and says, "We'll see."

"I'll be at the Rabbit Hole again tomorrow night. Ten o'clock," I call out to her.

She pauses, glancing back over her shoulder, her expression unreadable.

"It's Retro Rhythms night," I add with a playful grin. "A throwback to '70s and '80s music. There'll be dancing in the backroom. Come. Wear your dancing shoes."

For a moment, I think she might say something—but instead, she gives a small nod, her smile hovering like she knows exactly what she's doing to me.

I watch her go, a quiet thrill settling in, knowing she means to keep me guessing.

Chapter 7

Magnolia Steel

THE REVOLVING DOORS OF THE HARBOURVIEW GRAND sweep open with a soft whoosh, and just inside, the doorman greets me with a polite nod. The lobby, with its sleek marble floors and quiet luxury, feels familiar now, almost welcoming in a way it didn't before. It's just a hotel, but knowing it belongs to Caesar's family makes me see it differently—maybe even like it a little more. It feels more personal, like it holds a part of him, a glimpse into the world he comes from.

I cross the lobby and step into the waiting elevator, replaying our evening in my head—his easy smile, the way he looked at me like I was someone worth knowing.

The elevator arrives at my floor, and I step out, making my way down the hall. I'm halfway there when Sophie's door swings open, and Elijah steps out—shirt untucked and hair disheveled.

I stop dead in my tracks. Perfect. Exactly who I don't want to run into, but there's no avoiding him now.

He freezes when he sees me, fumbling to smooth his shirt as if that'll somehow hide the fact that he looks like he just crawled out of Sophie's bed. Could he not have the decency to stay until morning and then do the walk of shame like a normal person?

"Uh... hey... umm." He stumbles over his words, rubbing the back of his neck. "Just, uh, checking in with Sophie about our plans for tomorrow. The coastal walk is still on."

I raise a brow, biting back a smirk. "Glad to hear nothing has changed." Since dinner.

His obvious lie makes the moment painfully awkward. He shifts uncomfortably under my gaze, his eyes dropping to my blouse. I notice him zero in on the extra button I left undone, revealing a little cleavage, and his expression shifts.

"Have you been out?" His words carry a sharp edge, as if he actually believes he has the right to question my whereabouts.

The *fucking* nerve.

"Just went for a walk."

His frown deepens. "You shouldn't be out walking alone at night in a city you don't know. I would've been happy to go with you."

Disgust simmers inside me. He has the gall to say that, right after slipping out of Sophie's bed? And now he thinks he's somehow my protector, like I need *him* to keep me safe.

My smile remains firmly in place though it's brittle around the edges. "While I appreciate the concern, Elijah, I'm more than capable of taking care of myself."

What I don't tell him is that I learned how to handle men at a young age. Honestly, I could probably protect him better than he could protect me.

"Goodnight, Elijah." The finality in my words leaves no room for argument.

I turn on my heel and head toward my room, leaving him standing there with whatever excuse or charm he was about to throw my way.

The door clicks behind me, and I kick off my shoes, striding to the window. Sydney's breathtaking view sprawls before me, but my mind is tangled in what I did tonight with Caesar.

It was wrong. Meeting him is a direct violation of company policy, and if anyone at Soul Sync finds out, I could be terminated.

Twisting my hair absentmindedly over one shoulder, I wonder what Gabby would think if she knew. Gabby trusted me with this assignment, and here I am, risking it all.

Sitting on the edge of the bed, I rub my temples. I shouldn't have gone to meet him. I knew better, and I did it anyway.

But the truth is I'm not sure I'd take it back.

The attraction to him will pass—that's what I told myself, but it's even worse now that I've met him. Because Julius Caesar isn't just easy to talk to; he's impossible to ignore. The pull is stronger now, sharper, and being around him feels like stepping too close to the edge.

And that's a problem.

I don't know what to do. My head is spinning, and no matter how hard I try, I can't make sense of it. I need to talk to someone—someone who can help me sort this out before I make a bigger mistake.

Not Robin or Charlene. They'd both say the same thing: the guy has money, so go for it.

There's only one person in the world I can trust with this information—someone who will give me real advice, not tell me what I want to hear.

My phone rests on the nightstand, and I grab it, taking a deep breath. If anyone can help me figure this out, it's Violet.

She picks up almost immediately. "Mags? What the hell are you doing up this late? It's the middle of the night down under, isn't it?"

"One a.m.," I say, rubbing my eyes. "But your day's just starting, right?"

"Oh yeah, it's Fri-yay, baby!" she laughs, and I hear papers shuffling in the background. "You must be having one hell of a night if you're still up."

"Not exactly." Tonight has been a lot. "I need to talk."

Violet's concern cuts through immediately. "Uh oh. Wait, is this about Elijah? Did something happen?"

The image of him slipping out of Sophie's room, looking rumpled and guilty, flashes in my mind. But I don't want to get into it with Violet. Not tonight. "No, it's not about Elijah."

The words spill out of me, more like a confession than a story—something I need to release before it takes over. I tell her everything: how I met Caesar in the dating suite, how we talked longer than we should have. I recount every detail—from the way he asked me to help calm his nerves to the conversation that stretched on until his match finally arrived.

"Gabby asked us to take on extra roles for this assignment, so when Caesar asked to talk, I felt like I had to say yes. I was doing my job."

Saying it aloud doesn't make me feel any better.

"At least, that's how it started. Then I found myself drawn to him. But I swear, I never intended to act on it." The words make everything feel that much more real—and that much more dangerous.

I press a hand to my temple, trying to calm the chaos swirling in my head. "But then today, after we talked again, just as I was leaving the suite, he blurted out where he'd be tonight—like he wanted me to know, like it was an invitation."

"And you went." There's a hint of disbelief simmering beneath her words.

I sigh, feeling like a huge turd. "Yeah, I went."

"Oof." She inhales sharply, that familiar sound of hers—the way she always sucks in air through her teeth when things are about to get messy. "Damn, girl. That's next-level crazy... but also kinda iconic."

I let out a tired laugh, knowing she's right. "I know."

"Okay, so what did you think of him?"

I fall back against the pillows, letting out a soft sigh. "We didn't get much time to talk. It was already late by the time I got there. But oh, Vi..." I trail off, a grin tugging at my lips.

Violet's laugh crackles through the line. "Don't you dare stop there! Spill it, Mags. Is he gorgeous? What's he like? I need details."

My pulse quickens at the thought of Caesar. "He's half Swedish, half Samoan, with this inherent beauty... and black-ink tattoos."

I've always had a type, and he fits it so perfectly it's almost unsettling.

I can still picture him in that crisp white button-down, the fabric hugging his broad shoulders, the open collar displaying the edge of his tattoos—dark patterns curling along his golden-brown skin, warm and sun-kissed, like endless summers and ocean sunsets. "The way his skin contrasted with that white shirt..." I shake my head, a soft laugh escaping as I get lost in the memory. "God, it worked. And his glossy black hair—just messy enough to make you want to run your hands through it. And his dark eyes? Flawless, Violet. Chef's kiss."

There's a beat of silence before Violet speaks, her teasing edge unmistakable. "Wait... are you saying Dak might've slipped to second place?"

I let out a laugh, shaking my head. "I haven't thought about Dak once since I met this guy."

"This is huge," Violet says, exaggerating every word with playful dramatics. "You never get excited about guys."

"That's because I've never met *this* guy," I say, unable to keep the grin off my face.

I shift against the pillows, my smile widening. "He's rugged, Vi, exactly the way I like 'em. Not some polished pretty boy. He's got an edge about him—just rough enough to be dangerous but in all the best ways. And his voice—" I let out a small laugh. "That smooth, deep Australian accent could make anything sound like an invitation."

It could charm the panties right off a girl.

"Okay, but let's not forget—this guy's a client, Mags. And he's been matched with someone else. You're playing with fire here."

I sigh, the reality creeping back in. "I know, and I feel guilty. Caesar paid a ton of money for this match as did Cleopatra. And now, I might be the reason it's not working out between them."

Violet's words take on a practical edge. "This guy lives in Australia. You live in Charleston. In three months, you'll be back home. This could never develop into more than a fling."

"The logical part of my brain knows that."

Violet's laughter spills through the line. "Are you sure the logical part of your brain is still functioning?"

I laugh along with her, shaking my head. "Honestly? I'm not sure. This guy has me completely unhinged, and I'm low-key okay with it."

Violet's words are edged with gentle concern. "Be realistic for a second. What do you actually think can happen with him?"

"I don't know, Vi." I twist a strand of hair around my finger, the motion as aimless as my thoughts. "The only thing I know for sure is that I'm drawn to him—in a way that doesn't even make sense."

"Who is he?" she asks, shifting into full-blown detective mode.

"That's the thing—I don't know."

"Not even after meeting him?"

"*Especially* after meeting him." I let out a sigh. "He said he's in the hotel business. I strongly suspect some kind of hotelier magnate."

"Hmm." Violet perks up. "So, obviously he's not *famous*-famous? Are we talking billionaire-with-a-private-jet famous?"

"No idea. But his family owns the hotel we're staying in."

Violet hums thoughtfully. "Since you know he owns the hotel, finding out who he is would be easy enough."

I sit up straighter, frowning. "No. That would be crossing a line."

"Magnolia Steel," she says, balancing patience with a hint of reproach. "As if you haven't already crossed lines."

"I can't see him again, can I?" The moment the words leave my mouth, a pang ripples through me, unexpected and unsettling. The thought of never seeing Caesar again feels heavier than I'd anticipated, gnawing in a way I can't quite shake.

"You're asking the wrong question, Magnolia. It's not about whether you can see him again—it's about whether you should. You need to let this one go."

"Thanks, Vi. I needed a reality check." Violet always knows how to set me straight, pulling me back when I'm on the edge of making a bad decision. "It's late, and I'm meeting the others in the morning. I should go."

"Anytime. And whatever you decide, please be careful, okay?"

"No worries, Vi. I won't let this become a problem."

Who am I kidding? This is already a problem.

I end the call, and the silence in my room feels suffocating. The rational part of my brain knows this has to end before it even begins. But something deeper, something wild and reckless, whispers that I've never felt this kind of pull with anyone else before.

I clutch the phone tighter as if the connection to Violet might steady me. But no amount of logic can quiet the ache spreading through me at the thought of walking away from him.

And the worst part? I'm not even sure I want to.

Chapter 8

Magnolia Steel

THE COASTAL WALK WAS BREATHTAKING, AND THE MARKETS were filled with shiny trinkets and tempting sweet smells. Whitney and Sophie sampled every pastry in sight. But me? I spent most of the day wandering around in a daydream, replaying every moment from the night before with Julius Caesar—the way his voice curled around my name, the warmth in his laugh, and how he's gotten under my skin.

Dinner should've been enjoyable—a cozy restaurant tucked away with a warm, intimate charm. But Elijah ruined it, flirting with Sophie and then eyeing me when she wasn't looking.

Fuck, he gives me the ick.

As I suffered through it, my mind kept drifting back to Caesar and his invitation.

I'll be at the Rabbit Hole again tomorrow night. Ten o'clock. It's Retro Rhythms night. A throwback to '70s and '80s music. There'll be dancing in the back room. Come. Wear your dancing shoes.

His words have been stuck in my head all day, looping like a broken record.

It would be foolish to go. Seeing him again isn't worth risking everything I've worked for. I've invested too much of myself in this job to throw it all away on a man I just met, no matter how much he pulls me in. These are the things I keep telling myself.

Violet's words echo in my mind. *This guy's a client, Mags. And he's been matched with someone else. You're playing with fire here.*

By the time dinner ends, I feel resolute. I can't see him again. I won't. It's the only right choice if I want to keep my life intact.

Back at the hotel, I kick off my shoes and strip away the day, slipping out of my clothes so I can throw on pajamas and call it a night. But when I open the closet, my eyes catch on a dress—the shimmering one I packed on a whim.

Under the soft light, its metallic tones shift between champagne and gold, the fabric practically glowing. The sleek high neckline gives it a modern edge, while the sleeveless cut and mini length hint at both disco and new wave vibes. It would be ideal for Retro Rhythms Night at the Rabbit Hole.

I pull it out and hold it up in front of me, facing the mirror. I can already imagine it with platform shoes, bold red lipstick, and smoky eyes—blending eras, exactly like the theme of the night.

The shimmer catches the light just right as I smooth my hands over the fabric. "What a shame to let a dress like this go to waste."

I slip the dress back into the closet and sit on the edge of the bed, my thoughts swirling. Ghosting Caesar wouldn't be right—not after he invited me. That's not who I am. A small voice in my head insists I owe him at least that much.

I'll go—just for a little while—so I can explain. I'll make it clear that it isn't right to see him while he's matched with Cleopatra. She paid as much as he did. And no matter how much I want to explore what's between us, I can't.

Yes, that's the plan.

The gold dress glides over my skin, a shimmering second layer that catches the low hotel light in all the right places. It hugs my curves perfectly—just tight enough to show them off but with a high neckline that adds a touch of class, balancing the boldness of the hemline. I step into my platform heels, their height making my legs look impossibly long.

With a smoky eye, my gaze takes on a sultry, intense allure. A bold red lipstick makes my lips look even fuller. I tilt my head, studying the effect in the mirror. It's been a long time since I felt this sexy. The confidence I feel is the kind that straightens your spine and tells you that, tonight, all eyes will be on you.

I check the time—eleven p.m. Perfect. The later, the better. With any luck, Sophie, Whitney, and Elijah are already settled in for the night. I'm not in the mood to explain myself, or worse, weave a lie about where I'm headed.

With one last look in the mirror, I grab my clutch and take a steadying breath before opening the door. *Just one night*, I remind myself. *One night won't hurt.*

The Rabbit Hole is as dark and seductive as I remember, but unease creeps in the moment I step inside. I'm much later than planned, and a thought tugs at me—maybe Caesar has already left, assuming I wasn't coming.

I weave through the dimly lit space, my heels clicking softly against the worn wood floors. I find no familiar broad shoulders, no dark waves of hair, no rugged figure leaning at the bar waiting for me.

Maybe he never came at all because he thought better of it.

The disappointment hits sharper than I expected, a twist in my chest that surprises me. Why do I care this much?

The bass thumps from the back of the speakeasy, vibrating through the air, and I follow the rhythm, clinging to a sliver of hope that I'll spot him on the dance floor. But as I push through the curtain into the back room, he's nowhere in sight.

The lights pulse with the music, casting shadows over the swaying crowd. But only strangers are moving to the beat of retro rhythms.

A man steps out of the crowd, flashing me a smile as he leans in. "Fancy a dance, love?"

"Sorry. Not tonight," I say with a polite smile, stepping back without another word. I don't have the energy to fake it tonight.

The urge to leave sweeps over me. What am I even doing here? I feel foolish, going through all the effort to dress up, letting my hopes build, only to end the night alone.

I turn toward the door, heading back to the hotel. Disappointment settles heavy in my chest, and I can't shake the feeling that coming here was a mistake.

A hand wraps gently around my wrist—firm but not forceful. My breath catches as I turn, heart racing... and there he is.

Caesar.

He's dressed in a black button-down, the fabric snug against his broad chest and tucked into black pants that fit him perfectly, accentuating his frame in all the right ways. He's close, his dark eyes catching the dim light, and whether it's the music or just him, my pulse refuses to calm.

"Leaving so soon?"

"I thought you'd already gone. I was running late and figured you wouldn't wait."

He shakes his head, a faint grin curling at the corners of his mouth. "I knew you'd come. There's no way I'd leave and miss seeing you."

"Apologies for my tardiness. Dinner ran late, and then I had to wait on my coworkers to settle in for the night."

He leans in, close enough that I catch the scent of his cologne—something dark, woodsy, and dangerously intoxicating. "I'm glad you made it."

He takes my hand, his grip warm and steady. "Come on. Let's dance," he says, gently tugging me toward the dance floor.

The familiar beat of "Misled" by Kool & the Gang pulses through the room, funky and infectious. A grin tugs at my lips because I know this song well. My musical taste is all over the map, but I know this one to be a gem.

I slip out of his grasp, walking ahead before turning to face him, stepping backward in rhythm with the beat. With a playful lift of my finger, I give him a slow "come hither" gesture. His eyes narrow with a hint of amusement as he follows, matching my pace without a second's hesitation.

As the rhythm intensifies, I let myself go, moving with energy, every lyric slipping effortlessly from my lips. My gaze stays locked on him as I circle him slowly, my finger trailing lightly across his chest with each step.

Caesar's dark eyes follow my every move, his head turning as I glide past him during the song's slower beat, the tension between us humming like a live wire.

As the tempo shifts back to its upbeat groove, I give in completely, my body moving instinctively to the beat. There's something liberating about dancing to music from another era, like stepping into another time for a moment.

"You obviously know this song." A grin spreads across his face as he watches me.

"Of course I do." I catch my breath between steps. "You don't?"

He shakes his head, still smiling. "Never heard it before."

The music pulses through me, thrumming beneath my skin, my heart racing with the beat. I feel alive—more than I have in a long time. The seductive rhythm pulls us closer, and as the song slows to a sultry tempo, I turn and lean back against him. His arm slips easily around my waist, drawing me in.

His breath is warm against my ear, and for a moment, I forget everything—my job, Cleopatra, the consequences. It's just me, him, and the music.

I know I shouldn't be here, and I shouldn't be dancing with him like this. But for tonight, I want to let go. One night of fun before I walk away for good.

The next song flows from the speakers, the overlapping notes softening before transitioning into something tender and familiar. "Suddenly" by Olivia Newton-John and Cliff Richard drifts through the air. The tempo shift is immediate, slower, intimate, and I smile as the first notes settle around us like a warm embrace, wrapping us in the song's gentle rhythm.

"Ah, it's the original Aussie queen herself, Olivia Newton-John."

Caesar raises a brow, a spark of amusement in his eyes. "Had no idea."

I glance up at him, still swaying to the slow beat. "Never heard this one either?"

He shakes his head. "Not once, at least that I'm aware of."

Typical. Guys my age never know songs like these. I'm used to it, but that doesn't stop me from wishing, just once, to find someone who can keep up with my taste in music. Someone who doesn't flinch when I slide from '60s classics to '70s funk, belt out an '80s power ballad, or dive into '90s grunge and indie tracks that most people our age probably couldn't name.

One of these days I'll find that guy.

I reach up, wrapping my arms around his shoulders. It's a stretch — Caesar is tall, and even with these platform heels, I barely reach him. But I don't care. There's something about the way I feel in his arms—small, delicate, and feminine in a way I haven't felt before.

I lean in closer, and he pulls me tighter, his arm firm around my waist as we sway together. The world blurs and fades away until it's only us, the music, and this perfect moment.

"You're a good dancer." My cheek grazes his arm as the rhythm guides us closer together.

Most guys aren't into dancing—it's usually a grumbled excuse. They act like it's a chore, like they're too cool to let loose or step into the rhythm. It's rare to find someone who enjoys it, someone who moves like they actually feel the music.

He lets out a quiet laugh, his breath warm against my hair. "I don't look like someone who'd be so light on his feet, do I?"

I laugh, soft and genuine. "Not at all."

The next song kicks in, and the upbeat tempo pulls me back into the moment. "Maneater" by Daryl Hall & John Oates fills the room, and I can't stop the grin on my face. What a classic.

Without hesitation, I turn in Caesar's arms, my back brushing against his front as I move to the rhythm. His hands slide to my hips, guiding me, and I let myself get lost in the music.

The heat builds fast. My skin becomes slick with a faint sheen of sweat, and my heart races though I'm not sure if it's from the dancing or the way Caesar feels against me. Either way, my pulse refuses to slow.

As the song winds down, I lift a hand to fan myself, laughing breathlessly. "Okay, I need a drink."

Caesar tugs at the front of his shirt, using it to fan himself. "Definitely."

We weave through the crowd, making our way off the dance floor and toward the bar at the front of the speakeasy. Dim lighting casts a warm glow over the rows of bottles, their reflections dancing across the polished counter. Before I can say a word, he orders two old-fashioneds. The gesture brings a small smile to my lips—he remembers.

He gives me a slow, easy smile as the bartender starts mixing our drinks. "We make a pretty good team out there."

I grin, still catching my breath. "Not bad for someone who's never even heard of Kool & the Gang."

The music hums softly in the background now, a steady rhythm that keeps the energy alive without overpowering the room. The bartender places our old-fashioneds on the counter, and I take a slow sip, letting the burn slide down my throat.

Caesar leans in slightly, his dark eyes locked on mine, a quiet intensity in his gaze.

"How was your day?"

I swirl the drink in my hand, watching the amber liquid catch the light. "Pretty good. We did a late morning walk, checked out the market after that, and then went to dinner. But getting away from my coworkers wasn't exactly easy."

His brow lifts, a hint of curiosity in his expression. "Oh?"

I let out a soft laugh. "I was too chicken to leave my room before eleven. I kept imagining one of them catching me sneaking out and bombarding me with questions."

He gives me a surprised look, his brow furrowing slightly. "You're a thirty-year-old woman. Maybe they should worry less about what you're doing."

I laugh softly, swirling the drink in my hand. "Sneaking around felt like I was on some kind of secret mission. All I needed was a trench coat and sunglasses." The corner of my mouth quirks up. "But honestly? I liked it—sneaking out, all dressed up, like I was getting away with something."

Caesar chuckles, his dark eyes sparkling. "A secret agent by night and a design genius by day. You're full of surprises."

"What can I say?" I take a slow sip of my drink, meeting his gaze over the rim. "I'm a woman of many talents."

His eyes lock on mine, dark and steady, holding a heat that sends a ripple of awareness through me. There's something unspoken in the way we look at each other—an electric current passing between us.

I clear my throat lightly, breaking the spell. "I ran into Elijah last night on my way to my room, and he immediately started asking me where I'd been. Not that my whereabouts are his business, but that didn't stop him from interrogating me all the same. I guess that's why I was so on edge about being seen tonight."

Caesar straightens, his interest sharpening, a trace of something unreadable in his expression. "Elijah?"

"He's the carpenter. He builds the set pieces—the divider between each side of the dating suites, millwork, stuff like that. Basically, anything I need him to do construction-wise."

Caesar nods slowly, his expression thoughtful. "Hmm... I didn't figure you'd have a bloke along for a trip like this."

I raise a brow, half amused. "And what exactly do you mean by that?"

"I guess I figured Soul Sync would mostly have women on staff. Not to sound sexist, but it doesn't really seem like the kind of industry most men would go for."

"It's a common assumption." I give him an easy smile. "I'm not offended. Honestly, you're not wrong—Soul Sync *is* mostly staffed by women."

Caesar takes a slow sip of his drink. "Are your rooms close to each other?"

"Yeah, all of us have rooms right next to one another."

His gaze darkens slightly, something unreadable crossing his face. "Does your room adjoin his?"

"It does."

For a moment, there's a subtle shift in his expression—not quite jealousy but maybe something closer to him sizing up the competition. Except there isn't any competition. And even if there were, it wouldn't matter. Not really. Because after tonight, I won't be seeing Caesar again.

That thought settles heavy in my chest, unexpected and unwelcome. The idea of this being the last time I'll feel his gaze, hear his smooth, warm voice, or see that teasing smile—it stings more than I'd like to admit. I didn't come here looking for this, yet the idea of letting it go feels... wrong.

The song "If You Leave" by Orchestral Manoeuvres in the Dark drifts through the air, wrapping around us like a bittersweet promise. I draw in a steadying breath, forcing myself to meet his gaze. "I called my best friend when I got back to the hotel last night. She reminded me why seeing you isn't a good idea."

He doesn't respond, his dark eyes fixed on mine, his expression unreadable.

"I'd lose my job if anyone found out. And I can't lose my job."

His hand moves gently, brushing a loose strand of hair behind my ear. The simple gesture sends a shiver down my spine, unraveling my resolve a little.

"Go on," he says, calm and steady, his words almost daring me to finish.

I lay out every reason, stacking them like armor to resist the pull I feel toward him. "There's my job, the boundaries I can't cross, and the reality that you live here while I live halfway across the world." I shake my head, forcing myself to hold firm, determined to do what I know is right. "I'm only in Australia for three months. Anything we started would end before it even had a chance."

He leans in slightly, his dark eyes steady on mine, the intensity in his gaze making it impossible to look away. But he doesn't say a word. He just listens.

"You're looking for a wife. That's what this whole process is about—you finding someone to marry. I'm not looking for a husband. I'd only be in your way, keeping you from finding someone who wants the same things you want."

I pause, searching his face for any hint of a reaction, but his expression remains unreadable. "Marriage is not in the cards for me right now."

His jaw tightens briefly before he exhales slowly, giving a single nod. "That's not what I wanted to hear, but I understand. If that's what you've decided, I'll respect it."

He glances down, his thoughts clearly weighing on him, before lifting his eyes to meet mine again. His words come softer now. "Can I at least walk you back to your hotel and make sure you get there safely?"

I nod, my chest tight with a mix of gratitude and heartbreak. "Yeah, I'd like that very much."

I gesture toward the hallway leading to the restrooms. "I need to stop by the ladies' room first."

Inside, I catch my reflection in the mirror, resting my hands on the cool edge of the sink. The song playing softly through the speakers makes me freeze—"Fire" by the Pointer Sisters. A bitter laugh slips out. Could there be a more fitting song for this moment?

Whoever picked this playlist is absolutely on point tonight.

I take a deep breath, filling my lungs, and then slowly let it out. I didn't want to tell him I could never see him again. I didn't want to say any of it.

What I want—what I *really* want—is to walk back out there, look him in the eye, and tell him I was wrong. That we should see where this goes, give in to the fire that ignites inside me every time I'm near him.

But I can't. It's not possible. Not in this world, not in this moment.

The ache in my chest tightens as I push away from the sink and head back to the bar. When I step out, he's still there, finishing the last of his drink.

He sees me approaching and, without a word, grabs his jacket. In one fluid motion, he drapes it over my shoulders. The fabric is heavy and warm, wrapping around me like a cocoon. It smells like him— dark and woodsy with a hint of spice, a scent so distinctly *him* it feels like an embrace.

"The breeze off the water is cold this time of night."

I look up at him, my words barely more than a whisper. "Thank you."

The walk back to the hotel is quiet, the night air definitely cooler than it was when I walked from the hotel to the Rabbit Hole. I pull his jacket tighter around my shoulders, the warmth of it a welcome comfort against the chill.

"Has your stay at the hotel been all right so far?"

I glance up at him with a small smile. "It's been excellent."

"Is there anything I can get for you?" The sincerity in his words is unmistakable.

I shake my head. "No, everything's been spectacular." And it has been.

"Will you be staying at the hotel for the duration of your work assignment?"

"Yeah, Soul Sync worked out an extended stay rate with the manager." A playful grin creeps on to my face. "Was that your doing?"

He chuckles. "No. I don't handle guests."

I laugh, the sound light against the quiet night. "No, I suppose you wouldn't. Not when your family owns the hotel."

As we near the hotel entrance, Caesar glances at me, his expression thoughtful. "You really don't care who I am or how much money I have, do you?"

I shake my head. "I don't. Growing up with so little taught me to appreciate the small things. It really doesn't take much to make me happy. I guess that's why money doesn't impress me."

"Or fame?"

"Oh God, no." I laugh softly. "I'm perfectly fine never being in the spotlight. Honestly, I prefer it that way."

He tilts his head slightly, his gaze curious. "So, what does make you happy?"

I take a moment to consider his question. "Music, dancing, losing myself in a great book. Nature. Fresh, wholesome food—not the processed kind, which probably sounds bizarre, I know. I don't have a place for a garden right now, but I'd like to have one in the future. I want to grow my own food one day. And I'm ridiculously competitive, so I love beating someone at cards and board games." I grin, my smile widening at the thought. "Oh, and Dak Prescott. He definitely makes me happy."

Caesar halts mid-step, one brow arching in amused disbelief. "*Dak Prescott?*"

I laugh, but it's already too late to backtrack. "But I need to be clear about one thing: I'm a Dak fan, not a Cowboys fan. I've had a crush on him since my sophomore year in college. We had a class together."

Caesar chuckles, amusement sparkling in his eyes. "Do you like watching American football?"

I nod, smiling. "I love it. Football is the best."

"The *best*, huh?" He tilts his head, a painful smirk tugging at his lips. "Ever watched rugby?"

I shake my head. "Never."

"You should catch a game while you're here." His eyes sparkle with a challenge. "Think of it like American football but rougher. Tougher."

I arch a brow, mirroring his playful energy. "Intriguing. I'll have to add that to my list."

As we near the hotel, our steps slow, neither of us ready to reach the end of the walk. The cool breeze brushes against my skin, and I pull his jacket tighter around me, wanting to hold on to this moment a little longer. I'm not ready to let it go—not yet.

Without a word, Caesar takes my hand. "Come with me."

He leads me toward a gated courtyard beside the hotel. The quiet beep of the keypad fills the air as he enters a code, and the gate swings open, revealing a hidden garden beyond.

The scent reaches me first—sweet blossoms mixed with the earthy freshness of greenery. I inhale deeply, the air feeling lighter here, as though we've stepped into another world.

"Wow," I whisper, my eyes wide as I take in the scene before me. Soft lanterns cast a golden glow along the winding pathways, and vibrant flowers spill over the stone walls, lush and alive. "This is breathtaking."

Caesar glances around, a small, satisfied smile playing on his lips. "Popular venue for wedding ceremonies."

I nod, still in awe. "I can see why. It's absolutely stunning."

He tugs gently on my hand, leading me deeper into the garden, where the lanterns fade into soft shadows. In the far corner, the air grows still, almost reverent—a quiet sanctuary untouched by the world beyond. He leans in, his words a low murmur. "No cameras here."

Caesar takes both of my hands in his, his gaze locking on to mine with an intensity that roots me in place. His thumbs move in slow, deliberate circles over my skin, a touch both calming and electrifying.

"Please don't think I'm not hearing you. I understand what it would mean for your job if anyone saw us together. But unless I'm wrong..." His gaze searches mine, warm and unwavering. "I think you're as drawn to me as I am to you."

My breath catches.

There it is—confirmation that this pull between us isn't just in my head. It's real, undeniable, and shared. I came here tonight with every intention of ending whatever *this* is, of walking away before it went any further. But now, standing here before him, I feel something shifting, something I'm not sure I can fight.

I exhale slowly, my words soft but steady. "I came here tonight intending to end this, but it's clear this isn't something that ends so easily."

He hesitates for a moment, his thumbs still tracing slow, calming circles over my skin. "You're right—I am looking for a wife, and I know you're not looking for a husband." He pauses, his gaze steady, locked on mine. "I can live with that. What I can't live with is not seeing you again... not if it's something we both want."

The sincerity in his words tugs at something deep inside me, tightening my chest.

"I know that seeing you again is what I want," he says.

I close my eyes for a moment, summoning the strength to say what I know I need to. "I want to see you again too. But I can't. There's too much at risk."

Caesar's grip on my hands firms, his gaze unwavering, the quiet determination in his words cutting through the stillness. "We'd be careful. We'd meet in secret. No one at Soul Sync would ever find out."

I open my eyes, raising a skeptical brow. "So, you want to see me in secret while you continue pursuing a marriage with Cleopatra?"

"No, I would never do that." His expression softens, the sincerity in his gaze cutting through my doubts. "Regardless of what happens between us, Cleopatra isn't my match. I only went on that second date with her because it was the only way to talk to you again."

Cleopatra may not be his match, but he's still a client of Soul Sync. "So, you want to date me while you continue searching for a match?"

Caesar shakes his head, his gaze locked on mine, unyielding. "I'll pause the matchmaking process, tell them I need time to decide if it's the right path for me." He takes a step closer. "The conflict with your job... gone."

"I don't think Soul Sync would agree."

"Then the conflict is reduced." A small grin tugs at his lips. "I won't be an active client. Surely, they can't fire you for dating a *former* client."

I let out a small breath. "No, I suppose they wouldn't."

The thought bounces around, turning over in my mind. No active matchmaking, no client status... could it really be that simple?

His grin deepens, lighting up his features. "Come to dinner with me tomorrow night. We can discuss it—over *fresh food*, of course."

Despite the knot of uncertainty still coiled in my chest, a laugh slips out. "All right. I'll come to dinner." Having a meal together is innocent enough.

Caesar steps closer, so near I can feel the gentle heat radiating from him. His hands cradle my face, the touch tender and deliberate. His dark eyes search mine, and in them, I find a question—a silent, unspoken plea.

Permission?

My breath hitches, and I give a small nod. That's all it takes.

He leans in, slow and deliberate, his breath warm against my lips. When his mouth brushes mine, the world shrinks to this single, electrifying moment. His lips are soft yet sure, coaxing rather than demanding, moving with an unhurried rhythm that sends my pulse into chaos.

His hand slides from my cheek, fingers threading through my hair, the slight tug sending shivers down my spine. His kiss deepens, subtle yet deliberate, as if he's savoring every second, every touch, every breath.

God, this man can kiss.

The scent of his cologne mingles with the cool night air, subtle but intoxicating. It lingers in around us, intoxicating me.

I lean into him, matching his rhythm as the space between us narrows until it disappears. His thumb grazes my jaw, grounding me, even as the rest of me feels like it's floating.

A soft moan escapes me, and Caesar takes the opportunity to deepen the kiss, his tongue delving past my parted lips to caress and tease. I press closer, melting into his strong embrace. The initial tenderness gives way to rising passion as our kiss turns more urgent, more demanding.

Caesar trails his lips along my jawline and down the column of my throat, nipping and sucking at the sensitive skin. My body responds to his touch, arching into him as I become lost in the intense sensations. His hands explore my curves, gliding lower and lower until his fingers brush against my thighs.

His breath brushes my ear, the words low and deliberate. "What's it going to be, Charleston? Do I stop, or do I keep going?"

Shivering in anticipation, my body aches for more.

"Tell me to stop, and I will. But if you don't, I'm going to give you a small taste of what being with me will feel like."

It's been so long since I've been touched by a man. A part of me still yearns for that physical connection, but another part is terrified of being vulnerable. It's a struggle between my longing and my need to protect myself.

But I want this. I want a taste of what he's offering me. "Don't stop."

Caesar captures my lips again in a searing kiss as his hand slips beneath the fabric of my dress, gliding between my inner thighs.

I gasp into his mouth when his fingers barely graze my heated core through the damp lace of my panties. He swallows my moan, kissing me harder as he rubs me through the wet, flimsy barrier. Electric pleasure shoots through my veins and my hips rock instinctively against his touch, seeking more.

Caesar gently moves his hand to push my lacy underwear to the side, exposing me. A soft gasp escapes my lips as he grazes his fingers over my most sensitive spot, sending electric currents of pleasure through my body. I hold on to his shirt tightly for support as my legs threaten to buckle under the intense sensations coursing through me. My body feels like it's on fire, every nerve ending ablaze with desire and need.

He pulls back enough to watch my face as he slides a long finger inside me, then another, pumping them slowly. My head falls back against the brick wall behind me, my lips parting on a silent cry of ecstasy. Caesar leans in to trail hot, open-mouthed kisses along my neck as his curled fingers continue their sweet torment, driving me closer and closer to the edge.

"Just let go, Charleston," he murmurs against my ear, his breath warm and close, sending shivers cascading down my spine. "Give in to it. *Give in to me.*"

His words are my undoing.

I shatter in his arms, my inner walls clenching around his fingers as wave after wave of intense pleasure crashes over me. He captures my lips with his, muffling my cries while swallowing every whimper and moan.

My body trembles, my skin flushes, and my heart races as his fingers gradually ease up. I slowly float down from my high and he presses soft kisses along my cheekbone, jaw, and the corner of my mouth.

He whispers, his words carrying a quiet reverence, "You're absolutely radiant when you come."

He tenderly brushes my hair away from my face, his eyes shining with both wonder and adoration as they lock on to mine. I can only manage a shaky smile in response, still reeling from the intensity of my release.

Caesar seems to understand, pulling me into his arms and just holding me close. I rest my head against his chest, listening to the strong, steady beat of his heart as my breathing gradually slows.

We stay like that for a moment, wrapped up in each other, savoring the intimacy. Part of me wants this magical night to never end. Being in his arms feels so right.

But the spell is broken by the distant sound of a car horn, jolting us back to reality. He sighs, his breath ruffling my hair. "As much as I'd love to stay here with you all night, you should probably head inside before someone sees us."

He's right, of course. The risk of getting caught only adds to the thrill in the heat of the moment, but now, modesty and prudence make themselves known. Reluctantly, I untangle myself from his embrace, though I keep hold of his hand, not ready to let go yet.

I gaze up at him, the moonlight casting soft shadows across his chiseled features. "I had a wonderful time tonight. Thank you for a lovely evening."

The pleasure is all mine." He lifts my hand to his lips, brushing a kiss over my knuckles, slow and deliberate. His dark eyes smolder with the burn of something undeniable.

"Dinner tomorrow night?" he asks, his words low, carrying a quiet promise.

A smile teases the corners of my lips. "Yes. I'd love that."

He nods, satisfaction dancing in his gaze. "I'll pick you up at six. Meet me around the corner from the hotel, by the service entrance. Deliveries come during the morning hours so no one should be there."

My heart skips, the thrill of secrecy igniting within me. "All right," I whisper, barely louder than a breath.

For a moment, neither of us moves, as if the night itself is reluctant to let us part. But finally, he releases my hand, leaving behind the unmistakable pull of him even as he steps back into the shadows.

"Goodnight, Charleston."

"Goodnight, Caesar."

And the night ends, but the promise of tomorrow awaits.

Chapter 9

Alex Sebring

IT'S BEEN ONE OF THOSE LAZY SUNDAYS THAT SEEM TO STRETCH on forever. The day started as it always does—with my family, packed shoulder-to-shoulder at Sunday service. When your tinā tells you to show up for church, you show up. No excuses. No exceptions. In my family, there are two nonnegotiables: family events and Sunday morning service.

The same women were there, as always—the ones who've been circling for years. They smile a little too brightly, wait around a little too long, and try to strike up the same small talk they always do. Their mothers aren't any better, watching me like I'm a prize bull they've already decided belongs to them. If subtlety was ever part of their playbook, it's been completely abandoned.

You'd think they would've given up by now. If I were interested in one of them, I'd have made it clear a long time ago.

I spent most of the afternoon at home, sprawled on the couch with a rugby game on, trying—and failing—to focus on anything other than the conversation I need to have tonight with Charleston. No matter how hard I try, my thoughts keep circling back to what I need to say to make her agree to give us a shot.

I have to be careful. Thoughtful. I suspect Charleston isn't someone who can be swayed by charm or impulsive gestures. If I want her to say yes, I need to approach this the right way.

What will resonate with her most? Honesty? Reassurance? The promise of something simple and carefree? The truth is that I'm not sure. But there's one person who might have the answer.

Laurelyn McLachlan. She's the only woman I know who's ever agreed to something like what I'm about to propose.

Jack and Laurelyn's casual arrangement somehow turned into forever. If anyone can give me insight into how to approach this the right way, it's them.

I grab my phone and scroll until I find Jack's name. He picks up on the second ring. "Alex, mate. What's going on?"

"I was wondering if you and Laurelyn are doing anything this afternoon?"

"Not much. Just hanging out at home."

"Mind if I swing by for a bit? I need to talk to you and Laurelyn about something."

"You know you're always welcome here. What's going on? Are you in some kind of trouble?"

"Not yet," I say with a half laugh. "But I need a little advice."

"Say no more. Come on over, mate."

Jack and Laurelyn's place isn't far—just a short drive through Sydney's eastern suburbs. The house serves as their home base, though it's only one of many. Jack's wineries are scattered across Australia and New Zealand, so they're often on the move between vineyards. But no matter where their travels take them, this place remains the heart of their family.

Stepping inside, the silence feels almost unsettling. I shrug off my jacket as I glance around. "Where's the circus?"

Jack leans back against the kitchen counter, a small grin tugging at his lips. "With Mum and Dad."

No doubt they're having the time of their lives. Henry and

Margaret are the kind of grandparents every kid dreams of. They've mastered the art of grandparenting.

Someday, I know my parents will be the same. If Tinā's constant hints about wanting grandchildren are any indication, she's been ready to step into that role for a while.

As the eldest, I've been getting reminders from Tinā—more often than ever—about the importance of family. I can practically hear her voice now, laced with affectionate impatience: *Aleki, you've used rugby as an excuse for years. No more excuses. You're thirty-two. It's time to get serious about starting your family.*

The pressure hasn't let up since the day I retired. If anything, it's only grown. But I wasn't ready before—not for that kind of commitment. Not for a family of my own. And definitely not with Celeste Warrington. She wasn't the right woman to marry, not after everything she pulled. She didn't want *me*. She wanted the *idea of me*. The rugby star. The public life. The fame.

No, Celeste wasn't the one. But now, for the first time, I feel ready to be a husband. I'm eager to find something real and lasting.

"Sorry to interrupt your alone time," I say as we move into the living room.

Jack waves me off with a grin. "No worries. The kids have been with Mum and Dad the whole weekend. Plenty of alone time to go around." He glances slyly at Laurelyn, his grin widening. "And trust me, I've made the most of every second."

Laurelyn smacks his arm, her cheeks flushing. "Honestly, Jack Henry. Alex doesn't need to hear that."

Jack laughs, unbothered, while Laurelyn shakes her head, clearly amused despite herself.

He winks, completely unfazed. "Just letting him know how important it is for a man to seize the moment."

I watch them with quiet admiration. Their banter flows naturally, full of warmth and humor—the kind of easy rhythm that only comes with real love. It's the kind of connection I've been searching for—steady, genuine, built to last.

I clear my throat, shifting slightly in my seat. "Actually, I came by because I want to run something by you both."

Jack raises a brow, curiosity lighting his expression. "Sounds serious. What's going on?"

I shift in my seat, exhaling slowly. "The thing with Cleopatra isn't going to work."

Laurelyn's lips curl into a smile. "Of course it's not going to work. You're not even remotely into her. You're into Charleston. It's about as subtle as a neon sign."

I let out a low chuckle, shaking my head. "Yeah... you nailed that one."

Jack's expression sharpens with interest. "So, you made a move? With Charleston?"

I nod, gratification tugging at the corners of my mouth. "Yeah. I baited her to see if she'd show up at the Rabbit Hole. And she did—twice."

Laurelyn claps her hands softly, her excitement unmistakable. "Oh, Alex, that's fantastic."

My grin deepens as I lean back. "Yeah, it's been pretty damn good so far."

Laurelyn's eyes sparkle with interest. "You had no idea what she looked like last time we spoke. How did that go?"

"She's an absolute stunner." I shake my head with a smirk. "A proper knockout, if I'm honest."

Laurelyn's eyes brighten, her eagerness unmistakable. "All right, spill. Tell us everything about her."

Charleston's image is crystal clear in my mind. "She's gorgeous with long brown hair. Her eyes have this depth that draws you in, though I'm still not entirely sure of their color—I've only seen her at night." I glance between Jack and Laurelyn. "But it's more than her looks. She's got that Southern charm—kind of like you, Laurelyn. She has a way of putting you at ease, like you've known her forever. And now that we've met face-to-face, the connection is even stronger than it was in the dating suite with a wall between us."

I pause, gathering my thoughts. "The reason I wanted to talk to you is that Charleston and I are meeting for dinner tonight. We need to figure out what's happening between us and what it could look like over the next three months."

"What's your ultimate goal, mate?" Jack asks.

"Ultimate goal?" I exhale, searching for the right words. "I'm looking for my wife."

Laurelyn leans forward slightly. "Is she looking for a husband?"

I shake my head. "No, and she's made that very clear."

Her brows tighten, concern in her eyes. "Are you really okay with being with someone who isn't looking for a commitment?"

I pause, letting the question sink in. "She doesn't live here. She's only in Sydney for three months. If that's all I can have with her, I'll take it. Whatever time I can get will be worth it."

Jack and Laurelyn exchange a glance, something unspoken passing between them, before Laurelyn turns back to me. "You're *that* drawn to her? Enough to put your search for a wife on hold?"

I meet her gaze without a second's hesitation. "Yes. I'm that drawn to her."

Laurelyn offers me a small, encouraging smile. "You should go for it."

"Oh, I plan to. That's why I'm here—I need your help. You've been in a similar situation before, so tell me how I approach this. What's the best way to handle it?" I glance between them. "Your arrangement worked. I could really use your advice right now."

Laurelyn tilts her head, her gaze thoughtful, as if measuring her words. "First off, ask her what her concerns might be about starting something temporary. You need to understand what could hold her back before you try to move forward."

"I already have a good idea about her biggest worry. It's her job. She's afraid that if anyone at Soul Sync found out she's seeing a client, it could cost her everything."

Jack drums his fingers on the arm of his chair. "That's a legitimate concern. So, what's your plan?"

"I'm ending the match with Cleopatra and putting the process on hold."

Laurelyn raises a brow. "Do you think Charleston can get past the fact that you were a client there, technically dating another woman who was supposed to be your perfect match?"

I hadn't really considered that. She hasn't brought it up as an issue, but it's something we'll need to discuss tonight. "I think her biggest concern is still her coworkers. She's mentioned losing her job a few times. It would be devastating for her."

Laurelyn nods, empathy evident in her expression. "Of course it would. I understand that more than anyone. No one wants to lose what they've worked so hard for, and having it taken away would be even worse. At least for me, it was my choice to walk away. You have to be sensitive to her concerns and acknowledge them."

Jack gives a slow nod. "Given the circumstances, she's going to want to keep your relationship quiet."

"Very much so." It's the complete opposite of what I'm used to. Most women want the world to know they're with me.

Curiosity flickers in Laurelyn's eyes. "Are you okay with being her secret?"

"More than okay. I don't want her to know I'm Alex Sebring, former professional rugby player."

Laurelyn's eyes widen. "So, she still doesn't know who you are?"

"She doesn't. And I like it that way. Everything feels so much simpler without that part of me in the mix. The second she knows who I am, all the things I love about this stress-free thing we have going on will disappear. It'll become complicated."

Laurelyn's words are gentle but hit deep. "Alex, she's not Celeste. Give her more credit than that."

I exhale, nodding slowly. "Believe me, I know."

"To be fair, she's American. Being a professional rugby player in Australia probably doesn't mean to her what it means to Aussie women. Same as how Jack Henry's status didn't mean to me what it meant to the women here."

That's a perspective I hadn't really considered. Maybe Laurelyn's right—being a rugby player in Australia might not be impressive for an American like Charleston.

"I want to enjoy our time together without the complications."

Jack leans back, a knowing grin spreading across his face. "If anyone understands that, it's me. I loved every second of those first few months when Laurelyn and I were pretending to be other people, and we were hidden away from the public eye. I'm sure it's worse for you—being both a famous athlete and the son of Alexander Sebring, luxury hotel mogul. I was just Jack McLachlan, the bloke with a few wineries."

I shoot him a look. "I think you're a bit more than that."

Laurelyn smirks, nudging Jack's arm. "Definitely more than that."

Jack shrugs, feigning humility. "Maybe."

Laurelyn rolls her eyes, sarcasm lacing her next words. "Oh, so humble."

Jack laughs, shaking his head. "The point is, mate, you have much more fame than I ever did."

"It's better now than it used to be. I can actually leave the house without being followed and photographed."

"That's progress at least," Laurelyn says.

"Tell me, Laurelyn. What did Jack say to get you to agree?"

She crosses her arms, a mischievous smile tugging at her lips. "He took me to dinner to explain what he wanted. And, let me tell you, I was incredibly insulted by his proposition of fucking for three months and then cutting all ties."

Jack throws his hands up in wide-eyed innocence. "That's not how I said it."

Laurelyn arches a skeptical brow. "That's exactly what you said, just wrapped in prettier words."

Jack smirks, leaning back in his chair with a shrug. "I offered you the best three months of your life."

Laurelyn narrows her eyes. "You offered me a three-month fling and made it sound like I should be grateful for the privilege. Honestly, you made me feel like I was being propositioned like some kind of sugar baby."

"Ten years later and your wife still looks a bit put out about the conversation."

Her lips press into a thin line for a moment though I catch the hint of amusement dancing in her eyes.

Jack grins with casual confidence. "Well, I didn't lie, did I? Ten years later and I'm still giving you the time of your life." He covers his mouth and leans toward me, whispering with mock secrecy, "You should've heard her screaming my name last night."

Laurelyn sighs, her exasperation laced with amusement. "Don't think I didn't catch every word of that, Jack Henry."

He shrugs, feigning innocence as a sly grin tugs at his lips. "No idea what you're talking about, L."

Laurelyn shifts her focus back to me. "You need to let Charleston know that you understand the risk she'd be taking. And because of that, she's the one in control. You're at her mercy, and she makes the rules."

Jack raises an eyebrow. "Umm... I don't know if Alex has to go that far, giving her all the power."

Laurelyn cuts him a sideways glance loaded with more than words could say. "Don't listen to my husband if you really want this girl."

"Pfft. I seem to recall winning you over."

Laurelyn rolls her eyes. "Not before you managed to piss me off first. You seem to have forgotten, but I recall telling you no after that little dinner where you pitched your proposal."

"Fair enough. She did tell me no."

"*To hell with this shit. Call your driver to pick me up and take me home.*" A sly smile tugs at the corners of Laurelyn's mouth. "That's exactly what I told him."

I try to picture it. Jack—once one of Australia's most eligible bachelors—getting thoroughly shut down in such a grand fashion.

Laurelyn shakes her head, still amused by the memory. "He told me, '*When the three months are over, so are we. I'll move on, and so will you. Because you won't know my name or any information about me, you'll have no way to contact me. Ever.*'" She turns, leveling me with a knowing look. "That's not how you win a girl like Charleston over."

Jack shrugs, completely unbothered. "It worked plenty of times before."

Laurelyn huffs. "But it didn't work on the *one* who mattered."

There was a time when Jack wouldn't have admitted to being wrong. He was stubborn, confident to a fault, and always certain his way was the best way. But Laurelyn has softened him in so many ways, made him someone who can admit when he's not perfect. Watching them together, it's clear how much she's shaped him, how much better they make each other.

Laurelyn continues, "Listen, Alex. She needs to feel safe. She has to know you understand her position, especially when it comes to her job. And you need to make it clear that her feelings matter to you—so much so that you'll do whatever it takes to keep your relationship a secret. Because you want her that badly."

I nod slowly, turning her words over in my mind.

"I think she struggles with feeling safe. She had a tough upbringing. Her parents weren't reliable."

There's a shift of understanding in Laurelyn's eyes. "It sounds like this girl and I have more in common than just Southern charm. And if I'm right, you really need to listen to me, and not Jack Henry." She shoots her husband a pointed look, her tone making it crystal clear who the authority is here. "If she doesn't feel safe with you, she's out. No hesitation. No second chances."

"I'm starting to understand that about her."

Laurelyn's words carry deep empathy. "Poor girl. She probably had to learn to protect herself way too early. And even though she's strong and independent, I bet she'd appreciate someone who sees that —someone who respects her strength but also offers her a safe place to land when she needs it."

"How'd you become so wise, Laurelyn?"

She puffs her cheeks out and exhales slowly, her eyes widening with exaggerated drama. "Alex, I once was this girl you're describing. I know all too well what it's like to have an irresponsible parent and to be forced to figure out life on your own."

I nod, grateful for her insight. "Thanks for the pointers."

Laurelyn casts me a sly glance, lips twitching like she already knows the answer. "You really like her, don't you?"

I pause, the realization settling in deeper than I expected. "Yeah, I do. We haven't spent a lot of time together yet, but I think we could have something really special while she's here."

Jack's words take on a serious edge. "I have to ask. What's the plan if you fall in love with her? Because trust me, mate, it can happen."

I exhale slowly, rolling my shoulders as if trying to shake off the possibility. "That's something I'll figure out when the three months are up."

Jack's gaze sharpens. "If you ignore every other piece of advice I give you, at least listen to this: don't let her leave Australia without knowing her real name. Trust me, it's a nightmare trying to track down the girl you love after you've been a fool and let her slip through your fingers."

His words hit closer to home than I care to admit. "I don't think it'll come to that."

There's a knowing gleam in his eyes. "Don't underestimate how quickly the right woman can turn your life upside down. Ten years from now, you might be married to her, chasing around little people who look like you."

A seed is planted, the thought taking root. And it grows before I can stop it—me and Charleston, ten years down the road. Kids with golden brown skin, dark waves of hair, and eyes... maybe brown like mine. Or maybe hazel—if that's what hers are. And that laugh of hers, a light, infectious sound—I can imagine it filling every corner of my life.

Suddenly, a future with her doesn't feel so far-fetched.

Chapter 10

Alex Sebring

PULLING INTO THE SERVICE ENTRANCE OF THE HARBOURVIEW Grand, I park in a discreet spot behind the building. Hidden from view, it's the perfect place—no curious glances, no questions. Privacy, the way Charleston and I want it and need it to be.

The door opens, and she steps out, dressed head-to-toe in black—sleek, understated, and stunning. The crop top clings in all the right ways, while the wide-leg trousers flow with graceful movement. Draped over her arm, a leather jacket adding a bit of edge. There's a cool, unbothered confidence about her that I love, like she isn't trying to be beautiful or noticed.

Even in heels, she's still a good bit shorter than me, which makes the size difference between us stand out even more. She's petite but has this perfect mix of strength and softness—not the kind of woman you'd break if you held her too tight. Everything about her pulls me in, like she was meant to fit me every way that counts.

Bloody hell, it's like she was made for me.

By the time I step out and circle around to greet her, her gaze is already fixed on the car, a smirk tugging at the corners of her lips. "A blacked-out G-Wagon? Why am I not surprised?"

Holding the door open for her, I grin. "What else would I drive? I'm a big bloke. I can't exactly squeeze into a Fiat."

Her laughter spills out as she slides into the seat. "Fair enough."

The late evening sun filters through the branches of a nearby tree, casting shifting patterns of light. One stray beam breaks through, landing perfectly on her face—and the mystery is solved.

Her eyes—hazel. Light brown interwoven with green, flecked with gold that shimmers near the center, like sunlight scattered across amber glass. Her hair also surprises me. It's lighter than I'd realized, streaked with natural honey highlights that catch the sunlight, shimmering like glitter woven into silk.

I pause, my hand resting on the edge of the door, caught by her sheer beauty. For a moment, I forget to move, I forget everything but the woman sitting in front of me.

Her brow furrows slightly, a hint of curiosity softening her expression. "Is everything okay?"

"Yeah, I was just looking at your eyes. This is the first time I've seen them in daylight. They're beautiful."

She blinks, and a soft smile graces her lips. "Thank you."

I close the door and walk around to the driver's side, sliding in and glancing her way. "I have something special planned tonight. We're going to a restaurant owned by one of my closest friends. But don't worry—it's completely private. She's reserved a dining room just for us, so there's zero chance of anyone seeing us together. But the best part is she's an excellent chef and she'll be cooking the entire meal for us." I throw in a wink, adding, "Only the freshest ingredients for you, of course."

Her lips curve into a small, appreciative smile. "Oh wow. That sounds amazing."

I've taken Laurelyn's advice to heart, and it's time to show Charleston that I appreciate her concerns. "I want you to know that I understand how important it is to keep this under wraps."

Her nod is small but firm. "Thank you for acknowledging that."

"I don't want you to worry. I've got it handled."

"I believe you."

We pull away from the hotel, and I ease into some light conversation. "How was your day?"

"It started with brunch, then I spent the rest of the day holed up in my room. I'm still trying to shake off the time-zone adjustment."

I nod, watching the road. "Yeah, it can feel like you're living in two time zones for a while."

She laughs softly. "Exactly. I feel like I could sleep for days. But I think the worst of it is finally behind me. What about you? How did you spend your day?"

"Spent the morning at church with my family. After that, we had lunch at my parents'. All my siblings were there, so it was the usual loud, chaotic mess."

"Sounds like a beautiful, chaotic mess to me."

I chuckle. "Chaos, definitely. Beautiful? Not so much."

"To someone like me, it sounds wonderful."

Her words stir something deep inside me, a quiet reminder of how lucky I am to have the kind of family she's never had. Tonight, I appreciate them a little more than I did this morning.

I ease the G-Wagon into the narrow alley behind Chloe's restaurant, killing the engine. The kitchen's service entrance is ahead, tucked discreetly out of sight from the bustling main street. Stepping out, I make my way around to open Charleston's door.

She raises a curious brow. "You must know the owner pretty well if we're sneaking in through the back."

I grin, holding out a hand to help her out of my vehicle. "You could say that. Chloe and I grew up together. She's a close friend."

Charleston's heels click softly against the pavement as she steps out, smoothing her outfit. "A close friend who is a chef and happens to own a restaurant? Lucky you."

"Lucky indeed. She's an incredible chef. Trust me, you won't be disappointed."

Chloe wouldn't have had to work a day in her life if she'd chosen not to. Being a McLachlan comes with privileges, but it was her choice to work. She built this place from the ground up, pouring herself into every detail and earning every bit of her success on her own. Every plate served, every seat filled—it's all her success built with her own determination.

The service door swings open as we approach, and there she is—all smiles while wearing her crisp white chef's jacket. Her bright blue eyes light up when she spots us.

"Right on time," she beams, pulling me into a quick, familiar hug.

I return the hug with a squeeze. "You're a lifesaver, as always."

When she steps back, her gaze shifts to Charleston, her friendly smile tinged with curiosity.

I gesture toward the woman by my side, feeling an awkwardness settle over me as I search for the right words. "Chloe, this is... uh." I falter, my usual confidence momentarily escaping me. "This is my friend Charleston. Well, that's what I call her—because that's where she's from."

Chloe arches a brow, her words playful and carrying a hint of teasing. "Please tell me you aren't up to some of that weird shit like Jack used to do."

I chuckle, amused. "It might be something like that."

Chloe's lips twitch, amusement crossing her face as she holds back a full grin. Tilting her head slightly, her smile never falters. "Nice to meet you. Should I call you Charleston, too?"

Charleston nods, the corners of her lips curving enough to hint at a smile. "Sure, that works."

Chloe's eyes sparkle with mischief as she glances at me. "Charleston it is then."

Chloe guides us through the kitchen, weaving past bustling chefs and simmering pots, the air heavy with the mouthwatering aroma of garlic, fresh herbs, and roasting vegetables. Beside me, Charleston takes it all in, her gaze drifting with quiet interest over the organized chaos as we make our way toward the private room tucked at the back of the restaurant.

When we step inside, Chloe gestures toward the intimate setup—

soft, dim lighting, candles flickering gently on a small table for two, and a window offering a breathtaking view of the harbor. The room is quiet, a world away from the clatter of the kitchen and the hum of the dining room—exactly the atmosphere I'd hoped for.

"Do you have any allergies or dietary restrictions I should know about?"

Charleston shakes her head with an easy smile. "I don't."

"Perfect." Chloe's grin widens, her enthusiasm shining through. "Tonight's menu is completely farm-to-table. I sourced everything locally—some of it straight from the markets this morning." She ticks off the dishes with effortless precision: "Grilled lamb with rosemary, caramelized baby carrots, fingerling potatoes, and a beet and goat cheese salad to start. For dessert, a lemon tart with fresh berries. And to pair with the lamb, I'd suggest a bottle of Jack's shiraz—bold, peppery, and just right for the flavors. How does that sound?"

I glance at Charleston, her eyes lighting up and her smile widening. "That sounds incredible."

"Wonderful. I'll send Frederick in to take care of you. Whatever you need, just ask. I'll be in the kitchen making sure everything is perfect."

Chloe gives me a quick, playful wink before slipping out, the door clicking shut behind her.

"Thank you for bringing me here. This is such a lovely surprise."

"I'm glad you like it."

The private dining room feels like a secret tucked away from the world, a perfect retreat for a night like this. Charleston glances around, her gaze sweeping over the intimate space. "This is beautiful."

I nod, a small smile forming. "Chloe has a special talent for ambience, kind of like someone else I happen to know."

A mix of amusement and curiosity cuts through her expression. "Is that so?"

Her fingers trail lightly over the edge of the tablecloth as her gaze sweeps the room again, her professional eye clearly at work. "Well-chosen elements. The textures—velvet against dark wood—are inviting and harmonious. And the low lighting creates intimacy without feeling oppressive. It's perfectly balanced."

She looks at me, and her eyes are alight with that spark of passion I noticed earlier. "This space works because it's designed to make people feel connected and comfortable."

I watch her as she speaks, her words flowing with confidence, the language of her world. "You really love what you do, don't you?"

Her gaze shifts to mine, and for a moment, her expression softens —unguarded and open. "I really do."

Frederick moves in and out of the room with practiced ease, setting down water glasses and pouring the first round of a rich shiraz. Charleston lifts her glass, cradling it delicately as she takes a sip. Her eyes close briefly, savoring the taste. "Mmm. This is delicious."

I swirl the wine in my glass. "Chloe knows wine. She's got a real knack for pairing it with food just right."

Frederick returns with the first course, a beet and goat cheese salad drizzled with honey. Charleston takes a bite, her expression lighting up. "This is incredible. I didn't think I cared for beets, but this changes my mind."

I chuckle, cutting into mine. "That's Chloe for you—she can win over anyone with her food."

The main course arrives, and Charleston leans in with a contented sigh. "This is cooked to perfection. If all food in Australia is like this, I might never leave."

Her enthusiasm is infectious, and I find myself caught up in the simple joy of watching her savor the food.

Frederick tops off our wine and quietly slips out, leaving us alone again. I glance at Charleston, searching for the right way to ease into the things I need to say. But the words sit heavy in my chest, tangled with nerves. I'm not usually one to stumble over what to say, but with her, it's different.

We keep the conversation light—travel, the quirks of Australian slang, and the best dance clubs in Sydney—even though my mind isn't fully on it. Each time I try to steer things toward something more serious, the moment doesn't feel quite right, and I back out at the last second.

I take another sip of wine, hoping it'll settle the restless energy humming beneath my skin.

Frederick returns to clear the plates, leaving the soft glow of candlelight between us. Charleston leans back in her chair, letting out a contented sigh. "I'm stuffed, but I've never turned down a dessert in my life, and I don't plan to start tonight."

I like a girl who'll eat and doesn't pick at her plate or pretend she's not hungry.

Charleston is about to have her mind blown. "Dessert is Chloe's specialty. You're in for a real treat."

Frederick reappears with a delicate lemon tart, perfectly topped with fresh berries and a light dusting of powdered sugar. He sets it down with a quiet smile before slipping out, leaving us alone again.

Last course of the meal. The moment feels as close to right as it's going to get. "Have you given much thought to what we talked about last night?"

Her fork pauses midair, and she looks up at me through thick, dark lashes. "I don't think there's been a single moment since last night that I haven't thought about it."

"I haven't stopped thinking about it either."

The sincerity in her eyes draws me in, but there's also hesitation. "This is scary for me. Being in this private room eases my fear, but being in public with you is scary."

Her words reveal a fear deeper than I'd realized, slicing through my confidence. "What can I do to take that fear away?"

Her expression softens, her eyes searching mine, but she shakes her head. "I don't think you can."

I nod slowly, letting her words settle. Laurelyn's advice comes back to me, clear as day: *She has to feel safe if this is going to work.*

This isn't about finding the perfect thing to say—it's about proving it through actions. Trust isn't something you promise; it's something you build.

"We can avoid public places and stick to private settings where there's zero chance of your coworkers seeing us. How does that sound?"

Charleston hesitates, then nods slightly. "Private places would work."

Encouraged, I press on. "You wouldn't be able to stay in the room next to them since there's the possibility of them seeing your comings and goings. I would move you to one of the penthouses on the top floor which has its own private lift. That would eliminate running into them in the hotel."

Her eyes widen, a flare of surprise breaking through her composure. "No, I can't let you do that."

I shake my head, brushing off her concern easily. "You need to be in a place where we can move freely without worrying about running into your coworkers. You'll tell them there was an issue with your room, which isn't a lie—being so close to them is an issue. And for the trouble of moving from a room you've already settled into, the hotel upgraded you at no expense. No fuss. It won't raise suspicion—just a bit of envy."

She says nothing, her eyes wide.

I chuckle softly, holding her gaze. "What do you think of that?"

Her lips curve into a small smile. "It would definitely make things easier if the chances of bumping into them in the hallway or the elevator are eliminated. I hate being put in a position where I have to explain where I'm going, where I've been, or why I'm dressed the way I am."

It's not a yes, but not a no either.

A wave of relief settles in me, a quiet hope that we might actually make this work. "Things will come up along the way, but we'll handle them. We'll make smart decisions to keep this quiet and protect our relationship from being discovered. I know I'm asking for a lot, and I don't take the risk to your career or reputation lightly. I understand what's at stake for you, and I will protect you."

I hold her gaze, ensuring she feels the sincerity in my words. "You'd be the one in control every step of the way. If something doesn't feel right, you say the word, and it stops."

For a moment, she studies me, her anxieties and what-ifs visibly easing. The tension in her shoulders melts away, her face softening as the lines of worry fade. Watching her begin to relax stirs something deeper within me. This isn't only about staying hidden—it's about trust. And in this moment, I can see that a seed of trust has been planted, fragile but real, and I'm watching it start to take root.

For a moment, the quiet stretches between us, but it's not awkward. She seems to be turning over what I've said, her gaze thoughtful as if weighing the possibilities against her reservations.

"You've obviously put a lot of thought into how to make this work around my situation. And while I appreciate the lengths you're willing to go to keep this hidden from my coworkers, I'm still struggling with the fact that you're looking for a wife, and I'm not looking for a husband."

Her honesty stirs a surge of worry in me, but I push past it. I knew this was coming. "I understand that. I'm fully aware you're not looking for marriage, and that's okay. I'm not asking for any kind of commitment. I'm only asking for whatever time you're willing to spend with me while you're here."

Her expression shifts to something almost apologetic. "But I'd be keeping you from finding what you're truly looking for."

"You wouldn't be holding me back. This is my choice—to push my timeline back a few months. What's three months in the grand scheme of things?"

Her lips twitch as if she's fighting a smile. "You're going to have a counter for every reason I come up with, aren't you?"

"Abso-*fucking*-lutely." I flash her a grin, enjoying the way her guard starts to slip.

There's a spark of curiosity in her eyes now, a gleam that wasn't there before. "You've really thought this through every step of the way, haven't you?"

I lean forward, resting my forearms on the table. "I have. And I've got you, Charleston. If you'll take a chance and trust me, I'll keep you safe."

I can feel it—she's close to saying yes. Her hesitation is fading, her posture a little more relaxed.

It's time to seal the deal.

Recalling Jack's advice, I lean in slightly, a playful grin tugging at my lips. "And I'll give you the time of your life. The best three months you've ever had."

Charleston arches a brow, a smirk curving her lips as her eyes narrow slightly. "Cocky much?"

"I don't make promises I can't keep." My grin widens, meeting hers head-on. "You weren't disappointed last night, were you?"

"Oh... you... orgasm... giving... devil... you." Her cheeks flush a soft pink as she bites her lower lip, amusement dancing in her eyes. "I definitely wasn't disappointed. Which, honestly, was a first for me. Men don't usually get that so... right."

I chuckle, her words lighting a fire of satisfaction inside me. "You deserve every orgasm I give you. And trust me, there will be plenty more."

Her blush deepens as she laughs softly, shaking her head. "With promises like that, you're making it damn near impossible to say no."

"That's the plan."

There's a playful spark in her eyes, edged with thoughtfulness. "I see that."

I won't back down—I never do. Giving up simply isn't in my DNA. And it's time to lay all my cards on the table. "I'm going to tell you the whole truth."

Her confident gaze falters for a moment, a quake of nerves crossing her face. "I would have it no other way."

I take a steadying breath, the truth pressing against my chest, demanding to be spoken. "I want you, Charleston. I've wanted you since the first time we spoke in the dating suite, straight away, before I even knew what you looked like. And then when I saw you... you took my breath away. But it's more than the physical. It's the way we connect, the way you make me feel when I'm with you... and even when I'm not with you. This is easy—like I've finally found someone I can be myself with."

Her smile wavers slightly. For a moment, I question myself, wondering if I've taken it too far, if I've said more than she's ready to hear. But even if I have, I don't regret it. Not one word.

Charleston leans forward a little, her expression softening, a quiet smile playing on her lips. "You know what I like best about you?"

"My charm and dashing good looks?"

Her laughter bubbles up, light and easy. "While that's all quite appealing... no." She pauses, her gaze holding mine. "You make me feel seen and heard. And that makes me feel safe with you."

Everything Laurelyn said about Charleston was spot-on, and I owe her a heartfelt big thank-you.

"You're always safe with me."

If we're really going to do this, she needs to know the truth—at least some of it. I can't lay it all out yet, but she deserves a warning.

I take a steadying breath, preparing myself. "There's something I need to tell you."

She twists her mouth into an exaggerated grimace, her eyebrows shooting up. "Uh-oh."

"It's nothing bad, I promise. I just think it's important to be upfront about some things."

"Upfront—I like that."

This feels like the right moment to offer her a sliver of truth. "It's true that my family owns luxury hotels, and I've recently stepped into the family business. But before that, I had a different career—one that made me fairly well-known. Because of that, it's in my best interest to stay out of the public eye as much as possible."

"So privacy is something we both value."

"Very much so." The shadow of past experiences creeps in. "I don't like my relationships to be publicized. In fact, I can't stand it. My life—especially my personal life—should remain private."

Her gaze softens with understanding. "It absolutely should be private if that's what you want." She pauses, studying my face with a quiet intensity before letting out a thoughtful *hmm*. "And now you've got me completely curious about who you are."

I chuckle, shaking my head. "I will tell you if you want to know." But I'd rather not.

A playful glint sparkles in her eyes as she considers it. "We don't have to tell each other. It could be kind of fun if we didn't, don't you think?"

I'm pleased to see she's open to the idea of anonymity. "Can I tell you a story?"

"Of course." She leans in slightly, curiosity lighting her eyes.

"It's about my best mate—the one who recommended Soul Sync to me."

"Go on," she prompts.

"He had... let's just say, a complicated experience with a woman. It messed him up for a long time. He couldn't bring himself to trust women after that."

Sympathy softens her expression. "That sounds truly awful."

I nod. "It was. For years, he couldn't handle a traditional relationship. So instead, he started dating women through arranged agreements—set for a specific amount of time, no strings attached, no real names. Just two people, keeping it simple. That was his way of living for years."

Charleston's lips quirk up, amusement dancing in her eyes. "Much like what we're talking about doing?"

"Similar, yes. His arrangement had their differences—more like role play, I suppose you could say."

She props her chin on her hand, her fingers lightly curled against her cheek, curiosity dancing in her eyes. "What happened to your friend?"

I'm glad she asked. "He met *the one*. They've been married for ten years now. Got four kids. He's happier than I've ever seen him."

Her brows lift, surprise lighting her features. "Four kids? That's a lot."

I chuckle, the sound coming easily. "Yes, four's a lot, but it's not six."

A warm expression settles in her eyes. "Beautiful chaos."

The words settle over me "Yeah, beautiful chaos."

Charleston sits quietly, her expression thoughtful as she seems to weigh her options. After a moment, she gives a small nod. "Let's do this."

An explosion of satisfaction ignites in my chest. "Yeah?"

Her second nod is firmer, more certain. "Yeah, I want to do it."

I exhale a quiet sigh of relief. "All right. First order of business— getting your things moved to the penthouse. I can call now and have someone handle it while we're out unless you'd rather do it yourself." I flash a teasing smile. "Don't worry, nothing will go missing. You have my guarantee."

"I'm not worried about that. Go ahead and arrange to have my things moved. I trust your people."

A teasing grin tugs at my lips. "Should I warn them about dirty knickers on the floor?"

Her laughter lightens the moment. "I don't leave dirty *knickers* on the floor."

I pull my phone from my pocket, scrolling through my contacts. "What room are you in?"

"Oh, 7714," she says, her lips curving with a trace of amusement.

I tap the screen, dialing Gigi, the manager of the Harbourview Grand. The call barely rings once before she answers. "Good evening, Mr. Sebring."

"Hello, Gigi. I need a favor. The guest in room 7714 needs to be moved to one of the penthouses for the remainder of her stay— around ninety days. A complimentary upgrade."

There's a brief pause before she responds. "Certainly. May I have the guest's name?"

For a moment, I falter. "Her name is... you know what? It's completely slipped my mind. But the room number should give you all the details you need."

Gigi's laugh is soft and professional. "Not a problem, sir. I'll sort it out and handle the transfer."

"The guest isn't in the room at the moment, but she's given her permission for her belongings to be moved now."

"Understood, Mr. Sebring. We'll take care of it."

"She's a special guest. Treat her as a VIP."

"Of course, Mr. Sebring. Consider it done."

I hang up and slide my phone back into my jacket pocket. Charleston's gaze rests on me, her expression warm with gratitude. "Thank you."

"It's my pleasure."

Chloe comes into the dining room, wiping her hands on a towel draped over her shoulder. "So, what did we think of dinner?"

"The meal was great." I glance at our untouched desserts. "We've been so caught up talking we haven't even made it to dessert yet."

Charleston shakes her head. "It wasn't great—it was extraordinary. I've never had anything like it."

Chloe's grin widens. "I like this one, Big Al. You should keep her around."

Big Al. I cringe inwardly at Chloe using her pet name for me. It doesn't reveal my real name, but it wouldn't be hard for Charleston to figure out that Al is short for Alex.

"Thanks for coming in and doing this," I say, steering the conversation back to safer ground.

Chloe plants her hands on her hips, shifting her weight to one side. She takes a deep breath, her gaze lifting to the ceiling like she's trying to keep her emotions in check. "I had to do something to get my mind off Ben."

Her breath hitches, and she quickly presses a hand to her eyes.

"Shit, I'm sorry, guys." She sniffles, offering a weak smile as her gaze shifts from one of us to the other. "Charleston, you must think I'm a right drongo."

Charleston shakes her head, her voice warm and reassuring. "I don't know what's going on, but I definitely don't think you're a *drongo*... whatever that is."

I stand and wrap my arm around Chloe's shoulders, pulling her into a firm hug. "Come here, Clover." My words soften as I lean in. "I'm really sorry you're going through this."

Chloe exhales a shaky breath, melting into my embrace. "I'm sorry for ruining your date," she mutters against my shoulder.

"You haven't ruined a thing," I say firmly, leaving no room for doubt.

"Nothing is ruined." Charleston offers her a warm, reassuring smile. "Everything was perfect."

Chloe pulls back slightly, her eyes red but filled with gratitude. She glances at Charleston, her lips quirking into a playful smile. "This big bloke here is one of the good ones, you know."

Charleston's gaze meets mine, her lips curving into a soft smile. "I'm starting to see that."

Chapter 11

Magnolia Steel

THE PRIVATE ELEVATOR ASCENDS WITH A SOFT, STEADY HUM, BUT the tension between us is anything but subtle. I focus on keeping my breathing steady, but it's impossible to ignore his scent in this confined space—faint yet intoxicating.

Caesar stands beside me, close but not touching, his hands tucked casually into the pockets of his impeccably tailored trousers. He radiates an easy confidence, a presence that only amplifies the tension between us.

The floor numbers tick upward, our destination drawing near, yet time feels excruciatingly slow. Each second drags, stretching the charged energy between us closer to its breaking point.

I steal a glance at him, my heart pounding so fiercely it feels like it could crack a rib. He catches my gaze, and a slow, knowing grin spreads across his face—teasing, confident, as if he's perfectly attuned to the thoughts swirling in my mind.

The elevator feels impossibly small, the walls pressing in, and him... he's overwhelming, all-consuming. If he makes even the slightest move toward me, I'm not sure I'll have the willpower to resist.

And truthfully, I don't think I want to.

This man's not looking like a snack. He's a full-course meal.

The elevator doors finally slide open, and we step directly into the penthouse. My breath catches as the sheer grandeur of the space hits me—soaring ceilings, walls of glass framing the Sydney skyline, and an open-concept layout that feels like it's been pulled from the pages of a design magazine. Everything gleams—from the polished marble floors to the sleek, modern furniture.

"This is——" I trail off, struggling to find the right words. "This is way too much. You can't possibly let me stay here for three months."

"That's the beauty of owning the hotel. I can do whatever I like. And this place is yours for as long as you stay."

I wander toward the center of the room, drawn to the towering arrangement of fresh flowers. Roses, orchids, lilies—some so exotic I can't name them. I brush my fingers lightly over the petals, their delicate fragrance wrapping around me, soft and inviting. It's the kind of beauty that feels almost untouchable, yet here it is, real and within reach.

"This is mind-blowing." I say it more to myself than to him.

Caesar slips his hands into his pockets, at ease in the luxurious setting, looking every bit like he belongs here. "It's all yours."

My emotions waver between awe and gratitude. "Thank you."

He inclines his head slightly, the warmth in his eyes genuine. "My pleasure."

He steps closer, his presence filling the space between us. "Each morning, you can call the kitchen and request your in-room breakfast —only the freshest ingredients, of course. Or, if you'd prefer, you're welcome to dine at one of the restaurants. And if you ever want something from the bar sent up, it's yours. Whatever you need, whenever you need it."

I shake my head, stunned. "I can't let you spoil me like this."

"Oh, I'm definitely going to spoil you." A sly grin tugs at one corner of his mouth. "Best three months of your life, remember?"

For a moment, I'm at a loss. The depth of his sincerity and the way he looks at me leave no room for argument.

It's hard for me to wrap my head around someone wanting to give me everything. I've never had that before. I've always been the one taking care of myself, figuring things out on my own, never expecting anyone else to step in. The idea of someone being eager to spoil me is foreign, almost impossible to accept.

Caesar gestures for me to follow him, leading me farther into the penthouse. The open layout strikes a balance between sleek luxury and inviting warmth. The oversized sectional faces a wall of glass, perfect for taking in the glittering nighttime skyline. A modern chandelier hangs above a gleaming glass dining table, casting soft light over the space. The kitchen, with its polished marble and stainless-steel finishes, blends into the design—understated but impressive.

He stops near a section of built-in cabinetry, opening a panel to reveal a sleek control system. "This is the surround sound." His fingers glide over the touchscreen. "You can connect your phone via Bluetooth. It's wired throughout the penthouse—living area, bedroom, even the bath."

I arch a brow, intrigued. "You're telling me I can have my playlists follow me everywhere?"

He grins, the kind that's equal parts charm and pride. "Every room."

Without hesitation, I pull out my phone, excitement bubbling up. Music has always been one of my favorite escapes—a pure, unfiltered joy. I'd choose a good playlist over television any day.

Caesar leans casually against the wall, watching me with a faintly amused smile as I navigate through my phone's settings, pairing it to the penthouse system. A soft hum fills the room as the connection locks in.

"Got it," I say, more to myself than to him.

"Good." His arms cross over his chest as he tilts his head, his grin widening. "Let's hear it. Put on your favorite playlist—I'm curious to learn what kind of music gets you going."

I scroll through my playlists, landing on the one I always return to —the soundtrack that fits every mood. I tap shuffle, and within moments, the room fills with the unmistakable rhythm of "Straight On" by Heart. The beat pulses softly through the speakers, and I find myself shifting my weight from one foot to the other, a subtle sway in time with the music. My fingers tap lightly against my thigh, the smallest movements betraying how easily the song pulls me in.

Caesar listens for a moment before glancing at me. "I don't recognize this one."

I'm not the least bit surprised. "I didn't think you would. Most people our age are completely clueless when it comes to my music taste—'60s, '70s, '80s, '90s. I'm a little all over the place."

"You're into throwbacks?"

"Throwbacks, vintage vibes, timeless hits—call it whatever you want. Music from those decades has a special kind of magic to it. It feels raw and real in a way that sticks with you."

He nods thoughtfully, then flashes a knowing grin. "Retro Rhythms at the Rabbit Hole must've been right up your alley."

Loved every minute. "Oh, it was perfect. The playlist was spot-on —it was like stepping back in time."

His grin widens, satisfaction clear in his expression. "I could tell. You looked like you were in your element."

"What about you? What kind of music do you like?"

"Hip-hop or country."

I laugh, unable to hide my surprise. "Those are two very different genres but both very cool."

He shrugs, that easy charm of his on full display. "Sometimes you want something with a beat, and sometimes you need a good story."

I sink into the plush couch, letting the song wrap around me like a comforting embrace. Music has such a way of softening the edges, making everything feel a little bit lighter.

Caesar sits opposite me, leaning back comfortably with one arm resting along the top, his gaze steady and curious. "So, how did you end up falling for this kind of music?"

"It's kind of a funny story." The memory tugs at the corners of my mind. "I grew up in a trailer park. The people who owned it, Leonard and Janet, took me under their wing."

I catch the spark of curiosity in his expression and cut off the question before it even forms. "And no, before you ask, Leonard wasn't a creep or anything. He was a good man. He saw a kid who needed someone and decided to step up when no one else would."

Memories flicker like snapshots in my mind. "Robin and Charlene were gone a lot, so I spent most of my time with Leonard and his wife, Janet. They made sure I was fed and safe. But here's the funny part about how my taste in music started—one of the tenants at the trailer park was a hardcore music lover. She had this massive collection of vinyls and cassettes—'60s, '70s, '80s, '90s, you name it. She couldn't pay rent because she spent all her money on music. Anyway, she got caught selling meth and went to jail, so Leonard kept her stuff as payment for what she owed him. Whenever I stayed with Leonard and Janet, we'd dig into that collection and listen to everything. That's where my love for music really began."

His expression softens. "Leonard's the one who left you his estate, isn't he?"

"Yeah, that's right. Leonard and Janet lost their only child when she was young. It broke something inside them, something that never really healed. They needed me as much as I needed them. I thank God for them. They gave me stability when no one else did. They were good to me—better than anyone ever had been. Honestly, I don't know where I'd be today if they hadn't stepped in."

"I'm really glad you had them."

"Me too." There's still a bittersweet ache in my chest when I think about them. "I miss Leonard and Janet every day."

We sit in comfortable silence for a moment, the music weaving its way through the air, turning into more than background noise. It feels like a bridge—connecting me to the memories and people who shaped me.

I let the silence stretch for a beat before glancing at him with a small smile, breaking the quiet. "Okay, enough with the heavy stuff. Show me the rest of this place."

He pushes off the arm of the couch with a casual ease. "Right this way."

He leads me through the penthouse, casually pointing out features as we go, but it's the bedroom that truly steals my breath. Understated yet undeniably luxurious, the space exudes quiet elegance. A king-sized bed is dressed in soft linen bedding, flanked by sleek, minimalist nightstands, and a low bench positioned neatly at its foot.

But my eyes go straight past the bed to the floor-to-ceiling windows dominating the far wall.

He gestures toward the windows. "This view is one of the best in the city. You've got the whole harbor right in front of you."

Drawn to the glass, I step closer, my breath catching as the view unfolds before me. The water stretches out in endless ripples, dotted with boats gliding under the moonlight. In the distance, the Sydney Opera House gleams, its iconic sails shimmering with reflected light. It's the kind of view that could hold you captive, and for a moment, it does.

I sense him behind me. His warmth wraps around me from behind, not quite touching, but anchoring me all the same. He doesn't touch me, but his presence is impossible to ignore.

The soft hum of "Straight On" drifts through the hidden speakers. Its soulful melody fills the air like it belongs here in this moment, weaving itself around us.

"You weren't kidding," I'm caught up in the beauty of the scene. "It's breathtaking."

"So are you," he murmurs, his words low and intimate, behind me.

I don't turn. I just stand there, the city sprawling out before us, letting the moment settle deep in my chest. For the first time, I realize being here—being with him—is exactly what I want.

He steps closer, his breath warm against the nape of my neck, sending a delicate shiver down my spine. When his lips graze the sensitive spot below my ear, a wave of heat rolls through me, melting every last bit of restraint. His arms wrap around me, strong and secure, pulling me against his broad chest. In his embrace, I feel comfort, desire, and a pull I can't resist.

"I've thought about doing this all night," he whispers, trailing feather-light kisses along the column of my neck. Each touch of his lips lights my nerve endings on fire, desire igniting deep in my core.

His husky voice brushes against my ear, and a rush of heat flushes through my body. His tender kisses set off a firework of sensations, awakening every inch of my skin. A primal urge takes hold of me as desire courses through my veins, centered deep within me.

I glance back over my shoulder, meeting his heated gaze. His eyes are dark with desire, mirroring my own barely restrained hunger. "I've thought about it too."

"I was hoping you'd say that." Then, in a smooth, casual manner, he calls out, "Close window shades."

The window coverings glide down with a soft buzz, the city lights fading away as they close. The room transforms instantly—warmer, more intimate—while the music wraps around us like a gentle embrace.

He stands closely behind me, delicately brushing my hair to the side and baring the sensitive skin of my neck. A shiver courses through me as his warm exhalation dances over me, followed by the tender pressure of his lips.

His hands glide down my arms, igniting tingling sensations along their path. I surrender into his sturdy embrace, reveling in the warmth radiating from him. He nuzzles against my neck, the bristles of his short beard sending a delightful tremble throughout my body.

A soft gasp escapes my lips as he gently nibbles on my earlobe, and his fingertips glide along my hips, pulling me closer to him. His arousal presses against my lower back, igniting a flame within me. My breath quickens and desire builds in the depths of my core.

"You want this, right?" He pauses for a heartbeat. "I need to hear you say it so there's no confusion on my part."

I've never had a man ask for my permission. They're usually too eager to take what they can, rushing in before I have the chance to change my mind and say no.

I turn in his arms, my hands sliding up to cradle his face. As I draw him down toward me, our eyes lock, the moment stretching between us. "I want you to fuck me. Fuck me hard and fuck me good. And when you're finished, I want you to do it all over again. Is there any confusion on your part about that?"

A slow smile spreads across his face. "No... no confusion at all."

"Good."

He reaches down, grasping the back of my thighs and lifts me as though I'm light as a feather. My legs wrap around his waist, and my heels fall off my feet, dropping to the floor.

My breath catches as he presses me against the wall, his strong body pinning me in place. Heat radiates off his skin, and his intoxicating scent fills my nose. He presses his lips against my neck, trailing hot kisses down the side to my collarbone. Instinctively, I tilt my head to the side, bearing my neck to him.

Fuck, this is hot.

He holds on to my hips, pushing my back against the wall. I eagerly reach for his shirt, determined to feel his skin against mine. But those damn buttons won't cooperate, adding a playful but frustrating struggle to our heated encounter.

Buttons 1 | Magnolia 0

"God, I want to feel you inside me." Now. And my frustration multiplies as these fucking buttons fight me tooth and nail.

Caesar lets out a low, primal growl and tightens his grip on me. He carries me over to the bed and places me on the soft mattress. He flashes a mischievous grin as he stands over me, unfastening the last of the buttons on his shirt.

Pain-in-the-ass buttons from hell.

He removes his shirt and lets it fall to the ground before crawling on top of me. I don't get much of a chance to admire the muscular lines of his body or the intricate tattoos that span his chest, shoulder, and arm—but I'll definitely make time for that later.

I arch my back off the bed and remove my shirt, tossing it over my head to the floor. He focuses his efforts on unhooking and unzipping my pants, slowly pulling them down my legs until they are off, leaving me in only my bra and panties

He gently lifts my leg, his bristled cheek grazing the tender skin of my inner calf. "There's nothing in the world quite like the softness of a woman's leg."

His warm breath dances across my skin as he trails soft kisses up my calf and then thigh. A shiver of anticipation runs through me. His mouth moves higher, his tongue tracing delicate patterns along my inner thighs. I let out a breathy gasp as his mouth approaches the edge of my lacy underwear.

Shit.

Is he going there?

Is he not?

I don't know.

Do I want him to?

Maybe.

Fuck.

Of course, I want him to.

"I'm obsessed with every inch of you." He looks up at me with those nearly black eyes. "I haven't been able to stop wondering what you might taste like."

"Oh fuck," I say, mostly to myself, as I fall back on the bed and close my eyes, listening to the music around us, absorbing it. I swear that I'll never hear Heart's "Straight On" again and not remember this moment.

He presses his lips against the delicate fabric of my panties, his warm breath tickling my skin through the crotch as he kisses me gently. Then, he runs his tongue over the damp lace, following the cleft of my center. And then he does it again. And then once more.

My teeth sink into my lower lip, muffling my moans as he teases me without mercy. Despite the frustrating barrier of lace between his tongue and where I want to feel him most, it is an exquisite form of torture that only heightens my pleasure.

Raising my head, I gaze down at the top of his head nestled between my thighs. "You're loving this, aren't you? Delighting in my torture."

He looks up and a mischievous smile spreads across his face. "I must say, I'm rather enjoying myself."

"I believe you may have sadistic tendencies." And wow, what a beautiful sadist he is.

His tongue darts out and glides over his lips. "Do you want me to stop?"

"Don't even think about it."

He lets out a contemplative, low hum, his smile taking on a mischievous edge. "I believe you might have some masochistic tendencies."

I lie back down, allowing the music to seep into my soul. "If being a masochist means enjoying this kind of torture... then yeah. Guilty as charged. Carry on, sadist."

And he does.

His thumb traces over the wet lace of my panties, pressing against my clit in small, deliberate circles. My fingers tangle in his hair as he sends waves of sensation through my body.

I can't believe I'm already this close to coming and he hasn't even taken off my panties yet.

Don't come, Magnolia. Not yet, girl. I know it's been a long time, but it's too soon. This is only the beginning. You don't want to miss out on what's to come.

"Fuck, you smell good... but I can't play this game with you any longer. I'm torturing my own damn self. And I'm dying to taste you."

"I eat a lot of pineapple."

He stops and looks up at me. "*What?*"

God, Magnolia. Why did you say that—especially now? "It's nothing. I'll explain later."

He grabs the waist of my panties, and with a gentle tug, he pulls them past my hips and down my thighs. He then loops his fingers through the waistband and flings my panties across the bed like a slingshot. "You won't be needing those the rest of the night," he says, sporting possibly the sexiest smirk I've ever seen.

Lifting my legs and gripping my thighs, he pulls me toward him until my body is perched on the edge of the bed. Spreading my legs apart, he lowers himself onto his knees and nuzzles his face against my pelvis, taking a deep breath. A low mmm escapes from his lips as he savors the scent.

I shudder with pleasure as his warm breath teases my sensitive skin.

He delicately spreads my outer lips with his thumbs, then traces his tongue along the cleft between them. As soon as the tip reaches my sensitive clit, my body bucks with a jolt of pleasure.

He chuckles, a deep, throaty sound. "Oh, Charleston, I'm about to have so much fun making you come."

"I can't promise you I'll be quiet when I do."

"Scream if you like."

With my lips spread wide, he presses his tongue against my throbbing core. His tongue slides up and down my drenched petals, igniting intense sensations that consume me in ecstasy.

My fingers claw at the sheets as his mouth devours my clit, expertly teasing and tantalizing me. His lips seal over the sensitive nub, applying the perfect amount of pressure as his tongue dances and swirls around it.

I gasp and arch my back, grinding against his face. He slides two fingers inside me, curling them to stroke the most sensitive spot as he continues to feast. The combination of maneuvers sends waves of ecstasy through me, nearly driving me over the edge.

Almost... but not quite.

As his tongue explores, the tension in my groin intensifies, and I feel myself getting closer to the edge. I am completely consumed by the intense pleasure coursing through my body. My breaths become erratic as the anticipation builds, coiling tighter and tighter within me. The sensations are overwhelming, and I am on the brink of euphoria, longing for release.

Soft moans escape my lips as the intense sensations consume me. With his hands now firmly gripping my hips, I'm anchored as the pleasure continues to rise. My entire body trembles with anticipation, teetering on the brink of pure ecstasy.

My breath comes in ragged gasps as he tightens his grip and picks up the pace. Every stroke sends a surge of pleasure through me, building up like sparks, ready to ignite an inferno, until I can't hold back any longer.

I moan out loud, grasping his hair as the first waves of climax hit me hard. My body convulses and pulses with the intense sensations, reaching their peak. He doesn't let up, drawing out my pleasure until I'm quivering and breathless.

My body trembles as waves of pleasure wash over me. I'm floating, weightless, enveloped in a warm glow of blissful release. My skin tingles with electricity. I let out a long, contented sigh as the last tremors of ecstasy ripple through me.

My tense muscles slowly unclench as I melt into the sheets, utterly spent and deeply satisfied, savoring every moment of this euphoric haze. A dreamy smile plays across my lips as I bask in the afterglow, savoring every delicious sensation. I feel cherished, desired, alive.

In this perfect moment, all is right with the world.

He slowly moves up my body, his face coming into view above mine. "Well," he says with a sly smirk, "I'd say we did a pretty good job. Though I may have some lockjaw now."

I let out a breathless giggle and reach up to caress his stubbly jawline. "Poor thing. I guess I'll have to kiss it all better." I pull him closer for a deep, slow kiss, tasting remnants of myself on his lips and tongue.

His hand slides up my side, leaving tingles in its wake. He breaks the kiss and begins trailing his lips along my neck. "Mmm, I think I need more than kisses to recover," he murmurs against my skin.

I arch into him with a soft gasp as he finds a sensitive spot. "Is that so?" I manage to get out.

He hums in agreement, his breath warm against my neck. "Much more," he murmurs, his words thick with desire. His hand continues its journey upward, thumb brushing teasingly along the curve of my breast.

I can feel him hard against my thigh, stoking the fire building inside me once again. "Well then," I breathe, "I suppose I'll have to take care of you properly. But not with all of these clothes on. Let's fix that."

He gives me a brief kiss before standing up. In one swift motion, he unfastens his pants, and I sit up, quickly removing my bra. My eyes eagerly take in every inch of him as he removes his pants, revealing the throbbing length that I crave so desperately. I bite my lip with anticipation, ready to give myself completely to him.

His eyes are filled with longing as he comes back to me. I reach out and run my fingers over his skin, savoring the way his breath catches at my touch. He guides me down onto the bed and covers me with his body, the intensity between us palpable as he captures my lips in a passionate kiss.

As his fingers trace the curves of my body, a wave of pleasure washes over me. I arch into him, aching for more of his touch. His lips break away from mine and he trails kisses down my neck, leaving a fiery trail in their wake. A soft moan escapes my lips as I tangle my fingers in his hair, lost in the moment.

When he reaches my ear, he whispers, "I want you, Charleston. So much."

The raw need in his voice makes me whimper, and I tug him up for a passionate kiss. Our tongues tangle as his hips grind against mine. I feel how hard he is against my slick entrance.

"Please," I gasp, not even sure what I'm begging for.

But he knows.

With a gentle but firm push, he slides inside me, and I gasp at the sudden fullness. Our bodies mold together perfectly as we lay forehead to forehead, feeling our heartbeats synchronize with the rhythm of our movements. We both moan in unison, reveling in the overwhelming pleasure of being united in such an intimate way.

He shifts his weight on top of me, resting on his elbows and gazing into my eyes with an intense look. Our breaths mingle as he thrusts in a slow rhythm, gradually increasing in speed. I wrap my legs tightly around his waist, pulling him closer until our bodies are pressed together. The friction between us is electrifying, sending waves of pleasure through every nerve in my body as we move together in perfect synchrony.

Our bodies writhe together in a frenzy of passion, slick with sweat and tangled limbs. I dig my nails into the hard planes of his back as he devours my neck with his mouth. The heat between us rises to a fever pitch, sending waves of pleasure coursing through me.

His powerful thrusts bring me right to the edge, and with one final cry, I reach the peak of ecstasy. Again.

"Fuck, Charleston. Fuck."

He grunts and moans against my neck, finding his own release moments after mine. Our bodies tremble and our breaths mingle as we come down from our shared high.

Our bodies meld together as one, our breaths ragged and heavy. A sense of complete fulfillment washes over me, like I'm floating on a cloud of pure ecstasy. We lay intertwined, reveling in the tranquil aftermath of our passionate union, unmoving except for the rise and fall of our chests as we bask in the warm afterglow of our intimate connection.

He pulls out of me and rolls onto his back. I snuggle into the crook of his arm, feeling his chest rise and fall rapidly as his breathing slows. My fingers trace over the rippling muscles on his stomach, still heated from our passion.

I inhale deeply, savoring his musky scent mixed with sweat and sex, my body still tingling with residual pleasure. I trail my fingertips higher, swirling around his nipples and along his collarbone. He sighs contentedly, one hand stroking my hair while the other caresses the curve of my hip.

"That was—" I start, searching for the right words.

"Perfect," he says, the words a low rumble that seems to resonate through his chest.

A smile tugs at my lips as I tilt my head to meet his gaze. "Yeah, it really was."

His hand glides softly up and down my arm. "Skipping protection was reckless... but I can't say I regret a single second of it."

"So reckless," I agree, my smile widening. "But very, very good. No regrets here either."

He chuckles softly, the sound rumbling through his chest beneath my cheek. "I'm ruined now. How am I supposed to use condoms with you after having the best sex of my life without them?"

I lift my head slightly, a teasing smile playing on my lips. "The best sex of your life, huh?"

"Hands down." The certainty in his words wraps around me. "Nothing else even comes close."

A blush creeps across my face. "It was the best sex of my life too."

His hand strokes gently through my hair, the tender gesture sending a wave of warmth through me. "I'm happy to hear that."

"You don't need to worry about a pregnancy. I have an IUD."

He shrugs. "I'm not worried. I knew you'd be on some kind of birth control."

"You seem pretty sure about that." I prop myself up on one elbow to get a better look at him.

"You're clearly a woman who's got things figured out and doesn't leave important things to chance," he says with a wink.

"Oh really? And what else have you deduced about me, Sherlock?"

He pretends to ponder, his fingers still lazily threading through my hair. "Let's see. You're smart, ambitious, and you act like you don't need anyone. But deep down, I think you want someone who sees you—really sees you."

His words resonate deeper than I expect, brushing against a part of me I keep locked away. And I feel more exposed than I'm comfortable with. "That's a bold assumption."

His gaze holds steady, unwavering. "Not an assumption. Just an observation. And apparently *you eat a lot of pineapple?* Care to elaborate?"

I smirk, tilting my head. "You know what they say about women eating pineapple, right?"

One brow lifts in curiosity. "Enlighten me."

I lean in slightly, lowering my voice enough to tease. "It's supposed to make a woman... taste sweeter."

A slow, knowing smile spreads across his face. "Must be true then. Because you're pretty damn sweet."

Heat floods my cheeks, but I manage to keep my composure. "Oh? Is that so?"

He leans in enough to make my pulse stutter. "I'm happy to keep testing the theory... for the sake of science."

I bite my lip, letting the moment stretch between us for a moment. "Well, I'm always willing to contribute to scientific discovery."

The heat in his gaze makes it clear we're toeing a dangerous line. I swallow, searching for something—anything—to steady myself.

He's read me pretty accurately so far, but I want to know more about him. "You seem to have me all figured out. Tell me what you want in life."

He's quiet for a moment, his hand still lightly tangled in my hair. Then, with a quiet exhale, he simply says, "Peace."

The single word hangs between us, uncomplicated yet

profoundly heavy. It settles somewhere deep inside me, resonating in a way I understand far more than I'd like to admit.

The next song thrums softly in the background, wrapping around us as the silence stretches. In this moment, I realize something unexpected: being here with him, in this space, might be the closest I've ever come to finding peace myself.

And maybe—just maybe—*that's* what makes this so dangerous.

Chapter 12

Magnolia Steel

THE FAINTEST HINT OF MORNING SLIPS INTO THE ROOM, BARELY peeking around the edges of the blackout shades. The soft glow casts everything in muted shadows, just enough light to make out the shape of him beside me.

My eyes drift over him, taking in every detail, savoring the sight of him sprawled out on the bed. The sheet lies low on his hips, barely covering him. He's naked underneath—completely—and that knowledge makes my pulse skip. The dark waves of his glossy jet-black hair stand out against the stark white of the pillow, a contrast that draws my gaze, much like everything about him.

As my gaze roams, it traces the sharp line of his jaw, the proud slope of his nose, and the curve of his lips. His chest rises and falls with steady breaths, the intricate tribal tattoos etched into his skin shifting subtly with each inhale. My gaze trails down to his waist, the sheet clinging to his hips, teasing me with what lies beneath.

He's the most beautiful man I've ever been with. More than that, he's the sexiest... a literal dream. And last night? It was everything I imagined and then some.

Hotter than a skillet of cornbread.

Every fantasy I've ever had... he made them real. And then there were things I didn't even know I wanted until he gave them to me.

Caesar wasn't just good. He was a giver, not a taker, not the kind of man who's only interested in his own pleasure. He gave himself completely. And the way he touched me was like every inch of me mattered, even the imperfect parts. It was more than I ever dared hope for.

I lie here, drinking in the sight of him, knowing I've never experienced anything like last night. This man is special. That much I know.

He stirs beside me, shifting under the sheets. His dark lashes flutter for a moment, and then his eyes meet mine, a lazy smile spreading across his face. "Morning."

"Good morning," I whisper back, warmth spreading through my chest simply from the way he looks at me.

He stretches slightly, his muscles shifting under the sheet. "Didn't sleep well? Was the bed uncomfortable?"

I shake my head, my lips curving into a playful smile. "The bed was wonderful. And so was my bedmate."

His laugh is low and easy, the kind of sound that makes me want to hear it again. "I was pretty pleased with my bedmate too."

I prop myself up on one elbow, rubbing my hand over the sheet, appreciating its softness. "I don't sleep with men afterward. It's not something I do."

It takes a lot of trust to close your eyes and sleep beside someone. But that's not what kept me awake. It wasn't fear or discomfort, rather the rush of something I'm not used to. Dopamine, oxytocin, serotonin—a mix of all the feel-good hormones that happens after a night like we had. That's what kept me up.

After all, he made me come twice before midnight... and I lost count during the small hours.

Concern tugs at his features. "I hope I wasn't the reason you didn't sleep."

A laugh slips from my lips. "Oh, Julius Caesar. You absolutely disturbed my sleep but in the best way possible."

He shifts a little closer, the warmth of his body radiating through the thin sheet. "Good. That's exactly what I was going for."

Caesar glances over at the clock on the nightstand. "Five in the morning," he says, rubbing a hand down his face. "Too early for breakfast?"

I smile lazily, still enjoying the warmth of the bed. "I'm not an early eater."

"I'm an all-the-time eater."

I can see why. He's easily double my size—broad, powerful, every inch of him solid muscle. I can't even begin to imagine how many calories it takes to maintain a body like his.

"I'll take some coffee."

He raises an eyebrow. "I'll order extra food. You can have whatever you want."

Before I can protest, he reaches for the phone on the nightstand and dials room service. I listen, amused, as he rattles off the order—it sounds like enough food for four people, maybe six. Eggs, bacon, sausage, toast, fruit, pancakes, and everything else under the sun.

When he hangs up, a chuckle rumbles from his chest. "It takes a lot to keep me going."

"Yeah, I see that."

"You'll need to get the door when breakfast arrives. I can't be seen by the staff."

I hadn't even thought about that. Of course, he'd need to avoid being seen by his employees.

"You know they're going to realize I'm not eating all that food by myself."

"They'll assume you've got a man up here. It just can't be me they see."

I'm not the least bit offended. It makes sense. Just as I'm asking the same of him when it comes to my coworkers. "I absolutely get it."

He gives an understanding nod, and for a moment, we lie there, the easy quiet settling between us. Then I stretch, reluctant to leave the warmth of the bed but knowing I must. "I should get up and put something on before breakfast arrives."

"Turn on more of your weird music first to get the day started."

I narrow my eyes, grabbing my phone from the nightstand. "You *like* my music." I scroll through my playlists, setting it to shuffle on my favorite one.

He shakes his head, laughing. "No, I don't. I'm just amazed that you actually like it."

The familiar beat of a retro track fills the room, and I laugh, knowing full well he doesn't mind it as much as he pretends.

I slip out of bed and make my way to the bathroom, feeling the cool marble under my bare feet. The moment I close the door behind me, I stretch slowly—and wince. Yeah, I'm definitely going to feel this all day.

Every ache is a souvenir from an unforgettable night, reminding me that he fucked me good and fucked me long. I earned every ounce of this soreness.

I turn on the faucet, splashing cool water on my face to wake up, then glance around the space. The bathroom is all sleek lines, soft lighting, and luxury at every turn. A door catches my eye, and when I open it, I find a plush robe and matching slippers waiting inside.

The robe's fabric is as soft as a pillowy cloud, wrapping me in its luxurious warmth the moment I slip it on. The slippers are indulgent as well, cradling my feet with every step.

Adjusting the belt of the robe, I catch my reflection in the mirror. The perks of staying in a penthouse are definitely something I could get used to.

Stepping out of the bathroom, my eyes are immediately drawn to him. He's sprawled on the bed, lying on his back with his arms propped behind his head, his strong biceps on full display. And then there's the unmistakable evidence of his arousal—unrelenting and impossible to ignore.

"Apologies," he says, a mischievous glint in his eyes. "Thoughts of last night crossed my mind while you were in the bathroom, and... well, this happened." The playful curve of his lips leaves no doubt he's savoring every second of the memory.

A soft laugh escapes me as I step closer to the bed, stopping beside him. "Come here," I say, a smile playing on my lips.

He stretches his legs out, easing himself to the edge of the mattress until his feet rest on the floor. I approach him and straddle his lap, my arms encircling his neck as I settle onto him. My knees press against the sides of his hips, and our bodies meld together in a warm embrace.

From the speakers above, one of my favorite songs plays—"Look What You've Done to Me" by Boz Scaggs. The slow tempo is exactly what I need for what I have in mind, making it the perfect soundtrack for my plans.

My sore thighs quiver as I gradually lower myself onto him. As he slides deeper, I gasp and grip his shoulders, feeling every inch of him stretching me in the most exquisite way. I savor the sensation of being completely filled by his length, an intense feeling of both pleasure and pressure. My body trembles as I take him in fully, all the way to the hilt.

I lift myself onto my knees and lower myself, repeating the motion over and over. Our bodies move in unison, a slow and steady rhythm that consumes us both in an intense dance of passion.

His hands are gentle but firm as they hold on to my hips, guiding me and meeting my movements with subtle thrusts upward. His voice, deep and velvety, is filled with raw desire as he exhales the words, "The way you feel wrapped around me is un-fucking-believable."

With my arms draped around his shoulders, I move up and down, my hips rolling in perfect rhythm with the music. Every movement is deliberate and delicious, as I savor him moving inside me and embrace the moment fully. "You promised me the time of my life. But maybe I'm the one who's going to give *you* the time of *your* life."

"This is a damn good start." His words spill out in a low, husky murmur that sends shivers racing down my spine.

He grips my hips, his palms imprinting on to my skin as he guides my movements. Our eyes are locked in an unbreakable gaze, filled with primal desire and unwavering determination. The sound of our breaths fills the space between us as I ride him with a steady pace. Our bodies move together in a seductive rhythm, each movement igniting an inferno of pleasure that consumes us both.

"Fuck, I'm going to come," he says.

I nod, unable to speak.

His fingers dig into my skin, gripping me with a fierce intensity as his body moves in perfect synchronization with mine. Each thrust brings us closer to the edge, the heat between us building with every movement.

He lets out a deep groan, his movements becoming slower and deeper. I squeeze tightly around him, eager to bring him to the brink of ecstasy. In one last powerful thrust, he drives himself deeply into me and releases with a strong pulse. The overwhelming sensation consumes me, and I cry out as pulsating waves of pleasure wash over my entire body, fully embracing the moment.

He gently brushes my hair away from my face, placing a soft kiss on my forehead. A contented sigh escapes me as I nestle closer to his chest.

"That was amazing," he says, his lips lingering against my skin. "Again."

"Mm-hmm." The small murmur of agreement is soft and content as I snuggle deeper into his embrace.

"The chemistry between us is something else."

"Unmatched." I steal a quick kiss from his lips as the doorbell chimes through the penthouse suite. "Looks like your breakfast has arrived, sir."

When I return from answering the door, I stop in my tracks, laughter bubbling up. Caesar is standing by the bed wearing the other robe from the bathroom closet—or at least he's attempting to wear it.

It doesn't come close to closing over his broad chest, and the loosely knotted belt barely keeps it in place. At least he's got boxer briefs on underneath though they don't exactly conceal how impressively built he is.

My attention shifts to the absurd spread of food on the cart—plates piled high with pancakes, eggs, bacon, sausages, fruit, and at least three different kinds of toast. I stare at it, wide-eyed. "Are you seriously planning to eat all of that?"

Caesar's towering frame makes the dining cart look like a piece of dollhouse furniture. "I'm two centimeters shy of two meters tall and I weigh 109 kilograms. What do you think?"

I'm out of my depth on this one without some math. "I'm American. That means absolutely nothing to me unless I pull out a calculator."

"All right, yank babe. I'm just about six feet six and 240 pounds."

My jaw slackens. I knew he was big, but hearing the numbers said out loud proves how massive he is.

"Are you sure wrestling wasn't your old gig?" I give him a slow once-over. "Because you're looking an awful lot like Roman Reigns but with shorter hair."

He tips his head back, his laugh deep and unrestrained. "Not wrestling. And I can promise you I'm definitely not Roman Reigns."

"Well, you should've been a wrestler. You'd fit right in with Roman and The Rock."

"What I did was tougher than scripted wrestling."

Curiosity tugs at me. "*Who are you?*"

"Wouldn't you like to know?"

I roll my eyes, but I can't stop the grin that spreads across my face. "I could figure it out, you know. A quick internet search and I'd have all the answers."

A playful challenge burns in his gaze. "So why don't you?"

"Because I like the mystery. It's more fun not knowing."

He nods slowly. "I get that."

Caesar tears into breakfast like a man who hasn't eaten in a week, devouring pancakes, bacon, eggs, toast, and fruit like it's a warm-up round. I sip my coffee, quietly amazed at how much food he's packing away.

"You didn't eat like this last night," I say as he finishes the first plate.

He wipes his mouth with a napkin. "That's because Chloe's dinner portions were a joke. I went to bed starving."

"Starving, huh? You poor, deprived thing."

He winks, and my heart betrays me with that infuriating flutter it's been doing since I met him.

"Do you plan to shower here?"

He leans back, stretching his arms with a groan. "I have meetings today, so I'll have to go home for a clean suit. I'll shower there."

It's weird, but I already miss him even though he's still here. "Okay."

He glances at the clock, then back at me with a reluctant smile. "I hate to rush off, but I need to get going."

I nod, trying not to let my disappointment show. "Of course. The day waits for no one."

He slips into his clothes from last night. "I don't want to smother you, but I'd like to see you again... as soon as you'll let me."

A calm warmth spreads through me. "Text me after your meetings. We'll figure something out."

A playful glint lights up his eyes. "Happy to. But I'm going to need your number first."

I laugh, shaking my head at the absurdity. "Oh my God, we've already spent the night together, and I haven't even given you my number yet. That's absurd."

He chuckles, leaning in with a teasing smirk. "Seems fitting since we've been doing everything out of order and breaking all the rules."

We exchange phones, and I type my number into his. When I hand it back, he glances at the screen, smirking. "There. You're in. And you're already making it into my favorites list."

"A favorite already? That's pretty bold."

He shrugs, that teasing grin still firmly in place. "Bold and accurate."

I grin, typing his name into my phone. "Julius Caesar," I say aloud, shaking my head. "JC."

"My alias is starting to grow on me."

We hesitate by the door, neither of us ready to let the moment end. His eyes darken, and before I can overthink it, he pulls me close —one hand sliding into my hair, the other settling firmly around my waist. The kiss is slow, deep, and says everything we haven't put into words.

When we finally pull back, breathless, our foreheads rest together. "See you later, favorite," he whispers, his voice rough around the edges.

"Later, JC," I say softly.

With a longing look and a half smile, he steps onto the private elevator, leaving behind the faint scent of him and a smile that won't soon leave my face.

I glance at the clock on the nightstand: 6:15 a.m. Grabbing my phone, I open the weather app to check the time in Charleston. Perfect. Violet will be finishing work soon, and the conversation I need to have with her is definitely *NSFW*—not safe for work.

Setting the phone aside, I head to the bathroom for a quick shower, hoping to clear my head. The warm water cascades over me, washing away the lingering tension of the night. Once I'm out, I wrap myself in the robe, towel off my hair, and grab my phone again. Switching to speaker, I dial Violet's number while moving around the room, bracing myself for the conversation ahead.

The phone rings twice before she answers. "Well, well." Violet's words come through, sharp with playful curiosity. "Twice in one week? Either you've caused a scandal or uncovered one. Spill it."

I grin, propping my phone on the counter in the bathroom. "I haven't uncovered anything."

"Which means you've started one. All right, Steel, I'm ready. Hit me with it."

There's really no way to ease into this. "I went to dinner with Julius Caesar last night."

It's probably best to drop the headline and then give her a moment to process before I dive into the rest.

"Oh my God. You actually went for it." I can't tell if Vi is about to congratulate me or give me a lecture.

"Oh yeah. I went for it." All night long and then again this morning.

"I need the play-by-play—don't leave out a single detail. Was it sparks? Fireworks? Or are we talking full-on Fourth of July?"

I laugh, deciding to start at the beginning. "We went to dinner first. And then we had an in-depth conversation about what spending time together would look like. And we decided to enter into an *arrangement*."

There's a beat of silence.

"What kind of *arrangement*?" Suspicion practically drips through the line. "And don't you dare sugarcoat this, Magnolia."

"We'll have three months of fun together—just the two of us, completely under the radar. No one will know, especially not anyone from Soul Sync."

"Aren't the others staying right next door to you in the hotel?"

"Yes. That's why he moved me to the penthouse with a private elevator—to make it easier to keep things private."

"Wait, hold on one damn minute." Her voice shoots up an octave. "You're staying in a penthouse on the down-low? And he's going to fuck you while he searches for his wife?"

It sounds downright awful when she says it like that.

"No, Vi. He's called off the wife search for now."

"Well, damn. I've gotta hand it to you, Mags—you really know how to land yourself in the middle of some *shituations*."

She's not wrong. "What can I say? It's my superpower."

"Yeah, but this one's risky. You're getting involved with a client. What happens if someone finds out? Or worse—what if he decides to cut things off and you're left picking up the pieces? Have you thought about that?"

"I didn't plan for this to happen, Vi. But it did. And I like him. I really like him. It's only three months, and I'm okay with that. My heart is very aware."

She hesitates, her words gentler now. "That's surprisingly vulnerable for you. Seriously, Mags, that's not like you at all."

I pause, chewing on my bottom lip as her words settle in. "No, I guess not. But there's something about him, Vi. I know it's fast, but it feels so exciting."

Her words soften, carrying both warmth and caution. "Look, I'm glad you're letting someone in. That's a big deal for you. But promise me you'll be careful. Protect your heart, Mags. You're my best friend, and I don't want to see you get hurt."

"I won't let that happen." The words feel lighter than they should, hovering somewhere between determination and doubt.

"Please don't let yourself fall in love with him."

I roll my eyes as I lean against the bathroom counter. "Relax. There's no danger of that. I know exactly what this is. It's the here and now—nothing more."

Her words lose some of their playful edge. "It worries me because I've never heard you this excited about a guy before. Ever."

"That's because I've never met anyone like him. He's ridiculously good-looking. And, well... the sex is incredible."

"You know what my two cents are: don't fall in love. Don't fall pregnant. And don't fall victim to some kind of infection in your pussoir that none of us can pronounce."

Pussoir. That's a new one. Trust Violet to coin a term that's equal parts cringeworthy and hysterical. Leave it to her to make serious advice sound like a stand-up routine.

"And please don't make me use up my vacation days to fly halfway around the world to pick up the pieces if he breaks your heart, okay?"

While I appreciate her concern, it's not needed. "I know what I signed up for, Vi. Three months and then we're done. We walk away —it's that simple. I've got this."

Violet makes a small, doubtful sound but doesn't press further. "Okay. Just as long as you're sure."

"I'm sure." I will the confidence in my voice to be convincing.

"Fine. But I swear, if you land yourself in some international drama, I'm showing up with a megaphone and a hell of a lot of 'I told you so.'"

She absolutely would. "Noted."

"Love you, Mags. And remember—don't do anything I wouldn't do."

"That leaves me with a whole lot of nothing."

Her words carry a quiet plea. "Promise me you'll take care of yourself, okay?"

"I will, Vi. Love you."

"Love you too. Talk soon."

I hang up, still smiling, the plush penthouse robe draped over me and the faint scent of him lingering in the air—a reminder that no matter how I spin it to Violet, I've definitely found my way into trouble.

Chapter 13

Magnolia Steel

THE RHYTHMIC CLICKING OF KEYBOARDS GREETS ME AS I STEP into Soul Sync's office.

"Good morning!" Sophie's greeting is unusually bright and cheerful.

"Morning." I notice the coffee cup in her hand—the familiar logo from the café where Elijah sometimes surprises me with my favorite drink. I arch a brow, fighting a smirk. Sophie would never get coffee from there... unless Elijah made another visit to her room last night. It would explain the extra bounce in her step.

Not that I'm one to judge. After the night—and morning—I've had, I'm happier than a flea at a dog show.

I set my bag down beside my desk and fire up my computer, silently hoping for a quiet, uneventful start to the day.

No such luck.

Whitney appears out of nowhere, practically bouncing with excitement, her eyes wide and bursting with gossip. "You're not going to believe this. Julius Caesar emailed me this morning. He said Cleopatra isn't his match."

My heart skips.

He did it.

He actually did it.

"What else did his email say?"

"He wants to pause the matchmaking process and take some time to figure out if this is really the right path for him. Can you believe that?"

Actually, I can. "Wow."

Sophie's expression is dazed. "That almost never happens. I can recall maybe a handful of people who've ever been unhappy with their match. It's... odd, isn't it?"

"I don't think so. If he wasn't feeling it with Cleopatra, he wasn't feeling it. No point forcing it. I think he did the right thing."

Sophie shrugs, still baffled. "I guess. But Cleopatra? She's such a catch. If Julius Caesar knew what he was tossing aside, he'd kick himself."

Would he though?

I didn't meet Cleopatra or learn much about her beyond the surface details. Still, curiosity gnaws at me—what does she look like? Is she the poised, perfect type? The kind of woman who makes it hard to compete?

The thought stirs a faint jealousy in my chest. Silly, I know. He never even met her.

And he chose me. He's mine for the next three months, and that's all that matters.

I sit at my desk, scrolling through the Soul Sync profiles of the couple scheduled to arrive later this week. My notes are scattered across the top—color palettes, fabric swatches, and a few sketches for the dating suite decor. I tap my pen against the paper, brainstorming ways to make the space perfect for them based upon the profile I received.

The door suddenly swings open, startling me, as Elijah bursts in with far more energy than necessary. "Where were you this morning?"

I blink, momentarily thrown off. "*What?*"

"I brought you your favorite drink from the café. I waited outside your room, knocked several times, but you never answered. Didn't even hear the shower running."

A cold ripple of discomfort prickles down my spine. Was he seriously standing there, listening for me in the shower?

What the fuck is wrong with this guy?

I shove the thought aside and school my expression into something inscrutable. "There was an issue with my room. The hotel had to move me."

Elijah's frown deepens. "What kind of issue?"

I shrug. "I'm not sure. I didn't press for details."

His arms cross over his chest, his displeasure unmistakable. "Where'd they move you to?"

"Several floors up." There's no way I'm giving him my new room number, let alone telling him I'm staying in the penthouse. The last thing I need is Elijah knowing where to find me.

His eyes narrow, clearly not satisfied with my vague response, but I hold my ground, meeting his gaze without flinching. If he's fishing for details, he's not getting them from me.

"Do they plan to move you back to the room near us?"

"I don't think so. And honestly, I hope they don't. The new room has an amazing view of the harbor."

I battle the smile tugging at my lips. This morning's view was easily the most breathtaking thing I've ever woken up to. But it wasn't because of the harbor. JC, with his tousled hair and the sheet slung low on his hips, looked like pure, unapologetic sin. The way his dark eyes locked on mine, as if I was the only thing in the world he wanted, made the skyline disappear entirely.

"Being so far from Whitney, Sophie, and me will be a hassle for you."

"Well, they did give me a free upgrade for the inconvenience. I think I'll survive."

Elijah doesn't seem ready to drop the issue, but I am.

I lower my gaze to my desk, dismissing him. "I'm still pulling everything together for the new set. I'll let you know later today when I'm ready to discuss it."

"Sure thing." With a small nod, he heads out of my office.

The rest of the day passes in a blur of color swatches and furniture arrangements. I lose myself in the design, piecing together how everything will come together for the new clients.

My small staging warehouse in Sydney isn't nearly as stocked as the one in Charleston, and I'm missing a few key pieces that would make the space perfect. I'll need to go shopping tomorrow.

With the deadline looming, I hand off the building portion of the set to Elijah, who, thankfully, doesn't feel the need to talk it to death. At least when he's busy building, he's not hovering over me.

I'll give him credit where it's due—he's good at what he does. He always aims to get things exactly right, double-checking every detail to make sure I'm pleased with the final product. And he's never missed a deadline, which is probably why, despite all the reasons I have to complain about him, I know I'll never be rid of him unless he makes the decision to leave.

Still, I'm relieved when Elijah is finally out of sight, leaving me alone with my sketches and plans.

My phone buzzes on the desk, lighting up with a message.

> Hey, favorite. Got a business dinner tonight. Can I catch up with you afterward?

I smile, typing a quick reply.

> That's fine. I'll grab dinner with my coworkers. Enjoy your meeting.

His response comes almost immediately.

> Not likely. I'll be with my father and some others from the hotel industry. I'd much rather have dinner with you.

A grin tugs at my lips as I type back, feeling a little daring.

> Maybe you can come for dessert. 😏

> Or maybe I ditch this business dinner altogether and come for dessert now.

> > Patience, JC. 😏

> Patience isn't my strong suit. I'm going to think about you every second until I see you again.

> > Same.

By the time the workday ends, I'm completely wiped. It's always like this when new clients are scheduled to arrive—every single detail has to be flawless, from initial concepts to final touches. There's no room for error and juggling it all leaves me drained.

By the time I shut down my computer and pack up for the night, I feel like I've been wrung dry.

Everyone else seems to feel the same. Sophie, Whitney, Elijah, and I exchange weary looks as we gather our things. None of us have the energy to catch a taxi, hunt down a restaurant, and then drag ourselves back late. It's an unspoken agreement—we'll stick to the hotel restaurant tonight.

Dinner as a group has become routine. None of us like eating alone, and it's easier to stick together. Opting for the hotel restaurant means we can relax without the hassle of going out.

The food, as always, doesn't disappoint. We exchange satisfied smiles between bites, all silently agreeing that staying in was the best decision. I swirl my wine lazily in its glass, letting the conversation flow around me as I take a moment to savor the calm.

And then I see *him*.

Across the room, seated at a table with a group of impeccably dressed older men, is JC. He's deep in conversation as he commands the attention of everyone at the table.

He's wearing a sleek black suit, perfectly tailored to his broad shoulders and powerful frame. The crisp white shirt beneath it makes the dark fabric stand out even more. But it's the tie that catches my eye—*hot pink*.

I fight the grin tugging at my lips. Hot pink? I wouldn't have pegged him as the type, but it's breathtaking against his rich, warm skin tone, black hair, and those smoldering, intense eyes. The color somehow makes him even more striking.

I glance his way again, and our eyes meet. A slow, knowing smile tugs at the corner of his mouth as he lifts his wine glass in a subtle salute, his gaze locked on mine.

I arch an eyebrow, keeping my expression cool and composed. But inside my pulse is racing, and every nerve is humming with anticipation.

He is so damn hot. And for the next three months, he's all mine.

I try not to look in his direction. I really do. But it's impossible. Every time my gaze slips that way—and it slips often—JC is already watching me, his dark eyes unwavering, like he's daring me to meet his stare.

The soft vibration of my phone pulls me out of my thoughts. I glance down, the screen lighting up with a new message.

> You look beautiful.

I fight the smile threatening to break free and tap out a reply under the table, careful not to attract attention.

> Thank you. I must admit, I'm a little surprised by the hot-pink tie. 🩶 But it works.

I barely set the phone down before it buzzes again.

> Are you wearing knickers?

My cheeks burn, and I cross my legs under the table, squirming in my seat.

> Sorry to disappoint, but yes.

Another buzz, and I glance down quickly.

> I'm going to walk by your table in one minute. Tell your coworkers you're going to the toilet. Get up and follow me. You won't be wearing those knickers for much longer.

A shiver runs down my spine, and my heart skips a beat. How does he do this to me? I press my thighs together, trying to keep my expression flat as excitement bubbles under the surface.

> Yes, sir.

My phone buzzes immediately after.

> Just so you know, I like it when you call me sir.

I glance across the room in time to see him push back from his table, standing with grace. His eyes find mine, and the look he gives me—dark, smoldering, and full of promises—makes my breath hitch.

I lean forward, setting my wine glass down with deliberate ease. "Please excuse me for a moment. I need to visit the ladies' room."

Without waiting for a response, I stand, slipping my phone into my bag as my heart races.

But as I move away from the table, Whitney pushes her chair back too. "I'll go with you."

I falter, scrambling for a response. "Oh, uh—no need! You should stay and enjoy your wine."

She waves me off, already standing. "Nah, I need to use it too."

Dammit. Whitney is going to ruin this for me.

With Whitney trailing behind me, I silently pray to every higher power that JC notices her and realizes she's with me. At the same time, I pray Whitney doesn't notice him or, worse, recognize him as a client.

As we round the corner toward the restrooms, I find him leaning casually against the wall, exuding that sexy-as-fuck confidence like he owns the place... which, technically, he does.

His dark eyes lock on to mine, and I feel my pulse quicken. Widening my eyes in a silent warning, I give the tiniest shake of my head.

Don't. Say. A. Word.

But, of course, a slow, knowing smile spreads across his face, and before I can stop him, he opens his mouth to speak.

"So, Whitney," I say quickly, cutting JC off and turning abruptly to face her. "Did I tell you I had to move rooms?"

She nods, looking confused. "Yeah, we talked about it earlier."

JC's eyes dart to Whitney, and his expression shifts. It's subtle—just a flash—but I catch it. Without missing a beat, he quickly turns his back to us.

"Oh yeah. Silly me, I forgot."

I risk a glance at JC. He's holding his phone to his ear now, and as we pass by, I catch the low murmur of his voice: "Well, damn. Cockblocked."

My cheeks flush, and I pretend not to hear him as Whitney chats away beside me. I bite my lip, suppressing the grin threatening to break free. As I step closer to him, our pinkies brush for the briefest second—a fleeting, innocent touch that's nowhere near enough but will have to do for now.

Whitney pulls open the bathroom door, and I pause by the entrance, waiting until she disappears inside and is safely out of earshot. Only then do I tilt my head toward JC, lowering my voice to a soft murmur. "You should probably stretch... because I'm going to ride you so hard tonight... *sir*."

His smile breaks wide, dark and wicked. "Oh, you naughty, beautiful little thing."

I lean in, close enough to whisper, "And before I ride you, I'm going to suck your cock so hard you'll see stars."

His eyes smolder with desire, and before I can pull away, he delivers a quick, playful smack to my bottom. "You might want to call off work for tomorrow." His words are a low, dangerous promise. "You won't be able to walk."

I glance back at him with a smirk. "Don't make promises unless you plan on keeping them."

As I step into the restroom, his voice follows me, deep and sure. "That's one promise you can count on."

I lean into the mirror, smoothing on a fresh coat of lip gloss, giving myself a quick once-over. Just as I snap the cap back in place, Whitney emerges from the stall and heads to the sink, humming as she washes her hands.

"Did you hear what that guy on the phone said when we walked in?" She glances at me with a playful grin.

"What guy?"

"The muscular guy in the suit. I didn't see his face, but with a body like his, I don't need to."

I fight the urge to grin. "No, I guess I wasn't paying attention."

She pulls out her lipstick for touch-up. "He told whoever he was talking to that he got cockblocked." She shakes her head with a smirk. "I'd be more than happy to fix his problem."

Whitney obviously doesn't realize who he is—if she had, there's no way she'd be tossing around words like that so casually.

I force a casual smile though the thought of Whitney anywhere near JC sparks a prickle of annoyance. "Would you consider a short-term relationship with a guy here? Like, knowing it's only for a few months and then it's done when we go back to Charleston?"

Whitney adds a final swipe of lipstick with practiced ease. "Absolutely. Who wouldn't want a fling with a hot Aussie guy?"

Her answer eases my tension, leaving me feeling oddly reassured. "Right. Who wouldn't?"

We step out of the restroom and back into the hallway. He's still there, leaning casually against the wall, phone pressed to his ear, looking like he owns not only the hotel but the whole damn world.

He catches my eye, and a slow, wicked smile spreads across his face. "Listen, possum. I'll be at your hotel room as soon as this business meeting is over. Does that work for you?"

I slip my hand behind my back as we walk away, giving him a discreet thumbs-up.

Whitney glances at him, then leans closer to me with a smirk. "Some lucky bitch is getting laid tonight."

I grin, trying to suppress the giddy feeling bubbling up inside me.

It's me. I'm the lucky bitch.

Chapter 14

Alex Sebring

THE LEATHER SOFA FEELS TOO SOFT BENEATH ME, LIKE IT'S trying to swallow me whole. I lean forward, resting my elbows on my knees, fidgeting with the band of my Rolex—a habit I can't break when I'm here.

The room around me is calm with warm lighting. Every detail is designed to put me at ease. There's psychology behind design choices.

Charleston taught me that.

My thoughts circle back to last night with her. The way her laugh felt like it belonged to me, the way her fingertips traced along my skin, her voice soft and teasing... until it wasn't teasing at all. She didn't disappoint—not in the slightest. She kept her word, just as I did. And when she called me sir in that breathy, almost playful way, it unraveled every last thread of my composure.

I still feel the ghost of her touch, haunting me just beneath the fabric of my shirt, as if my skin refuses to forget.

I exhale slowly, dragging myself back to the present.

The door opens, pulling me from my thoughts. Dr. Whitfield steps inside, his usual warm, easy smile in place. He takes a seat across from me, notebook balanced on his knee, and leans back in his chair, his posture relaxed and inviting.

"Good to see you, Alex." He always speaks with the practiced ease of a therapist. "Tell me how things have been since our last session."

That familiar old discomfort creeps in, the one that always shows up when I have to talk about my feelings. It's not that I had a bad childhood. Far from it. I grew up in a wonderful family, but we weren't exactly the type to sit around and share our emotions. Feelings weren't ignored. They just weren't discussed much.

And on the rugby field? Emotions were a liability. There was no room for vulnerability in a game built on brute force and discipline. You played hard, kept your head down, and if something was bothering you, you dealt with it quietly on your own.

I shift slightly in my seat, fidgeting with my watch. "Things are good. Really good actually."

"Sounds like a new development in your life." He nods thoughtfully, giving me a moment. "Tell me what's making you happy."

I can sum it up in one word: Charleston.

"I met someone—an American in Sydney on a job assignment for three months."

Dr. Whitfield nods, jotting down a note. "Okay. Tell me how that's going."

"It's early on, but it feels good. She's uncomplicated. And for the first time in a long time, I feel at peace. Like she's exactly what I need right now."

"*Uncomplicated.* That's interesting, given what you've told me before. You said you want something serious and long-term—a marriage, a family, the whole package. So why this? Why choose a relationship that's likely to end when she goes back home in three months?"

Dr. Whitfield leans back in his chair, giving me space to find my words.

"For one, she's different."

"How so?"

"Everyone I've ever been with wanted the image, the status, the lifestyle that goes along with dating someone like me. But with her, there's none of that She doesn't care about what I've done or what I have. In fact, she doesn't know about it at all. She likes being with me."

Dr. Whitfield studies me for a moment, his expression thoughtful. "It's understandable that your past relationship, particularly with your former girlfriend, would influence how you approach things now."

I let out a slow breath, his words settling over me. "Unfortunately, it shapes everything I do when it comes to women." The words feel heavy, like I've been carrying them for far too long. "With Celeste, it was all an act. She pretended to love me, but the whole time she was using me—turning our relationship into content for likes and comments on social media."

My jaw tightens at the memory, the sting of betrayal still fresh despite the time that's passed. "The worst part? I didn't see it coming. She made me feel safe, like I could trust her, and then she gutted me." And that makes me feel stupid.

Dr. Whitfield lets the silence settle, giving me the space to untangle the knot of emotions that comes with saying it all out loud. That's his thing—he never rushes.

"But Charleston is nothing like that. I'm safe with her. For the first time in a long time, I feel like I can be the real me."

"It sounds like you've found something meaningful that truly matters to you."

"It's early, but yeah, I believe I may have."

"So, the real question becomes this—what happens when it's time for her to leave Sydney and return home?"

I shift in my seat, my fingers fiddling with the clasp of my watch. "I'm not thinking about that right now. If I let myself go there, I'll ruin what we have in the present. And I don't want that." I inhale and exhale to slow my racing thoughts. "Being with her is peaceful. I want to hold on to that feeling for as long as I can."

Dr. Whitfield nods, flipping a page in his notebook with the same calm, measured demeanor he always has. "All right then. Let's switch gears and revisit something we haven't talked about in a while. Where are you with your rugby career and processing how it ended?"

The familiar knot tightens in my chest, and I press my thumb harder against the clasp of my watch. "Badly," I admit, the words cutting sharper than I intended. "That's how it ended. And I still haven't processed it... or accepted it."

Dr. Whitfield doesn't push, doesn't prod. He watches me with that steady, practiced look that always seems to say, *There's more on your mind, and I'm not going anywhere.*

I exhale slowly, feeling the burden of memories I've kept buried for too long. "The injury wasn't bad luck. He did it on purpose. And I never said or did anything about it."

"We barely touched on your *inaction* before. Where are you with that now?"

Frustration rises, hot and simmering just beneath the surface. "At first, I couldn't do anything—I was too injured to go after him, no matter how much I wanted to. Then I convinced myself I'd heal, that I'd make a comeback, and going after him wouldn't help my career. But that comeback never happened. I didn't recover. And I told myself it wasn't worth it, that going after him wouldn't change anything. But here I am, two years later, still stuck. Still madder than hell. And I can't shake it."

"That anger is weighing you down. Have you thought more about what closure might look like for you?"

I drop my gaze to the floor, a sharp exhale escaping me as the corner of my mouth twists in a bitter, almost involuntary scoff. "What's the point? Confronting him won't undo what he did."

"Closure isn't about undoing the past. It's about releasing the control it has over you."

His words land like a punch I'm not ready to take, heavy with a truth I've been dodging for too long. I nod, barely, just enough to acknowledge what he's said though the idea of acting on it feels impossible. The anger still runs too hot. If I tried to confront him now, I wouldn't trust myself to keep it together. One smug look, one careless comment, and I'd lose it—completely. And then what? I'd be the one painted as the villain in the story he started.

The frustration bubbles over. "I get it, I do. But right now? If I saw him, I'd probably throw the first punch. I'm still too pissed off."

The familiar ache of regret stabs at me, sharp and unforgiving. I had at least three more years left in me—three years of playing the game I loved. And he stole that from me. I didn't get to decide when my career ended. He made that call, and I've been stuck with the fallout ever since.

Dr. Whitfield watches me, letting the silence stretch long enough for me to feel the impact of my own words. "You're not ready yet. And that's okay. But at some point, you'll need to deal with it— whether it's through confrontation or finding peace another way. Otherwise, it'll keep holding you back."

The tension loosens a bit, but the heaviness remains. *Someday*, I think to myself. Maybe someday. But not today.

Dr. Whitfield shifts in his chair, flipping to a fresh page in his notebook. "Let's talk about the family business. How's that going?"

Another knot tightens in my chest, frustration settling in. "The hotel business isn't what I want to do with my life. But I don't want to let my family down either. They expect me to step up now that rugby is over for me."

My parents don't get it. They don't understand what rugby was to me. It wasn't just a job—it was my identity, my purpose. And then, in an instant, it was gone. Ripped away from me without warning.

Now, as the eldest son, all eyes are on me to take over the family business. My father's ready to retire, and everyone assumes I'll slide flawlessly into the role of president as if it's the obvious next step. But it's not.

I can't bury everything I've lost and pretend this is what I want.

"They think I can handle it, but the truth is I'm drowning." The admission hits me hard, and I glance up, meeting Dr. Whitfield's steady gaze. "I don't want to let them down, but every day feels like I'm pushing a boulder uphill."

"What makes it feel that way?"

"My dyslexia." The confession is heavy, as if saying it out loud gives it more power. "In rugby, it didn't matter. On the field, I could hide it. But not in the business world. It's impossible to avoid. I had to hire an assistant to read and respond to emails. Without help, it would take me all day to get through them."

Hiding it feels like a job in and of itself. I know people think I'm lazy because I hand off simple tasks like asking someone to read an email out loud. They have no idea how much effort it takes for me to keep up.

But the worst part isn't what they think. It's what I feel. Stupid. Weak. Like a kid who never learned how to read properly, stuck pretending I've got it all together when the truth is I don't. Not even close.

"Alex, dyslexia isn't a weakness. It's a challenge, yes, but it's not a reflection of your intelligence or worth. You've spent your whole life excelling in an environment that didn't depend on reading—an environment where you thrived. That's no small thing. The skills that made you successful in rugby—resilience, problem-solving, leadership—can apply to your work now. You just need to approach it differently."

Dr. Whitfield pauses, giving me a moment to let his words sink in.

"It's not about hiding your dyslexia. It's about managing it in a way that works for you. There's no shame in using tools or relying on others for help. Real leadership isn't about doing everything yourself. And trust me, the people around you don't think you're lazy. In fact, they'd probably respect you even more if you let them know what you're dealing with."

Respect me more? Maybe in theory. But the reality is different.

Letting people know about my dyslexia isn't an option. I've seen what happens when you give others that kind of power over you—they twist it, use it against you. They make you feel small, broken, incompetent.

I've fought too hard to build the life I have, to carve out respect in a world that doesn't leave room for flaws. I'm not about to hand someone a weapon they could use to tear it all down. Some things are better left in the dark.

Dr. Whitfield's expression softens, his question turning more personal. "How have you been managing the depression and anxiety?"

"Better, thanks to Charleston, but both are still there. It hasn't been as heavy lately, but I feel it lurking beneath the surface."

"Like it's not gone but waiting for the right moment to rear its ugly head?"

"Exactly. Sometimes the anxiety blindsides me, especially at the office." My words falter, heavy with my next thought. "What if I can't get past this?"

"You're not supposed to conquer it all at once, Alex. Life doesn't come with a perfect plan. It's not about avoiding mistakes. It's about how you recover from them. You've been through a lot, and it's okay not to have all the answers right now."

"Easier said than done."

Dr. Whitfield offers a small, reassuring smile. "It is. But the goal isn't perfection, Alex. It's about finding ways to manage the pressure before it becomes too much. One step at a time. And there's an idea I've been wanting to suggest—canine therapy."

I raise a brow, half surprised. "You think I need a dog?"

"A dog could help more than you realize. They have a way of providing a calming presence, especially on tough days."

I consider it for a moment. "I like dogs a lot, but with everything going on, I don't think I have the time for one."

Dr. Whitfield nods, not pushing the matter. "That's fair. It doesn't have to be right now, but it's something to think about for the future. In the meantime, focus on the positives—like your time with this new woman in your life. Take it one day at a time. You don't have to solve everything all at once."

The simplicity of his words strikes a chord. One day at a time feels manageable, even if the bigger picture still looms uncertain.

"We should also talk about setting some boundaries with your family. It might relieve some of the pressure you're feeling. Expectations are much easier to manage when they're not running your life."

Easy for him to say. "Your mum isn't a spicy Samoan woman."

Dr. Whitfield smiles, the corners of his eyes crinkling. "Fair point, but it's still worth trying. Sometimes people don't realize how much pressure they're putting on you until you let them know."

He gives me a moment to absorb that.

"And as for your injury, finding closure might open up new paths you haven't considered yet. Whether it's a conversation, an outlet, or something else—it could be the key to moving forward."

Moving forward. That's what I need, isn't it? Not just for my family, or my career, but for myself.

Dr. Whitfield closes his notebook, signaling the end of today's session. "You're making progress, Alex. Even if it doesn't always feel like it."

We exchange a brief handshake as I rise to leave, his words still echoing in my mind. *Moving forward.* It's not a solution, but maybe, for now, it's enough.

"Just remember, Alex, healing is a process. It takes time. And it's okay to ask for help along the way."

I leave the office feeling lighter. My thoughts are still spinning, but the tight knot in my chest feels a little looser, like I can finally catch my breath.

As I step into the hallway, my phone buzzes in my pocket.

Hey big guy! How's your day going?

A small smile spreads across my face. For the first time in a long time, things don't feel so heavy, so hopeless. Maybe—just maybe—things will be okay after all.

I start typing a response, my fingers hovering over the screen longer than they should. Then, with a quiet sigh, I give in and switch to voice dictation, the way I prefer to send texts.

> Hey, favorite. My day's been great. Better now actually. Any chance you can slip away from your coworkers for the whole weekend? I have somewhere I want to take you.

> Hmm. Give me a little time to come up with something. I think I can pull it off. Where are we going?

> It's a surprise.

There's a beat of silence before her next message pops up.

> A mystery, huh? I like it. Sounds exciting, big guy.

> It will be. Promise.

I tuck my phone back into my pocket, that smile still playing on my lips. For the first time in a while, I feel like I have something to look forward to.

Chapter 15

Alex Sebring

A LIGHT SWEATER, BERMUDA SHORTS, A BALL CAP, AND DARK sunglasses—practical enough to blend in yet casual enough to keep things low-key.

It's been quiet lately—no sneaky photos, no reporters lurking—but experience has taught me the hard lesson of never becoming too comfortable. All it takes is one sleazy photographer with a long lens to turn a private moment into tabloid material.

Celeste thrived on the chaos. She fed off every flash, every candid shot sold to the highest bidder. The attention was her lifeblood.

The memory still churns in my gut, a bitter reminder of how I let her pull me into that circus—a circus she seemed to relish creating. It wasn't just the cameras; it was the way she turned small moments into full-blown dramas, escalating everything into a public spectacle and drawing even more attention to us.

Celeste has occupied more than her fair share of my headspace, and I won't let her take any more. This weekend is about spending time with Charleston. Work has been hectic, and it's time to kick-start the getaway I've been looking forward to all week. Friday evening to Sunday night. No plans, no distractions. Just us taking it easy and letting the world fade away for a while.

I told Charleston to keep it simple—low-key clothes, nothing flashy that might draw attention. A weekender bag with a couple of swimsuits, enough for a weekend on the water, and one outfit for a date. That's it.

Leaning casually against my Jeep, I glance toward the hotel doors, waiting. When they slide open and she steps out, it's like the air shifts.

For a second, my breath catches.

Damn.

She nailed low-key—cutoff denim shorts, a T-shirt, a ball cap pulled low with her ponytail peeking out the back, and oversized sunglasses covering half her face.

But here's the catch: she looks too good. Nothing about her outfit should stand out, yet somehow, she makes it impossible to look away. Maybe it's her legs. Or the way the sunlight catches her skin, wrapping her in that soft golden glow.

She strides toward me, bag slung over her shoulder, pulling off carefree while looking far too tempting for someone trying not to draw attention.

She stops in front of me, her oversized sunglasses hiding those playful hazel eyes, but a grin tugs at the corner of her mouth. "I was looking for the G-Wagon."

I gesture toward the Jeep. "This ride's a lot less conspicuous. The goal this weekend is to stay off the radar."

Charleston adjusts the strap on her shoulder, nodding with a knowing smile. "Low profile... I like that a lot."

We climb into the Jeep, and as soon as she's settled, I reach over, gently cupping her chin to turn her face toward me.

"What is it?" Her curiosity mingles with a playful smile.

I tilt my head. "Just trying to see your ball cap."

Her grin widens, and I can tell she's holding back a laugh. The hat has D4K embroidered across the front in bold letters.

"D4K? I don't know what that means."

She smirks, clearly enjoying my cluelessness. "It's Dak's emblem. You know, Dak Prescott? Number four?"

Her crush.

I chuckle, shaking my head. "Seriously? You show up for a weekend getaway with me, wearing a *Dak* hat?"

"Wait, it gets better." Mischief dances in her eyes as she tugs at the hem of her shirt. "Read it."

My eyes flick to the graphic on her chest—Dak Prescott front and center. Beneath his image, a line of text curves across the fabric, but the font, stretched over the curve of her chest, makes it impossible to read without a little extra effort.

Damn dyslexia.

I squint, leaning in slightly. "The font's a little distorted with the way you're sitting."

Frustration rises up, sharp and unwelcome. The fact that I can't even manage to read a damn T-shirt in front of her stings more than I want to admit.

Charleston twists in her seat, laughter bubbling up as she reads it for me. "It says, '*Big... Dak... energy.*'"

A laugh escapes me despite myself. "Oh fuck me."

"I plan to, JC... *good... long... and hard*," she says quickly, her grin widening into something far too smug. "What's the matter? Are you jealous of Dak?"

I scoff, trying for nonchalance, but even I hear how unconvincing I sound. "No, of course not."

Hell yeah, I'm jealous. I'd much rather see her wearing a ball cap and shirt with me on it instead of him. But she's completely unaware that I have my own line of rugby merch.

She tilts her head, a playful brow arching as she leans in, the brim of her cap grazing mine. With a smirk that sends a spark through me, she reaches up, adjusts both our caps, and closes the distance. Her lips touch mine—soft, sweet, and unhurried—the kind of kiss that hits deep, undoing something in me no amount of confidence could ever hold together.

"Feel better now?" Her words are soft, carrying a playful edge.

I rub my jaw, pretending to mull it over. "Marginally."

Her smirk deepens, satisfied but still playful. "Good."

The Jeep rumbles down the road, the tires humming against the pavement. Charleston props her feet up on the dash, her hair dancing in the wind. I steal a quick glance at her before turning my focus back to the road. She looks completely at ease, the very picture of carefree contentment.

"Hey, can you text me the links to some of those weird songs you listen to?"

She pulls out her phone, laughing. "I *knew* you liked my music."

I shake my head. "No, I don't. I want the songs available so I can play them for you when we're together."

She smirks, chuckling. "Liar. You're totally going to listen to my music when I'm not around."

I grin, shaking my head again. "No, you've got it all wrong. Music says a lot about a person. I want to know you better through your song choices."

"If you say so." She smirks as she types on her phone. A moment later, my phone buzzes in the cupholder.

"I sent you my log-in information. That's easier than sharing links to multiple songs." She glances at me with a playful glint in her eye. "Do you mind if I connect to this car's Bluetooth?"

I gesture toward the console. "I'd be disappointed if you didn't."

"I want you to know me better... *through my song choices.*"

She taps a few buttons on her phone, and the Jeep's Bluetooth chimes in response. A second later, one of her weird songs spills through the speakers, filling the car with a mix of beats and melodies that are so distinctly her.

Charleston leans back in her seat, a spark of mischief lighting up her expression. "I'm certain you've never heard this one."

I glance at her sideways, smirking. "News flash. I've never heard *any* of them."

She laughs. "This one's 'Naughty Naughty' by John Parr—a classic '80s vibe."

"Clearly."

The song kicks in, and before I know it, she's completely animated, singing along at full volume, her voice unapologetically loud and brimming with life. Her hands drum against her knees, her body bounces with the rhythm, and for a moment, she's not just singing—she's performing. There's no doubt in my mind she's danced to this song more times than she'll ever admit.

I occasionally glance over at her, and a thought slips through my mind: *God, I could get used to this.*

Her performance continues and another thought enters my mind. "You know, you remind me of my mate's wife... except she can sing well."

Charleston gasps in feigned outrage, punching me lightly on the arm. "Well, excuse me, but we can't all be musical superstars, can we?"

I grin, the corners of my mouth tugging upward. "Laurelyn was."

The moment her name slips out, I silently reprimand myself. It's probably a step too far—another breadcrumb leading her closer to figuring out who I really am. But honestly, I'm not too worried. She hasn't shown much interest in discovering my identity.

She furrows her brow. "Who's Laurelyn?"

I keep my eyes on the road. "My mate's American wife. She was a famous country-music star before they got married. Gave it all up to move to Australia and be with him."

"She really gave up her career?" The surprise in her words is unmistakable.

"Sure did. She still works in the music industry but not on stage anymore. Her priorities changed—building a family with Jack became the focus.

Charleston shifts in her seat, clearly intrigued. "When you say *country-music star,* are we talking about a struggling artist playing in dive bars in Nashville?"

"No. She was the original lead singer of a very well-known band. Hugely successful. You would absolutely know who they are if I said the name."

"Wow. That's pretty selfless, giving up something she must've worked so hard for."

"I doubt she sees it that way. Laurelyn's madly in love with Jack. Marriage and kids mattered more to her than fame ever did. And they're so damn happy. If I'm being honest, I envy what they have."

Charleston's smile turns a little wistful. "Sounds like they've built something amazing together."

I nod slowly, the thought of Jack and Laurelyn settling heavily but warmly in my chest. "It hasn't been without struggles—a lot of them actually. No marriage is perfect. But yeah, they've created something incredible."

The Jeep slows as I pull into the harbor, the scent of saltwater mingling with the faint hum of boat engines and the steady whisper of the wind through the open windows. Charleston sits up a little straighter, her gaze sweeping over the rows of sleek boats swaying gently on the water.

Her head tilts slightly. "We're going out on a boat?"

I glance her way, a sudden thought striking me: what if she gets seasick?

"Yeah, unless you don't do well on the water."

She shakes her head, her ponytail swinging. "No idea. I've never been out in the ocean on a boat before."

"I keep medication on the yacht for guests, just in case."

Her eyebrows lift, surprise crossing her face. "A *yacht*?"

I chuckle, pulling into a parking spot. "Yes, a yacht."

She narrows her eyes at me playfully. "Your family's yacht?"

I grin as I cut the engine. "Nope. It's mine."

Her eyes widen, disbelief mingling with curiosity as she studies me like I'm a puzzle she's still trying to piece together. "*Who are you?*"

The corner of my mouth lifts into a teasing smirk. "Wouldn't you like to know."

She leans back in her seat, crossing her arms, her playful skepticism on full display. "Am I out here running around with someone famous and don't even realize it?"

I laugh, shaking my head as I climb out of the Jeep, but I don't give her an answer.

I grab our bags from the back of the Jeep. "Keep your cap low and don't take off your sunglasses."

Her brow furrows as she studies me—really studies me—like she's trying to piece together a mystery she's only beginning to unravel. "You are, aren't you? You're famous."

The question is a curveball I'm not ready to swing at—not here, not now. "Used to be. I've spent some time in the spotlight. But not anymore."

She leans her hip against the Jeep, arms crossed. "I wouldn't like that at all—being in the spotlight. I'm content with not being seen or heard."

Her words sink in, bringing a strange, unexpected sense of peace.

I step closer, gently pushing back the brims of our caps, just enough to tilt her face toward mine. My lips brush hers in a soft, unhurried kiss—a silent thank-you for something I can't quite put into words.

When I pull back, her eyes meet mine. "What was that for?"

"For being you."

I take her hand, leading her toward the dock where the yacht awaits. The gentle hum of the engine vibrates beneath our feet as we step aboard. The yacht's caretaker runs through a quick checklist with me, confirming that all safety checks are complete before officially handing her over to me.

We're completely on our own now.

I glance at Charleston, her expression teetering between excitement and curiosity.

"Let me give you the tour before we head out."

She trails after me as I guide her through the layout, her wide eyes absorbing every detail. At the helm, she leans casually on the railing, a playful glint in her eye as she looks back at me. "Are you an experienced sailor?"

I smirk, amused by the question. "No, but I am an experienced *yachtsman*. The Royal Yachting Association declares that I'm more than qualified to skipper this beauty."

She laughs, light and teasing. "Just making sure you're not about to turn us into the stars of some based-on-a-true-story movie like *Adrift*."

I chuckle, the corners of my mouth lifting. "Considering how that movie ends, I think I'll pass."

"It would be wise."

I step closer, my hand brushing lightly against her back. "Don't worry. We'll never be too far from shore."

Curiosity flashes in her eyes. "Where are we going?"

"We'll spend the evening cruising along the coastline. Then we'll stop for dinner somewhere along the way. And by tonight, we'll drop anchor right outside Newcastle."

Excitement sparks in her eyes as she steps closer. Wrapping her arms around me, she tilts her head with a mischievous glint. "Drop anchor, you say?" Her voice dips, playful and teasing. "Are you also planning on dropping your anchor in me tonight?"

My naughtiness matches hers. "I'm definitely dropping my anchor in you tonight—and I'll make sure it's properly secured."

Her words drip with playful seduction. "Ooh, your yachting talk is so dirty. Keep it coming."

"I'll keep it coming."

I catch her mouth in a quick kiss, savoring her taste before pulling back. "We need to get moving. It's three and a half hours to Newcastle, and I want to anchor down at a decent hour."

"What will we do for dinner?"

"Taken care of. Chloe has hooked us up."

Her face lights up, excitement lighting her eyes. "Chloe cooked for us again?"

"Sort of. She sent food and recipes. But fair warning—if you leave me in charge of the kitchen, I'd probably set the yacht on fire. So, cooking's on you. I'll handle the cleanup."

"I'll happily cook and clean, as long as you take care of the sailing. And the *anchoring*."

Sliding a hand around her waist, I pull her closer, my words dropping to a playful murmur. "You can count on me."

The yacht glides smoothly out of the harbor and into open water. The sun dips lower on the horizon, casting a golden shimmer across the waves. Charleston settles into the cockpit seating near the helm, the wind tugging at the brim of her cap.

She reaches up, pressing her hand to the bill to keep it from flying off.

"We're out of the harbor now," I call over the wind, glancing down at her with a grin. "You can ditch that if you want."

She shoots me a knowing look, her lips curling into a smirk. "You're saying that because you hate my Dak hat."

I keep my eyes on the water as I steer us along the coastline. "Well, if that's the case then lose the shirt too."

"You wish."

"I'll get you out of it sooner or later." That much is certain.

Her eyes sparkle with mischief. "I hope sooner rather than later."

She reaches up, pulling off her cap and shaking her hair free. The breeze catches it, sending loose strands dancing around her face as she leans back in her seat.

Charleston's attention drifts to the rippling water beneath the yacht. After a moment, she turns to me, her eyes soft with curiosity. "How was your day?"

The question stirs up thoughts of my session with Dr. Whitfield.

For a moment, I consider telling her the truth. But in the end, I hold back. Because that's what I do.

Admitting I spend an hour in therapy every two weeks feels complicated. Embarrassing, even. With all the advantages I've had in life—and knowing how hard she's fought to get where she is—how could I ever complain to her about the injustices I've experienced?

She's so damn strong—the epitome of turning life's lemons into lemonade. Not just lemonade. No, she turns lemons into something extraordinary... like limoncello.

What she's endured and overcome is something I admire more than I've ever told her, more than she'll ever know. She's not just a survivor; she's a fighter. A thriver, the kind of woman who takes every curveball life throws her way and somehow comes out on top while still smiling.

"Same old, same old for me. Today was nothing special. Until now. What about you? Anything exciting happen at Soul Sync today?"

She lets out a small groan. "Actually, it was a pretty exciting day at Soul Sync."

"Let me guess—you got to design a new dating suite?"

"I did, but that's not the exciting part."

I wonder if someone famous came in. "Tell me."

"Cleopatra came in today."

That grabs my attention. "Why?"

Charleston shrugs. "To raise hell about you breaking off the match."

A laugh escapes me, and Charleston playfully narrows her eyes. "It's not funny," she says though her own laughter betrays her.

"Oh, it's definitely funny."

"I wasn't there, but they said she was irate—like, actually scary. Honestly, she might be a little unhinged."

"She gave off that vibe. I noticed she was obsessive about certain things. It was like nothing else existed when she locked onto something." Reminds me of someone else I used to know.

"It made me feel guilty, hearing how hurt she was."

"Hey, you're not to blame for any of that."

She shrugs, her thoughts visible in her expression. "Some would argue that I am. If I hadn't—" She stops herself, but the guilt is written all over her face.

"I told you, I wouldn't have gone back for a second date with Cleopatra. The only reason I even returned to Soul Sync was to talk to you."

She nods slowly, but I can see that guilt still dwells in her eyes. "I can't help feeling bad about it."

"That's because you're a wonderful human being with a huge heart." I glance at her, noticing how much she's overthinking it. "Come here."

She steps away from her seat, moving to stand between me and the helm, leaning her weight into me. I press a quick kiss to the side of her face.

"Now," I say softly, brushing her hair back, "put on some of that weird music of yours. I know it'll make you feel better."

"You already know me so well." Her grin returns, her spirit lifting. "All right, Captain Swoony. What kind of music are you in the mood for?"

"You're the DJ."

"Does this thing have cruise control?"

A laugh rumbles out of me. "I think you mean autopilot."

"Whatever," she says with a dismissive wave. "Does it?"

"It does." I scan the horizon, noting the calm waters ahead. "And yeah, we're in the clear now. It's safe to put it on for a bit."

She pulls out her phone and connects it to the yacht's Bluetooth, scrolling through her music.

Soft notes drift from the speakers, and I glance over. "What are we listening to?"

Her face lights up. "This one is 'Chances' by Air Supply. Fun fact—they're Australian."

I think my tinā listens to that band. "I couldn't name a single Air Supply song."

With a theatrical gasp, she clutches her chest, eyes wide. "You, my friend, are seriously deprived. But don't worry." She gives me a playful wink. "I'll educate you. By the end of this trip, you'll be a fan of all the greats."

I think we have different ideas about what makes great music. But before I can respond, she steps closer, wrapping her arms around my shoulders. Her touch is warm, calming.

"Dance with me," she whispers, the gentle invitation in her words stirring something I can't resist.

I oblige without hesitation, slipping my arms around her waist. The music fills the quiet between us as we sway together, moving in a slow circle beside the helm.

Everything about the moment feels right—her body pressed against mine, the gentle roll of the water beneath the yacht, the soft melody wrapping around us like a cocoon. I hold her close, letting myself savor the simple, perfect peace of being here with her.

We've been sailing for a couple of hours, the coastline still visible but drifting past as we move onward. Charleston rises from her seat, her fingers brushing lightly over my shoulder as she heads toward the cabin.

"I'm going to get dinner started."

"Sounds good. I'm hungry."

"You're *always* hungry," she says, giggling.

I ease the yacht to a slower speed, the hum of the engine fading as I shift it into neutral. The water is calm, the golden hues of the setting sun spilling across the surface. There's not another boat in sight—just us, the open water, and the endless horizon.

Charleston reappears, carrying plates to the outdoor dining area.

She's prepared everything Chloe sent—simple, elegant dishes perfectly suited for an evening like this. The sight of her setting up, her movements unhurried and natural, feels like its own kind of magic.

"Easy dinner tonight."

"What did she send?"

"Smoked salmon with dill, salad, several different cheeses, sourdough bread." She places the plates on the table. "Oh, and let's not forget the perfectly paired wine."

I kill the engine, letting the yacht drift lazily with the current. As I join her at the table, the sight of her framed by the endless ocean and the soft glow of the setting sun steals my breath for a moment.

We sit, clinking glasses of chilled white wine, and an overwhelming sense of peace settles over me. Out here, with Charleston beside me, it's as though the burden I've been carrying finally lifts.

The depression, the anxiety, the anger—all of it fades into the background, distant and powerless against me. With her, there's only joy. Only light. She makes me feel like the best version of myself.

Maybe I bring out the best in her too?

We savor the food and the view, the soft sound of the waves providing the perfect backdrop.

"So, why interior design? What made you choose that for a career?"

She takes a slow, deliberate sip of wine, nostalgia flickering in her eyes. "It's kind of funny actually. Growing up, everything I had—or rather, what little I had—mostly came from yard sales."

Her words hit me harder than I expect, a pang of sadness settling in at the thought of her having so little.

"When I got older, I'd do odd jobs around the trailer park. Leonard and Janet would pay me a few bucks here and there. It wasn't much, but at the time, it felt like a fortune. Eventually, I realized I loved taking other people's junk and turning it into treasure. I'd find an old, ugly décor piece at a yard sale, buy some paint or craft supplies, and turn it into something I was proud of."

She shrugs, but her eyes hold a glimmer of pride. "I got pretty good at putting lipstick on a pig."

See? Lemons to limoncello, I tell ya.

I smile, charmed by her story. "And now, here you are, turning that talent into a career. Impressive."

Her expression shifts to something thoughtful. "Funny how one of the things that used to embarrass me the most is actually what led me to where I am today."

Her eyes shine with pride. "Who would've thought painting other people's junk would one day land me a job that brought me to Australia... and to meeting an amazing *bloke* like you?" Her smile softens as her words come out in a quieter, more intimate murmur. "Fate works in mysterious ways sometimes."

I reach across the table, taking her hand in mine and giving it a gentle squeeze. "Funny thing, fate."

Suddenly, a smile breaks across her face, followed by a bubbling laugh. She gestures toward the song playing through the yacht's speakers. "This song—'Too Much Time on My Hands' by Styx— brings back memories. One of the very few happy ones with Robin. I don't have a lot of those, but this one? It's a good one."

Leaning closer, I rest my elbow on the table, intrigued. "Tell me about it."

She chuckles, settling back into her seat. "So, when I was little, Robin didn't have a car. She always borrowed Charlene's—a black 1978 Firebird, like the one Burt Reynolds drove in *Smokey and the Bandit*." She pauses, giving me a sidelong look. "You have no idea what I'm talking about, do you?"

I offer an apologetic smile. "Sorry, not a clue."

She waves a hand, dismissing it. "I'll show you later." A mischievous glint dances in her eyes before she continues. "Anyway, that car was fast. And Robin and Charlene both drove it like a bat out of hell."

I pause for a moment, taken aback by the way she speaks about these women who raised her. She always calls her mother Robin and her grandmother Charlene. It's not something I've heard often—most people would say Mom or Mum, Grandma or Nan. There must be a reason behind it.

For now, I let it go. It doesn't feel like the moment to ask.

She leans forward, her energy picking up, each word flowing with vibrant rhythm. "There was this gravel road we used to drive down, and it split into a Y. Right at the split, the road widened, and the gravel was thick—perfect for what she liked to do."

Her eyes are full of fondness. "Every time we got to that spot, Robin would crank this song up as loud as it would go and ask me, 'Do you want me to do it, baby?'" Charleston's laughter bubbles up, rich and unfiltered. "And there I was, standing in the passenger seat—not the back seat where a kid is supposed to be—shouting for her to do it."

My curiosity is piqued. "Do *what* exactly?"

She gives me a playful, almost daring look. "Do you know what gravel drifting is?"

"Enlighten me."

Her hands move animatedly, like she's back in that Firebird, as she tells the story. "It's when you whip the car into a spin on gravel—kind of like drifting, but messier. Robin would nail it every time, sending the tires sliding perfectly over the gravel in this wild spin." She shakes her head, laughing. "Honestly, I'm lucky she didn't kill me. I could've flown right out of those T-tops."

My eyes widen at the image forming in my mind. "That sounds bloody dangerous."

A shadow of seriousness crosses her face. "It was very dangerous."

The recklessness of it sits heavy with me. It's hard to reconcile that a parent would place their child in that kind of danger. But then I remember—Robin was just a kid herself when Charleston was born. Maybe she didn't know better, or maybe she simply didn't think it through.

Charleston's expression softens, her words filled with quiet determination. "I'll tell you this much—I'd never put my child in danger like that. Not ever."

There isn't a careless bone in Charleston's body. That much, I know. Everything she does is deliberate—and thoughtful—from the way she speaks to the way she moves through the world. Recklessness isn't in her nature. If she says she'll protect her future children, I believe her.

But something in her words sticks with me. *My child.* It's the first time she's mentioned having children.

"Sounds like you've thought about having kids someday." I keep the question casual, not wanting to press too much.

She shrugs, her gaze drifting to the horizon. "Yeah, maybe... if the circumstances were right."

The moment feels right to ask the question that's been on my mind. "You told me you weren't looking for a husband. Is that because you don't want one at all? Or because it doesn't fit into your life right now?"

She pauses, her expression thoughtful as she takes her time to answer. "I grew up watching a cycle with Robin, Charlene and the men who came through the revolving door of our trailer. They'd show up, stick around long enough to get what they wanted, and then they were gone." Her words lower, tinged with an unspoken pain. "But it wasn't one-sided. Robin and Charlene used those men too for whatever they could get out of them. It was a messy situation."

Her gaze fixates on the horizon as she continues, "I don't want to be like that. I will never depend on a man to take care of me, and I'll never be at a man's mercy. I will always stand on my own two feet and handle whatever comes my way."

Her words settle between us, and I take a moment to consider what it must be like for her—or for any woman—to carry that kind of fear, that determination to never rely on someone else. "I understand your need to be independent, but having a partner to do life with doesn't make you weak. The right man will stand *with* you, not above you. A relationship should never be about *needing* someone. It's about choosing to share the load so neither of you has to carry everything alone."

She goes quiet, her brow furrowed in thought. After a moment, she nods slowly. "That's a really good point, JC. I've never thought of it that way before."

She doesn't say anything else right away, just gazes out over the water, the corners of her mouth curving into a quiet, reflective smile. Her hand brushes against mine, and she gives it a light squeeze. "Thank you for showing me a different point of view."

It's not a grand declaration or some life-changing epiphany. It's a small, shared moment between us. And for now, that's more than enough.

Chapter 16

Alex Sebring

THE YACHT GLIDES TO A STOP, THE SOFT RATTLE OF THE ANCHOR chain cutting through the stillness of the night. Newcastle's coastline lies in the distance—a jagged silhouette softened by the faint glow of city lights. Close enough to glimpse, yet far enough to feel like a world apart. Out here, we're untouchable. Hidden. Exactly how I want it.

I step onto the deck, the night air cool against my skin, rich with the scent of salt and freedom. The sea is calm, gently rocking the boat in a rhythm that reminds me we're floating in our own private world. Overhead, countless stars spill across the sky, and the moon stretches a silver path across the water. It's a quiet invitation to nowhere but here.

Charleston stands at the bow, barefoot, her silhouette glowing softly in the moonlight. A weekend like this—her beside me every morning, hair tangled on the pillow, her hand drifting lazily over my chest—and I'm already forgetting what it feels like to be alone.

I step behind her, wrapping my arms around her waist as the breeze tousles her hair. She leans into me, her body fitting against mine. "It's just us out here."

She tilts her head slightly, her smile soft but teasing. "Think you can survive an entire weekend alone with me, Captain Swoony?"

My lips brush against her ear. "*Survive?* Charleston, I will *thrive.*"

She glances back at me, her eyes sparking with mischief. "Big words. You sure you're not overestimating yourself?"

I slide my hands along her waist. "Oh, I've got stamina. The real question is do you?"

She leans back into me. "Puh-lease. You'll be the one tapping out by Sunday."

I pull her a little closer. "Challenge accepted."

She laughs softly, the sound as tranquil as the waves lapping against the hull.

"Give me a minute. I'll be right back."

I head below deck to grab a couple of blankets and a few pillows. When I return, she's still at the bow, her hair catching the moonlight.

I spread the blankets and pillows across the sun pad, making it cozy. "Come here, favorite."

She turns, a small smile playing on her lips, and walks over with that easy, unhurried grace. When she reaches me, I settle onto my back and pat the spot beside me. "Perfect spot for you."

She sinks onto the sun pad with a smooth, effortless motion. "Do you always go to this much trouble to impress?"

I tug the blanket over both of us as she settles in beside me. "Only when it's worth it."

She stretches out, nestling closer, resting her head on my chest. Her breath is warm against my neck, and the steady rhythm of her breathing syncs with the gentle sway of the boat. The night air carries a cool edge, and I tuck the blanket around her shoulders. The soft hum of music drifts through the speakers, blending with the distant whisper of waves against the yacht.

Her hand rests lightly on my chest, her fingers tracing idle patterns over the fabric of my sweater. "Do you do this often?"

I glance down at her, brushing a stray strand of hair from her cheek. "Not like this."

"Not like *this*? You're telling me this isn't your signature move—bringing a girl out to the middle of nowhere, charming her with the moon and stars?"

Oh, if she only knew. "Hardly. My past dates were for show because that's the way the women liked it. Dinners, events, places where people could see us out on the town together. None of them cared about the quiet like this—or being with me with no one else around to see us."

Her fingers rest on my chest. "So, I'm the first woman who's ever wanted this—being with you without onlookers?"

"You're the first, Charleston. And that makes you different. You *see* me, and you care about the parts no one else has ever bothered to notice."

"Every part of you is worth noticing."

The words between us are heavy, and for a moment, neither of us speaks. She goes quiet, letting the stillness wrap around us, her gaze drifting upward to the sky.

I follow her line of sight, the stars scattered across the night like fragments of a story waiting to be told. "See that cluster there?" I point toward the horizon. "That's Orion's Belt—three stars perfectly aligned."

Charleston shifts, her head settling more comfortably on my shoulder for a better view.

"My grandfather used to show me the constellations when I was a kid. He'd tell me how the old Polynesian navigators used the stars to cross the ocean. No GPS, no maps—only the night sky."

"You know all the constellations?"

I grin, tracing another shape in the sky. "A lot of them."

"You're really intelligent, you know that?"

I huff a quiet laugh, shaking my head. "Women don't usually say that to me."

If she knew the truth, those words would likely never leave her mouth. Realizing I read like a young child—slow, stumbling, struggling to piece together words—might make her think again.

The thought stings, but I push it away. Right now, I'd rather focus on what she sees in me, not what she doesn't know.

"Maybe those other women weren't paying attention to the right things."

Her words wrap around me like the blanket tucked over us—warm, comforting, and undeniably her.

"Tell me more about Samoan culture."

I blink, the unexpected question throwing me for a moment. Most women stick to the polished parts—the rugby fame, the paparazzi flashes, the family business, flashy dinners, or the G-Wagons.

"Women don't ask about that side of me. They act like it doesn't exist."

"Then you've been dating the wrong women."

The moonlight casts a gentle glow on the curve of her cheek as she waits for my answer. There's something in her gaze, steady and unhurried, that tells me she's not asking to be polite. She truly wants to know. She wants to know *me*. All of me.

She shifts closer, her hand pressing more firmly against my chest. "Your heritage is a huge part of you. I want to know all the facets of who you are."

The way she says it, soft yet certain, hits deeper than I expected. I clear my throat and turn my gaze back to the stars. "My mom's a feisty Samoan through and through. Family means everything to her —our heritage, our traditions. She made sure we grew up connected to it. We're a big family. Loud. Loving. Completely chaotic. Every birthday, wedding, or reunion turns into a huge event. Everyone shows up, whether you want them to or not. And there's always enough food to feed an army."

"There would need to be plenty of food if they all eat like you do." She giggles. "Sounds like a nice kind of chaos."

"It is. Samoan culture is built on respect. Respect for your elders, your family, your traditions. There's a deep sense of responsibility, like you're always a part of something bigger than yourself."

Her hand drifts lazily over my chest. "And marriage? What does that mean in Samoan culture?"

"Marriage isn't only about two people. It's a bond between families. It's about trust, loyalty, and building something that lasts. There's a saying: *O le aiga e tumau le fa'avavau*. It means *family is forever*. When you marry someone, you're bringing them into that forever."

She's quiet for a beat.

"Forever sounds beautiful," she says, as though she's turning the idea over in her mind.

I lean down, brushing a light kiss against her hair. "It's a beautiful commitment, Charleston."

A beautiful commitment I'm ready for.

"My father is Swedish-Australian. Of course, my siblings and I took our dad's surname, but my mum always made one thing very clear: where we come from matters. She's never let us forget that. She takes us back to Samoa at least twice a year. No quick visits either— we stay for weeks so we can reconnect with the culture."

I chuckle softly, a smile tugging at my lips as I picture her. "My mum's a strong woman who doesn't take shit from anyone. And she's got plenty of opinions to go around. Fierce is the best word to describe her."

Charleston tilts her head up toward me, a sly grin playing on her lips. "Are you describing your mom or me?"

"The two of you have a lot in common."

"I'll take that as a compliment."

"Trust me, saying that you have a lot in common with a strong woman like my mum is a compliment." And it's the truth.

Strong women don't intimidate me. They keep me grounded.

We drift into an easy silence. The boat sways gently, the music a soft hum in the background. Her hand moves absently under the hem of my sweater, her fingers warm against my skin.

"Your tattoos are elaborate. Did they hurt?"

"It's a sharp, intense sting that doesn't let up. Not exactly pain—more like pressure and heat combined."

Her hand moves over my chest. "Tell me why you do it."

"Every line tells a story—family, heritage, moments that shaped me. It's not just ink. It's who I am."

Her fingertips trail along the curve of a design near my ribs. "How long did it take to finish them?"

"The pe'a—the traditional one—was done over a few weeks. Long days of sitting still, enduring it. Some of the others, like the personal ones, I've added over the years. My tattoos are a work in progress."

She hums thoughtfully, her hand continuing its lazy exploration. "Because your story continues, and you have many different stages of life ahead of you?"

I glance down at her, something tightening in my chest at how easily she understands. "That's it exactly."

Her fingers trace over one of the older designs, pressing gently, as if she can feel the stories etched into my skin. For once, I don't mind letting someone glimpse the parts of me I usually keep to myself.

As her hand glides over my skin, every nerve ending ignites, and my body reacts to her touch. I let out a low, guttural moan as she teases me. The pleasure builds and builds until I'm completely consumed by desire.

"Your touch is driving me wild."

"Sorry," she says, a faux apology, and then leans in closer so her breath brushes against my ear. "*Not...* sorry," she whispers, her words rich with seduction and mischief.

A fierce passion ignites within me, consuming my entire being and intensifying my longing for her. I can't fight the irresistible pull between us and I move closer, positioning myself on top of her. With very movement she makes and every breath she takes, the fire burning inside of me grows stronger.

"I don't think you realize the effect you have on me." I'm completely under her spell.

She pushes against my chest, and we roll, her body now on top of mine. Our legs tangle together as she settles on top, her soft curves pressing into me. I'm trapped beneath her, feeling the heat of her body pressed tightly against mine as she leans in for a kiss. Her lips meet mine with an urgent hunger, sending warm tingles through my body.

She presses her index finger against my lips, her words a soft whisper. "Hold that thought for a minute."

She pulls away, rising gracefully to her feet. The cool night air and sultry melody fill the space, wrapping around her as she moves to the music's rhythm. Her body sways with a sensual confidence, every roll of her hips mesmerizing, each movement drawing me in more.

One by one, layers of fabric slip from her skin, fluttering to the deck like whispers in the dark. Her flawless curves stoke the fire inside me, the tension tightening with every piece she lets fall.

We're like two flames burning in the darkness, drawn together by a force we can't resist. My hands ache to pull her back down to me, to let go of restraint and lose myself in her completely. But somewhere deep inside, a thread of control holds me back, whispering that something better awaits.

Her figure, bare and inviting, beckons me with a slow, seductive finger, her lips curling into a tempting smile. "Come here."

I do as she says, moving slowly as I get to my feet. My eyes are locked on hers, the space between us shrinking with every step I take. The way she looks at me—like she knows exactly what she's doing to me—makes my pulse quicken. By the time I reach her, my heart is pounding, every step pulling me further away from the edge of control I'm barely holding on to.

The music weaves around us, guiding her movements as she slowly undresses me, each touch a teasing, delicious torture. The anticipation builds as she reveals more skin, her grin widening at the effect she has on me.

Abruptly, the song playing comes to a halt and the next one begins. This time, it's a slow, romantic tune. Bathed in the moon and starlight, we stand side by side, completely exposed. Our bodies sway in rhythm with the music, as we intimately explore each other's bare skin through gentle kisses and caresses.

Our fingers dance over each other's skin, tracing every contour and crevice. Each touch is a spark igniting between us, the heat from our bodies mingling in the cool night air. Her soft sighs fill the space around us, a symphony of pleasure as I gently caress her most sensitive areas. As my thumb glides over her hardened nipples, they respond eagerly to my touch, rising to meet me with a yearning desire.

I pull her to me, my hands exploring the curves of her bare back as we melt into each other's embrace. Our lips meet in a searing kiss, tongues tangling and igniting a fire within us. She trails featherlight kisses down my neck, sending shivers down my spine. I bury my fingers in her soft hair, delighting in its silkiness.

We lower ourselves onto the sun pad, our bodies entwined in a perfect union. Every movement is met with a matching response, our connection never breaking. Skin meets skin as we sink into the plush surface, the cooling night air a delightful contrast to the burning desire between us. Her hands explore my body, sending shivers through me with her gentle touch. I caress her spine, savoring the delicate sound of her gasp when I reach the curve at the small of her back.

Our lips meet again in a passionate kiss, tongues exploring, tasting. I roll her beneath me, drinking in the sight of her in the moonlight—hair tousled, eyes dark with desire, chest heaving. She wraps her legs around my waist, pulling me closer, the friction eliciting a groan from deep in my throat.

She presses her body against mine and gently moves in a sensual rhythm. Her breath tickles my ear as she murmurs, "Take your time tonight. Make love to me—slow and tender."

"Happily."

I lean in, my hand gently cradling her cheek as I tilt her head upward, lips meshing together in a soft and warm embrace. My tongue brushes against hers, and they intertwine in a slow and sensual dance. She tastes like white wine, and I can't get enough of her.

Her fingers entwine in my hair, gently pulling me closer to her, and I explore every corner of her mouth until we're both breathless. As our lips part, she tilts her head back, exposing the smooth curve of her neck, and I cover it with light kisses, cherishing the way she trembles under my touch.

She lies back, her legs spreading slightly to make room for me. My body presses against hers in a primal embrace. Our eyes meet and a silent understanding passes between us before I slowly enter her, savoring the warm tightness that surrounds me. As our bodies intertwine, we find a rhythm that feels natural. Every thrust is met with an equal force from her, our movements synchronized as if we've been dancing together for years. In this moment, nothing else exists but the two of us.

Our bodies move in perfect rhythm as we rock together. Our lovemaking is tender and adoring, worshipping every part of each other.

"JC." She says her nickname for me like a prayer, her fingers tangling in my hair. This time it's a pleasure building gradually—a slow burn—rather than a raging inferno.

I run my lips along the delicate curve of her collarbone, savoring the tangy salt on her warm skin. As I trace a pattern of kisses, she grips my shoulders, fingers digging into my flesh as I brush over a particularly sensitive spot. I return to that spot again and again, each time eliciting soft moans of pleasure from her lips. Her inner muscles contract around me, urging me.

With each gentle movement, our bodies mold together in a perfect rhythm. The outside world fades away as we focus solely on each other. The soft touch of skin against skin, the building heat between us, and the delicate sounds of our shared pleasure fill the air. Our breaths synchronize as time stands still in our intimate cocoon, and I gaze into her eyes, seeing my own passion and adoration reflected back at me. I cup her face in my hands, brushing my thumbs across her flushed cheeks before leaning in to place a loving kiss on her lips.

"I don't understand how this can be so good, so different, with you." I whisper against her ear.

"I don't know either, but it is."

The pressure builds slowly but steadily, like waves lapping at the shore. Her breathing quickens and her movements become more urgent. She trembles beneath me, on the precipice of ecstasy.

With a soft cry, she comes undone in my arms. The sight and feel of her release trigger my own, and we cling tightly to each other as waves of pleasure wash over us. Our bodies shudder in unison as we ride out the aftershocks together.

Gradually, our movements slow and then still. I remain inside her, unwilling to break our intimate connection just yet. We lie tangled together, our ragged breaths mingling as we come down from our shared high. I pepper her face with soft kisses—her forehead, her cheeks, and finally the tip of her nose. She sighs, a dreamy smile playing on her lips.

"That was—" she trails off, seemingly at a loss for words.

"The best," I finish for her, brushing a stray lock of hair from her face.

She nods, affirming our mutual understanding, and leans into my touch. We savor the warm feeling of contentment, exchanging soft kisses and tender touches. There's no need to hurry; we have all the time in the world.

The peaceful night envelops us, the gentle movement of the yacht soothing us in rhythm with the waves. Her head is nestled on my chest, her skin still radiating warmth against mine under the tangled covers. We lay there in quiet bliss for some time, both lost for a while in the aftermath of our passion.

"No one's ever made love to me before." She pauses like she's testing the words aloud for the first time. "It's always been fucking and not even *good* fucking. To be honest, none of it has ever been good. Until you."

Hearing that she enjoys sex with me makes me happy, but at the same time, it also stirs up some uncomfortable feelings. Obviously, I was aware that she'd been with other men before me. That's not a surprise. What is a surprise is how that makes me feel.

I shift slightly, my hand brushing along her back. "I don't like the thought of you being with other blokes."

She laughs, light and teasing. "Are you jealous, JC?"

I am, but I don't want her to know that. She might not find jealousy an attractive trait. "I'm not."

"You sound a little jealous." She props herself up on one elbow, her eyes studying my face.

I raise an eyebrow, smirking. "Do I?"

"Mm-hmm," she murmurs, her grin widening.

She has me, but I'll never admit to it.

I brush a hand through her hair, tucking it gently behind her ear. "Have you ever been in a serious relationship?"

"I've been in a few relationships, but they all fizzled after a few months."

"So you've never been in love?"

"No. Not even close."

A quiet sense of satisfaction settles in my chest. I don't say it, but I like that she's never loved anyone. Knowing her heart has never belonged to someone feels like there's a part of her still untouched, waiting for the right man to claim it.

"What about you? Ever been in love?"

My fingers trail gently along her arm. "I've been in situations that felt close but no... not love." I pause, letting my admission settle between us. "I want to be in love though."

She hums softly as if turning my words over in her mind. Then she lifts her head, resting her chin lightly on my chest. "I hope you find the love of your life someday, JC. You deserve that."

Her words carry a sincerity that stirs an unexpected ache deep inside me, leaving me momentarily unsure how to respond.

"You deserve the perfect wife, someone to be the perfect mother for all those beautiful little Samoan babies you're going to have one day."

The life she's describing feels distant, like it belongs to a version of me I haven't met yet. A version that hasn't existed up till now.

It's true—I want a wife and children someday. But right now, all I care about is what the next three months look like with her.

The thought of how quickly three months can slip away creeps in, tightening something deep in my chest. I shove my anxiety down before it can take hold of me.

Not now.

Not tonight.

She nestles against me, her warmth a quiet balm against the edges of my restless thoughts. For now, this moment with her is enough. I'll let the future come when it's ready.

I press a kiss to the top of her head, breathing in the faint, familiar scent of her hair. With her curled against me, the stars stretching endlessly above, and the ocean rocking steadily beneath us, everything feels exactly as it should.

Even if it's only temporary.

And for tonight, that's enough.

Chapter 17

Magnolia Steel

THERE'S SOMETHING SURREAL ABOUT WATCHING THE SUNRISE out here, suspended between sky and sea. The colors ripple over the water, shifting from deep purple to a warm gold that stretches as far as I can see. I've watched plenty of sunrises, but somehow, this one feels different. This is one I'm always going to remember.

JC is next to me, his arms wrapped around my waist, holding me close as we lean against the yacht's railing. The world is so incredibly quiet right now, just the sound of waves lapping against the yacht and the occasional call of a seabird somewhere out in the mist.

I sip my coffee, savoring the warmth as the cool morning wraps around us.

"Not a bad way to start the day." His voice carries the lingering rasp of early morning.

His profile is softened by the first rays of sunlight. "Not bad at all. I could get used to this."

He hums in agreement, and we stand there in silence, watching as the sun climbs higher, casting light across the water until everything glows. Sharing this moment with him feels special, a quiet kind of magic.

"What's the plan for today?"

"We'll stay on the yacht most of the day. Swimming, music..." He leans in a little closer, his words lowering to a softer, more intimate pitch. "*Privacy*."

I grip the railing, the new day's sun warming my skin as the breeze toys with my hair. "Ah, *privacy*." I parrot his words, mirroring his playfulness.

"Lunch and dinner are already sorted, thanks to Chloe. And tonight, we'll head into Newcastle for a surprise."

"You really do love keeping me in suspense, don't you?"

His eyes glint in the morning light. "Gotta keep you interested somehow."

I lean closer, a playful smile on my lips. "No need to worry—you keep me more than interested."

There's something in the way he looks at me that sends a flutter straight to my chest.

By midmorning, the sun is high, its warmth spilling across the deck as I head below to change into my swimsuit. I pull on the red bikini I packed, adjusting the straps and smoothing the fabric before catching a quick glance at myself in the mirror.

I take in my reflection for a moment, noting the soft curves that attest to my love of good food and living life fully. I'm not the kind of girl who picks at salads or starves herself to fit some impossible standard. I eat, I enjoy, and it shows. These are things I've come to appreciate about myself. And JC seems to appreciate it too, judging by the way his hands linger when he touches me, like he can't get enough.

He's a big guy, broad and solid, and I can't imagine him being with someone stick-thin or delicate. He's never said it, but the way his gaze follows me, the way his grip tightens slightly when he pulls me close, tells me everything I need to know. He likes me the way I am. And that thought brings a smile to my lips.

When I step back onto the deck, his eyes meet mine, holding

steady for a beat before drifting over me. His lips curve into a slow, appreciative grin.

"Bloody hell, you are a knockout. But, lovie, you better put on some sunscreen before you fry in that sun."

Lovie?

I roll my eyes, grabbing the sunscreen from the nearby bench. Before I can start, he holds out his hand with a teasing glint in his eye. "Come here, small pale one."

"Small? Nah, I don't think so." I arch a brow, stepping closer, bottle in hand. "And I'm not pale."

He looks me up and down, entirely unbothered by my protests. "From where I'm standing, you're very much both of those things."

I hand him the bottle with a resigned smile, turning around to let him get to work. His hands are warm as he spreads the sunscreen across my shoulders, gliding over my back in firm strokes. His fingers press just enough to make my breath catch, and as he moves lower, his hands sneak under the edge of my swimsuit bottoms, massaging my butt cheeks. Then he toys with them, making them jiggle.

"What the hell are you doing back there?" I smirk, glancing over my shoulder at him. "Pretty sure that's covered by the swimsuit. No chance of a sunburn in that area."

He grins, utterly unrepentant. "I'm looking out for your safety."

"Uh-huh." I let out a small laugh, amused by his playfulness with my butt.

He finishes, and I turn to face him, one eyebrow raised. "Are you going to lay out with me?"

He chuckles, crossing his arms as he looks down at me. "My tan was well-established years ago. And I didn't have to cook in the sun to get it."

"You have those good genes." I shake my head, smiling. "All you had to do was incubate in your mother's womb."

"Something like that," he says, watching me settle onto the sun pad.

I stretch out, letting the sun seep into my skin, but I don't have long to settle before he steps beside me, casting a playful shadow. "While you soak up some sun, I'll be your cabana boy for the day."

I raise an eyebrow, smirking up at him. "Is that so? All right then, cabana boy, what's on the drink menu?"

He glances over his shoulder at the drink cart parked on the far side of the deck in the shade. "I'm not sure what's stocked, so we'll have to take a look. But I'll say this—the yacht's caretaker usually keeps it well supplied."

Together, we stroll over to the drink cart. I lean in, scanning the array of bottles and mixers. "How about a classic mai tai?"

He pauses, brow furrowed. "Sounds good, but I have no idea how to make that."

"JC, you're a sad excuse for a cabana boy."

I grin as he gives me a playful scowl, gesturing toward the bottles and ingredients in front of us. "It's simple. Light rum, dark rum, orange curaçao, fresh lime juice, and orgeat syrup. Even you could pull it off."

A grin tugs at his lips. "I may be your cabana boy, but I'm no bartender."

"No worries." I wink, grabbing a few bottles and the bar tools, already feeling in my element. "Lucky for you, I happen to be a very well-trained mixologist."

He steps back, watching with an amused glint in his eyes as I get to work. I shake, stir, and pour with practiced ease, throwing in a little flair as I spin the shaker and flip it back with a flick of my wrist. When I finish the drink with a flourish and toss him a playful wink, he lets out a low whistle.

"I'm not gonna lie. That was hot."

He watches me as I mix the second drink.

"Where in the world did you learn to do that?"

"Robin and Charlene—both bartenders." I pause, seeing his reaction shift. "I learned how to mix drinks at a tender age."

He shakes his head, not looking particularly amused this time.

"The more I hear about Robin and Charlene, the less I care for their parenting skills."

His jaw tightens, a storm in his gaze. Maybe protectiveness?

"You were a kid, Charleston. And they didn't protect you."

There's something about the way he says it—so firm, so sure—that makes my chest tighten. It's not pity, and it's not judgment. It's genuine concern, and that does something to me. Knowing he cares, that he's angry on my behalf, feels strangely comforting. I'm not used to someone worrying about my well-being like this, and I can't deny how much I like it.

"True. But at least I had Leonard and Janet looking out for me. They installed a padlock on my bedroom door—from the inside—and taught me how and when to use it. I learned how to protect myself at a very early age from the creeps Robin and Charlene brought into our home."

Thank God for Leonard and Janet and their foresight. That padlock saved me more than once. I lost count of the times I heard the jiggle of my bedroom doorknob in the middle of the night, a not-so-subtle reminder of the dangers outside my door when Robin or Charlene let some lowlife stay over.

His expression hardens, his gaze dropping to the drink he's holding. "You shouldn't have been exposed to that kind of danger."

"Well, unfortunately, I was. That was my life growing up. There's nothing to be done about it now except take the lessons I learned and do better. Because when you know better, you do better."

He watches me, admiration softening the edge in his eyes. "You're such a wise and forgiving person. I want to be like you when I grow up."

It hasn't always been this way. It's taken years—years of heartache, of learning, of forcing myself to let go of things I couldn't change. I've had to unlearn the resentment, rewrite the story I told myself about what I deserved. Forgiveness didn't come easy, but I realized something along the way: holding on to anger only gives it more power. And I refuse to let the past define me.

"Look, I could spend the rest of my life angry about my childhood, but that would only make me a bitter, miserable person. And that's not who I want to be."

I look up at him, feeling strength in the words I'm about to say. "I choose to be the heroine in my story, not the victim."

He goes quiet, his gaze fixed on me as he processes what I've said. And in the pause that follows, I see something shift in his eyes—something that tells me he's taking that to heart.

He's quiet for a long moment, his eyes drifting away. When he finally speaks again, there's a heaviness in his words, a tension that wasn't there before.

"Something happened to me a couple of years ago at my former job. A colleague did something—intentionally—that caused me a serious injury. That injury meant I couldn't keep working in that profession."

He pauses, his jaw tightening as his gaze fixes on the horizon. "Nothing ever came of it. He wasn't reprimanded, and I never confronted him. Even now, two years later, I'm still so angry that if I did confront him, I'm afraid I'd lose control. Afraid I'd choke the bloody hell out of him."

Frustration seeps from his words. "How do you move on from something like that? How do I adopt the attitude you have?"

His words hit me squarely, their meaning impossible to ignore. I draw in a steady breath, choosing my response with care. "What Robin and Charlene did wasn't intentional. Neglectful and dangerous? Yes. But it wasn't meant to hurt me. They're stuck in their own toxic cycle, doing what they were taught by someone else who was just as broken. It's a survival mechanism they don't even realize they're repeating."

He shifts slightly, his gaze turning back to me. There's a look in his eyes, something raw and unresolved, as if he's trying to understand.

"It takes a special kind of... I don't know, *darkness*, to make the choice to hurt someone deliberately. What you went through is entirely different from what I experienced."

He nods slowly, processing my words. "So how am I supposed to move on from it?"

I watch him, sensing the depth of his pain. "Can you tell me more about what happened? That is, if you're comfortable sharing it with me."

He hesitates, eyes distant, before finally speaking. "A ruptured Achilles. It happened in a split second." He pauses, jaw tight, like he's holding back part of the memory. "I've seen the footage. He came in from behind, hit low, deliberately aimed at my ankle. It felt like a snap, like something tore right through my leg."

I watch him, hearing the tension, the frustration barely hidden beneath the words. "The tendon was shredded, and the force of the impact damaged the nerves. After surgery, months of rehab, and every physical therapy exercise they could throw at me... I still wasn't able to get the stability back." His hand tightens into a fist. "Some days, I don't know if my ankle will hold steady or give out. It's like it has a mind of its own now."

He looks down, his expression hardening, the bitterness impossible to miss. "And the worst part? Nothing happened to him. He walked away—no apology, no consequences—while I was left figuring out how to rebuild my life." He pauses, a shadow darkening his face. "And it wasn't the first time he'd tried something like this. Just the first time he was successful."

I take a breath, letting his words settle, then reach for his hand, giving it a reassuring squeeze. "I know you're a good person, someone who'd never hurt anyone intentionally. But I get it, and I understand the need for closure. Anger like that can eat at you. Do you think some form of retaliation would give you the peace you need to move on?"

He falls silent, his gaze distant, fixed on something I can't see. "Sometimes, I think it would help. Other times, I'm not so sure. But I can't leave it as it is. It's been festering for too long, eating at me piece by piece. This feeling that I've failed somehow—that I haven't handled it as a real man should—is tearing me apart."

My chest tightens because I hate seeing him like this—lost in a battle he shouldn't have to fight alone. He doesn't deserve this kind of heaviness or pain. He deserves laughter, lightness, and a reason to smile that reaches his eyes and stays there.

"If you ever need someone to take care of it, you just say the word. I can go from a classy Charleston lady to full-on Mississippi redneck in 1.3 seconds if that's what you need." I give him a wink.

The laughter that escapes him is genuine, lighting up his face, if only for a moment.

"I'm not entirely joking, you know. I'd gladly make this guy pay for what he did to you if I were ever in a position to do so. I mean that from the bottom of my heart."

"You're a whole lot of trouble wrapped in a sweet, Southern-talking little package, aren't you?"

There's honesty beneath the banter. "I'm just saying, if this guy ever crosses my path, he better watch out. I might decide to handle it for you."

His amusement fades. "Would you think less of me if I lashed out at him?"

"Not even a little. I'd think you're human—and a man still carrying the scars of what he did to you." I squeeze his hand, my thumb brushing over his knuckles. "Everyone has a breaking point, JC, and sometimes enough really is enough."

I take a deep breath, letting my words come carefully. "There are a lot of people in this world who would tell you to get over it. But if life's taught me anything, it's this: don't let anyone who hasn't walked in your shoes tell you how to tie your laces. Only you know what will bring you peace."

"You're wiser than your years, you know that?"

"I've been lucky to learn from a few good people along the way."

The conversation drifts into a peaceful silence as I stretch out on the sun pad, the sun's warmth sinking deep into my skin. He settles beside me, and together we let the day unfold unhurried, the gentle rhythm of waves against the yacht our only companion. As the heat intensifies, a sheen of sweat forms on my skin. I sit up, running a hand through my hair, welcoming the soft breeze as it plays through the strands, offering a brief, refreshing reprieve.

"It's so hot out here even my sweat is sweating. I think I can actually feel my soul evaporating."

He glances over, a playful glint lighting his eyes. "Want to cool off in the water?"

"Sure."

Why not? What's the worst that could happen?

I eye the endless expanse of ocean around us, and my imagination, unhelpfully vivid, starts spinning scenarios. Jellyfish could swarm out of nowhere. A sneaky current might tug me under. Sharks—oh, yes, let's not forget the possibility of becoming an impromptu seafood platter.

But what are the odds of all that happening? Slim, right? I hope so.

I glance back at JC, whose teasing smirk says he's ready to dive in. He's here to save me...hopefully.

We walk to the back of the yacht, and he counts down before we leap in together. The cool water is a sharp, invigorating contrast against my sun-heated skin, making me gasp as I surface. I glance around the endless expanse of blue, my mind conjuring flashes of sharp fins and unseen shadows lurking below.

"What do we do if a shark shows up?" I try to sound playful, but I'm unable to fully mask my unease.

He laughs, the sound light and carefree as it echoes over the water. "I'll sacrifice myself to save you."

The way he says it, so easy and offhand, makes me smile. But deep down, I know he actually means it. He'd do it without hesitation, no second thoughts, if it meant keeping me safe. That's who he is—the kind of man who'd protect the people he cares about even at his own expense. That thought sends a warmth spreading through my chest, one I'm not quite ready to analyze.

"You're actually worried about sharks, aren't you?"

Caught, I look down, a little sheepish. "Maybe a little. I mean, we are playing in their backyard."

He nods, his teasing replaced by something softer. "We can hang out on the floating pad if that'll help you feel more comfortable."

Relieved, I smile and nod as we climb onto the floating pad. It wobbles beneath us, a little flimsy, so it feels more like we're sitting directly in the water than on a solid floating surface. Water pools around us, keeping our skin cool despite the heat of the sun. Every movement sends a gentle ripple through the pad, rocking us softly, the water lapping at our sides and legs.

The sound of the ocean fills the comfortable silence until he glances over at me, his expression curious. "I've noticed you're not one of those people who is glued to her phone. Do you have social media?"

I shrug. "I have accounts on a few platforms, but I rarely post. Broadcasting my life for validation from people I probably didn't like much to begin with is not my thing. The whole thing is bizarre to me —how people who judged or ignored you in school suddenly want to connect on social media to keep tabs and keep judging. It's all so fake, not even remotely close to real life. Social media means nothing to me."

A brief silence follows, sparking my curiosity. "I've noticed you're not glued to your phone either."

"Social media has zero appeal for me. I have accounts, sure, but someone else manages them."

I sit up, laughing and giving him a skeptical look. "You have someone who manages your social media? Seriously?"

He grins, his eyes glinting with a trace of mystery. "Perks of the job."

"Omigod." I shake my head, amused. "*Who are you?*"

He leans back, his smile widening with a teasing glint in his eyes. "Wouldn't you love to know."

I laugh, but a thought crosses my mind, and I study him more intently. "We're avoiding Newcastle in daylight because there's a good chance someone might see you and recognize you, aren't we?"

He shrugs, his expression flat, giving nothing away—but his silence says it all.

I let out an exaggerated sigh, leaning back. "I'm going to feel so ridiculous if the truth ever comes out and I realize I've been hanging out with a superstar this whole time."

He chuckles, clearly amused, but still offers no confirmation.

And yet he doesn't deny it.

Great. Now I have to mentally prepare for the possibility that his ex is a supermodel.

The sun sinks lower in the sky, and he docks the yacht at the harbor, stepping over to help me disembark. His hand is warm and steady as I step onto the dock, my lightweight white dress fluttering in the evening breeze. I kept it simple per his request—sandals and a loose braid to pull it all together—but polished enough for wherever the night might take us.

He's dressed casually in Bermuda shorts, a light sweater, and his usual confident ease.

Such swagger.

We stroll along the harbor, the lively hum of Newcastle filling the air, until we reach our destination: a small, boutique cinema tucked into the heart of town. Its vintage marquee glows softly, the old-world charm drawing me in with the promise of something special.

I pause, taking it all in. "A vintage cinema? I didn't see this coming."

He watches my reaction with a satisfied smile. "I had a feeling you'd like it. I'm starting to figure you out."

"Oh really? And what exactly have you figured out?"

"You're not into the flashy stuff. You appreciate the kind of charm most people overlook. Thoughtful, unique, a little nostalgic—this seemed like your kind of place."

I'm surprised by how spot-on he is. "Okay, I'll admit, you're getting to know me better than I expected. What are we seeing?"

"A rom-com."

"A rom-com? That's what you picked?"

"Hey," he says, feigning offense. "I enjoy a good laugh, and I thought you'd appreciate something lighthearted."

Wow. I'm touched by the thoughtfulness behind his choice. "You keep surprising me, you know that?"

"I hope so."

I'm instantly enchanted. The cozy, nostalgic atmosphere wraps around us, and I spin slowly, taking it all in—the plush armchairs, the velvet drapes, the soft glow of the sconces lining the walls. "This place is incredible. It's like stepping back in time."

He smiles, clearly pleased by my appreciation. "I had a feeling you'd like it. It's one of my favorite spots when I want to keep things low-key."

It's the perfect place to stay under the radar.

As the movie starts, he reaches over, lacing his fingers through mine. His touch is warm, steady. I try to focus on the screen, but my thoughts keep drifting back to him beside me, his hand in mine, and the quiet, unspoken connection that seems to grow between us with every passing moment.

Onscreen, the two leads bumble their way through a budding romance, tripping over misunderstandings, quirks, and an undeniable pull toward each other. As I watch, my thoughts drift to us—how, in such a short time, he's done more thoughtful, meaningful things for me than any man ever has. He's so openly shared pieces of himself, and it stirs something deep inside me.

I glance over at him, taking in the quiet confidence in his posture, the ease in his expression. A wave of appreciation washes over me— for who he is and for the space he's carved into my life. He deserves everything good this world has to offer. And he deserves all the things he yearns for but might be too proud to say aloud.

As the movie ends and we step back into the cool night air, a thought settles over me, soft but unshakable. I want him to have it all —peace, fulfillment, love. Every last bit of happiness he's chasing.

Sliding my hand back into his, I let myself savor this moment, realizing something I hadn't before. Even if this—whatever this is—is only temporary, I'm grateful to be part of his story right now. For as long as it lasts, I'm content to be here, walking beside him, sharing these fleeting moments.

Chapter 18

Magnolia Steel

THE SOFT PATTER OF RAIN AGAINST THE YACHT'S ROOF PULLS ME from sleep before the sun has a chance to. Not that it matters—the overcast sky and thick clouds make it clear the sun won't be making much of an appearance today. Outside, the world is draped in muted shades of gray, the kind of morning that whispers, *Stay in bed a little longer*. And with this man beside me, I don't need much convincing.

Snuggled beneath the warm covers, JC's arm draped lazily around me, I let myself sink into the moment. I could get used to mornings like this—waking up to the steady rhythm of his breathing, the heat of his body pressed against mine, and the feeling of being completely, utterly safe.

There's something so settling about waking up beside him, like the chaos of the world can't touch me as long as I'm here. It's not just his presence—it's the way he holds me, even in his sleep, as if letting go isn't an option.

I close my eyes for a moment, savoring the peace, the quiet intimacy of it all. For the first time in a long time, I feel like I'm exactly where I'm supposed to be. With him.

The rain grows heavier, a rhythmic tapping against the yacht's roof, a steady reminder that today won't go as planned. No swimming, no smooth sail back to Sydney. Just us, tucked away in this cozy little world while the storm unfolds outside.

I glance toward the windows, watching the rain ripple down the glass, blurring the view of the water beyond. It feels as though the world has drawn a curtain around us, leaving the two of us cocooned in this quiet, timeless space.

He stirs beside me, his raspy morning voice still heavy with sleep. "Looks like we're staying put for a while."

I'm perfectly content with the idea. "No complaints here. Not a bad excuse to stay cozy."

His arm tightens around me, and he lets out a soft laugh. "Good because I'm not eager to sail through a downpour. Anyway, I've got the best company."

A comfortable silence wraps around us, the kind where words aren't needed. We stay in bed, nestled together, listening to the rhythmic patter of rain against the windows and the relaxing sway of the yacht beneath us. The moments blur, the quiet so calming it feels like time itself has slowed. Before long, my eyes grow heavy again, and I let myself drift back into the warmth of sleep, safe in his arms.

Eventually, the pull of the day tugs us from the cocoon of blankets. JC stretches, his movements slow and unhurried, while I stay for a moment longer, savoring the warmth of the bed. The rain hasn't let up, creating a soft, steady rhythm that seems to set the tone for the rest of the day.

By midday, the rain shows no sign of stopping, casting a soft gray glow over the yacht. Lunch is simple yet perfect for the day: sandwiches, fresh fruit, and a bottle of bubbly. The quiet intimacy of the morning stretches into the afternoon as we settle in the living area, the steady patter of rain providing a lulling backdrop.

I rummage through my bag and take out a small deck of cards.

"What's that?"

"A conversation-starter game. I found it while I was shopping for the dating suite and thought it might be fun. It will help us to know each other better faster."

"Do we get to do dirty things to each other?" He leans back against the cushions, looking far too pleased with himself.

I laugh, shaking my head as I hold up the deck. "Sorry to disappoint, but it's not that kind of game. It's about actual conversations."

His grin holds a hint of intrigue. "Ah, so it's a talking game. Got it."

"It has three levels—close, closer, and closest." I give him a playful look. "And just so you know, there's no wimping out when things get personal."

He raises his hands in playful surrender. "Wouldn't dream of it."

Settling back beside him, I shuffle the deck, the anticipation making me smile. I've been looking forward to this since I bought the cards. "All right, should I read the questions, or do you want to?"

He leans back, looking entirely too relaxed. "I'll let you do the honors."

I glance at the first card and smile. "What is your love language?"

His eyebrows lift. "I don't even know what *love language* means."

Shaking my head, I bite back a grin. "It's basically the way you prefer to show love to others—and how you feel loved in return."

Holding the deck in one hand, I start explaining. "First, there's words of affirmation. That's when someone expresses love through compliments, heartfelt notes, or even a quick text to say they're thinking of you."

He chuckles, shaking his head. "Nope, definitely not me."

"Okay. Then there's gift-giving. It's not about the money—it's more about thoughtful gestures, like a small keepsake or a meaningful book."

He considers it for a moment, then shakes his head again. "Still not me."

"How about physical touch?"

A grin spreads across his face. "Now that's more like it. That's definitely mine."

I nudge him playfully. "Just so you know, physical touch isn't only about sex—it means being affectionate in general. Not just a sex partner."

He shrugs, smirking. "In that case, I'm revising my answer. Definitely not that one, either."

"All right, how about acts of service? That's when someone shows love by doing helpful things—running errands, fixing something, or lending a hand when needed."

He frowns slightly, crossing his arms as he thinks it over. "Hmm, maybe...but it still doesn't feel like it fits."

I smile, holding up the final option. "Then I think I've got yours: quality time. It's about being present, without distractions, enjoying time with the people you care about."

A genuine smile spreads across his face as he nods. "Yeah, that's me. I love spending time with my family. And," he pauses, his gaze meeting mine, "I really love spending time with you."

Warmth blossoms in my chest, and I smile back. "Quality time is my love language too. And I'm really enjoying our time together."

I draw the next card and glance at it, my smile faltering slightly as I read the question. "Why did your last relationship end?"

He shifts, an uncomfortable look crossing his face. "You go first, if you don't mind."

I nod, giving him a small smile. "Sure."

Taking a deep breath, I let out a soft exhale. "Things went downhill fast when the last guy became obsessed with a self-proclaimed *alpha male* influencer. You know the type—one of those guys spouting toxic nonsense about how men and women are supposed to act."

I shake my head, still baffled by the way Hunter was sucked into that insanity.

"At first, it was harmless motivational stuff. But then he started talking like he'd joined a cult, going on and on about how *real women should know their place* and how I'd be *happier if I wasn't so independent.* It was like I was suddenly dating someone who saw me as inferior to him because of my gender."

I shrug, resigned but resolute. "I gave him a choice: stop the nonsense, or I was gone. He didn't stop, so I left. No regrets."

His expression softens, respect in his eyes. "Good on ya. No one should cop that kind of rubbish."

I tilt my head toward him. "Your turn. Why did your last relationship end?"

He hesitates, his gaze falling to the cards for a moment. "Well, she was a social media influencer obsessed with her following, always posting everything she could think of to keep them engaged. At first, I thought it was a side project for her, something she did for fun, but no." He pauses, a shadow crossing his face.

"When we started dating, she'd post little things about us—a picture here, a cute caption there. Her followers loved it, and I didn't mind it so much. But then she realized she could use our relationship to grow her following, and things spiraled. One day, she filmed me without my permission—without me even knowing—and posted it."

I can see the pain in his eyes as he recalls what happened.

"I won't go into what the video was about, but it was deeply personal. For her, it was staged. For me, it was my true reaction. The video was one I would never have wanted out there for anyone to see. And she shared it without a second thought for likes and comments."

I bite the inside of my cheek, a wave of sympathy washing over me. "I'm so sorry. That's awful. How long ago was it?"

He exhales sharply, glancing down. "It's been a couple of years. Right before my injury. So not exactly the best year of my life."

My chest tightens at the gravity of his words. "That really sucks."

"Yeah," he says, letting out a short laugh that carries no humor. "It did."

"*She* sucks," I say softly, sliding the card back into the deck.

After a moment, he clears his throat. "You know, for a game I didn't expect to like, this isn't half bad. Keep going—I'm curious to see what's next."

I glance at him, his openness sparking a smile of my own. "All right."

I draw the next card, curiosity mingling with something deeper as I read it. I lift my gaze, giving him a playful look. "This one's all yours, Mr. looking-for-a-wifey."

"Hit me with it. I'm ready."

I grin, reading it aloud. "What does the ideal marriage look like to you?"

He pauses, his expression thoughtful as he considers his words. "For me, an ideal marriage would be a true partnership. Two people who are there for each other no matter what, through the good and the bad. Someone I can count on, who has my back, who I can laugh with and be myself around. No masks. Just real."

He leans back, his words taking on a gentler edge as he continues. "I think an ideal marriage feels like home. It's about loyalty and trust, where you don't just love each other—*you know* each other, flaws and all. And you still choose each other every day. Supporting each other's dreams, sticking together even when it's not easy. A marriage should weather life's storms and still come out stronger."

His words settle in my mind, their clarity and sincerity striking something deep within me. The kind of relationship he's describing feels almost too good to be real—built on trust, loyalty, and a partnership that endures through everything. It's the kind of connection that would be incredible to have, to know someone that deeply and trust them completely.

"What about you? What's your version of the perfect marriage?"

The question hits harder than I expect, his vision of marriage so beautiful yet so far from anything I've ever known. I take a breath, shifting slightly, trying to untangle my thoughts. "My ideal marriage—" I pause, the words feeling heavier than I thought they would. "Honestly, I don't really know what a healthy marriage looks like."

I glance down, shrugging lightly, a twinge of embarrassment creeping in. "I didn't grow up seeing that. Maybe that's why I've always struggled with the idea of getting married. I don't have much to base it on."

I exhale, looking up at him. "But I really like what you just described. I like it a lot actually. More than anything, I want to be with someone who feels like home." I pause, taking a moment to find the right words. "And if I ever get married, I'd want to be *very married*. All in, forever."

"*Very married*. I like that."

Our eyes meet, and for a moment, there's a quiet understanding—something unspoken but deeply shared. I let myself imagine it—the kind of marriage he described, the kind that feels more like a fairy tale than real life. And yet, sitting here with him, it doesn't feel so unattainable after all.

I shuffle the cards, glancing down at the next one. My eyebrows lift in surprise. "Okay, here's a fun one. Or at least it's supposed to be. What's a humiliating moment you've experienced in the past?" I look up with a small smile. "Want to go first?"

He sighs, shaking his head with a wry smile that doesn't quite reach his eyes. "Oh, that one's easy. Without a doubt, it was that video my ex posted of me."

I reach over and give his hand a quick squeeze. "Well, mine's not exactly fun, either. Senior year of high school, Robin brought home this guy one night..." I trail off, feeling the familiar wave of embarrassment rise. "Which wasn't unusual, by the way. Honestly, Robin's a smoke show and always bringing guys home, so I didn't think much of it at first. Except this time, it turned out he was my classmate. And not just any classmate—the boy *I* had a massive crush on."

His eyes widen, and he winces, already catching on. "*What?*"

"Oh, yes," I say with a dry, humorless laugh. "And it gets worse.

He recorded it and showed it to his friends. Naturally, word spread like wildfire. The next day, a ton of guys came up to me, asking if I fucked as good as my mom did." I cringe, shaking my head at the memory. "It was mortifying. Even now, I could crawl into a hole thinking about it."

His jaw tightens, disbelief and anger flashing across his face. "Is that legal in the U.S.?"

"Immoral and humiliating? Absolutely. But illegal? No," I shrug. "He was eighteen, so they were both consenting adults."

He watches me, the anger fading into something softer. "I'm really sorry that happened to you."

"It's still embarrassing. Bad enough that I skipped my high school reunion—not that I had any desire to see those assholes again."

I glance at the next card, then up at him with a playful grin. "Another one?"

He shrugs, leaning back with an easy smile. "Why not? Keep going."

I pull the card and read it aloud, "Where do you see yourself in five years?"

He pauses, his gaze growing thoughtful. "In five years... I'd like to be married. Hopefully with a couple of kids—maybe a third on the way if it's what my wife wants. Content with life, you know? Just settled and happy."

The sincerity in his words makes something flutter in my chest, and for a moment, I watch him, absorbing his words before he turns his attention to me. "What about you?"

"It's hard to say. Maybe I'm married, maybe I'm not. Maybe I'm a mom, maybe I'm not. It's tough to picture myself five years down the road."

He studies me. "Would you get married if the right man came into your life?"

"Absolutely. I'm not against marriage, but I'm also not chasing it. If it happens, great. If it doesn't, that's okay too. I'm enough as I am on my own."

"Yes, you are."

I slide the last card back into the deck. "Okay, I think that's enough of the heavy stuff for now."

"Agreed. But I have to admit, I don't hate this game."

I glance toward the door, an idea sparking, and turn back to him with a grin. "How spontaneous are you feeling right now?"

"What have you got in mind?"

Instead of answering, I grab his hand and pull him to his feet, leading him outside without hesitation. The rain falls steadily, a cool drizzle that cloaks the world in mist. As we step onto the deck, the fresh, rain-soaked air greets us, and we're instantly soaked. He laughs, the sound full and unguarded, as I tug him farther into the open.

I lift my arms to the sky, spinning slowly, letting the rain wash over me, its coolness invigorating, wiping everything else away. When I glance back at him, he's standing there, watching me with that warm, familiar smile, rain dripping down his face.

"Dance with me." I laugh as I reach for him.

He doesn't hesitate, his hands sliding around my waist as he pulls me close. His touch is warm against the chill of the rain. We sway together, our movements unhurried, guided by the rhythm of the rain. My laughter blends with his, the world around us fading as we move. His fingers trace gentle circles against my back, and though we're soaking wet, it doesn't matter. Nothing else matters but this moment.

For a moment, we pause, our eyes locking in a way that makes the rest of the world melt away. His hand moves to my face, gently brushing a rain-soaked strand of hair from my cheek. Before I can catch my breath, he leans in, his lips meeting mine in a kiss that feels as natural as the rain falling around us.

The world fades into a blur of gray, the steady rhythm of the rain our only soundtrack. It's just the two of us, drenched and completely wrapped up in each other, holding on like nothing else matters, like there's nowhere else we'd rather be.

He lifts me up in one swift motion and I instinctively wrap my legs around his waist, holding on to his strong body. He carries me to the dining table and sets me down gently on the cold, wet surface, sending shivers through my body as it touches my skin.

Dressed in only a T-shirt and underwear, my soaked shirt clings to my body, revealing every curve. He carefully pulls down my lacy panties and settles himself between my legs. With a soft stroke, he enters me, and we both let out a primal moan of pure joy. Our bodies meld together, giving ourselves over to the intense pleasure that engulfs us.

Our bodies move in perfect harmony, the union of our souls igniting a fiery passion. In that moment, nothing else exists but us as we give ourselves over to the intense pleasure coursing through our veins. His hands grip tightly on to my hips, pulling me closer as we lose ourselves in each other's embrace. As he moves inside me, time stands still, and the rest of the world disappears

"You feel so fucking good," he says, looking down at me.

He pushes my legs, bending them at the knees and spreading them apart. The table groans beneath us as our bodies move together in a flawless rhythm. His strong body presses against mine, each deliberate thrust sending waves of pleasure through me. In this moment, I'm utterly lost in sensation, lost in the feel of him filling me with slow, powerful strokes. Our pace is deliberate and unhurried, drawing out every moment of ecstasy and creating a delicious friction that brings us both to the edge of ecstasy.

He meets my gaze and leans in, pressing his lips against mine. Our foreheads touch as he moves in and out of me at a deliberate pace. "Please don't stop," I whisper, knowing that I never want this feeling to end.

His hands press firmly on my hips, keeping me still as he comes inside me. His strength and intensity take me deeper than ever before.

As our bodies merge, his hips come to a halt, and he draws me nearer. His lips, warm and inviting, press against mine. "Fuck, I can't get enough of you."

JC leans in, his fingers gently moving my wet hair from my face. Our gazes connect, and suddenly the world seems to narrow to only the two of us. In that moment, I realize something.

I can't get enough of him either.

What's going on with me?

Chapter 19

Alex Sebring

THE ROAR OF THE CROWD WASHES OVER ME, AND IT'S LIKE stepping back in time. The scent of fresh-cut grass and the charged hum of anticipation stir memories I thought I'd buried, now rising to the surface with startling clarity.

I settle into the stadium suite, my eyes drawn to the field below. Familiar faces surround me—former teammates and industry big shots—laughing, sipping drinks, and swapping stories. Once, this was my world. These were my people. But now, the suite feels more like a fishbowl, their polite nods and sidelong glances tightening a knot in my chest. They all know why I'm not out there anymore—or at least, they think they do.

Most chalk it up to bad luck—a freak accident or the inevitable toll from brutal years on the field. But the truth is far uglier. Tyson McRae ended my career with a single calculated, dirty shot. That moment didn't just shatter my body—it unraveled everything I'd worked for. And no one understands how a betrayal like that rewires everything you thought you knew about loyalty, the game, and yourself.

I can't breathe.

I cannot fucking breathe.

I school my features and wear the mask they expect—one that says I'm fine, and I've moved on. But every cheer from the stands, every familiar sound, every faint hint of fresh-cut grass is a sharp reminder of what's gone.

And of how much I've lost.

"Good to be back, yeah?" My old teammate Nate nudges me with a grin, his easy demeanor a stark contrast to the storm inside me. "Like the good old days, eh?"

No, Nate. It's not at all like the good old days.

I manage a small smile. "Yeah, good to be in the stadium again."

He nods, taking a sip from his drink, his eyes scanning the field below. "It's different, though—watching instead of playing."

"Quite." The word slips out sharper than I intend.

"I get it, Sebring. I retired on my terms. My body gave me a few warnings, and I knew when it was time to call it quits. But you——" He glances at me, the rest of his thought hanging unspoken between us, clear without him needing to say it.

"No, I didn't get a choice." Bitterness claws at the edges of my words, threatening to break through.

Nate nods, giving my shoulder a quick clap. "That's rough, mate. I don't envy that."

"You don't know the half of it." Memories flash through my mind —grueling recovery sessions, sleepless nights, and the endless frustration of knowing everything I'd worked for was ripped away. But I shove it all back down, unwilling to let it surface here.

Nate leans back in his seat, his gaze distant. "Still, it's good to see you here."

"Yeah, well, I didn't think I'd be sitting here as a spectator this early in life."

Nate gives a small nod, his lips pulling into a half smile. "At least you had a good run. A great run actually."

"It was good." A part of me can't fully embrace the words. "But it didn't end the way it should have."

The players charge the field, their cleats striking the turf with a rhythm that feels alive, each movement sharp, deliberate, powerful. My eyes follow the action until they land on him—my replacement. He's good, I'll give him that. Strong, fast, disciplined. But he's still missing something, the finesse, the instinct that only comes with time.

My thoughts drift as I watch him, unbidden memories pulling me back to those first days after the injury. The crutches, the endless cycle of physical therapy, the constant ache that dulled with time but never truly disappeared. And the questions—always the questions. Would I recover? Could I come back? And the hardest one of all—what would I do if I couldn't?

Nate nudges me, pulling me out of my thoughts. "Been a while since we caught up. You probably haven't heard, but Julia and I are expecting! It's a boy."

"That's brilliant." I manage a genuine smile for him. "Congrats to you and Julia."

He grins, practically radiating pride. "Thanks, mate. Wasn't exactly planned—getting pregnant right before the wedding—but hey, it happens."

I chuckle, shaking my head. "That's one way to keep things interesting."

Nate laughs, the sound easy and unbothered. "You're falling behind, you know. Time for you to find a missus now that you're retired. Gotta get some sons while you're still young—so we can turn them into rugby stars before we're too old to keep up."

I smirk, shaking my head lightly to brush off the comment though the thought persists, heavier than I want to admit.

"If you spot a missus for me running around out there, let me know."

Nate chuckles, turning his attention back to the game. My gaze is fixed on the field, but a quiet thought sneaks into my head—what would it be like to have a son out there one day? To pass on everything I know. The idea tugs at something deep, but it's quickly joined by another image—a daughter. A little girl I'd protect with everything I've got, who'd no doubt grow up tougher than I could ever imagine. Especially if Charleston were her mum. That kid would be steel-willed, no question.

The game wraps up, and before I know it, I'm swept along with Nate and a few others to one of the usual post-match gatherings. It's the kind of scene I used to thrive in—music, laughter, drinks flowing, a blur of teammates, fans, and women eager to be part of the celebration. The kind of night where everyone blends together into one big, buzzing, chaotic family.

But now it feels different. Off. Like I'm watching it all from behind glass. The laughter, the clink of glasses, the hum of conversation—it's just noise, amplifying the realization that I don't belong here anymore.

I sip my drink, barely tasting it, scanning the room out of habit. The women flirt and laugh, leaning into conversations with the guys who soak it all up, the kind of easy, carefree attention I used to enjoy. But now? It feels hollow, like a version of myself I've left behind.

And then, through the blur of movement and noise, I see her. Across the room, she catches my eye, and everything else fades.

Celeste. She's dressed to be noticed, her smile sharp and deliberate, cutting through the room like a blade. Our eyes meet for a fraction too long, and that's all the invitation she needs. Her gaze locks on to mine, predatory intent in her eyes as she moves through the crowd. The room seems to part for her as if she commands it. Every step, every glance, is calculated—charm wielded like a weapon, designed to get exactly what she wants.

"Alex." She draws out my name, her hand grazing my arm—a touch I don't want.

I stiffen, polite but distant. "Hello, Celeste."

Her smile widens as her gaze sweeps over me. "Oh, come on, Alex. Don't be like that. We've always gotten along, haven't we?"

"'Gotten along' might be a stretch."

She laughs softly, seemingly unfazed. "We had some good times, didn't we?" Her hand slides down my arm, her touch deliberate, testing. "And I'm sure you must miss what only I can give you."

It's just like Celeste to think she has a magical pussy.

"Celeste, some things are better left in the past. You're one of them."

Her confident smile falters for a moment before she smooths it over, charm snapping neatly back into place. She steps closer, her voice dropping to a low murmur, clearly aiming to create an air of intimacy. "Maybe we should slip away for a bit. I could remind you of what you've been missing."

My patience thins. "Not interested."

Her smile tightens, a crack in her polished exterior starting to show. "Why not?" She tilts her head as her gaze sharpens. "Are you seeing someone?"

The question hangs between us, her eyes probing for a reaction.

"Does it matter?"

She narrows her eyes, her forced casualness slipping. "Guess that's a yes then."

Now is the perfect moment to end this conversation. "Celeste, I really should get going." I step around her, heading toward the edge of the room.

And then I see him.

Tyson McRae.

He's across the room, laughing with a group, his demeanor as casual and carefree as if the past had never happened. The sight of him makes my pulse spike, anger surging through me in a wave so intense I can barely breathe.

My heart pounds with every bitter thought, every reminder of what he stole from me. Seeing him so at ease, so smug, while I'm haunted by the aftermath of his actions, twists something deep in my gut. My fists curl tightly before I even realize it.

Our eyes meet, and for a moment, something cold flashes across his face. Then his mouth curves into a slow smirk. He starts toward me, his steps deliberate, his confidence rolling off him like a challenge.

"Sebring, didn't expect to see you here. Finally grew the balls to stop hiding, did you? So, tell me—what's it like watching from the stands, mate? Tough luck, eh?" Every word drips with mocking sympathy.

My jaw tightens, the muscles in my neck straining as I fight the urge to respond. Every instinct screams at me to wipe that smirk off his face with one solid blow, but I force myself to stay still. I can't give him what he wants.

He leans in closer, his words dropping to a near whisper that carries a serrated edge. "Should've been more careful out there on the field." His smirk sharpens into something outright malicious.

A flash of rage blinds me, my fists clenching so tightly that my nails bite into my palms. Every nerve in my body screams to shut him up, to silence his smug arrogance with one decisive move. But I breathe through it, steadying myself. I won't let him win—not like this.

But *fuck*, it takes everything in me to hold back.

I step away, forcing myself out of the moment before the anger consumes me. As I push through the crowd, the noise swells, the space feels tighter, and the walls seem to close in around me. Memories and fury twist together, coiling tighter with each step until it feels like my skin might split from the pressure. Each breath comes harder, heavier, the burn beneath my skin refusing to fade no matter how hard I try to shake it off.

It's overwhelming—every ache of what I've lost, every sneer and memory stirred up by being here, by seeing him. I stop, dragging a hand through my hair, trying to steady myself as my pulse races. The edge feels dangerously close, sharp and impossible to ignore.

And then, cutting through the haze, one thought steadies me with startling clarity.

Charleston.

Her name alone shifts something inside me, steadying me in a way nothing else can. She's the only one who could pull me back from this. Before I fully realize it, my fingers are already reaching for my phone. I tap the microphone icon and bring my phone to my mouth. "I hate it here. I wish you were with me."

I send the text, my heart pounding. Hearing from her is the only thing that might pull me from the anger and regret consuming me.

Her response comes almost instantly, and the tightness in my chest begins to ease as her words appear on the screen.

> Are you okay?

No.

> I'm here for you. Come to the penthouse when you leave... if you feel like it.

Simple.

Unassuming.

Exactly what I need.

The breath I've been holding slips out, and the rage begins to ebb, the tension loosening its grip. She's the pill that takes away my pain. For the first time since stepping into this stadium, I feel something steady, something real. Just knowing she's there for me pulls me back to myself.

Without a word to anyone, I leave. An Irish goodbye feels fitting —no explanations, no farewells. The cool night air greets me as I step out of the after-party. The tension in my shoulders persists, knotted and tight, but Charleston's message dulls its edge. The hum of the city surrounds me, a quiet rhythm that steadies my thoughts as I take a few breaths. Slowly, the anger settles, receding piece by piece.

Celeste and Tyson don't get to have this power over me anymore. They're relics of the past—parts of my life I need to leave behind if I'm ever going to build something real, something good. The life I want? It doesn't exist here, tangled in a world I've outgrown.

With each step, my resolve hardens. The past doesn't define me anymore.

On my way.

The penthouse is still when I step inside, a sanctuary from the chaos of the night. I move quietly toward the bedroom, pushing the door open to find Charleston already in bed, her hair spilling over the pillow like a chestnut halo. She stirs, turning toward me with sleep-heavy eyes and a soft, welcoming smile.

"Hey, big guy. Everything okay?"

The sight of her undoes the last of the tension in my shoulders, and I exhale deeply. "It is now."

I strip off my shirt and pants, letting them drop to the floor, and slide into bed beside her. Pulling her close, I fit myself against her, the warmth of her body soothing me like nothing else ever could. In her arms, I find a sense of ease I haven't felt in years.

She shifts slightly, her hand finding mine and resting over it. "You're sure everything's okay?"

For a moment, I hesitate, unsure if I should even bring it up. But the thought of keeping it to myself feels heavier than it should, and I know talking to someone as understanding as Charleston is exactly what I need. "I ran into my ex tonight."

She rolls over to face me, her eyes sharpening with curiosity and concern. "Did something happen between you two?"

"She flirted a bit. Made some suggestions."

Her brow furrows. "What kind of *suggestions*?"

I let out a dry chuckle, the memory more irritating than amusing. But the slight edge of jealousy I catch in Charleston's voice...... I can't deny liking it. "She wanted us to slip away so she could remind me of what I've been missing."

Charleston's eyes narrow. "What exactly was she wanting to remind you of?"

"Exactly what you're thinking."

Her expression grows unreadable, the pause stretching a beat too long before she finally responds. "Of course she wanted to hook up. Why wouldn't she? The sex is amazing."

Sensing her growing jealousy, I feel the need to make things clear. "I left and came here. My ex doesn't mean a thing to me. You know that, right?"

Her eyes search mine, her features softening. "I believe you." Her words are heavy with something unspoken, something that reaches beyond the surface. "I know we haven't known each other long, and I don't have any right to tell you who you can or can't see, but—" She pauses, drawing in a breath. "I can't stay in this if you're interested in being with anyone else. I should've said it sooner, but this is new to me. While I'm really enjoying this—us—I won't share you with anyone else while we're together."

I won't share you with anyone else. The quiet intensity of her words strikes me, vulnerable yet firm, sinking deep in a way I didn't expect. I like hearing it—more than I probably should. Knowing she cares enough to set that boundary is reassuring, giving me a sense of certainty I didn't realize I wanted. With her, it's not about control. It's about clarity. She's drawn her line, and I respect it. Hell, I admire it.

There's a shift between us, something sharper, clearer than before. "I'm not interested in that life anymore. I've done it—juggled dates, spread myself thin, kept everything casual. That's not what I want right now."

I pull her closer, brushing a kiss against her forehead. "You're the only woman in my life, Charleston."

Her hand finds mine, her fingers threading through, her touch warm and sure. "And you're the only man in mine."

Charleston tilts her head, studying me in the dim light. "You still seem upset. Is that all that happened tonight?"

I take a breath, steadying myself. She deserves to hear it all. "No. The guy who caused my injury—Tyson—he was there too. He taunted me, got up in my face and tried to push every button he could find."

Her eyes flash with a sudden fierceness, and her grip on my hand tightens. "This guy injures you, ends your career, and then has the nerve to taunt you about it? That's a fuck ton of horse shit right there."

My jaw tightens as the memory resurfaces. "It took everything in me not to lose it. I wanted to knock that arrogance right off his face, but everyone was there. If I'd retaliated, it would've only made things worse."

"I don't think he confronted you in public because he felt safe there. I think he wanted to provoke you, to make you react and look bad in front of everyone. This asshole's not done messing with you."

Her words hold an unsettling clarity. I'd assumed Tyson taunted me there because he knew I wouldn't risk a scene, but maybe she's right. Maybe he wanted me to snap.

"Why does this jerk have it in for you?"

"I took his job. The... *organization* wanted me because I was better at the job, and he got transferred. Simple as that."

"So he was settling a score by injuring you? Like, if he couldn't have the job, then neither could you?"

"Exactly."

She sighs, her expression softening. "I'm so sorry you had to deal with that tonight. Are you okay?"

The warmth in her words and the genuine concern in her eyes touch something deep within me. "I am now. Talking to you makes it manageable. My anger doesn't feel so overwhelming."

Her smile softens as she brushes her thumb over my cheek, the slow, calming motion easing what's left of the tension inside me. "I'm glad," she whispers, leaning her forehead gently against mine. "You deserve peace."

For the first time in what feels like forever, I feel peace. With her beside me, the anger fades into something smaller, quieter, easier to manage. I close my eyes, letting her presence wash over me—the very thing I've been needing and looking for even when I didn't fully understand what it was.

Chapter 20

Magnolia Steel

WE PULL UP TO THE HOUSE, AND I STARE, GOBSMACKED, AS THE sprawling estate comes into view. Nestled among lush greenery, the house is bathed in soft golden sunlight, its grand yet unpretentious design exuding a welcoming warmth. It's the kind of place that could easily grace the pages of a magazine.

"Well, shit a brick and build a house with it!"

JC chuckles, glancing over at me. "Don't hold back, Charleston. Tell me how you really feel."

I laugh, shaking my head. "What do your friends do for work again?"

"Jack owns several vineyards across Australia and New Zealand. Laurelyn's in the music industry—a songwriter for country artists."

"Oh right." I nod as it clicks. "She's the one who used to be a big country-music star, isn't she?"

"That's right. And she also runs a nonprofit called Healing Melodies. It's a foundation that uses music therapy to help kids, especially those dealing with tough family situations, like parents struggling with addiction."

"All that while raising four kids? They must have their hands full all the time."

"That's putting it mildly. But somehow, they make it work. You'll see—they're incredible."

This is a side of his world I haven't seen before, and from what he's told me, Jack and Laurelyn are more than friends—they're family. Letting me into this part of his life feels significant, like he's opening a door to something deeper.

As we approach the front door, I steal a glance at him, the question slipping out before I can think better of it. "Do they know all about our... *situationship?*"

His grin comes easy, amusement lighting up his face. "They know, and there's zero judgment. Promise. They've been where we are, so they understand exactly what's happening between us."

Relief washes over me, smoothing out the tension. "So I can talk to Laurelyn about it?"

"Absolutely. Ask her anything. She's been in your shoes, and I know she'll tell you the truth."

I think about Violet, the one who's been with me through so much, always ready to listen. But she's thousands of miles away, too far to see what's unfolding here or fully grasp the strange, unexpected connection JC and I have built. It's hard to put into words, even for myself sometimes. With Laurelyn, though—someone who's lived this kind of whirlwind—I won't have to explain it at all.

JC reaches out, his hand giving mine a brief but steady squeeze before we enter the McLachlan home. Together, we step into a space that feels like a breath of fresh air—a kind of comfort where our situationship doesn't feel quite so complicated.

The rich scent of aged wood and something faintly floral greets me as we cross the threshold. Warm lighting spills across the room, highlighting the soft gleam of polished surfaces and the subtle charm of framed family photos on the walls. There's a faint hum of music just loud enough to blend into the background.

"Jack! Laurelyn!" JC calls out, his voice carrying easily through the open space.

"Hey." Laurelyn appears from around the corner, her smile bright and genuine as she strides forward, her arms already outstretched. She wraps JC in a warm hug first, patting his back as she pulls away with a beaming grin. "It's so good to see you."

JC steps aside, his hand gesturing toward me. "Laurelyn, this is Charleston."

Her gaze shifts to me, her smile widening as she steps closer. She pulls me into a hug that's firm and welcoming. "Charleston, we're so glad you're here." Her easy, natural embrace instantly melts away any nerves I've been holding on to.

Jack follows behind her, his handshake strong and steady, followed by a quick pat on JC's shoulder. "Made it just in time. Hope you're ready for a feast."

Laurelyn steps closer, her arm looping through mine with an ease that feels natural. "Come on, let me show you around."

She moves gracefully through the space, pointing out small details—a photo here, a piece of art there—each accompanied by a story that feels like an invitation into her world. I follow her to a gallery wall filled with framed photos, my gaze catching on one in particular. It's a wedding picture—Laurelyn and Jack, radiating happiness, surrounded by friends and family. But it's not them that stops me.

"Wait a second." I lean in closer, my finger hovering near the image. "Is that... Jake Beckett? He came to your wedding?"

Laurelyn glances at the photo, her lips curling into a wry smile. "Only because he's my sperm donor."

My head jerks back, and I stare at her, my jaw practically on the floor. "Your father is Jake Beckett? As in *the* Jake Beckett? Legendary country-music star, *that* Jake Beckett?"

"Yep," she says, popping the p in a way that's almost dismissive. "Don't be too impressed." Her expression tightens. "He's an asshole."

I blink, her words sinking in. The casual way she says it makes it hit even harder, like it's a truth she's long since come to terms with. My thoughts spiral, pulling me back to my own life, my own father.

I know what it's like to have an asshole for a parent, but at least Jake Beckett doesn't sound like mine. Whatever mistakes he's made, I doubt they include dragging his daughter into dangerous messes or insisting she lock her door at night in order to stay safe from the fallout of his bad choices.

The thoughts stick, heavy and unresolved, like they always do when my father crosses my mind. I glance at Laurelyn, wondering what stories she carries about Jake Beckett, how she manages to talk about him so matter-of-factly. "I get it. I have my own version of an asshole for a father."

Laurelyn's gaze meets mine, a faint understanding passing between us before she gestures to another photo, shifting the conversation back to something lighter. But my thoughts loom, a quiet storm beneath the surface, one I'm not willing to share.

Jack picks up a wineglass, filling it with the last of what remains in the bottle. "Here you go, Charleston. The good stuff. Guaranteed to make you feel like part of the family—or at least tolerate us until dessert." He raises his own glass in a playful toast, his humor tugging a smile from me.

The gesture is casual and welcoming, easing the knot of nerves in my chest a little more.

"You have a beautiful home." My eyes travel to the high ceilings and open layout. The understated elegance is warm and inviting; nothing about it feels overly showy.

"Thank you," Laurelyn says. "I really do love it here. This home has so much of our story in it—it's where we've built our life, raised our kids, and made so many memories. It's different from living in the U.S., but I wouldn't trade this for anything."

Jack claps JC on the shoulder, grinning. "First things first, mate. Let's hit the wine cellar and find another bottle of vino."

JC flashes me a quick wink before following Jack, leaving me alone with Laurelyn. I take a steadying breath, surprised at how nervous I'd been on the drive here. Those nerves, though, are beginning to fade.

Laurelyn moves with grace around the kitchen, finishing the final touches on the meal. There's no staff bustling about, no air of formality—just a wife and mother in her element, creating a space that feels warm and authentic. It's comforting in a way I didn't expect, and to my surprise, I feel at ease, like I truly belong here.

She glances up, catching my eye with an easy smile, the kind that instantly makes you feel welcome. "Just so you know, we're not formal around here. Relax, make yourself at home. If you feel like jumping in, go for it—if not, no pressure. Whatever makes you comfortable."

"Honestly, I was a little nervous, but you've made tonight feel really easy."

"Good. That's what we're about here—no pressure, no expectations, just family." She sets a dish on the counter, brushing her hands on a towel before glancing back at me, a playful spark lighting her expression. "And speaking of family—" Her smile widens mischievously. "I told the kids you two are playing a little game, and they're supposed to call him Julius Caesar while you're here. But they're kids, so who knows how long they'll actually stick to it."

I laugh, taking a sip of the wine Jack poured for me.

She raises an eyebrow, a playful challenge dancing in her gaze. "Are you ready to learn his real name if one of them lets it slip?"

"It wouldn't be the end of the world if they slipped up. The alias thing is for fun. What we have is about making the most of the time we've got while I'm here in Australia."

She nods, a glimmer of understanding in her eyes. "You're okay with not knowing more about him?"

I pause, considering the possibility. "I know he's someone well-known in the public eye. That's not something he can hide, but I actually like the mystery. Even if I learn his real name tonight, it won't change anything for me."

Understanding crosses her expression. "This all takes me back to when Jack Henry and I first met. I'm sure you've heard we had our own little arrangement when we started seeing each other."

I grin, feeling an easy camaraderie settle between us. "JC told me all about it. Your arrangement has definitely been an inspiration for us."

"Well, I hope you're enjoying your time together as much as we did. Those early days were something special. Unforgettable, really."

Laurelyn laughs, nostalgia lighting her eyes. "I found out Jack Henry's real name completely by accident. There was a medical emergency with his father, and I was unexpectedly thrown into the middle of the McLachlan family. When we arrived at the hospital, his mother called him Jack Henry, and to cover the fact that I didn't know his real name, I called him that too." She grins, her eyes sparkling with mischief. "His mother nearly lost it because she was the only one who ever called him that. She took it as a sign he must love me if he let me get away with it. And, well, he's been my Jack Henry ever since."

I smile, charmed by the tale. "Such a great start to your love story."

She nods, her laugh soft and warm. "Like you, we had aliases when we first met. His was Lachlan, after McLachlan, and mine was Paige—my middle name. It was supposed to keep things uncomplicated, at least in the beginning." She shrugs, her smile softening. "But it didn't stay that way for long. Complicated snuck in pretty quickly—but it was the best kind of complicated."

"Has he told you how we came up with our aliases?"

"He did, but I have to tell you—Julius Caesar doesn't suit him at all to me."

I laugh with her, shaking my head. "I've started calling him JC. It fits better."

Her eyes warm with amusement. "It's funny how those things take on a life of their own. Makes it all the more special."

"Exactly! Our aliases are tied to this little bubble we've created. It's silly, I know, but it's meaningful in its own way."

"It's not silly." Laurelyn takes a sip of her wine, her gaze thoughtful. "So, how far along are you two in this three-month arrangement?"

"About a month in." I'm surprised by the unexpected pang I feel at how quickly the first four weeks have flown by.

"That's when the real fun starts—the awkward newness has worn off, and you finally get comfortable with each other."

"So true."

It's so nice to have someone to talk to who understands where I am. This isn't exactly the kind of situation you can explain to just anyone.

"The next two months are going to fly by, trust me. Before you know it, your time together will be up. So, make the most of it. Enjoy every moment."

Her words strike a quiet chord, settling into the part of me that's been avoiding thoughts about how fleeting this arrangement is. But before the reality of it can fully settle, Jack and JC emerge from the wine cellar, each carrying a bottle and wearing easy smiles, their presence shifting the mood to something lighter.

Jack grins, a teasing glint in his eyes. "So, the emperor tells me you're into some... *unusual* music?"

I place my hands on my hips, narrowing my eyes at JC with dramatic disapproval. "*Eclectic*, not unusual. My playlist is highly curated, thank you very much."

JC raises his hands in surrender. "Fair enough—I stand corrected."

"I like a woman who's passionate about her music," Laurelyn says, raising her glass.

Jack leans back, a proud glint in his eye. "Speaking of music, did Caesar mention that my beautiful wife is a musician?"

"He might've mentioned it."

Jack's grin widens. "But I bet he left out the part where she was the original lead singer for Southern Ophelia."

My jaw drops, my gaze snapping to Laurelyn. "Southern Ophelia? Are you kidding me?"

Jack chuckles, clearly enjoying my reaction. "Not kidding. She's the real deal."

I turn back to Laurelyn, a mix of awe and surprise on my face. "That's incredible."

Laurelyn waves it off with a modest smile, though there's a sparkle in her eyes. "That was a lifetime ago, but it was definitely a wild ride."

I tilt my head, studying her closely, and suddenly it clicks—the voice, the face. My mouth falls open. "Wait. I remember you."

A melody springs to mind, and before I can stop myself, I'm humming the chorus of one of Southern Ophelia's biggest hits. The lyrics flow naturally, spilling out in a low murmur as I mouth the words:

> *I'm waiting for your heart to wake*
> *So you will ask me to stay.*
> *My heart is impatiently waiting around*
> *To hear the words it's begging you to say.*

I glance at Laurelyn, my eyes wide with realization. "That was you."

"I wrote that song about Jack Henry." She lets out a laugh, waving a hand as if to brush it off. "It feels like another life. I stopped performing years ago. Now, I write songs for other people—and wipe snotty noses."

Even as she downplays it, there's a quiet warmth in her expression, a glow that speaks of pride. And a twinge of awe settles in my chest.

Jack strides across the room with an easy grin, wrapping his arms around Laurelyn and pulling her close. "This amazing, gorgeous woman doesn't give herself enough credit. Three of her songs have already hit the top 10 this year. And let me tell you, if she were the one performing them, they'd have gone straight to number one."

"Jack Henry," she says with a laugh, swatting his chest lightly, her cheeks tinged with a warm flush. "Stop it. Those days are long gone."

She turns to me, her smile softening, raising her glass in a gesture that feels more like an invitation than a toast. "Maybe we'll give the piano a workout later."

I tap my glass gently to hers. "Now that's something I wouldn't miss."

The four of us settle around the beautifully set table, and I feel a little spoiled by the care put into every detail. The soft glow of candles and the savory aroma of the meal create a cozy, inviting atmosphere. Just as conversation begins to flow, a loud thud echoes from upstairs, drawing Laurelyn's attention. She glances up with a knowing smile.

"I asked the babysitter to keep the kids busy upstairs so we could have a little adult time."

Jack chuckles, pouring more wine. "She's probably up there running triage."

Another thud follows, paired with muffled giggles and hurried footsteps. Laurelyn shakes her head, her smile widening. "See what I mean?"

JC leans in slightly, his words dropping to a playful murmur. "It's always like this—basically, a circus on any given day."

Jack grins, filling JC's glass with wine. "But you have to admit, it's a pretty cute circus."

Laurelyn nods in agreement. "It's a *very* cute circus."

JC raises a brow, his gaze darting between them. "Sounds like you need another one to add to the fun."

Without missing a beat, they both answer in unison, "No!" before bursting into laughter.

Jack shakes his head. "Have four of your own and then let me know if adding a fifth sounds like a good idea."

JC chuckles. "Fair enough. I'll take your word for it."

We settle into the meal, and Laurelyn glances over. "Have you been able to get out and explore the city together?"

JC gives her a wry grin. "It's tricky in Sydney. Too many eyes. You two probably understand that better than anyone."

"What kind of things have you managed?" Jack asks.

"We've been to the Rabbit Hole a couple of times and took the yacht up to Newcastle for a weekend. We also went to Chloe's restaurant—used the private dining room, of course. Honestly, we've spent most of our time in the penthouse."

Jack and Laurelyn exchange an amused glance, the nostalgia practically visible in the softening of their expressions, as if they're both replaying the early days of their story.

"Lots of eyes and wagging tongues in Sydney," Jack says with a shake of his head. "I took L to the Sydney Opera House, and the paparazzi were shoving cameras in our faces before we even made it inside. The next day, our pictures were plastered everywhere."

"I didn't understand why on earth they were taking photos of us." Laurelyn laughs, her eyes sparkling with the memory. "Oh my God, that was such a great night at the opera."

Jack raises his glass, smirking as his gaze locks with hers. "An *amazing* night, if I remember correctly."

The look they share feels layered, their words hinting at a story too personal, too deeply theirs to invite questions. It's not about the opera; it's about a moment in their history, one clearly meaningful enough to hold significance without further explanation. Whatever the story is, it belongs to them, and I decide not to press.

Jack chuckles, turning back to us. "It wasn't long after that night when all the secrets came out. Once everything was in the open, our relationship changed. For the better."

Laurelyn nods, her eyes lighting up with the glow of a cherished memory. "That's when it went from fun to incredible. No more hiding in the shadows."

Jack tilts his head, a teasing glint in his eyes. "Not that the shadows were so bad. I did enjoy having you all to myself."

"True. But we had so much more freedom once we went public. And while the aliases were fun, things shifted once we knew each other's real names. Everything changed."

After a pause, she waves a hand, her expression softening, as if brushing away the nostalgia. "But enough about us."

We finish dinner, and as I reach for a plate to help clear the table, Jack waves me off with a grin. "Don't even think about it. The emperor and I have this covered. You ladies go relax. We'll be there in a few."

I glance at JC, who gives me an easy smile. "This won't take long."

"Fine, I'm not going to argue," I say with a laugh, letting Laurelyn lead the way into the living room.

My attention is immediately drawn to the beautiful piano tucked into one corner. Its sleek black surface gleams under the soft lighting, exuding elegance. I wander over, lightly running my fingers along its polished edge. "This is stunning."

She notices my interest and smiles. "Do you play?"

"Oh God, no. I wouldn't even know where to start."

Laurelyn settles onto the bench and lets her fingers brush gently over the keys. "I wasn't sure." She plays a few soft notes, "Julius Caesar mentioned you love music."

I smile, watching the way her elegant long fingers move gracefully. "I do, but I didn't grow up in the kind of family where music lessons were even a possibility. Let's just say my lessons were a little more practical—and a lot less fun."

She nods, her expression softening. "I understand that more than you can imagine. People assume I had this picture-perfect upbringing, but it wasn't like that. There were struggles—maybe not the same ones you had but struggles all the same. Honestly, I didn't know happiness until I met Jack Henry."

A chill runs through me, and I can't help the small smile that tugs at my lips. "That gives me goose bumps."

She glances up, her eyes holding a knowing look. "Is that because you feel the same way about Julius Caesar?"

I glance toward the kitchen, making sure the guys are still occupied. "Maybe something like that."

Laurelyn smiles, her eyes warm with understanding. "I know you didn't come all the way here expecting to find a relationship on the other side of the world, but sometimes fate has other plans. And we don't always get a say in it."

Her words stir something deep inside me. I want to respond, but the truth feels too big to put into words right now. Instead, I offer a small smile, hoping it's enough to convey that I understand exactly what she means.

Laurelyn seems to sense my hesitation and shifts gears with a warm smile. "What's your favorite music?"

I relax as I lean against the piano. "Oh, definitely '70s and '80s. Occasionally, some '60s. Some '90s. "I'm a little all over the place."

Her fingers glide over the keys, and within moments, the soft, familiar opening notes of "The Rose" fill the room. My eyes light up, and Laurelyn notices, a smile tugging at her lips.

"Know this one, do you?"

I nod, smiling. "Of course. It's only one of the greatest songs ever written."

"I agree. Come on, sing it with me."

I laugh, shaking my head quickly. "Oh no. I could never sing with you."

She waves a hand, her eyes sparkling with encouragement. "Nonsense. In this house, singing isn't reserved for professionals. Everyone sings."

Her playful insistence draws another laugh from me, and for a moment, I let the idea settle. Maybe—just maybe—I could give it a try. But for now, I simply listen, the music wrapping around me like an familiar old friend.

Laurelyn continues playing, and I notice a small figure peeking around the corner, her wide eyes fixed on us with quiet curiosity. Smiling, I lean in toward Laurelyn. "Looks like we have company."

Laurelyn glances up, her face brightening as she spots the little girl. "You can come in, sweetheart."

The girl dashes over and hops up beside her mom at the piano. "I heard you playing."

Laurelyn wraps an arm around her, smiling down at her daughter. "We're about to sing. Want to join us?"

The little girl nods. "Yes, ma'am."

"This is our daughter, Maggie James. We call her MJ."

I crouch slightly, meeting MJ's bright, curious gaze. "Hi, MJ. Some of my friends call me Maggie."

MJ's eyes widen, her interest piqued. "I'm named after my grandmother Margaret. Is your real name Margaret?"

I glance around and then lean in as if revealing the juiciest gossip. "Well, between us girls... my real name is Magnolia." With a playful wink, I press a finger to my lips. "But let's keep that between us."

Laurelyn leans in, her smile brimming with mischief. "Now that's just for us girls to know. The boys can't know—especially Uncle—" She catches herself with a soft laugh. "Uncle *Julius.*"

MJ's face lights up, clearly thrilled to be part of an adult secret. "I won't tell."

I chuckle, leaning closer to MJ. "Good. We girls gotta stick together."

Just as we finish sharing our little secret, Jack and JC step into the living room, their easy laughter breaking the quiet hum of the piano.

"Take a seat, gentlemen. You're about to be thoroughly delighted," Laurelyn says with a playful grin, her hands poised over the keys.

JC raises a brow, his mischievous grin aimed at MJ. "Sing nice and loud, MJ. You'll need to carry Charleston—let's just say delight isn't the first word I'd use to describe her singing."

I laugh, shaking my head. "*Rude...* but fair."

"We're doing 'The Rose,'" she announces, letting her fingers drift into the opening melody. She glances over at her daughter. "Think you remember this one?"

"I remember it, Mum!" MJ says, her enthusiasm lighting up the room.

As Laurelyn's fingers dance over the keys, the three of us begin to sing. The music flows easily, and to my surprise, I don't feel self-conscious at all. Singing with them feels natural, like being welcomed into something warm and familiar.

Laurelyn's singing is breathtaking—deep and vibrant, carrying the melody with natural grace. MJ's voice adds a youthful sweetness, and somehow, my less-than-perfect notes don't feel out of place.

Midway through, I catch JC watching me. His gaze is steady, soft, and unwavering. It sends an awareness through me, a quiet wonder at what he might be thinking.

The lyrics take on an intensity I didn't expect, resonating with something deep inside me. They speak of dormant love, fragile but enduring, blooming even in uncertain times. The way Laurelyn sings it, every note feels personal, almost like a promise whispered into the air.

As the final notes fade into the stillness, I find myself holding on to the moment. There's a thought dwelling in the quiet—knowing JC's true identity wouldn't change this. If anything, it might make it even more extraordinary. But that decision isn't mine to make.

For now, this is enough. The beauty of the unknown, wrapped in the warmth of music and connection, feels like everything I need.

Chapter 21

Alex Sebring

THE SOFT HUM OF CONVERSATION AND THE FAINT CLINK OF glasses welcome us as we step into the restaurant. The cozy buzz of diners fills the space, their voices blending with the gentle background music. The lively atmosphere is a stark contrast to the last time I was here—tucked away in the private dining room with Charleston, hidden from prying eyes.

Once we're seated, Laurelyn flips open the menu. We order drinks, and as soon as the waiter steps away, she folds her hands on the table, her gaze settling on me with a calm intensity.

"I thought it would be a good time to steal a moment with you since Jack Henry is out of town this week." Laurelyn's casual delivery hints at something more thoughtful underneath.

"I appreciate the invite." But I can tell this isn't just a friendly catch-up.

Her smile softens. "I'm so glad you brought Charleston to dinner the other night. I really enjoyed meeting her."

A small smile tugs at my lips. "She enjoyed meeting you."

"I wanted to check in and see where things stand between you two." Laurelyn's usual playfulness gives way to an unexpected seriousness.

"Things are great. We're having a lot of fun together."

A smile spreads across her face, lighting her features. "Good. Because I really love Charleston. Can we keep her?"

I laugh, and her expression shifts to something more serious. "I'm actually not kidding, Alex. Hear me out."

Her words grab my full attention. "All right."

"She's wonderful. She'd fit into your life—and your family's life—so naturally. Malie and Alexander would adore her, and I know all your siblings would too. Especially Leilani and Sefina."

Warmth spreads through me at the thought of having something more with her. "Yeah, I know they would. But she's not looking for that kind of connection right now."

"Maybe she's not looking for it, but that doesn't mean she wouldn't be open to it if it unfolds organically. Sometimes the best things in life aren't planned. They just happen."

I pause, letting Laurelyn's words sink in for a moment.

Her expression softens as she studies me. "Where's your head at with all of this?"

"It's still early, but I really like her. More than I expected to. And I already know it's going to hurt like hell when she leaves and I lose her."

Laurelyn studies me for a moment. "What if you didn't have to lose her?"

"What do you mean?"

"I've been in your shoes, Alex. I know how easy it is to let something good slip away because you're scared or convinced it won't work. But letting her leave without telling her how you feel would be a mistake."

I shake my head slightly, a quiet laugh escaping. "I can't ask her to change her world for me. She's got her life in Charleston, her work, her friends."

Laurelyn doesn't waver. "I'm not saying you have to ask her to stay. I'm saying you owe it to both of you to be honest. Let her know how much she means to you. If she still chooses to leave, at least she'll know. And if she doesn't... well, maybe fate has other plans."

Her words stir something undeniable in me. "Charleston's here for work, Laurelyn. When her assignment ends, she'll go back to the U.S. It's not like she can simply extend her stay. And she's not going to drop her life for me—not without a real reason."

Laurelyn's gaze sharpens, her determination unwavering. "Then give her a reason."

I shake my head. "She's made it clear she's not interested in marriage. That's not what she's looking for."

"Maybe not right now. But she's here with you, Alex, spending her time with you. That tells me she's open to something more, whether she realizes it yet or not. The question is this: are you brave enough to show her what that could look like?"

Laurelyn's smile is soft, almost amused, but there's a knowing edge to it. "Jack Henry wasn't looking for marriage either, but look at him now. No one could be more married than he is today. Things change, Alex. People change. And I see the way you two look at each other. She might not be there yet, but that girl is falling for you. And I know you're falling for her too."

Her words stir something deep within me, a thought I've been too cautious to fully embrace. I let out a slow breath, deciding to be honest. "You're right. I can't lie—I have growing feelings for her. I can see a life with Charleston, but only if she wants it too. I can't force her into something she doesn't want."

"You have, what, seven weeks left with her?"

A pang of anxiety tightens in my chest. Each week that passes feels sharper, the countdown looming over everything. "Right. Seven weeks and then I have no idea what happens after that."

Her expression softens. "Make those seven weeks count. Show her what a life with you could be like. Let her see what she'd be leaving behind."

She studies me for a moment as if weighing her next words

carefully. "Charleston is different. You can trust her. She's not Celeste, and she's not like the other women who chase you for all the wrong reasons."

My thoughts drift to the moments Charleston and I have shared, moments that were raw and real, untouched by the shadows of my past.

"She showed up at the Rabbit Hole to meet you without knowing a thing about you. She genuinely likes you for who you are—not Alex Sebring, the rugby legend. Not Alexander Sebring III, heir to Sebring Hotels. Just you."

Relief loosens the tension in my chest. "I know she isn't like Celeste or the others—not even a little. And I do trust her. She's everything I was hoping for when I signed up with Soul Sync."

I chuckle softly, shaking my head as a small smile tugs at my lips. "You know it took me a bloody week to fill out that compatibility assessment—tripping over every question, every word. My brain was a mess. But somehow I ended up finding her. Charleston is exactly who I was describing in every answer on that questionnaire."

"That doesn't surprise me one bit. She's the one for you, Alex. I know it deep in my soul." Her expression shifts, turning serious. "I know the aliases have been fun, but at some point, you're going to have to tell her who you really are. Once the role-play ends, that's when you'll know if this is something real—something that could last."

Laurelyn's words sink in, their truth undeniable. She's right. Charleston has more than earned my honesty. She deserves to know it all.

"You have to admit she's passed every test. She's proven herself and deserves to know you—fully, completely, down to the core." Her gaze softens, warmth threading through her words. "Jack Henry and I love you, Alex. We want to see you happy—you're so deserving of it. And if it means sticking my nose into your business to make sure of it, well, I'll do that happily."

"You're starting to sound an awful lot like Margaret McLachlan right now."

She grins, her eyes sparkling with pride. "Thank you. I'll take that as the highest compliment."

There's a mischievous twinkle in her eye. "I want to do for you and Charleston what Margaret did for Jack Henry and me."

My curiosity is piqued. "And what exactly was that?"

"To help open your eyes to the possibilities of true love. Now, do I have your blessing to invite Charleston to lunch? I'd love the chance to get to know her better... and maybe plant a few seeds."

Planting seeds—that's Laurelyn's specialty. She introduces an idea so subtly that it starts to grow before you even realize it. I'd bet Jack Henry didn't see it coming until he was already in too deep.

"Of course. Charleston would love that. She told me a couple times how much she enjoyed hanging out with you last weekend."

"She seems like a strong woman, someone who's had to build walls to protect herself. Don't let your time together slip by without showing her who you really are and how you truly feel. Heaven forbid, she's like I was and decides to leave because she can't bear the thought of saying goodbye."

Her gaze softens, her expression tinged with a memory that seems to ache. "It took Jack Henry months to find me after I ran. And during that time, I was living in hell."

Her words settle over me with a heaviness I can't shake, cutting deeper than I expected. The thought of Charleston leaving, slipping through my fingers, leaves an ache in my chest I can't ignore. Watching her walk away never knowing how I truly feel would be unbearable.

As Laurelyn continues talking, her voice fades into the background, and my thoughts drift to Charleston. It would be so easy to tell her the truth, to lay it all out and believe she'd keep it safe. I do have faith in her—more than I've had in anyone in years.

The secrecy, the aliases, the constant tension of being someone else in public—it's exhausting. With Charleston, the idea of stepping out from behind the mask feels less terrifying and more like relief.

I want her to see the real me. No pretenses, no walls—just me. And more than that, I want to see what we could be together if she knew everything.

As the evening winds down, the quiet hum of Laurelyn's words drifts into silence, but her message remains. A newfound certainty takes root, steady and undeniable. Charleston is worth the risk. She's different from anyone I've ever known.

I may have found the one I've been waiting for.

Chapter 22

Magnolia Steel

It's been a week since JC and I had dinner at Jack and Laurelyn's house, and I was surprised when she reached out to invite me on a girls' day. We've only just met, and while she's been warm and welcoming, I didn't expect to hear from her. When her message popped up, asking if I wanted to go shopping, I found myself saying yes without hesitation.

I pictured high-end boutiques and exclusive storefronts, the kind of places that fit her polished life. Instead, we're at a lively shopping center, the kind of place where real people—people like me—come to shop. It's not what I imagined, but it's perfect.

Not that I'm struggling—I'm doing fine for myself. But growing up with barely enough to get by has left its mark. I'm careful with money, always thinking ahead, always weighing what's necessary versus what's frivolous. Splurges are rare, reserved for something truly special... or something I can't stop thinking about.

My attention keeps straying—unwillingly, irresistibly—to a particular lingerie set in the store we've wandered into. Deep emerald with delicate lace, it's unlike anything I'd normally buy. But it's got my attention in a way that's both surprising and hard to ignore.

Laurelyn's eyes sparkle as she plucks a lacy black piece from the rack, holding it up with a mischievous grin. "Now this would send Jack Henry straight over the edge if I showed up wearing it tonight."

I laugh, nodding. "It's hot. You should absolutely get it."

She drapes it over her arm, her smile turning satisfied. "I think I will. It's perfect for my next dance."

"Next dance?" I ask, raising an eyebrow, my curiosity piqued.

Her eyes twinkle with playful confidence. "I pole dance—only for Jack Henry, of course. It keeps things fun." She says it casually as though she's talking about what she had for breakfast. The way she owns it, completely unapologetic, is both surprising and admirable.

She moves on, sifting through delicate lace and silk, humming softly as if this is simply another ordinary errand. Her ease is magnetic.

Singing, dancing, raising four kids, and still looking like a million bucks—seriously, is there anything this woman can't do?

We comb through the racks, the soft rustle of fabric filling the air as curiosity gets the better of me. "So, what's it like being married for —" I pause, realizing I don't remember the number.

"Ten years," she supplies with an easy smile. "And it's... well, it's imperfect. But it's also magical in its own way. It's the kind of bond that's hard to describe unless you're living it—filled with moments of absolute joy and others that test every ounce of patience and love you have. It's not always a fairy tale, but the magic is in the realness, in knowing someone has your back, flaws and all. There's beauty in the mess, in building a life together piece by piece."

I let her words sink in, feeling the depth behind them.

"And your career? You were the lead singer for one of the biggest country bands in existence. Do you ever regret giving that up?"

"Not for a second." Her expression softens, a faint smile tugging at her lips. "Jack Henry will always be my first choice. I love him, and I love the life we've built together. My family means everything to me. Nothing—no stage or spotlight—could ever compare to what I have at home."

A pang of admiration settles in my chest. "I can see it. The way you two look at each other—you can feel the love between you. But how did you know?"

"That Jack Henry was the one?" She glances at me briefly, her smile deepening with fondness, before her eyes drop to the piece of lingerie in her hand,. "I just knew. With him, it felt like coming home. Like every part of me was understood and accepted, no questions, no conditions. He saw the real me—flaws, quirks, everything—and loved me anyway. It's the kind of love that makes you know you can face anything together."

Her words settle over me, stirring something deep and quiet. And her description leaves a soft imprint in my thoughts. "That makes sense."

Laurelyn's eyes light up as she pulls a striking red lingerie set from the rack—a delicate lace bralette with matching, barely-there bottoms edged in soft satin. She holds it up, giving me a knowing grin. "This would look incredible on you."

I glance at it, the vibrant red lace practically daring me to step out of my comfort zone. "Honestly, I didn't even pack lingerie. I mean, why would I? I didn't come to Australia expecting to—" I pause, realizing there's no graceful way to finish that sentence.

"To *get laid*?" Laurelyn fills in, her smile playful. "Julius Caesar would lose his mind if he saw you in this. You should get it. It would make his night—and yours."

I hesitate, the lace dangling from her hand as if it's challenging me. It's not something I'd normally choose, but there's something about it—bold, daring, the kind of thing Magnolia Steel wouldn't give a second look.

But Charleston?

Laurelyn raises a brow, her expression full of encouragement. "Do it."

Before I can talk myself out of it, I grab the set, draping it over my arm with a grin that surprises even me. "Why not?"

We wander through the aisles, conversation flowing as easily as the shopping. Laurelyn glances over, her expression curious. "How are you feeling about everything?"

I smile, the thought of JC warming me from the inside out. "He's amazing. Patient, selfless, and genuinely giving. He's special. And it doesn't hurt that he's hotter than a two-dollar pistol."

Laurelyn laughs, her eyes sparkling with amusement. "You spend a lot of time together, don't you?"

"We're together every night and entire weekends. He's practically moved into the penthouse with me. My coworkers probably think I'm holed up in my room depressed and moping." I chuckle, shaking my head. "If they only knew. I'm having the time of my life. And the sex? Incredible. Best I've ever had." My cheeks heat slightly as I realize how easily the words slip out. "But you probably don't want to hear about that, considering how close you are to him."

Laurelyn waves a dismissive hand, her laugh light and easy. "Doesn't bother me one bit. Say whatever you like about your relationship."

Her easy acceptance softens something inside me, and I grin. "Thanks, Laurelyn. Honestly, it means a lot. I don't really have anyone I can talk to about him. It's not like I can bring it up with my coworkers."

Laurelyn studies me thoughtfully before nodding. "You know, you and Julius Caesar seem like a really good fit."

Warmth blooms inside me. "I've never felt this compatible with anyone before. It's surprising, honestly, considering how different our backgrounds are."

"I think you'd feel even closer if you knew more about him and could see the parts of his life he hasn't shown you yet."

The thought takes root. "Sometimes, I long to know more. Not because I need to pry, but because I yearn to understand him better. I want to see the pieces of him kept out of reach."

Laurelyn reaches out, her hand resting gently on my arm. "Maybe it's time to think about being honest with each other. The aliases were a fun way to start—safe, playful, and exactly what you needed then. But you've built something stronger now, something real. You've outgrown the game, as Jack Henry and I did."

You've outgrown the game. The words settle deep inside me, stirring a quiet ache of uncertainty.

Am I ready for what comes next?

"JC knows me more than any man ever has. The real me." Well, almost the real me. The exception, of course, being my name—and the truth about my father.

"So, you've been comfortable revealing your true self to him?"

"I am. It's strange, but with him, it feels easy. Natural."

"And you're not opposed to learning who Julius Caesar is?"

"Not at all." No hesitation. "But it has to be his decision. If he wants me to know, I'll be ready. If he doesn't, that's his choice to make."

"You should tell him that. Don't wait. It'd be a shame to spend the rest of your time with anyone other than the real man he is."

Her words settle over me, a quiet but firm nudge toward honesty. "How were you able to leave Jack when your three months were up?"

Her expression softens. "I was stubborn and scared. I'd built so many walls that I couldn't let myself be vulnerable enough to tell him how I felt. So, I slipped away without a goodbye, telling myself it was easier than risking the pain of hearing him say he didn't feel the same."

Her gaze drifts, a soft smile playing on her lips as though she's caught in a distant memory. "What I didn't know was that Jack Henry was already coming for me. He was ready to tell me everything—how he felt, what he wanted. But I'd already run off, and we missed each other by a few hours."

Her words resonate like an unspoken warning. "Being apart from the person you love is a kind of misery you can't prepare for. It hollows you out in ways you don't expect. I lost so much time with him—time we could've spent building the life we have now."

Her words carry a hint of urgency. "Don't make the same mistake I did. Don't let fear or pride keep you from being honest. If you care about him—and I know you do—then tell him. Speak your mind, even if your voice shakes. And don't let something as fragile as doubt rob you of something real."

Her lips curve into a small, knowing smile. "Trust me, Julius Caesar cares deeply for you."

He cares deeply for you. Those words hit me with a quiet intensity, sparking a flutter in my chest.

Laurelyn picks up a delicate white lingerie set, all lace and silk accents, holding it up with a playful grin. "Imagine this with stockings and heels, the whole shebang. Trust me, he won't stand a chance."

I run my fingers over the soft fabric. "I'm afraid."

Laurelyn rests a hand on my arm with a quiet assurance that only someone who's walked this path can offer. "I've been there. And I'm telling you from a place of *knowing*... don't let fear drive your choices. Regret is worse than any risk you'll ever take. It's better to regret the things you've done than regret the things you haven't."

Her words sink in, stirring something deep within me, a fragile place I've tried to keep untouched. "And if it all falls apart?"

She smiles, soft but sure. "Sometimes things fall apart so that better things can come together."

Laurelyn's words settle into something resembling courage. Three months—that's all I signed up for, all I let myself hope for.

But now, I realize, I want so much more.

Chapter 23

Alex Sebring

OF ALL THE GAMES I'VE PLAYED, THIS ONE HAS BEEN THE MOST fun. But now? It's time to stop playing.

Charleston is beside me, but the weight of what I'm about to do presses harder than ever. Tonight, the truth comes out. No more hiding. No more masks.

I grip the wheel, pulse hammering as I steal a glance at her. The soft glow of the dashboard lights casts shadows across her face, her expression calm, unaware that everything is about to change.

This moment is fragile, electric, like a held breath before the plunge into the deep end. Once I say the words, there's no going back.

Some games end with a whistle.

This one ends with the truth.

Before we left, I told her to pack a bag for the weekend, throwing enough intrigue into the mix to keep her guessing. Now, as we drive deeper into the countryside, her lips curve into a small, knowing smile. "You love surprising me."

I grin, glancing her way. "I do, but this one's different. Tonight's the biggest surprise yet."

We turn off the main road and on to a long, tree-lined driveway that winds gracefully toward a house nestled into the landscape, its lights glowing softly in the distance. Charleston's gaze shifts, taking in every detail, her curiosity sparking like a live wire. "Where have you brought me?"

I glance at her, the corner of my mouth tugging into a grin I can't quite hide. "Be patient. You'll find out soon enough."

She narrows her eyes, a teasing glint mixed with curiosity. "Let me guess—it's an Airbnb. You rented this place for a private weekend getaway."

Her hand slides over my leg, and her eyes dance with mischief. "A weekend away from the world. Just the two of us. I'm very into that."

I smirk, keeping my cards close. "Good to know."

I steer the G-Wagon into the garage and cut the engine, the soft hum fading into silence. As I look over at her, I catch the spark of curiosity lighting up her face. She glances around, clearly intrigued.

"This is a great surprise."

We step out of the car, the air fresh and slightly cool. As we make our way inside, the space wraps around me like a warm embrace. Stepping into the kitchen, a sense of ease settles over me.

This isn't just a house. It's my home.

Charleston's eyes brighten as she looks around, her gaze sweeping over the room. "This place is stunning."

"Go on. Explore."

Charleston glances around the kitchen, running her fingers along the cool marble countertops. "I'm going to cook for you this weekend. Something Southern, of course. I bet you've never had cooking like mine before."

I lean casually against the counter. "Look forward to it. I'm sure it'll be incredible." I hold back from mentioning that Laurelyn has cooked Southern food for me more times than I can count. There's no way I'm bursting her bubble.

She wanders from the kitchen into the living room. Her gaze

lands on a framed photo resting on the mantel, and she picks it up, her expression softening as she studies it. "This is you and your family?" she asks, staring at the photo.

"Beautiful chaos," I say, waiting for her to put the pieces together.

Her gaze sweeps the room again, taking in the small, personal touches scattered throughout and the warmth that speaks of a lived-in home. Slowly, she turns back to me, her eyes widening slightly as realization dawns.

Her laugh comes soft, almost disbelieving. "This is *your* house?"

I nod, the truth lifting even as I brace for her reaction. "This is home."

"Julius Caesar!" She scans the space again, her laughter growing as she shakes her head. "You're filthy stinking rich."

I step closer, cradling her face gently in my hands, my eyes locking with hers. "My name's not Julius Caesar."

Her gaze sharpens, searching mine. For a moment, everything else fades, the world narrowing to the two of us. "Are we really doing this?"

I nod, the gravity of my decision settling firmly in my chest. "I want you to know all of me. Not just the parts I've let you see."

Her lips part slightly, and I catch the faintest tremble in her breath. Her eyes, usually so steady, are filled with uncertainty, betraying a vulnerability I've never seen in her before. It twists something deep inside me, the urge to reassure her nearly overwhelming.

"But only if you're ready," I add, hoping to ease the fear I can see rising in her.

Her breath catches, and hesitation crosses her face, something raw and unguarded. "I'm scared." The words are so quiet they barely reach me.

My thumb brushes softly against her cheek. "So am I."

The honesty of my confession is heavier than I expected.

The silence stretches, every second pulling tighter until she exhales. "I want to know everything—the good, the bad, all of it."

Her words hit me harder than she realizes. She wants all of me, but a small voice in the back of my mind wonders if she truly knows what she's asking for. There's so much I've kept hidden—the anxiety that grips me without warning, the depression that drags me down when I least expect it, the constant frustration of living with dyslexia in a world that doesn't slow down for it. And the anger—always there, simmering beneath the surface, fueled by the man who stole my career and the dreams I'd built my life around.

What if she sees it all and decides it's too much?

Or decides *I'm* not enough?

The thought twists like a knife in my chest. She deserves better—someone without the shadows I carry. Someone who isn't weighed down by the mistakes and scars of his past. But the idea of letting her go feels impossible. I know it's selfish, but I want her. Even if I'm not enough, even if I should let her find someone who is, I can't let her go.

The thought of her slipping through my fingers is unbearable.

Not yet.

Not now.

"I'm ready to tell you everything."

Steadying my breath, I brace myself for what comes next. "My... name... is..." I pause deliberately, watching her face for any sign of hesitation. If she wants to stop, this is her last chance.

But her gaze holds firm, unwavering and open, silently urging me forward.

"Alex." My name feels heavy yet freeing on my tongue. "Alex Sebring. Alexander Björn Sebring III, actually."

A beat of silence follows, stretching longer than I'm prepared for. Her face is unreadable, and dread creeps up my spine, tightening its grip. What if this is too much for her? What if she sees the name, the legacy, the sheer magnitude of it all, and decides I'm not worth the trouble that accompanies me?

Then, to my surprise, she bursts into laughter. It's soft and melodic, light and playful, cutting through my fears.

"I'm sorry," she says between chuckles, her eyes sparkling with amusement. "But I have absolutely no idea who you are, Alex Sebring."

The tension in my chest unravels so fast it almost knocks the air out of me. Relief floods in, tempered with disbelief, and I find myself laughing with her.

"Not even a clue?" I ask, shaking my head with a half smile.

"None. Should I? Are you, like, royalty or something? Should I be curtsying right now?"

Laughter rumbles in my chest. "No, not royalty. Let's just say my name tends to come with a lot of... unnecessary attention."

She leans in. "Well, none of that matters to me. I'm here for you, not for whoever the world thinks Alexander Björn Sebring III is supposed to be."

Her words settle over me, grounding and liberating all at once. For the first time in weeks, I feel lighter—like I'm finally stepping into the light with her.

"You have no idea how relieved I am. I was so convinced my identity would change everything."

She tilts her head, her smile soft but teasing. "I mean, I already knew you were wealthy and mysterious. The whole 'Alexander Björn Sebring III' thing confirms you're way fancier than I thought. But none of that changes how I feel about you, JC—sorry, Alexander."

Hearing her say my name—my real name—sends an unexpected wave of warmth through me, like something clicking into place. Laurelyn was right. Charleston isn't part of the world I've been so guarded against—Australian rugby, the constant spotlight, or the expectations of society.

She's from a world entirely her own, untouched by the noise and pressure that's always surrounded me. And in her world, none of the things I've feared seem to matter at all.

I let out a long, steady breath, feeling lighter than I have in years. For the first time, it feels like we might finally have the chance to be real. "Just Alex. That's all I want to be with you."

"*Alex.*" She repeats my name, tilting her head with a soft smile, letting it settle in the air between us. "Alex," she says again, this time slower, as though savoring it, letting it take shape. "You definitely look more like an Alex than a Julius Caesar."

The tension in my shoulders eases. "My mother and her side of the family don't call me Alex. For them, I'm *Aleki*—the Samoan form of Alexander. It means defender of the people."

Her eyebrows lift with interest. "Aleki. I like it. And your father is obviously Alexander?"

"That's right. And my tinā's name is Malie."

"Does your *tinā* know about me?"

"Skipping Sundays with the family hasn't gone unnoticed. Tinā started asking questions, so I had to tell her I was seeing someone."

Her lips curve into a wry smile. "I don't imagine she's too happy with me for keeping you from Sundays with the family."

"You've got it all wrong. Tinā's thrilled I'm seeing someone. Her exact words were, 'as long as she's not like Celeste.'"

Her smile falters. "Celeste is your ex—the one who posted the video?"

Now is my chance to lay it all out, no matter how messy or uncomfortable. If we're going to have a shot at a future together, Charleston must know everything.

"Celeste Warrington. If you look her up online, you won't see the video on her socials anymore, but it's still out there. Nothing ever really disappears online."

She shakes her head. "I'm not interested in watching some staged video she posted to rack up likes and comments."

A small wave of relief washes over me, but I know this conversation isn't over. "I'm glad to hear that, but there's more to it, and I don't want this hanging between us. I need to tell you exactly what happened so there's no misunderstandings."

"Okay. I'm listening."

I take a steadying breath and dive in. "Celeste called me over one day, saying she had something important to talk about. When I got there, she held up a positive pregnancy test, waiting for my reaction."

The memory comes into focus with startling clarity. "I didn't handle it well—not because of the baby. I've always wanted children, always known I'd love being a father. But the thought of having a child with her, especially when I'd already made the decision to end the relationship, was overwhelming. It was the permanence of it, and the way it could ripple through any future I might build with another woman. It felt like my entire world tilted, like the ground was shifting beneath me. The idea of being tied to her forever through a child hit me harder than I could've imagined."

I watch Charleston's reaction, willing her to understand. "None of it added up. Celeste is calculating. A pregnancy wouldn't happen unless she planned it. And I said as much."

I pause, bracing myself for the worst part. "What I didn't know was that she was recording me—without my consent. An hour later, she posted the video online, along with another of herself crying hysterically, claiming I was abandoning her because she was pregnant. The narrative was set: I was the villain, and she was the victim."

Charleston's eyes narrow. "You have a child with her?"

"No." I raise my hands quickly. "I probably should've led with that."

She frowns, confusion plain in her expression. "Then what—?"

"Celeste was never pregnant. It was all fake. She had her sister, who was pregnant at the time, take the test for her."

Charleston's jaw drops. "She faked a pregnancy? For what?"

The absurdity is still hard to process. "Followers and attention—she couldn't get enough. It was another stunt to keep herself trending."

"That's insane. She dragged you into it like it was nothing?"

"Exactly. And when it all fell apart, I was left to deal with the fallout."

Her brow furrows as she shakes her head. "Did it not occur to her that at some point, she'd have to explain why there was no baby?"

"She faked the positive pregnancy test and then claimed it was a false alarm. Honestly, I think her original plan was to fake a miscarriage to keep the spotlight on herself. But then she must have realized she could milk even more sympathy by spinning it into a story about how I *mistreated* her." Saying it out loud makes it sound even more absurd, like some over-the-top plot twist in a bad soap opera.

Charleston's disgust is unmistakable. "That's vile. Not just to you, but to anyone who's experienced that kind of loss. It's cruel and disrespectful to women who've suffered miscarriages or struggled to have children."

"I couldn't agree more."

"How could you date a woman like that?"

The sting of regret is sharp even now. "She wasn't like that at first. Or maybe I just didn't see it. She was charming, confident, always the life of the party. For a while, I thought that was what I wanted. But over time, the cracks started to show. I learned that Celeste is one of those people who can become whoever she needs to be. She's like a chameleon—she knew exactly what to say and how to act, like she'd rehearsed it all. I thought I knew her, but I was fooled."

Charleston's gaze softens. "I know that type all too well. Robin and Charlene are the same. They can shape-shift into whoever they need to be in the moment."

Her hand shifts, resting lightly over mine. "Even though we've been playing this game with aliases, I want you to know I've always been real with you. Everything I've told you about myself is the truth. I've never pretended to be anyone else. But there's one thing I haven't shared—not because I was hiding it, but because it didn't feel relevant before. Now that I understand you attract public attention, if someone ever decided to dig into my life, they might uncover something about my family."

I grip her hand. "Whatever it is, you can tell me."

She hesitates, taking a deep breath. "My father is not a good man. He's serving life in the penitentiary for killing someone during a drug deal gone wrong." Her eyes drop briefly, then rise again, steady but uncertain. "I would understand if you don't want ties to the daughter of a convicted murderer."

"I don't care what your father's done. His actions aren't a reflection of you."

A small, shaky sigh escapes her, her fingers tightening slightly around mine. "I know that logically. But it's still embarrassing. Admitting all of this about my family is hard."

She hesitates, her gaze dropping for a moment, embarrassment crossing her face. "Honestly, my family is like a never-ending train wreck. Every time I think I've escaped it, something drags me right back, reminding me of where I come from."

"There's no need for you to feel embarrassed or ashamed. It doesn't change how I see you or how I feel about you."

Her shoulders relax, relief softening her expression. "Thank you for not judging me for things beyond my control."

"There are things I haven't told you either. Not because I didn't want to, but because I was afraid that your knowing who I really am might change what we have. This connection has been so good and so real. I didn't want anything to ruin it."

Her eyes meet mine, unwavering. "I want to know everything about you."

There's no turning back once I tell her. "My family is wealthy, but that's not where my fame comes from. My career was in rugby. I used to play professionally, and not to brag, but I was kind of a big deal. Highest-paid player in the league actually."

A spark of amusement lights up her face, her lips curling into a playful grin. "So, you had big Dak energy?"

I can't help but laugh, nodding. "Yeah, something like that."

She leans back, her laughter ringing out as she shakes her head in surprise. "Unbelievable. I've been dating the Australian Dak Prescott and didn't even know it. That's actually kind of hot. Honestly, I'm not surprised. You've got an athlete vibe about you."

Her gaze softens a bit. "I must admit, though, I feel a bit clueless.

I could talk football all day, but rugby? I don't know the first thing about it."

"That's all right. I'm more than happy to teach you. I think you'd love it."

"If it's anything like football, count me in."

Her gaze softens, her expression growing serious as she studies me. "Is there anything else I should know?"

I take a deep breath, choosing my words carefully. "There are personal things I'd like to share with you, things that matter. But I'll tell you in time when it feels right."

"I can take any truth. Just don't lie to me."

"I'll never lie to you."

She studies me for a moment, her eyes searching mine. "Are we okay?"

I don't hesitate, reaching for her. She slides onto my lap, wrapping her arms tightly around me.

"We're more than okay, favorite."

Her closeness melts away any doubts. Our lips meet, the kiss starting slow but quickly deepening, charged with something electric. My hand glides along her thigh, my touch instinctive, as the moment between us grows hotter, more intense.

She shifts, repositioning herself until she's straddling me, her body fitting against mine like it's where she belongs. The air between us is heavy, wordless, but full of meaning. After a beat, I pull back slightly, a grin tugging at my lips. "Feel like skipping the house tour and heading straight to the bedroom?"

She laughs, her eyebrow arching playfully. "No grand tour of the Sebring estate?"

I wrap my hands around her hips, pulling her even closer. "The bed's the only tour you're getting tonight. The rest can wait until tomorrow."

Her smile turns mischievous. "All right. But I'll need a minute. I have a surprise for you."

"A surprise for me?" I shift beneath her, a mix of anticipation and impatience bubbling up. "And I have to wait for it?"

She grins, leaning in close. "Only for a minute. Promise."

Untangling herself, she slips off me, heading toward her bag. My heart races with the thrill of what's to come, but then it hits me—she still hasn't told me her real name. The thought tugs at my curiosity for a moment, but I let it go, caught up in the rush of the moment. Her name can wait a little longer.

Chapter 24

Alex Sebring

Each second stretches longer than the last, anticipation winding through me like a taut coil ready to snap. Charleston is just beyond that bathroom door, and the wait is torturous. She promised she wouldn't take long, but every tick of the clock feels like an eternity. My mind races, painting vivid images of her—of what's to come—until my body is practically vibrating with the ache of wanting her.

When the door finally creaks open, I sit up straighter, the breath catching in my throat. And then she steps out.

Barely-there white lingerie, delicate lace hugging her curves, sheer material teasing glimpses of smooth skin, and thin straps that somehow manage to look both elegant and sinful. She's radiant, a vision that steals every coherent thought from my brain.

Worth. The. Wait.

I swallow hard, unable to say anything, my throat dry, my words caught somewhere between disbelief and desire. She takes a tentative step forward, and it's all I can do to stay seated, my hands itching to reach for her, to feel the reality of her against me.

My breath hitches as she moves toward me, every step deliberate, drawing me in with an irresistible pull. The sharp click of her stilettos on the hardwood resonates in the quiet room, a steady rhythm that ignites something primal within me, sending my pulse into overdrive.

Her hips sway with each step as she moves closer, her already-hot-as-fuck figure looking even more enticing in the body-hugging lingerie she wears. I move to the edge of the bed and wrap my hands around her waist when she reaches me, pulling her closer, feeling the soft curves of her body lean into mine.

"What a fucking stunner you are in this."

"It was worth the wait?"

"Oh, very much."

Her eyes flash with a mischievous glint as she leans in, her lips hovering above mine, close enough to drive me insane. "Let's see if I can make it even more worth your while." Each word drips like honey, smooth and slow, wrapping around me and sinking deep into my core.

She presses her body against mine, her arms encircling around my neck. Our lips meet in a passionate embrace, our tongues dancing in unison. I savor the taste of her cherry lip balm and the hint of mint from her toothpaste. She's intoxicating, a perfect blend of sweet sin and temptation.

Her fingers tangle in my hair, pulling me deeper into the kiss. I lose myself in the sensation of it all—her taste, her smell, her warmth, the way our breaths intermingle. It's enough to unravel me completely.

In one swift motion, I pull her onto the bed and she lands with a soft thud on top of me. Her hair falls forward, forming a curtain around our faces. Her eyes lock on to mine, shimmering with desire, her chest rising and falling with each unsteady breath. A smug grin tugs at my lips, knowing it's my touch that sets her ablaze.

My grip tightens on her hips as I flip her on to her back. She gazes up at me with passion-filled eyes, her chest rising and falling with each breath. A smirk curls on my lips as I revel in the power of knowing that I am the cause of this desire within her.

Starting at the corner of her mouth, my lips glide down the smooth line of her neck. She arches her back, a willing offering for me to explore every inch of her. I shower her skin with gentle kisses and teasing nibbles, savoring every sweet gasp that escapes her parted lips. My tongue dances in lazy circles, tracing a map of desire on her sensitive flesh, punctuated by feather-light bites that send shivers through her body.

Her fingers dance across my skin, leaving a trail of fire in their wake. Her touch is both gentle and intense, igniting a visceral desire deep inside me. I growl as her nails graze over my shirt, the fabric becoming a barrier between us that only adds to the tension. And when she presses harder against me, it's like an explosion of pleasure that consumes my entire being.

"You're wearing too many clothes," she whispers, tugging at the buttons of my shirt with urgent hands.

I smirk against her neck, placing one more kiss before meeting her eyes. "Who's the impatient one now?"

"I can't help it. I want to feel your skin against mine."

Aching to please her, I sit up, kneeling between her legs, and unfasten the buttons of my shirt. She watches with an insatiable gaze as I remove it, revealing my bare chest. Her hands reach out, caressing every inch of skin they can touch. Sparks of electricity shoot through me as her fingers roam over my muscles. I close my eyes and bask in the sensation, her touch igniting an inferno within me.

As my eyes flutter open, I'm immediately transfixed by the intensity of her gaze. It's as if she's baring her soul to me, a delicate balance of vulnerability and desire that pulls at my heartstrings. Without hesitation, our lips meet in a tender kiss. We take our time, savoring every moment, pouring all our unspoken emotions into it. My hands travel up to caress her face, deepening the kiss with each shared breath.

My lips trace a tantalizing path down her skin, reveling in her satin-smooth flesh beneath the intricate lace of her lingerie. With each kiss, I explore every curve and crevice, from the rise of her breasts to the dip of her ribcage, before moving lower to the valley of her stomach. She quivers under my touch, her eager anticipation evident as she arches into me, begging for more.

The aroma of sweet vanilla and delicate cherry blossoms weaves through the air, intertwined with our heated attraction. I savor each caress, tracing tantalizing patterns with my tongue while reveling in the symphony of her moans and gasps. Every inch of her body is a masterpiece begging to be worshipped, and I'm determined to leave no part untouched by my adoration.

I glide down her form, settling my face between her legs. The delicate lace of her panties beckons to be removed, yet I resist, relishing in the buildup. With a gentle pull, I shift the crotch of her panties aside. My pulse quickens as I expose her flushed, slick petals, begging for my touch and exploration.

I close my eyes, inhaling her intoxicating scent as a shiver shoots down my spine. This delicious anticipation, the moment before I taste her nectar, is always the sweetest.

My tongue flicks out, testing the waters, savoring the musky essence of her arousal. She moans, grabbing handfuls of the sheets, and I hold on to her hips as she wiggles against me.

Fuck, I love how responsive she is.

"Right there, Alex. Right there."

Her hand suddenly grips the back of my hair, urging me closer to her core as she presses herself against my mouth. Her hips undulate against my eager tongue, her pleasure building with each tantalizing lick.

My tongue dances around her clit, savoring the taste of her arousal. Two of my fingers delve into her wetness and her body shivers in response. Her thighs quiver as she nears the edge, and I eagerly push her closer to release.

"Oh God, Alex," she moans, her hips lifting off the bed. Nothing in this world compares to hearing her call out my name—my real name—while she experiences such ecstasy.

I lose myself in the sensations—the slickness of her folds against my mouth and fingers, the softness of her skin under my touch, the heady scent of her arousal filling my senses. The world disappears, leaving us in this moment of pleasure and passion.

I've never felt this with anyone else—only her.

As I continue to lick her with my tongue, her breath quickens, and her hips grind against my mouth with an insatiable rhythm. With two fingers deep inside her, I add a third one and then her walls squeeze and relax around my fingers every few seconds.

"Oh! Oh! Oh!" she shouts.

There's never any question with Charleston. I always know the exact moment I've hit the spot that makes her melt in pleasure.

She squirms beneath me, her body coiled and ready to explode. With a sharp cry, she arches off the bed, fingers clenching at the sheets as her breath comes in gasps. When she finally subsides, I press my lips against her inner thigh before trailing up her trembling form. Her eyes are heavy with desire, cheeks flushed with pleasure. I devour her lips in a fervent kiss, savoring the taste of her on my tongue.

"That was..." she trails off, still breathless.

"Just the beginning," I murmur against her neck, nipping lightly at her pulse point. She shivers beneath me, her hands sliding down my back, nails lightly scraping my skin.

"Mmm... is that so?"

In one fluid motion, she pushes me on my back, pinning me to the bed. The sight of her above me, hair tousled and lips swollen from our kisses, is enough to make my breath catch.

She trails her fingers down my chest, feather-light touches that leave goose bumps in their wake. When she reaches the waistband of my boxer briefs, she pauses, a teasing smile playing on her lips. Her fingers dance along the edge, dipping beneath the elastic before retreating. The anticipation is exquisite torture.

"It's my turn to make you come," she whispers.

She leans down to capture my lips in a searing kiss as her hand slips inside my boxers. I gasp into her mouth as her fingers wrap around my cock, stroking slowly.

"Oh fuck." I let out a low groan as her hand moves up and down, each stroke deliberate and slow.

"You like the way that feels?"

"Oh yeah. Love it."

"Just wait," she whispers, her hand continuing its enchanting movements. "I haven't even begun the true sorcery yet."

Her soft lips leave mine and wander, leaving a trail of kisses along my jawline down the column of my neck, stopping to swirl her tongue around each sensitive nipple before moving lower. I thread my fingers through her silky long hair, my hips bucking up into her hand wrapped around my cock. She looks up at me through her lashes, a wicked smile on her face, as she slides farther down my body.

With a smooth movement, she pulls down my boxers. My cock feels the cool air briefly before being engulfed in her warm, wet mouth. I let out a strangled noise, gripping her hair tightly as she takes me farther into her mouth. Her tongue dances around the tip before she moves back down, creating suction with her cheeks as she sucks on me.

How can her mouth feel so damn good?

My breath comes in ragged pants as she works me with her lips, tongue, and hand in perfect harmony. The combination of sensations is almost too much to handle. A warm sensation spreads throughout my body, as pleasure intensifies with each movement of her head. Heat builds in the pit of my stomach, driving me closer to the edge of ecstasy.

"Fuck, you're amazing," I manage to gasp out between ragged

breaths. She hums in response, the vibrations sending shock waves of pleasure through my body.

Fuck. Fuck. Fucccck.

She takes me deep, the wet heat and suction driving me wild. My hips thrust as I feel myself reaching the brink. She must sense it too because she grips me tighter, moving her hand up and down in time with her mouth. My hips buck, meeting her movements.

"I'm close. So fucking close," I warn her, my voice strained.

She looks up at me, her eyes dark with desire, and gives a small nod. Her gaze locked on mine, she takes me as deep as she can and swallows around me. And that's all, folks. The swallowing sensation pushes me over the fucking edge.

With a hoarse cry, I find my release, waves of intense pleasure washing over me as she continues her ministrations, milking me.

Every. Last. Drop.

When I'm completely spent, she slowly pulls away, placing a tender kiss on my hip. She crawls back up my body, a satisfied smile playing on her lips. I pull her close, our mouths meeting in a deep, unhurried kiss that lingers, soft and full of connection. When we finally break apart, the room feels warm and still, the perfect quiet wrapping around us.

We lie beside each other, her head resting on my chest, her fingers lightly tracing patterns across my skin. Her touch is calming, and I find myself exhaling deeply, content in a way I haven't been in a long time.

My hand brushes her hair away from her face. "You never told me your name."

She lifts her head slightly, her gaze meeting mine. "My name is Magnolia... Magnolia Steel. Magnolia Elizabeth Steel, actually."

Hesitation crosses her face before she adds, "Why aren't you laughing?"

I frown, not in on the joke. "Why would I laugh?"

"Because of the movie *Steel Magnolias*. My grandmother thought it would be clever to name me Magnolia Steel. She thought it was charming, but I've always found it embarrassing. My name has been one long-running joke my entire life."

I tilt my head, studying her. "First of all, I've never heard of that movie. Secondly, your name is beautiful. Just like you."

Her lips part slightly, as if she wasn't expecting that, and the faintest smile tugs at the corner of her mouth. "You mean it?"

"Absolutely."

Magnolia Steel. Her name settles in my mind. "It's very nice to meet you, Magnolia Steel. And what you just did was incredible."

My lips brush hers in a kiss I can't resist.

She laughs softly, her eyes sparkling with mischief as her fingers trail lightly down my chest. "I'm very glad you enjoyed it, Alex Sebring."

Her gaze holds something deep that makes my chest tighten in the best way.

After a beat, I clear my throat, my heart pounding a little harder than I'd like to admit. "Magnolia, I have a wedding to attend tomorrow evening. A former teammate's. I'm supposed to bring a plus-one, and... I'd like you to come with me."

Her eyes widen slightly, surprise rippling through her expression. "Your date? You mean... go public?"

I nod, holding her gaze steady, hoping she can see how much I want this. "Yes. I want you there with me, if you're willing. It's a private ceremony, and I'll make sure we avoid any paparazzi. You'll be completely protected."

She bites her lip, fighting a smile. "I'd love to go, Alex, but I don't have anything to wear to a wedding—especially not to a wedding of a professional rugby player."

"That's an easy fix. Tomorrow, we'll go shopping and find something stunning for you to wear. What do you say?"

Please say yes.

Her hesitation melts into a smile, her excitement bubbling beneath the surface. "Okay, then. I'd love to be your plus-one."

Hearing her say yes sends a surge of warmth through me. I lean forward, capturing her lips in a soft kiss, savoring the sweetness of this moment and the possibilities it holds.

This is a turning point for us. Taking her to the wedding, going public, letting the people in my life see us together—it's more than a date. It's a quiet but undeniable statement: she's the one I've chosen, the one I want. As I look into her trusting eyes, there's no doubt in my mind that this is the right move.

The thought of walking into that wedding with her on my arm stirs a mix of excitement and nerves. It's a step toward something bigger, something deeper. This is about letting her into my world completely.

I reach for her hand, lacing my fingers with hers. "Thank you for saying yes."

"Thank you for inviting me."

My hand cups her cheek. "Having you there means more to me than I can put into words."

Her lips curve into a smile, and before I can say more, she shifts, closing the small space between us. Her kiss is slow and deliberate, her hands sliding to rest on my shoulders as she presses against me.

I deepen the kiss, pulling her closer, my hands tracing the curves of her back. Every kiss, every touch feels like a promise, one we're both more than ready to keep.

She pulls back, uncertainty swirling in her eyes. "Don't you need more time before you can... do it again?"

"Not with you." The simplest touch from her has the power to reignite the flame she's just extinguished.

I flip us over, pinning her beneath me, and her hair fans out on the pillow—a halo of chestnut in the dim light. She looks like an absolute angel.

I gaze down at her, marveling at how perfectly she fits into my world, and trace the curve of her cheek with my thumb. "I love having you here in my space."

Her eyes soften, a tender smile gracing her lips. "I love being here."

My lips hungrily graze against hers in a fiery embrace. My hands eagerly explore every curve of her body, fueled by an unbridled desire. With delicate movements, I slide her panties down her smooth legs and toss them aside. My eyes devour the sight before me—her lacy lingerie hugging her figure, stockings accentuating her shapely legs, and those dangerously high heels that make her even more alluring. The delicate lace against her bare skin is like a tantalizing temptation, driving me wild with longing.

"Tell me how you want it. Slow and gentle, or fast and rough?" I kiss my way down to her collarbone, waiting for her answer.

Magnolia runs her fingers through my hair, pulling me closer until our eyes meet. "I want to make love tonight. I want to explore every inch of you and savor every moment."

"You can have every part of me."

I belong to you tonight, Magnolia Steel.

Her captivating eyes—a mesmerizing blend of brown, green, and gold—hold me captive. In this moment, I am willing to do anything for her. She doesn't even have to ask; the way she looks at me is enough to make me want to fulfill her every desire.

I release a deep, guttural groan as I enter her with aching tenderness. As our bodies become one, she gasps and arches against me, urging me to go deeper. Our movements are fluid and synchronized, each touch and thrust sending waves of pleasure through our bodies. Every sensation is heightened in this sensual dance between us, our bodies perfectly attuned to the other's desires. It's an exquisite moment that we savor, lost in the intoxicating sensations coursing through us both.

With my weight supported on my elbows, I look down at Magnolia's stunning face and carefully move within her. Our eyes lock, an intense connection forming between us that goes beyond the physical. It's as if I can see into the very depths of her soul, and she into mine.

The world fades away until there is nothing but the two of us, joined together in this intimate moment. I savor every sensation—the warmth of her body, the softness of her skin, the way she moves with me in perfect harmony.

"Magnolia," I whisper, her name a prayer on my lips.

"Alex," she says, my name whispered with tenderness and desire.

We continue our unhurried lovemaking, lost in each other's eyes and the intensity of our connection. Every thrust is slow and purposeful, building our pleasure gradually. In this moment, we are one—body, heart, and soul intertwined.

Our bodies move together in a slow, sensual rhythm, every motion deliberate and filled with meaning. I feel Magnolia's heart beating in time with mine, our breath mingling in the small space between us. The intimacy is almost overwhelming, and I never want it to end.

As I gaze into her eyes, I see a kaleidoscope of emotions—desire, vulnerability, trust. It's as if her very essence is laid bare before me. And I hope she sees something similar reflected in my eyes.

The pleasure builds gradually, like a slow-burning fire, as we continue to move as one. Every nerve ending feels alive, hyperaware of each point where our bodies connect.

In this moment, nothing else matters but the two of us, lost in our own world of sensation and emotion. Time seems to stand still as we savor each exquisite moment. The outside world fades away completely, leaving only us.

As our passion builds, our movements become more urgent yet still retain that sense of lovemaking. Her quiet gasps and sighs of pleasure are the most beautiful music I've ever heard.

"Alex," she moans softly, her nails raking gently down my back. The sensation sends shivers through my entire body.

We're both nearing the peak of ecstasy, yet I want to prolong this perfect moment and stay suspended in this blissful connection for as long as possible. I slow our pace once more, drawing out each movement.

Magnolia's eyes flutter, dark with desire, as her legs tighten around me. "I'm so close," she whispers, the need in her words undeniable, leaving no doubt about what she's asking for.

With a controlled and teasing slowness, I withdraw my length enough to let the head of my cock brush against that special spot inside her with each thrust, eliciting a gasp of pleasure from us both. Our bodies move together in a sensual dance, our movements fluid and synchronized as we climb higher and higher toward that ultimate peak of bliss.

The tension between us builds exquisitely like a tightly coiled spring ready to release its energy in one explosive burst of ecstasy.

Magnolia's breath comes in short, sharp gasps now. Her fingers dig into my shoulders as she clings to me. I feel the tremors running through her body, matching the trembling in my own limbs.

"Oh... oh... oh," she cries out, her voice breaking.

With a shuddering exhale, she reaches her release, her body arching in pure ecstasy. The sight of her lost in pleasure ignites a fire within me, and I can feel myself being pulled toward the edge.

Every nerve in my body tingles with white-hot pleasure as we both reach our climax, leaving us breathless and shaking in each other's arms. The world around us becomes a blur of sensations, and all that exists is the overwhelming rush of pleasure coursing through us.

For long moments, we remain entwined, our hearts racing in tandem as we slowly drift back down to earth. I pepper soft kisses across Magnolia's face—her closed eyelids, her cheeks, the corner of her mouth. When she finally opens her eyes, they're filled with such tenderness that it makes my heart ache.

As I gaze at Magnolia's flushed face and tousled hair, a realization dawns on me. This woman, who can appear so angelic and pure, possesses a devilish side that sets my blood on fire. She's not only the sweet, innocent girl next door. She's also the seductress who can reduce me to a primal, lustful creature with a simple look or a touch. The angel and the devil, both wrapped up in one intoxicating package. And I'm utterly addicted.

Magnolia gives me a coy smile. "What are you thinking about?"

"You. And how you manage to be both the sweetest and the sexiest woman I've ever known."

She laughs, a musical sound that makes my heart skip.

I pull her closer, reveling in the warmth of her soft skin against mine, and press a kiss to her forehead. "You're incredible, you know that?"

Magnolia hums contentedly, snuggling into my chest. "You're pretty incredible yourself," she says, her breath tickling my skin.

As we lie in the afterglow, I'm struck by how right this feels. It's not just the sex though that certainly doesn't hurt. It's the way Magnolia fits so perfectly in my arms, how her laughter bubbles up so easily, how her eyes sparkle when she looks at me. I trail my fingers lazily along her spine, savoring the little shiver it elicits.

She arches into my touch. "Mmm, that feels nice."

"Yeah, this is nice."

With Magnolia, I find myself craving more than the physical connection. I want lazy Sunday mornings and shared inside jokes. I want to know her hopes and fears, her dreams and regrets. I want to be the one she turns to when she needs support and the one she celebrates with when she succeeds.

Sensing the shift in my mood, Magnolia props herself up on an elbow. She studies my face, a hint of concern in her eyes. "Is everything okay?"

I gaze into her eyes, captivated by the flecks of gold. "Yeah," I say, reaching up to tuck a stray strand of hair behind her ear. "Just thinking about how good this feels."

She smiles softly, her fingers tracing idle patterns on my shoulder. "It feels really good, doesn't it?"

I nod, but inside, a storm of thoughts brews. In five weeks, she'll be gone—back to the States—and the idea of losing her feels unbearable. She's more than I ever expected to find; she's everything I've been searching for.

I can't let this slip away. Not without trying to make her stay, to show her that what we have is worth holding on to. The distance, the challenges—they all seem insignificant compared to the thought of not having her in my life.

As she nestles back against me, I make a silent vow. I'll find a way to convince her that this connection between us is just the beginning of something extraordinary. Letting her go when the time is up isn't an option.

Not anymore.

Chapter 25

Magnolia Steel

THE EMERALD-GREEN GOWN HUGS MY BODY PERFECTLY, ITS bold elegance a stunning mix of refinement and allure. Alex chose it himself, insisting it was the one, and now I see why. The mirror reflects more than the dress—it shows a woman ready to step into a new chapter, into Alex's world, even if it feels a little daunting.

In the living room, he stands by the window, adjusting his cuff links with practiced ease. The tux fits him flawlessly, accentuating his broad shoulders and exuding a quiet confidence. For a moment, I pause in the doorway, taking him in. This is Alex Sebring—poised, polished, completely at home in a world of elegance and refinement.

For him, this is normal. It's second nature.

For me, this is intimidating.

He turns as I step forward, his gaze sweeping over me before locking on to mine. His smile is subtle but loaded with meaning. "You're breathtaking."

"Thank you." I smile back, a mix of nerves and anticipation fluttering in my chest. "You don't look so bad yourself. You clean up pretty well, big guy."

His grin widens as he closes the space between us. "Only *pretty well*, huh? I was hoping for something more like devastatingly handsome or maybe dangerously debonair."

"Fine, Mr. Dangerously Debonair." I laugh, shaking my head. "You're a solid ten, tux or not."

"Much better," he says, pulling me closer.

His hand settles at the small of my back, his thumb grazing the satin fabric with a touch that sends a ripple of warmth through me. "I know tonight might feel overwhelming, but I want you to know something. No matter what anyone thinks or says, you're the only one I care about. You're the only one I see."

A lump rises in my throat. "You realize this is it, don't you? No aliases, no hiding. It's you and me, out in the open for everyone to judge."

"I know." He nods, his gaze unwavering. "You should also know we're going to steal the spotlight from the bride and groom tonight." His lips curve into a proud, playful smile. "But I don't care. Walking in with you—showing the world how incredible you are—feels right. Nothing else matters."

The mix of nerves and excitement churning inside me finds a new edge. "I want to make you proud." I feel my vulnerability breaking through. "This is your world, not mine. I don't want to misstep."

Unrelenting doubt takes root. His high-profile life, his polished friends, and the elegant world he moves through so easily—it feels like a galaxy away from mine. What if I say the wrong thing? What if I embarrass him?

His hand shifts, cupping my cheek. "Magnolia, you're perfect as you are. There's nothing you could do that wouldn't make me proud."

His words settle over me like a promise, pulling me from the edge of uncertainty. Tonight might be daunting, but with Alex at my side, it feels like the start of something bigger. Something real. Something worth every risk.

The low hum of the limo pulling up outside interrupts the moment. Alex glances toward the window, then back at me, his hand finding mine. His grip is firm and steady, his thumb brushing lightly against my skin. "Are you ready for this?"

I meet his gaze, letting the warmth of his confidence seep into me. A small smile tugs at my lips as I squeeze his hand. "As ready as I'll ever be."

The city lights blur by outside, casting fleeting patterns of gold and white across the interior as the limo glides through the streets. "By the way, that green dress? Perfect. It was made for you."

"Thank you." His compliment soothes some of the butterflies in my stomach. He picked this dress for me, and knowing he loves it makes all the difference.

Still, a thread of unease winds through me.

Earlier, he felt it necessary to warn me about the likelihood of both Celeste and Tyson being at the wedding. The thought is an unwelcome shadow in the back of my mind. What if they find a way to disrupt the night? What if old tensions rise to the surface?

But even as those doubts creep in, I remind myself why I'm here. I'm not doing this for Celeste or Tyson, or for anyone else. I'm here for Alex. No matter what happens tonight, I'll stand by his side.

He's been honest with me—raw and vulnerable in ways that have left me in awe of his strength. Tonight, I want to be that same source of strength for him. If the ghosts of his past rear their heads, I'll be here. Steady. Unwavering. His lighthouse in the storm.

The wedding venue is straight-out-of-Pinterest breathtaking—towering marble columns, glistening chandeliers, and intricately arranged floral displays that look like they belong on a top-tier bridal blog. As we step inside, my hand slips into Alex's, the touch a quiet reassurance that steadies me.

The moment we cross the threshold, heads turn and whispers ripple through the crowd. Their gazes settle on us, heavy with curiosity, as though we're a mystery waiting to be unraveled.

Alex leans in, his breath a warm whisper against my ear. "This is only the beginning, Magnolia. A few glances here are nothing compared to what lies ahead."

I glance up at him, finding comfort in his calm, unwavering presence. "Just promise me you won't leave my side."

His grip tightens slightly, his expression softening with resolve. "Never."

As we take our seats, Alex's hand moves to the small of my back, a touch that feels both protective and intentional, as though he's subtly declaring to anyone watching that I'm more than his plus-one. Once seated, his hand finds my leg, resting there with a quiet confidence that steadies the swell of unease in my chest.

The gesture sends a message—to everyone here and to me—that I'm not just accompanying him tonight; I'm *with* him. It's an act that holds meaning, not ostentatious but quiet and powerful, reminding me of his unwavering presence and the statement he's making simply by having me at his side.

The ceremony begins, and as the bride and groom exchange vows, my thoughts drift into uncharted territory. This is what Alex wants—a future built together, a life shared in its entirety. The thought stirs something deep, equal parts longing and fear.

Marriage isn't just a partnership; it's the complete surrender of your heart, the willingness to let someone see every hidden corner of your soul. The vulnerability it demands feels like walking a tightrope with no safety net.

My gaze shifts to the couple before us, their faces glowing with a love so sure it feels unshakable. The thought of standing in their place sends a ripple of unease through me. The towering marble columns, glittering chandeliers, and sea of poised guests make my chest tighten.

This isn't just a wedding; it's a glimpse into a world I'm not sure I belong in—a world Alex navigates with ease, but one that leaves me feeling exposed and uncertain. I close my eyes for a moment, drawing a deep breath. The truth is, the life Alex wants—the life he deserves—terrifies me.

When the ceremony ends, we move to the reception, which is every bit as breathtaking. Tables draped in crisp white linens sparkle with glimmering candles and intricate floral arrangements. We're led to a table near the front, where two couples are already seated, their laughter filling the air with a lively warmth. Alex squeezes my hand, his touch steady, as if offering silent reassurance.

"Magnolia, I want you to meet a few people. These are my teammates, Bradley and Jonathan. And their better halves, Megan and Callie. Everyone, this is Magnolia."

I smile warmly, offering a nod as Alex makes the introductions. "Hi there. It's nice to meet y'all."

Megan's face lights up, her grin growing wide and genuine. "Magnolia... I've never known anyone with that name. I love it. And your accent! I could listen to you talk all night."

Callie's brow lifts with interest, her eyes sparkling. "You've got a drawl that could charm a crocodile—whereabouts are you from?"

I relax into their easy warmth, the tension I had been carrying starting to ease. "I live in Charleston, South Carolina, now, but the accent? That's all Mississippi."

Megan and Callie seem genuinely kind. They're nothing like the image I had in my head of professional athletes' wives—no air of superiority, no distant politeness.

"Ah, Mississippi—that explains it," Callie says, snapping her fingers like she's solved a mystery. "That's why it has that sweet cadence to it."

When people find out I'm from Mississippi, their reactions usually fall into one of two extremes. Some get stars in their eyes, conjuring images of magnolia trees, sweet tea, and front porch swings creaking in the humid breeze. Others arch an eyebrow, as if picturing me strolling out of a trailer park barefoot in dirty overalls, a six-pack tucked under one arm and a possum on a leash. And to be fair, they're not entirely wrong about the trailer park part. Middle ground doesn't seem to exist, but I've learned to lean into it with a little charm—it keeps things easier for everyone.

"You all have such lovely accents. And the slang? Don't even get me started. Half the time, I'm convinced y'all are making up words to see if the American will nod along."

Megan laughs, nodding in agreement. "Fair, but yours takes the cake, Magnolia. You could read the ingredients on a box of cereal, and we'd all be charmed."

Callie's eyes sparkle with curiosity. "So, what brings you all the way from Charleston to Sydney?"

"Work. I couldn't resist when the chance for a short-term assignment in Australia came up. It felt like the perfect excuse for an adventure."

Megan's grin spreads wide as she shoots Alex a teasing look. "Adventurous *and* gorgeous. Alex, you've hit the jackpot."

Alex rests his hand lightly on the back of my chair, looking at me with adoring eyes. "Trust me, you have no idea."

Callie winks at me. "I think you've got *The Iron Wall* wrapped around your finger, Magnolia. It's written all over his face."

Megan nods in agreement. "She's right. I've never seen him like this."

Bradley shakes his head with a good-natured groan. "All right, ladies, cut the man some slack."

Their laughter surrounds me, warm and genuine, melting my nerves with ease. The teasing feels like a welcome embrace, drawing me into their circle.

I share bits of myself, answering their questions, while Alex's steady gaze reminds me I belong here. I'd worried about fitting into his world, but their kindness puts me at ease. By the time cake is served, I'm smiling at how unnecessary my nerves were. Tonight feels unexpectedly right.

The band begins playing Etta James's "At Last," the smooth, soulful melody spilling into the room and drawing couples to the dance floor. The familiar tune catches my ear, and a smile tugs at my lips. "I love this song."

Alex's gaze meets mine, a teasing smile curving his lips. Rising to his feet, he extends a hand toward me with a slight, playful bow.

"May I have the honor of this dance, Miss Steel?"

My smile widens as I slip my hand into his. "Yes, you may, Mr. Sebring."

Alex leads me to the center of the floor, the golden lights casting a soft glow that feels warm and intimate. His hand settles at the small of my back, his other holding mine firmly as he pulls me close. The rest of the room fades into a blur, leaving the two of us in a world of our own.

The music is gentle and steady, and for a moment, it feels like time has paused. My heart skips as I glance up at him, captivated by the way he looks at me—like I'm the only thing that matters.

"You've been incredible tonight." The admiration in his eyes matches the warmth in his words.

I blink, surprised by his appraisal. "Incredible? Nah, I was just trying not to trip over my own feet."

He spins me with an effortless grace that makes my pulse race. "It's so much more than that. You carry yourself like you've done this a hundred times. Like you belong here."

His words settle deep within me, warm and unexpected. I search his face for any hint of teasing, but there's none—just pure sincerity. "I only followed your lead."

"You didn't follow anyone's lead," he says, pulling me close once more. "You made it look easy. Like this world—this life—is meant for you."

The thought sinks deeper, clawing at me. Maybe I didn't realize it before, but what if I'm just like Robin and Charlene? What if I'm a chameleon too, slipping into this role, pretending to fit? Able to play the part, smile in all the right places, but it's not real.

I swallow hard, my breath hitching as I meet his gaze. There's something in his eyes—unspoken, powerful, and far too tender. It wraps around me, slipping past every wall I've built, and I don't know how to handle it. Warmth spreads in my chest, but it doesn't last. Unease follows, twisting it into something heavier, something I can't quite name.

And it terrifies me.

Because in moments like this, the reality of who I am feels unbearable. I'm just a girl born into chaos, and not the beautiful kind—but the kind that sticks to you, leaving jagged scars you can't hide.

I wasn't born for a life of chandeliers and sprawling estates, of private jets and penthouses perched above glittering cityscapes. Eight- or nine-figure bank accounts—hell, maybe even ten—are as far from my reality as the moon.

This isn't my world, and it never will be.

It's temporary. Three months to be exact.

His gaze holds mine, steady and unrelenting. It's too much. The intensity, the rawness, the possibility of being truly seen.

And as "At Last" swells into its final notes, the lyrics feel like they're taunting me.

"I need to visit the ladies' room," I say, slipping free of his grasp. My smile feels brittle, barely held together.

His brow furrows, confusion flashing across his face, but he doesn't press. "Of course."

As I turn away, the last notes of the song fade into the background, and with every step, the ache inside me grows heavier, threatening to consume me whole.

I slip away from the dance floor, his words echoing in my mind, heavy and unsettling.

Like this world—this life—is meant for you.

My pulse races as I grab my bag from the table, clutching it tightly as I make my way to the bathroom.

The romantic haze of the evening clings to me, but as I push open the bathroom door, I'm flooded with relief at the solitude waiting inside. Within the stall, I pause, standing still as the quiet wraps around me. I close my eyes, my heart pounding against my ribs. His words settle over me with a heaviness I hadn't anticipated, far more than what tonight was supposed to hold. This was meant to be light—fun. So why does it feel like the ground beneath me has shifted? Why does it feel like he's offering me something I'm not sure I know how to hold?

I exhale shakily, stepping out and making my way to the sink. The cool counter beneath my fingertips steadies me as I glance at my reflection in the mirror. My cheeks are flushed, my breathing uneven. I take a slow, deliberate breath, trying to steady myself. Pulling a lipstick from my bag, I touch up my makeup, focusing on the familiar routine—a small attempt to regain control over the moment.

As I finish touching up my lipstick, the bathroom door swings open. A striking tall blonde strides inside, her presence demanding attention. She pauses, folding her arms with casual arrogance as her sharp gaze zeroes in on me.

Unsure of what else to say, I offer a polite but wary, "Hello."

Her smirk curls into something sharp, cutting. "Ah, the Southern belle," she drawls, her tone thick with mockery. "I see Alex has gone international. Guess no woman in Australia wants him after they got a glimpse of the real Alex Sebring."

It doesn't take much to piece together who she is. "Celeste."

Her smirk deepens, her satisfaction practically radiating. "Oh, he's mentioned me? I hope he gave me a glowing review."

I cross my arms, my stance firm. "Only as someone desperate for likes and views. Pathetic really."

Her smirk falters for a split second before it sharpens again. "You should do a search on him, read the stories, watch the video. Then you'll see for yourself what kind of man you're really with."

I shake my head. "I haven't seen the video, and I don't care to. You know why? Because it reveals more about you than it ever could about him."

Her eyes narrow. "You think you know him? Trust me, sweetheart, you've barely scratched the surface."

I meet her gaze head-on, my voice unwavering. "You're right—I don't know the Alex you once knew. But I know the man he is now, and that's all I care about."

Her smirk falters for a heartbeat before she recovers. "You're making a mistake," she hisses, each word laced with venom.

I tilt my head, a slow, confident smile curving my lips. "If it is, it's *my* mistake to make—not yours. So don't lose any sleep over it."

I turn toward the door but pause, glancing back over my shoulder with a slow, deliberate smile. "Oh, and Celeste? It's clear you haven't forgotten how good Alex is in bed. He told me all about your little attempt after the game. *'Maybe we should slip away for a bit. I could remind you of what you've been missing.'* Pathetic doesn't even begin to cover it. That's embarrassing—for you."

With that, I stride out, my heels clicking purposefully against the marble floor, leaving her bitterness—and her desperate attempts to rattle me—far behind.

My stomach twists as I step back into the reception and spot Alex across the room, locked in a tense exchange with a man I've never seen before—but I know exactly who he is. The energy between them is charged, sharp enough to cut through the air, drawing a small crowd of curious onlookers. Alex's jaw is set, his fists clenching at his sides, the calm control I've come to rely on unraveling right in front of me.

This is bad. Really bad. The storm inside him is visible in every taut muscle, every shift of his eyes, and I can tell he's moments away from losing the grip he's barely holding on to.

I weave through the onlookers until I'm right in front of Alex. Without hesitation, I step between him and the man, a barrier against the tension that feels ready to explode. Placing my hand gently on his chest, I can feel the thunderous booming of his heart beneath my palm—wild, unsteady, and barely contained.

"Hey, babe."

His eyes snap to mine, recognition cutting through the storm brewing inside him.

"You know how much I love the song 'Endless Love.'" I offer a small smile, tilting my head as if nothing is wrong. "Come dance with me?"

Behind me, Sir-Picks-a-Fight scoffs, his smug laughter slicing through the thick air. "That's right, Sebring." His words drip with venom. "Stick to dancing. Leave the real game to those who can actually handle it."

I don't flinch, refusing to give him the satisfaction of a reaction. My gaze stays locked on Alex's, unwavering. "I'll be so sad if we don't dance to *our* song."

I slide my hand into his and give it a gentle squeeze.

Leaning in closer, I whisper, my words meant only for him. "Remember what we talked about? He's baiting you, trying to make you snap in front of everyone so he can paint you as the villain. Don't give him that satisfaction, Alex. Come with me."

His jaw tightens, tension radiating off him like a physical force. But slowly, I feel the fight drain from his body. His shoulders ease, and his grip on my hand shifts—not in anger, but in quiet surrender.

I lead him away from the crowd, his steps heavy, reluctant, but following. The strain of everything he's holding inside clings to him, his silence louder than any outburst.

When we reach the center of the dance floor, surrounded by a sea of swaying couples and safely out of sight of his nemesis, I stop and turn to him. My hands find his face, gently cradling it, his jaw tight beneath my touch, his breaths coming in shallow, uneven pulls.

"Alex," I whisper, brushing my thumbs along his jawline in reassuring strokes. "It's over. Look at me. Just me. You're in control."

His gaze locks on mine, the turmoil in his eyes fading as he steadies himself. His breathing slows as his tension unravels. I rise onto my toes, pressing a soft kiss to his lips. He hesitates for a moment, then exhales deeply, his body softening as he lets go of the storm brewing within him.

When I pull back, his words come out rough, barely controlled. "You're my peace in the madness. I don't know what I'd do without you."

The music surrounds us, soft and steady, as we move together in a slow rhythm. His grip on me is firm yet somehow tender, as though letting go would shatter something fragile between us. The room, the crowd, the tension—all of it fades away until it's only the two of us, steady and inseparable in a world of our own making.

Alex presses his lips to my ear. "Do you want to get out of here?"

I tilt my head up to meet his gaze, offering a gentle smile. "I'll do whatever you want."

His brow arches slightly, the faintest smirk tugging at the corner of his mouth. "*Whatever* I want?"

"Anything. Just say the word."

His eyes dart over his shoulder toward Tyson, his jaw tightening as his expression hardens. "What I want is to leave before he pushes me to a place I can't come back from."

"Then let's go," I say without hesitation, giving his hand a reassuring squeeze.

As we weave through the crowd and step outside to the waiting car, I steal a glance at Alex. His profile is taut, his thoughts clearly heavy, the pull of unspoken emotions dragging him into silence. He doesn't deserve this—not tonight, not ever. Whatever darkness Tyson stirred, whatever storm is brewing inside him, I'll make sure it stops here. By the time this night is over, the chaos will be a distant memory. I'll make sure he remembers only the calm I gave him.

Chapter 26

Magnolia Steel

THE SILENCE WRAPS AROUND US IN THE BACK OF THE LIMO, heavy and unyielding, a melancholy neither of us can seem to lift. Alex sits beside me, his posture rigid, his gaze fixed on the city lights blurring past the window. The tension radiating off him feels like a fortress, keeping me out.

I can't stand it.

I shift closer, placing my hand gently on his thigh. He doesn't react, doesn't move, and the ache in my chest tightens.

"Alex." I lean into him. "Don't do this."

His eyes land on me, guarded and distant. "Do what?"

"Shut me out." My fingers brush over his hand, a silent plea for connection. "I'm right here. Don't disappear on me."

He exhales sharply, his jaw tightening as he drops his gaze to where my hand rests on his. "I don't choose to, but the way he gets under my skin—"

I slide my hand up to his chest, feeling the rapid rhythm of his heartbeat beneath my palm. "You don't have to carry that alone, not with me."

His hand moves to cover mine, his thumb brushing over my knuckles. "It's not that I want to." His eyes drop to our hands, as though searching for the words. "But it feels like I don't get a choice. My head runs away with thoughts I can't slow down. The noise, the pressure... it's constant."

His chest rises sharply beneath my palm. "I'm fighting a battle I don't know how to win. And sometimes, Magnolia" —he looks up, his eyes heavy with vulnerability— "it feels like I'm losing."

This isn't a clash of egos or a pissing contest between two men— it's something deeper. Alex isn't just angry. He's hurting. Tyson's words might have lit the spark, but the fire comes from something far older, far more consuming—something he's carried silently for a while.

My chest aches because I see it, even if he refuses to say it out loud. This isn't about Tyson. This is Alex fighting to keep himself from breaking.

"You're not losing," I whisper, desperate to reach him. "Not with me. You don't have to carry this by yourself, Alex. Let me in. Let me help."

His grip on my hand tightens, his gaze lifting to meet mine. The intensity in his eyes is almost unbearable, a quiet storm that tears at me. He looks like a man carrying the world on his shoulders, and the sight of it breaks something inside me.

His jaw tightens like he's forcing himself to stay in control. "I can handle Tyson. This isn't something you should have to worry about. I need to keep you away from this."

The words hit like a blow I wasn't expecting, their impact sinking deep. He's not just resisting me—he's shielding me. Protecting me from whatever darkness he's battling within himself. And it tears at me because I know he doesn't realize that keeping me out doesn't protect me. It only keeps us apart.

"I want to help you through this. Let me take this from you... in *my* way. Whatever you're feeling—let me help you let it go."

His fingers tighten around mine. "I don't understand."

"You're holding on to so much inside." My eyes search his. "But you don't have to. Not with me. Let it out *with* me. I can take it."

A storm of doubt, confusion, and resistance crosses his face. "What? No—"

"Sometimes people reach a point where they need to scream. But not necessarily with their voice—maybe in other ways. Think of it like releasing the pressure before it explodes. You can do that with me. Let me be the one you let go with."

I slide my hand higher, cradling the side of his face. "You don't have to hold it all in. Not tonight. Not with me."

His eyes search mine, clouded with uncertainty and something else—something raw and unguarded. The silence stretches between us, heavy with unspoken emotions, and I hold my breath, willing him to see the truth in my words.

I see it—clarity blooming, breaking through the doubt. Hesitation fractures, revealing something raw and untamed beneath the surface. His gaze sharpens, and a storm gathers in his eyes as he leans into my touch, his voice rough and unsteady. "Are you sure you want that?"

I don't flinch. Instead, I close the distance between us, my lips hovering above his, and whisper, "I've never been more sure. Give me all of it."

His breath catches, his hand sliding up to cradle my cheek, his thumb brushing softly along my jaw as he searches my face, looking for doubt. He won't find any. I meet his gaze head-on, my heart pounding in my chest.

"I know exactly what I'm asking for—I want all of you, Alex. The good, the broken, the beautiful... even the dark parts you're afraid to show me. *Especially* those."

The tension between us is electric, pulling taut like a string about to snap. His eyes darken, his jaw tightening as if he's holding back. But I don't let go, pressing my hand over his heart, feeling the thunder of it beneath my palm. "You don't have to handle this alone. Let me in. All the way."

Something in him shifts—a decision, a surrender—and the

moment stretches, heavy with the magnitude of what's about to happen. Then, slowly, he exhales, his hand sliding around to the back of my neck, drawing me closer. And when his lips finally crash into mine, it's not gentle. It's raw, hungry, and filled with everything he's been holding back.

His hand tangles in my hair, his grip firm, and I know he's letting go—giving me the parts of himself he's been too afraid to share.

As the limo glides through the city, the world outside blurs. His touch is urgent, his movements possessive, but beneath it all, I feel his gratitude, his trust. And as I meet him with equal intensity, I know we've crossed into something deeper—something that binds us in a way neither of us can deny.

"Fuck me any way you want to," I breathe against his ear. "I can take it. Let me be your release."

A deep growl rumbles in his chest as he pulls me onto his lap, his lips meeting mine in a passionate and urgent kiss. I let out a moan, moving my hips in sync with the hardening bulge in his tuxedo pants.

"You want me to use you?" he rasps, nipping at my lower lip.

"Think of me as your... *outlet.*"

I want to be his release, his escape—the place where he can lose himself completely and find solace in my arms. I want to be the warmth that eases his pain, the balm that soothes the wounds life has left on him. I ache to trace gentle fingers over his scars, both the ones I can see and the ones I can't. I yearn to murmur quiet words of comfort and acceptance against his skin until the heaviness he carries feels lighter.

When he finally lets his guard down, when he allows himself to be vulnerable, I want to be his safe harbor—the one he turns to when doubt or despair threatens to pull him under. I want to listen without judgment, to offer quiet strength. To be the soft place he can fall when the world feels too heavy. Not just his lover, but the one he knows he can count on.

And I want to be fucked raw.

He leans back slightly, his jaw flexing as if he's biting back the words already forming on his tongue. I see the war inside him, the push and pull of wanting to protect me from his chaos and the desperate need to let it out.

His lips part, and for a moment, I'm certain he's going to say no, to shield me from whatever storm he's battling, to protect me from the darkness he thinks is too much for me to bear. His gaze clouds with hesitation, his fingers brushing mine in a way that feels almost apologetic.

But then something shifts. It's subtle at first—a sharp inhale, the way his shoulders ease, the hard set of his jaw softening ever so slightly. His eyes meet mine, and I see it—something breaking, something raw and unguarded finally pushing through the layers.

His chest rises and falls, a shallow, shaky breath leaving his lips. And then, like a dam giving way, he reaches for me, his hand slipping to the back of my neck as he pulls me close, his grip firm but trembling.

"No more walls," he says, almost to himself. "No more holding it in."

His lips crash into mine with a passion that's overwhelming and wild—a controlled storm, intense but deeply reverent. It's not just a release; it's a surrender, a moment where he's choosing to trust me, to let me share the burden he's been carrying. I meet him fully, my hands sliding up to hold myself against him, knowing this is as much about us as it is about him finding himself again.

"How do you want me?"

"On your knees, bending over the seat."

"Anything you want."

Alex leans forward, turning up the volume on the sound system, the chords of "Breath" by Breaking Benjamin blasting through the car. I recognize it instantly because Violet used to play it on repeat.

The heavy beat fills the space, drowning out everything else, ensuring the driver won't hear a thing. My heart races, the pounding rhythm syncing with my pulse as I follow his command. The leather seat beneath me is cool against my flushed skin as I lean over, feeling my dress ride up to expose my thighs.

Alex's hands grip my hips, his fingers digging in as he positions himself behind me.

His fingers trace along the edge of my lace thong, pulling it aside as he positions his throbbing cock at my slick entrance. His deep groan rumbles through me as he plunges into me with one powerful thrust. The intense sensation floods my body, and I struggle to catch my breath. But Alex doesn't slow down, his hips moving in a relentless rhythm, keeping time with the song.

Alex's hips snap forward with relentless force, each thrust driving deeper than the last. The sound of skin slapping against skin fills the back of the limo, punctuated by our shared moans and gasps. His fingers dig into my hips, using the leverage to pull me back onto him with each powerful stroke.

I can feel every inch of him as he pounds into me, stretching and filling me completely. The intensity builds with each passing moment, pleasure coiling tighter in my core.

"You have no idea what you do to me, Magnolia."

"Show me."

His pace increases, becoming almost frantic. The roughness of his movements, the raw need behind each thrust, pushes me closer to the edge.

Alex's hand snakes around to my front, his fingers finding my most sensitive spot with practiced ease. He begins to stroke in tight, rapid circles, perfectly in sync with his relentless thrusts. The dual stimulation is almost too much to bear, and I feel myself rapidly approaching the precipice of ecstasy.

"Come for me, Magnolia. I want to feel you come around me."

His words, combined with the exquisite sensations coursing through my body, push me over the edge. I cry out, my back arching as waves of pleasure crash over me. My inner walls clench around him rhythmically, intensifying the feeling of fullness.

Alex growls, his movements becoming erratic as he chases his own release. With a final, powerful thrust, he buries himself to the hilt inside me, his body shuddering as he finds his climax.

For a moment, we stay frozen in that position, both of us panting heavily as we come down from our shared high. Slowly, he withdraws from me, and I feel a sense of loss at the absence of his fullness.

Alex slumps back onto the leather seat, his chest heaving as he gulps in air. He runs a hand through his hair, pushing it back from his forehead as he tries to steady his breathing. "Fuck."

I take a moment to smooth down my dress, wincing slightly at the delicious soreness between my thighs. Once I've made myself presentable again, I turn the music down and slide into the spot beside him.

He turns to look at me, his eyes dark and intense, the heat between us still smoldering. A slow smile spreads across his face, equal parts satisfaction and tenderness. Without hesitation, I move to straddle his lap, settling into him like it's the most natural thing in the world. My arms loop around his shoulders, and his hands find their place on my waist, steadying me.

I lean in, pressing my forehead to his, breathing in the mix of cologne, sweat, and something that's purely Alex. For a while, neither of us speaks. We simply hold each other, the rhythm of our breathing gradually syncing, the quiet intimacy filling the space between us.

The scent of sex lingers in the air, mingling with the fogged windows and the soft hum of the music in the background. In this moment, the world outside doesn't exist—it's just the two of us, wrapped up in the aftermath of something that feels bigger than words.

"I hope I didn't hurt you. I was rougher than I meant to be."

I shake my head, a small smile playing on my lips. "You didn't hurt me. I liked it. A lot actually."

His eyebrows raise slightly in surprise. "You did, huh?"

"Mm-hmm," I hum, snuggling against him. "I liked the roughness, the urgency, knowing that I could be an outlet for your frustrations. It was incredibly... *arousing*."

Alex is quiet for a moment, then cups my chin, tilting my face up to his. "You're amazing, you know that? But you don't have to do that. I don't want to use you as some kind of stress relief."

I reach up, tracing my fingers along his jaw. "But what if I want you to? What if I enjoy being that for you?"

"You're serious?"

I nod, holding his gaze. "Completely. Alex, I care about you. I want to be there for you in every way possible. If this is something you need, something that helps you, I want to give that to you."

He searches my face for a moment. "God, you have no idea what you do to me."

I smile, nuzzling into the crook of his neck, pressing a soft kiss to his pulse point. "I think I have some idea."

Alex pulls me close, wrapping his strong arms around me. For a while, we simply hold each other, basking in the afterglow. The world outside our little bubble seems distant and unimportant.

"Do you have any vacation days you can take?"

I glance up, curiosity sparking at the question. "Some. Why?"

"I need to go out of town the week after next. I want you to come with me."

"Another surprise?"

"Maybe." His grin deepens, his fingers brushing over mine. "Think you could work something out with Soul Sync and come with me?"

A thrill courses through me, excitement bubbling up as I nod. "I think I can make it happen."

"Good."

His arm tightens around me. His hand rests warmly on my back as we settle into the quiet intimacy of the ride.

As the car moves through the dark streets, I glance up at him, his profile softened by the glow of the city lights. For the first time tonight, the tension in his face seems to ease, and I feel it too—a sense of peace, fragile yet undeniable.

Whatever comes next, I know we'll face it together. And in this moment, that's all that matters.

Chapter 27

Magnolia Steel

A WHIRLWIND OF EXCITEMENT AND DOUBT CHURNS INSIDE ME, my stomach twisting with every mile that brings us closer to Alex's childhood home. Meeting his parents feels monumental—too monumental for a relationship with an expiration date. Isn't this the kind of step you take when you're planning to stay, not when there's a countdown hanging over you like a ticking clock?

Alex reaches over, his hand warm as it closes around mine, his thumb tracing slow, deliberate circles over my knuckles. It's a small gesture, but it soothes me, his touch steady even as my thoughts spiral.

"Relax, Magnolia. My parents are going to love you."

I force a smile, trying to let his confidence wash over me, but the pull of one single question tugs harder. *Why are we doing this?*

We're living in a fantasy, pretending that three months can stretch forever, that meeting his family isn't a milestone meant for a relationship we don't have. I glance at him, his profile sharp and steady, his grip on my hand unwavering. He looks so certain, so unshaken by the reality we're staring down.

But I'm not.

Because deep down, I know this is more than a visit. It's a step forward in a relationship that isn't supposed to move beyond the boundaries we've set. And yet, here we are—me about to step into his world, about to meet two of the most important people in his life.

The closer we get, the harder it is to ignore the truth: we're pretending the clock isn't ticking, as if the time we have left isn't slipping away with every passing second.

A fresh wave of nerves unfurls as we approach the front door, dredging up memories I've tried to bury. I was never the girl a guy brought home to meet his mama—not when everyone in town knew exactly who Robin Steel was. Bartender, bad mom, occasional husband-stealer. No guy's mother wanted her son anywhere near the daughter of a woman like her.

I swallow hard, forcing air into my lungs, and glance sideways at Alex. He doesn't know how deeply those roots run, how they've wrapped themselves around parts of me that still ache, no matter how far I've come.

As if sensing the storm brewing inside me, Alex squeezes my hand, his thumb brushing over my skin in a way that feels like both comfort and promise. "My parents are down-to-earth. You'll see."

I try to hold on to that, let it calm the anxiety swirling inside me. But the ghosts of my past are hard to shake, whispering doubts I'm not ready to face.

You're not good enough.

You have no business here.

As we make our way up the sidewalk, I tighten my grip on the bouquet of flowers I picked out this morning—vibrant and tropical, a nod to Alex's Samoan roots. At the time, I considered them a thoughtful gesture, something to show his mom I cared. But now, as I stand here, they feel more like a bundle of nerves wrapped in cellophane and ribbon, every bit of my anxiety carried straight to the door and presented like a lamb to the slaughter.

Before I can second-guess myself, the door swings open, and warmth spills out like a welcome embrace. Alex's mom, Malie, steps forward, her face lighting up with a smile so radiant, it momentarily leaves me speechless. She's stunning in a way that's both natural and commanding—glossy black hair streaked with silver cascading over her shoulders, her features soft but interwoven with a quiet strength.

"Tinā," Alex says, filled with reverence as he greets her in Samoan. "This is Magnolia."

Her smile widens, and before I can stammer out a polite hello, she steps forward and wraps me in a hug that's surprisingly firm and filled with unmistakable warmth.

"Magnolia, it's so lovely to meet you." Sincere warmth radiates through her words.

"It's wonderful to meet you too." I lift the bouquet, the blooms trembling slightly in my grip. "I thought you might enjoy these."

Malie's eyes brighten as she takes the flowers, her expression one of genuine delight. "Oh, Magnolia, these are stunning," she says, turning the bouquet to admire the vivid, tropical hues. "They remind me of home. How thoughtful of you. Thank you."

Her reaction is so heartfelt, I feel some of my nerves ease. As far as first impressions go, maybe I'm not as out of place as I feared.

Beside her is Alex's father, Alexander, a striking contrast to his son. Where Alex's dark, rugged features reflect his Samoan heritage, Alexander's fair skin, sharp blue eyes, and light blond hair hint at his Swedish roots. He's tall, though not nearly quite as broad or commanding as his son.

He comes forward with a warm smile. "Magnolia, it's a pleasure to finally meet you."

"It's so nice to meet you both," I manage, my nerves softening under the warmth that seems to flow from both of them.

Mr. Sebring's expression immediately puts me at ease—like I've stepped into a place where I'm already welcome.

Alex and I follow his parents through the house, and despite its grandeur, it's the inviting warmth that strikes me most. Soft lighting bathes the space, accentuating decor that feels more thoughtful than showy—family photos on the walls, well-loved furniture, and small touches that speak of a home built on love rather than wealth.

We step into the kitchen, and the rich, tantalizing aroma of a home-cooked meal wraps around me like a welcoming embrace. The counters are laden with vibrant dishes, each one more inviting than the last.

Malie moves gracefully by the stove, focused on the final touches of what looks like a true feast. I glance at the spread, then at her, feeling a little out of place but eager to contribute. "Can I help with anything?"

Malie's eyes crinkle with kindness. "You're our guest tonight, Magnolia." Then she winks, adding with a playful lilt, "But you can help next time."

Next time.

Malie motions to the colorful spread with a proud smile. "I've prepared a traditional Samoan meal for us. We have faiai eleni, fa'apapa, and sapasui."

My smile widens as I take in the vibrant dishes. "I've never had Samoan food before, so I'm really looking forward to this."

Alex steps behind me, his hand brushing lightly against my back. "You're in for a treat. No one does it better than Tinā."

Malie laughs softly at his praise, waving him off. "Of course he says that. I raised him on this food." She gestures to the dishes with an inviting nod. "Let's move everything to the dining room. Family-style is the only way to eat this meal."

I instinctively step forward, reaching for one of the serving platters. "Here, let me help."

Malie raises an eyebrow, the hint of a smile tugging at her lips, but relents with a small nod. "Thank you, Magnolia. Just be careful—the fa'apapa is hot."

Together, we carry the dishes to the dining room, where a long table is set with understated elegance. White linens drape gracefully, neatly folded napkins rest at each place, and the soft glow of candles creates an inviting warmth. Once everything is in place, we settle in, the atmosphere shifting into something even cozier, more intimate.

Malie gestures to the large bowl in the center of the table. "This is faiai eleni—mackerel baked in coconut cream with onions and vegetables. It's a dish that always reminds me of home."

She motions to a plate of golden bread beside it. "And this is fa'apapa—coconut bread with a touch of sweetness. Perfect for scooping up the other dishes."

Alex leans forward, his excitement evident. "You've got to try it with the sapasui. It's Samoan-style chop suey. My favorite."

Curiosity piqued, I take a bite of each, the flavors bursting on my tongue—rich, sweet, savory, and completely unique. "This is incredible."

Malie beams at the compliment, her pride unmistakable. "I'm so glad you like it. Food is a way of bringing people together—it's how we share our hearts. And food is one of the best ways to share our love and culture. It's what mothers do—feed everyone until they're stuffed."

Her words stir something bittersweet inside me. That's not what my mother did. Robin Steel's idea of love was always about taking care of herself, not nurturing others. My grandmother, Charlene, was no different. Love wasn't baked into casseroles or poured into homemade pies; it was fleeting, selfish, conditional. The kind of warmth and care Malie radiates feels foreign, like something plucked from the pages of a novel I once read but could never imagine living.

Malie's voice gently pulls me from my thoughts. "Where are you from, Magnolia?"

"I grew up in Mississippi, but I live on the East Coast now, in South Carolina."

"Aleki says you work in interior design?"

"I do—specifically, the psychology of decor. I love what I do. Every project is different, and I get to think about how spaces affect people's moods and energy. There's a lot of psychology involved—

choosing colors, textures, and layouts that make people feel welcome, calm, or even inspired."

Malie nods, her interest clear. "That sounds fascinating. I've never thought about how much intention goes into a room."

"It's incredible how much impact a well-designed space can have. It's not only about aesthetics—it's about how a space can make someone feel safe, happy, or even empowered. It's subtle, but it matters."

Alex's hand brushes mine under the table, a small but reassuring gesture.

Alexander's eyes brighten with intrigue as he exchanges a glance with Malie. "What an intriguing concept. We're planning a remodel of the hotels next year, and someone with your skills could make a real difference."

"It sounds like an exciting project."

"We want to refresh the spaces. Our goal is to create an atmosphere of elegant luxury—where guests feel not only pampered but also valued. It sounds like you'd know exactly how to make that happen."

Malie's lips curve into a smile as she looks between us, her eyes sparkling. "Perhaps you should hire Magnolia. I bet she'd bring a fresh, unique perspective to the Melbourne locations."

Her expression softens with curiosity. "Do you see yourself staying where you are, or could you be lured away?"

I hesitate, her question settling over me as I glance down at my plate. "Actually, I'll be returning to the U.S. in a month when my assignment here wraps up."

A gentle quiet settles over the table, the moment tinged with something unspoken. "Well, that's too bad. I hope your time in Australia has been unforgettable."

My gaze drifts to Alex, catching the way his eyes fix on me, soft and filled with something that makes my chest tighten. "It's been more memorable than I ever could've imagined."

Malie's smile widens, her words carrying a gentle excitement. "We're all so happy you'll be joining us in Samoa next week. The rest of the family is eager to meet you."

Alex groans, rolling his eyes as he shoots his mother a playful look. "Ugh, Tinā! That was supposed to be a surprise."

"Oops." Malie claps a hand over her mouth, her eyes widening with guilt. "Sorry, Aleki."

Surprised, I glance between them. "You didn't tell me it was time for one of your trips to Samoa."

"It wasn't supposed to be this soon, but my grandfather's health has been declining, so we want to move the trip up. And" —he pauses a moment— "I couldn't imagine being away from you for a whole week when you only have a few weeks left here. I want you to come with me."

I look back at Malie and Alexander, their warm, expectant smiles easing the nervous flutter in my chest. "Of course I'll come. I'm looking forward to it—truly. Thank you so much for including me."

After dinner, I follow Malie into the kitchen, eager to help with the cleanup. She nods in approval as I start stacking plates and transferring leftovers into storage containers while she loads the dishwasher. The quiet rhythm of our tasks fills the space, but I can feel her eyes on me—a gaze that's warm yet probing, like she's peeling back layers to see what lies beneath.

She raises an eyebrow, a teasing glint in her expression. "You know, I've never seen Aleki this smitten before. He talks about you constantly—always with that special look in his eyes."

Heat rushes to my cheeks, and I glance down, a shy smile tugging at my lips. "I really enjoy being with Alex. He's... well, he's incredible."

Malie's expression softens, her pride shining through. "Perhaps I'm biased, but I'd say incredible is the right word. He's always been a good man, but with you, he seems happy for a change."

Her words give me pause, a quiet ripple of surprise moving

through me. Alex, unhappy? It's hard to picture the confident, self-assured man I know being anything less than content. But then again, I've seen flashes of something deeper in him—moments when his jokes faltered, when his silence spoke volumes. He hides it well, but he carries some kind of torment, one I don't fully understand yet.

Has he been pretending for everyone else's sake?

She glances down at the container she's sealing, her movements slowing as if she's weighing her next words. "What happens when you go back to the U.S.?"

Her question takes me by surprise. "I'm not sure."

Malie doesn't know about the agreement Alex and I made—three months of uncomplicated fun, a fixed end date with no strings attached. It was supposed to be simple, but nothing about what we have now feels simple anymore.

She studies me for a moment. "Well, I hope the two of you figure out something. It would be a shame to let distance decide for you. So, dear, put your ear down close to your soul and listen hard."

Her words hit me harder than I expect, their weight settling over me like a heavy, unshakable truth.

"I'd hate to see you part ways. You're good for Aleki... unlike the last girl he dated."

As the evening winds down, I find myself watching Malie and Alexander more closely. There's something about the way they move together, an unspoken rhythm that speaks of decades of trust and love. A shared glance, a fleeting smile—they're a portrait of what I've always imagined a family should be.

I like them more than I expected to, more than I should. There's a comfort in their presence that feels so foreign yet so magnetic, like stepping into a world I didn't know I was missing out on.

For a fleeting moment, I let myself wonder what it would be like to belong to a family like this. To have Malie and Alexander not only as Alex's parents but as my family too?

But reality cuts through the thought like a sharp edge, pulling me back to the plan. This is temporary. The life I've begun to picture—the one where I'm part of this family, where Alex and I are building something lasting—isn't part of the deal we made. It's a beautiful dream, but that's all it can ever be. A fleeting fantasy, destined to dissolve the moment my time here is over.

Chapter 28

Alex Sebring

ANTICIPATION CHURNS BENEATH MY NERVES AS WE DRIVE toward the airport. This isn't just another trip to Samoa—it's a leap, a test of sorts. Magnolia is about to meet my entire extended family, the whole loud, close-knit, wonderfully chaotic clan. And while I hope she'll embrace it, there's no denying the significance of the moment.

My grandparents—Tinā's parents—are the heart of our family, and they live a life worlds apart from the one Magnolia knows. While my father and I have built lives surrounded by luxury and success, my grandparents have stayed true to their roots, living in a traditional Samoan home. It's a life built on love, tradition, and simplicity. It's beautiful, but it's not for everyone.

Celeste wouldn't have lasted five minutes there. She'd have waved off their home as quaint and unsuitable, opting instead for a suite in Apia, complete with air conditioning, a mini-bar, and Wi-Fi. She wouldn't have understood the quiet strength in my grandparents' way of life—the pride, the history, the connection. To her, it would've been nothing more than an inconvenience.

But Magnolia isn't Celeste. Magnolia is... Magnolia. Genuine, adaptable, and far from pretentious. She grew up in her own kind of chaos, and that's given her a depth most people never find. She's the kind of woman who can appreciate what really matters—not the facade, but the heart of things.

As I glance at her beside me, a small smile playing on her lips as she watches the scenery rush by, my confidence in her swells. I know she'll respect my family's world, see its value, its beauty. She'll understand.

Still, the nerves persist. Because this isn't just about her meeting my family. It's about me too. I've never brought anyone to Samoa, never shared this part of my life with a woman before. It's sacred to me and letting her in feels like laying my soul bare.

But with Magnolia, it feels right. It feels like the first step toward something real. Something that, even with the clock ticking on her time here, I can't let slip away.

As the small airport comes into view, I take a deep breath, anticipation tightening in my chest. Magnolia is about to step into my world—not the polished, public version, but the sacred, unvarnished parts I keep guarded. And yet, I know she'll meet it all with that quiet strength and unshakable grace that's uniquely hers.

We pull up to the terminal, and before I can even grab the first bag, Magnolia is swept into the Sebring-Malietoa fold. My sisters descend with their usual whirlwind energy, flanking her with bright smiles and rapid-fire chatter. Their warmth is electric, making it impossible for her to feel anything but welcome.

They weren't like this with Celeste. Not even close.

They know how important Magnolia is to me, and they're treating her accordingly, welcoming her with the kind of warmth and care they reserve for someone who truly matters.

Tinā, ever the heart of the family, takes the lead with a hug that radiates love and acceptance. "Magnolia, we've been so looking forward to this."

Leilani and Sefina aren't far behind, their laughter bubbling as they pepper Magnolia with questions and stories.

Leilani's grin is downright devilish as she fixes her gaze on me while addressing Magnolia. "Alex has been talking about you nonstop. Magnolia this... Magnolia that." She draws out the words with exaggerated drama, clearly relishing my discomfort. "It's about time we finally got to meet you."

Magnolia's laughter is light, cutting through my embarrassment. "Well, I must've made quite the impression if Alex is out here singing my praises. I'll take it as a compliment." She throws me a teasing glance that sends a twist of warmth straight through me.

Leilani cackles, delighted to stir the pot. "Oh, Magnolia, it's more than compliments. My brother's practically writing poetry about you."

"Keep it up, Lei, and I'll tell everyone about your One Direction fan-fiction phase." I narrow my eyes in a half-hearted attempt at intimidation.

Leilani flips me off with both hands. "I think you just did, loser. Thanks a lot."

Magnolia tilts her head, her grin widening with playful curiosity. "Wait, wait. Back up. I need to know more about this poetry."

Leilani forms a heart with her hands, mimicking a dramatic heartbeat as her eyes gleam with mischief. "Alex is in looooove," she declares, dragging out the word with exaggerated flair.

I groan, dragging a hand down my face. "Leilani, I swear—"

Leilani doubles over with laughter, completely unbothered by my weak threat.

Magnolia meets my gaze, her eyes sparkling with amusement, and for a moment, the world shrinks to the two of us.

I sigh, shaking my head, a reluctant smile breaking through. I should be mad at Leilani, but I can't bring myself to care. Not when I'm this damn happy.

Behind me, a low whistle catches my attention. I turn to see Niko grinning, his brows raised. "She's a real stunner, mate," he says, nodding toward Magnolia.

Elias chuckles, clapping me on the back. "If she weren't with you, I'd be trying my luck."

"As if," Asa cuts in with a smirk, crossing his arms. "She's way out of your league, Eli. And let's be honest, Alex—she's more down-to-earth than anyone you've brought around before. Not to mention, easy on the eyes." His gaze sharpens as he looks at me, clearly angling for a reaction.

I shake my head, laughing despite myself. "You three done with the commentary?"

Asa leans in, his grin widening. "You've never brought anyone to Samoa before. That says a lot, doesn't it?"

They exchange knowing glances, their smirks threatening to grow. I sigh, holding up a hand. "Fine, here's the deal." I glance over my shoulder, catching a glimpse of Magnolia laughing with Tinā and my sisters, blending into the chaos. "She's genuine—no act, no pretense. She actually cares about this part of my life, and more importantly, she respects it."

Elias slaps my shoulder again, his grin turning approving. "Good on you, Alex. Sounds like she's got more than just looks—sounds like she's got her priorities straight too."

I nod, my gaze drawn back to Magnolia. Across the terminal, she meets my eyes, her smile softening into something quieter, something that feels like it's just for me. A slow grin spreads across my face as I turn back to my brothers. "She's the real deal."

Niko leans in, his smirk unrelenting. "Good thing too because she'll need all that 'real' to survive this family."

The flight crew announces it's time to board, and one by one, we step onto the private chartered plane. Magnolia stays close as we settle into our seats. With six hours of flight time ahead, I slide my arm around her, drawing her closer.

The hum of the engines grows louder, a persistent backdrop to the quiet buzz of my family getting settled. I glance up to see my siblings seated up front, far enough away to give us a little privacy.

"Shame my whole family's on board." I lean closer to her ear. "Because, believe me, I'd love to join the mile-high club with you right about now."

Magnolia arches a brow, a playful glint lighting her eyes. "Would that be a first for you?"

"It would be. Never thought about it much—until now. And what about you? Am I sitting next to a mile-high member?"

Her laughter rings out, soft and genuine, her cheeks tinged with a faint blush. "Not even close."

The unexpected sweetness of the moment surprises me. I squeeze her hand, her fingers lacing with mine, and the simple warmth of her touch steadies me as the plane begins to taxi down the runway.

As the hum of the engines settles into a steady rhythm, I glance at Magnolia. She leans comfortably against me, her presence calming me in a way I've never known, and for a moment, it feels like the rest of the world has disappeared.

Now feels as good a time as any to tell her what I must. "Magnolia, there's something important I need to explain before we get there."

She tilts her head, her attention fully on me. "What is it?"

"In my family, fa'aaloalo means everything. It's more than a word —it's a way of life. It's about showing respect to our elders and honoring our culture." I pause, my eyes holding hers, wanting her to understand the importance of what I'm saying. "That means while we're staying at my grandparents' house, we won't be sharing a bed. It's considered disrespectful unless we're married."

Her gaze doesn't waver, and after a beat, her expression softens, a small smile curving her lips. "I understand. I wouldn't want to do anything to go against your family's values. It's important to me that they feel respected."

"Thank you for understanding. That means a lot to me." Relief washes over me, and I press a kiss to her forehead. "I hope you got enough of me last night to tide you over for a while."

Her laughter breaks the quiet, the sound light and teasing, carrying that irresistible spark she always has. "I hope *you* got enough of *me*," she fires back, her eyes glinting with playful defiance.

I lean in, my words a rough whisper. "I'll never get enough of you."

After six hours in the air, the plane touches down, and we step into the warm, fragrant embrace of Samoa. The sunlight here feels alive—richer, softer, and golden as it spills over the swaying palms and glistening ocean. The air carries the scent of salt and flowers, a blend that always feels like home.

Magnolia steps out beside me, her eyes wide with wonder as she takes it all in. The way her gaze roams over the vivid greens of the palm trees, the impossibly blue sky, and the rolling hills makes me see it all anew. Her awe stirs something deep inside me—pride, knowing I get to share this part of my life with her.

Laughter and voices rise as a group of my cousins comes rushing toward us. Their greetings in Samoan ring out like music, arms wide open as they envelop us in their embrace. It's a chaotic, joyful welcome, one that's impossible not to smile at.

Masina, one of my younger cousins, is holding a vibrant red hibiscus flower. She grins up at Magnolia with wide, bright eyes before tucking it above her left ear. "Welcome to Samoa, Magnolia. I'm Masina. It's good to meet you."

Magnolia touches the flower lightly, her smile warm and genuine as she meets Masina's gaze. "Thank you. It's beautiful. And it's so lovely to meet you as well."

Emotion swells in my chest as I take her in—standing here with the hibiscus tucked behind her ear, her smile soft and radiant, the island sun casting a golden glow over her face. She's breathtaking, more than I ever dared to hope for. This moment etches itself into me, one I know I'll carry with me forever.

We pull up to my grandparents' home, and a mix of excitement and nerves churns in my chest. Magnolia's hand tightens around mine as we step out, her wide eyes taking in the scene before her—the simple beauty of their home framed by swaying palms and vibrant flowers.

On the porch, my grandparents wait with bright smiles, their warmth radiating even before a word is spoken. "Aleki!" Nana calls, her voice strong despite her years, pulling me into a hug that feels like home.

When she turns to Magnolia, her smile softens, and I can see the tension in Magnolia's shoulders ease a little. Nana takes her hands gently, speaking first in Samoan before switching to English. "We are so happy you're here. Malie has been telling us all about you, and now I see why."

"Magnolia, this is my grandfather, Tui."

Tui smiles warmly. "Welcome, Magnolia. We're glad you've come."

"Thank you so much for having me. It's truly an honor to be here and meet your family."

Nana nods, her approval clear as she squeezes Magnolia's hands and then pulls her into a brief but affectionate hug.

Family arrives in waves, filling the yard with laughter and warm embraces. Names and faces blur as cousins, aunts, uncles, and neighbors pull me into their orbit. Even I feel a bit overwhelmed, but when I look for Magnolia, I find her blending in smoothly. She's laughing, chatting, and holding her own like she's been part of this world forever.

Her gaze catches mine from across the crowd, her smile soft and radiant. It stirs something deep in me—pride, maybe, or awe. She's not just fitting in; she's thriving.

When we sit for the umukai, Magnolia takes it all in with quiet curiosity. I lean closer, pointing out the dishes as they're passed. "Try the palusami."

I watch as she takes a bite. Her face lights up, and she glances at me with genuine appreciation. "Wow."

"Told you," I say, grinning. And for a moment, everything feels exactly as it should.

"Alex, this is incredible." Her eyes are bright with wonder. "Being here with you, seeing this side of your life... it's beautiful. I can tell how much your family means to you. They're such a big part of who you are."

Her words are unexpected. For a moment, I glance around at the faces I've known my whole life, at the laughter and stories flowing between generations. This is home—the part of me that remains constant no matter where I go.

The steady rhythm of drums pulses through the air, drawing everyone toward the clearing for the Siva Samoa. My cousins and sisters form a semi-circle, their bodies moving in harmony with the beat. Torchlight casts flickering shadows across their faces as they sway and step, their movements fluid and storytelling in every gesture.

Beside me, Magnolia is spellbound. Her eyes track each motion, wide with awe, her lips slightly parted as if she doesn't want to miss a single moment. Without thinking, I glance at her profile, the firelight catching the edges of her features. She doesn't just watch—she absorbs it, her quiet intensity making the pride swelling in my chest almost too much to contain.

She reaches for my hand, her fingers curling around mine without a word. It's a simple gesture, but it settles something deep inside me—seeing her embrace my world like it's becoming hers too.

The tempo builds, and my sister Leilani steps forward, breaking the circle with a playful smile. She motions to Magnolia, her grin wide and welcoming. "Come, Magnolia! Dance with us."

Magnolia's eyes dart to mine, her hesitation clear, but I nod, grinning. "Go on. You'll love it."

With a small laugh, she stands, taking Leilani's outstretched hand. My sister begins showing her the basic steps, and while Magnolia starts out tentative, she quickly picks up the rhythm. Her movements become looser, her smile brighter as she sways to the beat, the torchlight highlighting her every graceful turn.

Unable to resist, I move to her side, stepping behind her and resting my hands lightly on her waist. "Just relax," I say against her ear. "Feel the music—it'll guide you."

She glances back at me, her eyes sparkling with laughter. "Easier said than done."

Within moments, she's moving gracefully, her body aligning with mine, every sway and turn perfectly in time. The warmth of her beneath my hands, the rhythm of the drums, and the electric charge between us make the moment feel surreal.

The drums fall silent, and for a moment, the night holds still before my family erupts in cheers and laughter. My mother stands nearby, smiling proudly as she watches Magnolia, who fits, blending into the celebration.

Magnolia turns to me, her cheeks flushed, her eyes sparkling. And I know this moment is one we'll both hold on to—something bigger than just tonight.

"There's one more dance. The Siva Afi. It's about strength, courage, and honoring tradition. This one's high-energy—a bit more intense."

I glance toward the group of cousins and brothers preparing nearby and turn back to her with a grin. "Don't go anywhere. I've got a surprise for you."

Her brows lift, her smile growing playful. "Should I be nervous?"

"Not at all." I give her a wink before stepping away.

I join the others, slipping into the traditional costume—a lavalava skirt adorned with intricate Samoan patterns and a band tied across my chest. My arms are bare, showcasing the warrior tattoos that weave over my skin and the faint burn scar on my bicep—a mark from when I was learning the Siva Afi. The crowd stirs as we step into the circle of firelight, the murmurs growing louder with anticipation.

As the dance begins, the flames leap to life, the knives glowing as they slice through the air. The drums thunder in a fierce, steady rhythm, their vibrations pulsing through the night. Magnolia's eyes widen, her expression shifting to awe as I twirl the flaming blade, tossing it high and catching it with fluid precision. The heat radiates against my skin, every movement deliberate and controlled.

I spin the fire in tight, sharp arcs, sweeping it low to the ground before launching it skyward again. The flames hiss and crackle, illuminating the captivated faces of the crowd. My body moves in perfect sync with the pounding rhythm, each step and turn honoring the legacy of those who came before me.

The firelight casts long shadows across the sand, their shapes rippling and shifting with each movement. Sweat glistens on my skin, the heat and intensity of the performance demanding everything from me. But I find her face in the crowd—Magnolia, her eyes locked on me, her hands pressed to her chest as if she's holding her breath.

The flames feel alive in my hands, their power coursing through me like a heartbeat, but her gaze is what steadies me. Each toss, each spin, each precise step is for her as much as it's for the tradition that flows through my veins. As the drums reach their crescendo, I throw the blade high one last time, the fire tracing a brilliant arc against the night sky before I catch it with a final, powerful flourish.

My family erupts into cheers, their voices filling the air as the drums fade. My chest heaves as I step out of the firelight, the echoes of the dance still thrumming through me. Magnolia rises, her eyes shining, her smile radiant, and in that moment, nothing else exists but her.

When the final flame dies out, I make my way back to her. She's staring at me, equal parts awe and disbelief. I lift my arm, showing her the faint burn scar on my bicep. "This is where I earned this. Fire knife dancing isn't forgiving when you're learning."

Her smirk grows as she looks me up and down. "Well, that was hot. And so is what you're wearing."

I raise an eyebrow, stepping closer. "How hot?"

She laughs, shaking her head. "Nice try. But I'm not starting something we can't finish—not at your grandparents' house, practicing... what's the word again? Fa..."

"Fa'aaloalo." The word rolls smoothly off my tongue.

Her playful smile widens. "Right. Fa'aaloalo—which means no fooling around."

I chuckle, pulling her close but keeping enough distance to be respectful. "It doesn't mean no fooling around at all. It means no fooling around under their roof."

"Oh, okay, Mr. Technicality." Magnolia's eyes sparkle with mischief. "And here I thought my aerial silk dancing was edgy. But no, you had to upstage me with flaming knives."

I shrug, grinning. "To be fair, the nifo'oti—the blade—is wrapped. It's mostly for show. *Aerial silks*, though—what's that?"

Her face lights up as she explains, her enthusiasm captivating. "It's where you climb long fabric suspended from the ceiling and use it to perform acrobatics—twists, poses, shapes. It's graceful, but it takes a lot of strength and control."

The image of her suspended midair, twisting through silks, holds me captive. "You're telling me I've been missing out on you defying gravity all this time? Now this, I *have* to see."

She laughs softly. "It requires a proper setup—a studio, silks, rigging. I can't just do it anywhere."

I lean in with a mischievous grin. "I'll build you a studio."

Her brow arches, amusement playing at her lips. "Right. And you'll manage that in three weeks?"

The teasing fades as her words hang in the air, and our smiles falter. Three weeks. The dread of it settles between us, unspoken but heavy.

"No, I suppose not," I say quietly, reaching for her hand, intertwining our fingers. "But I would like to make every second count."

Her eyes search mine, her expression softening into something tender. "Every second," she whispers.

And as the firelight dances around us, casting warm shadows on her face, the night stretches endlessly above. In this moment, I'm certain of one thing: I'll make every moment with her matter, no matter how fleeting our time may be.

Chapter 29

Alex Sebring

THE TRAIL WINDS DEEPER INTO THE LUSH FOREST, SUNLIGHT filtering through the canopy in dappled, shifting patterns. The hum of the outside world fades, replaced by the tranquil melody of birdsong and the gentle rustle of leaves in the breeze. The air here is cooler, rich with the earthy scent of rain-kissed soil and tropical blooms.

I brush aside a low-hanging branch and glance back. Magnolia steps over a rocky patch, her eyes wide, her expression caught somewhere between awe and curiosity. She's seeing Samoa through fresh eyes, and I can't get enough of the way it lights her up.

"You doing all right back there?"

Her gaze snaps to mine, a playful challenge sparking in her eyes. "I can handle a hike, Alex. Don't worry about me."

I reach up and pluck a ripe guava from a nearby branch. "Good, because you're about to experience the freshest snack on the island."

She takes the fruit, sinking her teeth into it, and her lips glisten with juice as her eyes close in bliss. "Oh, wow. I didn't know anything could taste this good."

Her reaction holds me captive, the way she savors something so simple. "That's Samoa. Untouched. Pure. Unlike anything else."

Her gaze sweeps over the vibrant green all around us. "It feels like we've stepped into another world."

Reaching for her hand, I lace our fingers together, the connection as natural as the path beneath our feet. "Just wait. You haven't seen the best part yet."

The sound of rushing water grows louder as we follow the path, the foliage thickening around us. Hand in hand, we climb a small ridge, the trail narrowing as anticipation builds with each step.

Magnolia glances at me, her cheeks flushed from the hike, her eyes bright. There's an energy about her that makes me smile without meaning to.

"Almost there." I push aside a curtain of vines, revealing the clearing.

The waterfall cascades over dark rocks into a crystal-clear pool framed by bursts of vibrant tropical flowers. The sunlight catches the water, scattering beams of light across the lush greenery.

Magnolia freezes, wide-eyed. Her gaze sweeps the scene, focusing on the falls, the shimmer of sunlight on the surface, the untouched beauty surrounding us. "This is like a dream. A beautiful dream."

"I knew you'd love it. Not many people know about this place— locals only."

When she turns to me, her expression is soft, her gratitude unmistakable. "Thank you for bringing me here."

I pull my shirt over my head. "Come on. The water's waiting."

"You don't have to tell me twice." Her smirk deepens as she shrugs off her cover-up, revealing a bikini that sends my pulse into overdrive.

"Careful," I say, reaching for her hand. Her fingers slide into mine, warm and steady, trusting me to lead her into the shimmering pool.

The first step makes her gasp, her sharp inhale breaking into a laugh. "Colder than I expected."

I send a splash her way, the water catching sunlight in glittering arcs as it lands.

Her gasp turns into laughter. "Oh, you're in for it now, big guy," she says, sending a wave of cool spray back at me.

The cool water hits my chest, and I throw my hands up. "Truce! You win!"

Her eyes narrow, playful and challenging. "Giving up already? That's disappointing, Alex."

I wade closer, grinning. "I know when I'm outmatched."

The playful energy fades as we drift toward the falls, the mist surrounding us, cool and sparkling. I reach for her hand and pull her close, the quiet between us deepening. She meets my gaze, her face framed by the dappled light breaking through the spray.

Gently, I tuck a wet strand of hair behind her ear, my fingers hovering.

For a moment, the world narrows to this—the sound of the falls, the rhythm of our breathing, the unspoken connection hanging in the air.

"I've never brought a woman here before."

"To this waterfall?"

I shake my head. "To Samoa."

"Not even Celeste?"

"*Especially* not Celeste. This place—my family, my culture—it's who I am, and I didn't want to share it with someone who wouldn't understand." My hand finds hers beneath the water. "Because with you, it's different. I don't have to explain or worry you'll see yourself as above it. You just... get it."

Her fingers tighten around mine, her smile soft and sincere. "Thank you for trusting me with this, Alex. I love being here."

The water flows around us, but all I feel is her hand in mine, steadying me. "We haven't known each other long, but I swear, you know me better than anyone ever has."

Her smile shifts, touched by something deeper. "I see you, Alex—all of you. And I love every part."

I lean in, resting my forehead against hers. Our breaths mingle, the quiet between us thick with unspoken emotion. The world blurs, leaving only the steady rush of the falls and the gentle beat of her pulse beneath my hand.

When my lips meet hers, it's slow and deliberate, a kiss meant to convey everything I can't put into words. It's tender, unhurried—a silent promise. In this moment, nothing else exists. Just her. Just us.

When we pull apart, her eyes hold a softness that stirs something deep in my chest. I smile and swim back, diving beneath the cool water.

Resurfacing, I spot a delicate flower floating nearby. I catch it, returning to her to tuck it behind her ear.

"Perfect." I'm struck by how naturally she fits here, as though this place has been waiting for her all along.

Her fingers graze the flower, her smile bright and unguarded. "I never want to forget this moment."

"Neither do I."

We drift in the water until we both prune. Here, in this hidden oasis, nothing else matters—no expectations, no plans.

We eventually climb out and settle on a blanket near the edge of the pool. I unpack the small picnic I brought and hand her a slice of mango. She takes a bite, her eyes closing as the sweet juice drips on to her lips.

"This is relaxing," I say, watching her. "No phones. No deadlines. Just us."

Magnolia leans into me, resting her head on my shoulder. "Very peaceful."

She glances up, her eyes holding a quiet intensity, like we're both quietly acknowledging the shift between us—something neither of us names but both feel.

We lie back on the blanket, side by side, the sound of the

waterfall filling the stillness around us. My arm slips around her, her head finding its place on my shoulder.

Sunlight dances across the rippling water, and her fingers thread through mine, fitting so naturally it's like they were always meant to. She doesn't say a word, but her touch speaks of everything we're both holding close, everything unspoken.

I glance at our joined hands, my thumb rubbing her knuckles. This isn't just a moment—it's something bigger, something I'll carry with me long after we leave this place.

The steady rhythm of the falls surrounds us as we sit together, letting the quiet stretch. But faint laughter filters through the trees, growing louder with each step. I glance up, already recognizing the unmistakable energy of my siblings and cousins.

She laughs. "Well... so much for our private moment. Looks like the family fa'aaloalo squad is out in full force today. Not a chance at fooling around."

I squeeze her hand lightly. "At least we had a little time before they found us."

The clearing bursts into life as my family arrives. My brothers head straight for the cliff, their eyes lighting up as they size it up, clearly planning their next jump.

Leilani, Sefina, and a few of my female cousins make their way to Magnolia, their laughter bright as they draw her into their group. She glances back at me, smiling, and I watch how she connects with them, already part of their circle.

My brothers launch into their usual antics, daring each other to make the wildest jump, their laughter and banter filling the clearing.

Niko's voice rises above the noise, his grin sharp. "Alex! Don't tell me you're chickening out in front of your girl."

I glance over as Magnolia raises a brow, her smirk amused. "Afraid of heights, are you?"

I shake my head, chuckling. "Afraid? Not a chance. I grew up jumping off this cliff."

My brothers keep up their relentless taunts, their competitive grins making it clear someone's about to do something ridiculous— probably me.

Climbing the rocks with my brothers, I glance back and see Magnolia with my sisters and cousins, their laughter rising above the sound of the falls. Leilani is teaching her how to weave a flower crown from wild blossoms, her hands guiding Magnolia's as she picks up the technique with ease.

From above, I take a moment to watch the way she leans into their laughter, her focus on the delicate folds of the flowers. There's something captivating about how she connects with them, drawing them in, her joy shining through every gesture.

Niko leans in, his expression sure with a knowing glint in his eye. "You're in love with her. Admit it—it's written all over you."

I laugh, crossing my arms in a half-hearted attempt to deflect. "It's too soon to start throwing around words like love." I try to sound convincing, but even I hear the crack in my voice.

Asa's grin deepens. "You might not see it yet, but we do. Bringing her here, sharing this part of your life—it's not nothing, Alex. We're your brothers. We know what this place means. It's a big deal for any of us."

I glance away, my eyes finding Magnolia. She's laughing with Leilani and Sefina, her head tilted back as the sunlight catches the golden strands of her chestnut hair. She looks at ease, fully present in the moment. Something tugs in my chest, and I wonder if my brothers are right.

"I'm taking things as they come."

Niko claps me on the shoulder, his grin a mix of teasing and something more serious. "Sometimes, mate, you're the last one to see what's staring you right in the face."

"And since when are you an expert on love?"

He shrugs, his smirk widening. "I've learned a thing or two. But that's a story for another time."

As their laughter fades, my eyes drift back to Magnolia, and the edges of a realization press in. It's a truth I can't say out loud yet, but it feels unavoidable, like the tide drawing back to the sea.

My brothers go quiet. These rare moments of silence remind me that they know me better than anyone. And as much as I hate to admit it, they're right.

I glance at Magnolia again. She leans into Leilani, whispering something that sets them both laughing, their heads thrown back in easy joy. She isn't simply blending in—she's shining here, adding something to this place I never knew was missing.

The thought crashes into me, undeniable and all-encompassing. This isn't simple attraction or a fleeting connection. It's solid, unshakable.

I've fallen for her.

The realization hits me, both exhilarating and terrifying, spreading through my chest like a steady pulse. Standing here, surrounded by my family in the place that shaped me, there's no denying it.

I love her.

It's a simple truth, but it shifts everything.

I draw in a deep breath, letting it fill every part of me. Watching her now, full of life and light, I know this isn't something I can fight— not that I want to. She's woven into me, into this life, into everything that matters.

No matter what lies ahead, this love is mine to hold. And right now, surrounded by the people and the place that mean everything to me, one thing is clear: she's the one.

Chapter 30

Magnolia Steel

THE MALIETOA FAMILY HOME HUMS WITH LAUGHTER AND SOFT voices, a melody that blends with the natural rhythm of the place. The air carries a comforting warmth, its earthy scent—a mix of dried grass, coconut, and something rich yet unnameable—wrapping around me like an unspoken welcome. It feels like a world apart from anything I've known, yet there's a strange comfort about it.

My gaze sweeps the room until I find Malie seated on the floor. Her hands move with practiced precision, weaving a large mat. When her eyes lift to mine, her smile radiates a warmth that instantly puts me at ease.

"Come join me, Magnolia." She pats the space beside her.

She holds out a bundle of dried leaves, her fingers demonstrating the first steps. "Have you ever woven anything before?"

I laugh as I settle beside her. "Not unless a few lopsided friendship bracelets from middle school count."

Malie chuckles. "That's a start. It just takes patience and practice. You'll get the hang of it."

Her steady confidence draws me in, and I mimic her movements, though my fingers fumble against the unfamiliar material.

Meanwhile, her hands work with quiet grace, each fold and twist deliberate. Slowly, I begin to find a rhythm, my fingers moving a little more confidently.

"This mat is for Sela's wedding next month."

Sela. I've heard her name mentioned a few times—Alex's cousin, vibrant and full of life, if his stories are anything to go by. She's marrying the son of a high-ranking chief, a union steeped in Samoan tradition and significance.

Malie shifts closer, her hands steady as she guides mine. The dried leaves, pliable under her skilled touch, feel awkward in my fumbling grip. She adjusts a piece with the patience of someone who's done this countless times.

"We make these mats for special moments—weddings, funerals, births," she says, her hands never slowing. "They're not just decorations; they carry a piece of the person who made them. A gift of yourself, something that lasts long after the moment has passed."

I follow her hands, mimicking her movements. "A gift of yourself. I like that. Too often, people focus on things that don't matter."

Her smile warms, pride glimmering in her eyes. "It is. And it's something we pass down, teaching each generation how to give of themselves."

Her expression brightens, a playful edge creeping into her words. "My niece, Sela, is a fiery one. Mark my words, her poor husband's going to have his hands full. But she'll be a good wife. This mat will remind her of home and the family that stands behind her."

"From what Alex has told me about Malietoa women, a fiery spirit seems to run in the family."

"Oh, it absolutely does. The men think they're in charge only because we let them believe it. Right, girls?"

Laughter ripples through the women, nodding and shaking their heads with knowing smiles.

There's a quiet strength in the way the women move together—sharing glances, laughter, and unspoken understanding. Their camaraderie feels unshakable, like a bond that transcends words.

I glance down at the mat forming beneath my hands, a small smile tugging at my lips. There's something about the Malietoa women—their fierce independence, balanced with deep roots in family and tradition—that draws me in. I want to learn from them, soak up everything they have to teach.

Malie's hands still, and she stretches her fingers, flexing them as if seeking relief. "What about the women in your family, Magnolia? Do you have that same bond with them?"

My fingers falter for a moment before I recover. "My family is... different."

"Different how?"

I keep my eyes fixed on the weaving, avoiding her gaze, keeping my emotions in check. "I've been in Australia for over two months, and I haven't spoken to my mother once."

Malie's expression clouds with quiet sadness, but she doesn't press.

"My mother's not like you. She's always been more focused on herself and the men in her life. That's how she is." I shrug, forcing a small smile. "But it's okay. I've learned to live with it."

Malie's brow furrows, compassion etched into her expression. "It's not okay, Magnolia. Not by any stretch. But despite it all, you've grown into someone remarkable. That kind of strength is all yours."

Her words settle deep, wrapping around me like a balm. "Thank you."

She smiles, her hands resuming their steady rhythm. "Family comes in all forms. Sometimes, it's the one we're born into, and sometimes, it's the one we choose. You'll always have a place here."

I nod, swallowing against the unexpected lump in my throat. "That means more than I can say."

She pats my hand gently, her smile warm and knowing. "If you ever need a mother's ear, you know where to find me."

It strikes me then how remarkable Malie is. Her grace, the quiet strength rooted in kindness and tradition, radiates in everything she does. She pours so much into her family, shaping them with a love that feels unshakable. Watching her now, I understand where Alex gets his quiet confidence and fierce loyalty. How lucky he is to have grown up with someone like her shaping his world.

I shift my focus back to my mat, determined not to let my thoughts wander too far. But my fingers fumble, and a few loose strands slip out of place. Malie glances over, her soft chuckle breaking the moment.

"Not bad for a palagi."

I pause, glancing up. "What's a palagi?"

Her laugh deepens, humor sparkling in her eyes. "It's what we call foreigners. Outsiders." She reaches over, her practiced hands deftly fixing the strands I'd loosened.

"Good to know I have an official title here."

"Oh, don't worry about being called an outsider, dear. My beloved Alexander is a palagi too."

I bet there's a good story here. "How did you two meet?"

She sets her mat aside, settling in with a storyteller's ease. "Let's just say it wasn't love at first sight—at least not for me."

A playful glint shines in her eyes as she crosses her arms, drawing me into the moment.

"This is a good one, Magnolia. Picture this: I'd just arrived in Australia, full of wide-eyed excitement to see the world. I picked up a job waiting tables at a small restaurant to make ends meet. One night, in walks this serious-looking tall blond man. But here's the twist," she pauses, her voice brimming with mischief, "he was on a date."

My eyes widen, and a grin tugs at my lips. "No way."

"Oh yes," she says, her laughter spilling out. "He was dressed to impress, doing his best to charm this lovely girl. But the moment he saw me? That poor woman didn't stand a chance. He kept sneaking glances every time I walked by. She might as well have been invisible."

I laugh, shaking my head. "Did he manage to get your attention?"

Malie raises a teasing brow. "Oh, I noticed him. But I kept it professional—polite, charming, maybe a smile or two. Still, I felt his eyes on me every single time. When they left, I figured that was the end of it. But wouldn't you know it? He came back and asked for my table."

"Tell me he didn't bring the girl back with him."

Malie waves her hand, her laughter bubbling over. "Oh no. He came back alone after that. Sat there like a lost puppy, ordering everything on the menu as an excuse to keep sitting at my table. Eventually, he worked up the nerve to ask me out."

Her laughter fills the room, and I picture a lovestruck young Mr. Sebring, trying to charm his way into her heart.

I shake my head, grinning. "He must've been thrilled when you said yes."

"Oh, he was. He may be a palagi, but he loved me enough to learn about my culture, to understand what matters to me. That means more than any grand gesture."

Her words settle over me, quiet but full of meaning. "That's really beautiful. Thank you for sharing that."

"Life has a way of surprising us, and love's often one of those surprises. When it's real, you know. But it isn't a fixed thing. It grows. It changes. It's never the same from one year to the next. No one tells you that, but it's true."

Her words take root, quiet but certain. "And you'd know. You've been married... how long now?"

"Thirty-four years. And I'd do it all over again—bumps, bruises, and all."

Malie's smile turns wistful, a warmth in her eyes that speaks of great love. She gives a small sigh, as if lost in a memory, before focusing back on me.

"I can see that you and Alex share something special. Don't overthink it. Love is simpler than we make it out to be." She winks, leaning in. "But don't tell Aleki I said that. Let him sweat a little. It builds character."

I laugh, glancing down at my mat as my fingers continue weaving. "I think he's figuring me out more than I expected."

"Good." Malie pats my hand. "Let him. Don't close yourself off. Life's too short to spend it guarding yourself because you're afraid of being hurt. Love isn't about staying safe—it's about taking the leap, knowing there might be a few bruises, but trusting it'll be worth every scar."

As we near the end of our weaving, Malie reaches over to adjust the corner of my mat, her skilled fingers smoothing the loose strands with ease. "This is good work, palagi."

Pride swells in my chest. "Thank you for teaching me. I really enjoyed this."

"You're a quick learner. And you've got spirit—like us. Don't ever lose that. No matter where life takes you."

Her words carry a depth I can't quite put into words. I look at her, feeling the sincerity of her kindness. She's more than Alex's mother— she's a mentor, someone with the rare ability to recognize the walls I've built and the strength it takes to hold them in place.

I set my finished mat beside hers, the two works lying side by side. Malie meets my gaze, her expression full of understanding and encouragement. In that moment, something shifts—a sense of belonging, not just to this family, but to a part of myself I'm only beginning to discover.

Chapter 31

Magnolia Steel

SOFT MORNING LIGHT STREAMS THROUGH THE WINDOWS, casting the room in a warm, golden hue. Alex's arm is draped around me, his presence a quiet reassurance, steady and familiar. Waking up like this—wrapped in his warmth—feels like a secret I want to hold on to forever.

He stirs, his arm tightening slightly as a sleepy chuckle rumbles from his chest. "Morning, blanket thief."

I laugh, tilting my head to meet his gaze. "Blanket thief? I think you've got that backward. I spent half the night reclaiming my side after you stole the covers."

His lips curve into a slow, easy grin as he brushes a stray lock of hair from my face. "So, you're the victim now, huh?"

"You're built for rugby, and I'm built for... arranging throw pillows. Cover battles are not exactly a level playing field here, big guy." I arch an eyebrow, feigning seriousness. "Rude."

His chuckle is low and soft as his hand lazily traces circles on my back. "Fair."

A comfortable silence settles between us, the memories of our week in Samoa still fresh in my mind. Each one vivid, treasured—a reminder of how deeply we've fallen into this rhythm together.

"I'm still not over the fire-knife dance. Seriously, how did I not know you could do something like that?"

Pride lights his eyes. "Didn't scare you off?"

"Scare me?" I laugh, shaking my head. "Not even close. You were incredible. Honestly, I could barely breathe watching you. I'm still trying to wrap my head around it." My fingers glide along his arm, a playful glint in my eyes. "You know you're going to have to do it again for me, right?"

"Oh, is that so?" he teases, one eyebrow arching. "Just for you?"

"Absolutely. And next time, I'll try not to forget how to breathe."

He brushes a kiss against my forehead. "Just say the word, favorite, and I'll give you a private show."

"Careful. I might take you up on that."

He pulls me closer, the quiet intimacy of the moment settling in. I shake my head lightly, still caught up in the memory of his fire-knife dance. "I'm not sure how anyone could watch you and not be impressed."

"Glad to know I made an impression. But honestly, you impressed my family more. They love you."

A smile tugs at my lips as memories of the past week surface— Malie's warmth, the easy banter of his siblings, the way his cousins welcomed me like I'd always belonged. "I adore them. Your family's incredible. I've never known what it feels like to be part of something like that. It's special, Alex. You're lucky to have them."

His arm tightens around me, his expression soft and full of quiet gratitude. "I know."

Eventually, the morning insists we leave the bed. Reluctantly, we slip from the covers, our bare feet padding across the floor to the bathroom. The shower fills the room with a soft, steamy haze, and we fall into step with one another—exchanging lazy smiles, the occasional laugh, and unhurried touches that make even mundane moments feel special.

Later, we stand side by side at the sink, caught in the quiet rhythm of routine. He brushes his teeth while I comb through my damp hair, the ease of it all settling around us like second nature. Our glances meet in the mirror, a fleeting moment that feels like we've been doing this forever.

He heads to the closet, and I follow, my eyes roaming over the neatly hung shirts. A playful idea sparks, and I can't resist. "How about I pick your suit today?"

"All right. Impress me."

I sift through the shirts, my fingers skimming over the fabrics until I land on a sapphire blue button-down. The vibrant color will make the warm, rich brown of his eyes even more striking and will look incredible against his sun-kissed skin. Holding it up, I turn to him with a grin. "This one. Trust me—instant double takes."

He takes the shirt from me, his smirk softening. "As long as it gets your seal of approval, I'm good."

I reach for a sleek charcoal suit that I'm certain is tailored to fit him with perfection. "This will set it off—clean, classic, and just the right amount of sharp." I pluck a navy silk tie with a subtle sheen, holding it against the shirt. "This pulls it all together. Trust me, you'll look like you walked straight out of a magazine."

He takes the tie from my hand, his gaze bouncing between me and the outfit. "You know, I think I need you around every morning to pick out my clothes."

I smooth a hand over the fabric. "Well, I do have an eye for choosing the perfect textures and colors for decor. It stands to reason that I'd have the skills to choose what drapes you too."

"Yeah. That makes sense."

In the kitchen, Alex hands me a steaming cup of coffee, a playful glint in his eyes. "Your java, my lady."

I accept it with a smile, leaning against the counter as the warmth seeps into my hands. "Thank you, sir. Such chivalry this early in the morning."

He mirrors my stance, leaning casually against the counter beside me. "Always gallant where you're concerned."

I smile over the rim of my coffee, the memory of last night tugging at the corners of my lips. "You were certainly gallant last night."

His smirk deepens. "If by gallant you mean completely at your mercy, then yeah... that's what I was."

A smile tugs at my lips as I take a slow sip of my coffee, letting his words settle. So, we go a week without sex while observing fa'aaloalo at his grandparents', and suddenly he's reduced to a man who's at my beck and call in the bedroom.

Duly noted.

Coffee in hand, we step out into the morning air. Alex opens the car door for me, the quiet gesture something I've come to cherish.

As we settle into the drive, the deep bass of a song I don't recognize fills the car. Curious, I glance at the screen on the G-Wagon's dash. "Luther" by Kendrick Lamar & SZA. The smooth blend of introspective verses and soulful vocals creates a vibe that feels both intimate and powerful. I tap my finger against my coffee cup in time with the beat, letting the music wrap around us like a cocoon.

Alex glances over, catching my small smile. "Finally coming around to my kind of music?"

I laugh softly. "Something like that."

His gaze flickers back to the road. "Told you I have good taste."

"Let's not get carried away."

He lets out a low chuckle, the sound blending with the music. "So, am I lucky enough to steal you away for dinner tonight, or do your coworkers get their turn with you?"

"You had me for an entire week. Did you not get your fill?"

"Of you? Never. I'd spend every second with you if I could."

I can't say that I'll ever get my fill of him either. "All right, what's the pitch? No takeout, no microwave meals—I have standards."

"Perish the thought."

"Consider it perished."

"Fresh, chef-prepared cuisine, just for you. Candlelight, a little wine... and I promise we'll be completely uninterrupted."

I let the silence stretch, tapping my finger to the beat of the song like I'm really considering it, though the curve of my smile gives me away. "Hmm. Candlelight is tempting. But what's the catch?"

"No catch. Just a perfect evening with me."

Any evening with him is perfect. "You know, I don't think I can say no to that."

A slow smile of satisfaction spreads across his face. "I like the way you think."

As we pull up to the office, Alex leans over, catching me by surprise with a soft kiss. There's no rush in it, just the kind of tenderness that makes my heart flutter and my breath catch.

"Have a good day, favorite."

I brush my fingers lightly over his hand, my smile growing. "You too, big guy. See you this evening."

I step into Soul Sync's building, the warmth of Alex's kiss still buzzing through me. My mind drifts back to the car for a moment before Sophie's and Whitney's voices pull me back.

"Well, look who decided to return!" Sophie greets me with a quick hug, her energy as bubbly as ever. "Hope you had a restful week off."

Whitney gives me a once-over, her brow arching as suspicion gleams in her eyes. "We didn't run into you once—not even at the coffee shop. That's so unlike you." She pauses, tilting her head slightly. "And look at you—sun-kissed and glowing. Did you live at the beach this week?"

I pause, a small smile tugging at my lips as flashes of Samoa drift through my mind: walking along golden shores, the rush of waterfalls, Alex teasing me about tan lines as I lounged in the sun.

It wouldn't be a lie to say I spent a lot of time surrounded by sand and water.

Meeting Whitney's curious gaze, I shrug. "I did spend quite a bit of time at the beach."

As I settle into my desk, Elijah's familiar voice slices through the hum of the office, his footsteps purposeful as he heads straight for me. He leans casually against the doorframe, arms crossed, his brows arched in that signature nosy way of his.

"So, where'd you disappear to? Some kind of romantic getaway?"

I glance up, offering him a smooth, practiced smile. "Just a change of scenery and some time to recharge. Nothing too exciting."

Elijah tilts his head, his gaze sharpening, as though trying to read between the lines. "Well, since you're all recharged, why don't you clue me in on the new dating suite? Got any plans yet?"

The afterglow from my time with Alex wraps around me like armor, impenetrable and unyielding. Nothing could sour my mood today—not Elijah's nosiness, not even a full day of deadlines. "I've been back five minutes, Elijah. Give me a second to breathe, and I'm sure I'll conjure something brilliant."

He smirks, clearly unfazed by my response. "Fair enough. But if you need a second pair of eyes—or hands—don't hesitate to call me."

I offer him a polite smile, shaking my head lightly. "Thanks. Just need a little time to get back into the groove."

"This'll be the last one we do together in Sydney. Two weeks, and we're back to Charleston."

His words hit me hard, settling like a stone in my chest. I nod slowly. "The last one in Sydney," I echo softly, almost as if I'm still trying to grasp the reality of it.

"Thank fuck, right?" he says casually and matter-of-fact. "I'm so ready to get out of here. Aren't you?"

I hesitate, the truth catching in my throat and refusing to budge. "I think I could stay forever. I've fallen in love..." I pause, glancing away to collect myself before finishing, "with Australia of course."

Elijah doesn't seem to notice the crack in my voice, but I feel the truth of it deep in my chest. Leaving Sydney—leaving Alex—feels like stepping off a cliff I'm not ready to face.

Elijah's sly smile pulls me back to the present. "I don't know what you could possibly love about this place."

I shrug like it's the most obvious thing in the world. "What's not to love?"

He shakes his head, obviously dissatisfied with my answer, and dives into a string of design details. But his words barely register, blurring under the despair left behind by his earlier statement. Two weeks. Just fourteen days, and I'll be back in Charleston. The life Alex and I have built will be nothing more than a memory.

I clear my throat, forcing myself to focus, and cut Elijah off gently. "I'll take a look at the specs and get started. I just need a little time to work through it."

After a beat, he nods. "Fair enough. Let me know if you need anything."

The day drags on, tasks blending into each other in a dull haze as I go through the motions. My mind refuses to stay on track, drifting constantly to Alex, to the life we've been living here, and the ache of knowing it's all temporary.

By late afternoon, a quiet anticipation starts to bloom. I wonder if Alex will be waiting outside to pick me up or if we'll meet somewhere for dinner.

Just as I glance at the clock, my phone buzzes with a message from him.

> Pick you up at 5:15? Same place I dropped you this morning?

My fingers fly over the screen, the reply coming without a second thought.

> Yes, 5:15 would be great. 😊

> See you then.

Even his simplest messages have a way of brightening the longest days. It amazes me how easily we've fallen into this routine—one that feels so natural.

As the workday winds down, I gather my things and make my

way to the exit, my thoughts already drifting to Alex. There's no message to say he's here yet, but I know he's close. Stepping into the crisp evening air, a small smile tugs at my lips as I imagine what he might have planned for tonight.

Then I see her, and my steps falter.

She stands outside the entrance, impossible to miss. A striking blonde with sharp eyes and a posture that radiates confidence. Everything about her—the impeccable clothes, the cool indifference in her expression—screams power, and it sends a ripple of unease through me.

Her gaze locks on to mine, unwavering, and recognition slams into me like a punch to the gut.

Celeste.

She strides toward me, her expression unreadable but undeniably focused. Every step she takes sharpens the dread pooling in my stomach, but I force myself to stay still, refusing to give her the satisfaction of seeing me falter.

"Who... the... fuck... *are*... you?" she asks, low and icy, each word drawn out like a deliberate threat.

Her surprise arrival throws me for a moment, but I compose myself. Straightening my posture, I lift my chin. "How did you find me here?"

Celeste's lips curve into a slow, calculating smirk. "Oh, I have my ways."

The hair on the back of my neck rises as her sharp gaze sweeps over me, dissecting me as though I'm some kind of puzzle she's determined to solve. "Then why not use those *ways* to figure out *who the fuck* I am?"

Her smile doesn't falter, her confidence unwavering. She doesn't reply, just keeps studying me, her silence heavier than any response. The tension between us hums like a live wire, sharp and unrelenting.

Finally, she turns on her heel, striding away with the same cold, deliberate precision she arrived with, the click of her heels against the pavement echoing long after she's out of sight.

What a bizarre encounter.

I'm rooted in place, my heart racing, a knot of unease tightening in my stomach as I watch her disappear around the corner. The echo of her heels fades, but the chill she left behind remains.

Alex's car pulls up to the curb, the sight of him washing relief over me like a tide. I slip into the passenger seat, closing the door with a shaky exhale. He glances at me, his brow furrowed with concern. "Everything okay?"

I hesitate, glancing over my shoulder as if expecting her to materialize out of thin air. The words feel heavy as I finally meet his gaze. "She knows where I work, Alex."

His expression hardens instantly, his grip tightening on the steering wheel. "Who? What do you mean?"

"Celeste," I whisper, her name slipping out like a ghost. My eyes dart toward the window, half expecting her to be lurking around somewhere.

Alex stiffens, his jaw clenching as his knuckles whiten against the wheel. "Celeste was at Soul Sync?"

I nod, swallowing the lump in my throat. "She didn't say much, but it was enough. If she's watching us... if she even suspects you're a client, she could destroy everything."

His jaw flexes as he processes my words, his gaze fixed ahead. "There's no way she knows I was a client."

"But what if she's digging? What if she's following us?" My voice wavers despite my effort to keep it steady.

Alex reaches over, his fingers wrapping around mine, their warmth steadying me. "Hey." His thumb brushes over my knuckles in circles. "Let's not get ahead of ourselves. She doesn't know about Soul Sync, and there's no reason to think she's pieced anything together."

I take a deep breath, his calm presence easing the turmoil even as the knot in my chest refuses to fully loosen. As he pulls away from the curb, I hold on to his words like a lifeline, trusting—for now—that we'll figure this out.

Alex glances over at me. "I can see how rattled you are. How about we skip going out for dinner tonight? We'll go back to my place. It'll be quieter."

I nod without hesitation. "I'd prefer that."

As the city lights blur past the windows, his hand stays wrapped around mine, steady and reassuring. The shadow of Celeste's presence looms, but with Alex beside me, it feels bearable. Whatever she's planning, I know we'll face it together.

For the first time tonight, that thought loosens the knot in my chest enough to let me breathe.

Chapter 32

Alex Sebring

THE CLOSER WE GET TO THE END, THE TIGHTER THIS UNEASE coils around me, gripping harder with each passing day. But nothing changes the truth: Magnolia is leaving in a week, and I don't know how to let her go.

Hell, I'm not sure I *can* let her go.

My therapist's words play on a loop in my mind, calm and measured, urging me to focus on what I can control. To treasure the time we have left. But logic can't touch the ache in my chest or silence the part of me screaming for her to stay.

Logic isn't enough. I need something more—clarity, perspective. And if anyone can help me find it, it's Jack and Laurelyn. They've faced this same challenge, the kind that tests you, and they came out stronger, together. I've seen their bond firsthand—steady, unshakable, the kind of love that doesn't falter.

The decision is made before doubt can creep in. I grab my phone and scroll to Jack's name.

"Hey, mate. Are you and Laurelyn free tonight? I could use some advice... and maybe a glass of that wine you keep bragging about."

"Absolutely. We'll be here. Come by when you're ready."

I pull up to Jack and Laurelyn's house. Taking a steady breath, I step out of the car and head to the door. Jack is already there, his easy smile tempered by the concern in his eyes as he studies me.

"Alex," he says, gripping my hand in a firm shake before pulling me into a brief hug. Jack's been like an older brother to me for years—steady, unflinching, the person I know I can count on when I need honest advice.

"Hey, mate," I say, managing a small smile.

Laurelyn appears, wrapping me in a gentle hug. "Good to see you, Alex."

"Thanks for letting me come over. I know you've got a lot on your plate, so I really appreciate it."

"You're always welcome here." Laurelyn's gaze moves past me, her brow furrowing slightly. "Where's Magnolia? Isn't she with you?"

I shake my head. "She's having dinner with coworkers tonight."

Laurelyn glances at Jack, their silent exchange quick and seamless—the kind of communication that comes only from years of marriage. Jack gives her a small nod before stepping aside, motioning me in.

"Come in and let's talk about it," Laurelyn says.

They lead me into the living room, and I sink into the chair across from them. For the first time all day, I feel like I can breathe. I'm in good hands with them.

Laurelyn goes first. "Alex, you look like you're carrying the weight of the world on your shoulders. What's going on?"

Am I that easy to read?

The dread presses against my chest, heavy and unrelenting. Admitting it feels like unlocking a door I've been holding shut for too long. But the fear and frustration are too loud to ignore any longer.

"Magnolia's leaving in a week... and I don't know how to handle it. There's a knot in my chest that won't go away, and I'm scared out of my mind that—" I glance between them, my voice faltering. "I don't know how to let her go."

Jack leans forward, cutting straight to the heart of it. "What do you actually feel for her, Alex? Do you love her?"

The question lands like a blow. My chest tightens, and for a moment, I can't breathe. "I do, but it feels too soon."

While the admission is terrifying, it's a relief to finally admit it.

"Alex, love doesn't follow a timeline. When it's real, you don't wait for the perfect moment. You seize it, even if it's messy, even if it's not part of the plan. The best things in life never happen on schedule." Laurelyn's words sink in, but the fear clings. The what-ifs loom large—the risks, the possibility of pushing too hard, too fast. They're not so easy to let go.

Jack clears his throat. "I know how you feel. I've been there. I hesitated with Laurelyn because I thought I had all the time in the world to figure things out. And I almost lost her because of it. If you love Magnolia, don't let fear stop you. Pride and hesitation aren't worth the regret."

Laurelyn studies me as though searching for the answer herself. "What's stopping you? What's holding you back from telling her how you feel?"

"What if it's too much too soon? What if it scares her off?"

Laurelyn immediately fires back. "And what if it's exactly what she's waiting to hear? You can't predict her reaction. But holding back because you're afraid? That's a regret you'll carry far longer than anything you might say wrong."

Her words soften my doubt, but I can't shake the fear in my mind. "What did you say when Jack told you how he felt?"

Her gaze slides to Jack. "It wasn't some perfect declaration. We'd been apart for months by then, and so much had been left unsaid. When he finally told me how he felt, I was elated to hear he'd been miserable without me. It made the time we lost a little easier to forgive."

"I almost lost L because I let my fear take over. Don't make my mistake, Alex. If you feel it, say it. Don't let hesitation cost you what matters most."

Their words settle over me, each one clicking into place like the final pieces of a puzzle I've been struggling to complete. "You're right. I need to tell her."

Laurelyn nods. "Trust yourself, Alex. Trust her. Speak your truth."

I stand, and Jack claps me on the shoulder. "Don't let her be the one that got away. Trust me. You'll regret it."

Their advice echoes in my mind as I head for the door. For the first time, the fear gripping me begins to loosen, replaced by something else. I know what I need to do, and this time, I won't let doubt hold me back.

As I drive away, the city lights blur into streaks of gold and white, distant and unfocused. My thoughts, however, are razor-sharp, honed in on one thing: Magnolia. Anxiety twists in my chest, its familiar pull impossible to ignore, but this time, it's tempered by something stronger—hope. It's faint, fragile even, but it burns steady, pushing me forward.

This decision feels different—solid, unshakable, like a foundation I can trust. I'm done hesitating, done letting fear steal my voice. Magnolia deserves to know how I feel, and I'm ready to tell her.

No matter what happens, I'll face it head-on. Because love isn't about waiting for perfect timing. It's about diving into the unknown, risking everything, and believing that some people, some moments, are worth it all.

On my way to the penthouse.

See you there.

I take a deep breath, my grip firm on the wheel, determination steadying me.

I'm not letting her slip away.

Chapter 33

Magnolia Steel

THE DEEP CRIMSON WINE CATCHES THE SOFT LIGHT AS I SWIRL it in my glass, the dim glow casting gentle shadows across the room. It's the perfect setting—intimate, quiet, and full of unspoken longing. But beneath the calm, there's an ache—a reminder that Alex and I are almost out of time.

Eleven weeks replay in my mind like a cherished melody—the laughter, the stolen moments, the nights that stretched into dawn with stories and confessions. Alex has a way of making the world fade. With him, I've felt seen, understood, and held in a way I never have before.

The ache sharpens, knowing there's only one week left before this chapter ends. Every second feels like it's slipping through my fingers. Tonight, I want to freeze time, to hold on to every smile, every glance, every way he makes me feel like I'm home. Just for tonight, I want to savor it all before it's gone.

The soft hum of the elevator rising pulls me from my thoughts, each passing floor heightening my anticipation. By the time the doors slide open, my pulse is already quickening. I set the glass down, my focus shifting to the sound of his footsteps as they draw closer.

A smile tugs at my lips, unbidden, because he's here. For tonight, he's still mine.

When he steps into the bedroom doorway, the world narrows to just him. His gaze sweeps the room before settling on me. The warmth in his expression softens something deep in my chest, replacing the ache with a quiet certainty. In this moment, it feels like we have everything.

"Wow." His voice dips low, a slow smile spreading across his face. "Stunning doesn't even begin to cover it."

The silky red baby-doll gown drapes over me, every curve visible through the sheer fabric, offering a tantalizing glimpse of the matching G-string beneath—a subtle promise wrapped in bold sensuality.

Before I can respond, he closes the distance between us, his arms wrapping around me with a warmth that steadies my racing heart. His lips find mine, slow and deliberate, a kiss that melts everything else away. The world outside fades, leaving us in the quiet cocoon of his embrace.

When he pulls back, his gaze remains locked on mine, a mix of tenderness and heat. His hands rest lightly at my waist, his eyes tracing over me, leaving no doubt about the effect I have on him. "You look stunning in this."

I lean in enough to feel the warmth of his breath. "I wanted to look beautiful for you tonight."

His expression softens, his gaze wrapping around me like a promise. "You're always beautiful, Magnolia. Lingerie or not."

The sincerity in his words settles over me, momentarily stealing my breath. But then his expression shifts—tender, serious, a quiet intensity replacing the lighthearted rhythm we usually share. His hand finds mine, and he guides me to sit beside him on the edge of the bed.

A prickle of worry surfaces, my thoughts leaping to Celeste and what she might have done.

"Alex." My fingers tighten around his instinctively. "Is something wrong? Has Celeste—"

He lifts a hand to cradle my face, his thumb brushing softly over my cheek. "No. This is about us."

The serious tone in his voice makes my pulse race. I hold my breath, waiting, caught up in his words before they even come.

His gaze locks on to mine, open and unguarded, a vulnerability that sends a pang straight to my heart. "I can't stop thinking about you leaving. And the truth is... I don't know how to let you go, Magnolia. I'm not ready. I don't think I ever will be."

His raw honesty leaves me breathless. His eyes hold a tenderness that narrows the world to the two of us, and I feel my defenses crumbling, the walls I've kept so carefully in place slipping away.

My voice trembles, barely louder than a whisper. "I'm not ready to say goodbye either." The confession feels more profound than I anticipated. But when I meet his gaze, I see the same ache, the same struggle mirrored back at me.

He takes my hand in his, his steady touch reassuring me. "I love you, Magnolia Elizabeth Steel. I'm completely in love with you. Being with you has changed everything for me."

His words fill every corner of my heart. Shock ripples through me, quickly giving way to a rush of joy so profound it nearly takes my breath. But at the edges, a quiet fear lingers. No one has ever loved me like this—completely, without hesitation. It's as if he's seen every part of me, even the ones I've kept hidden, and decided I'm exactly what he wants.

And that terrifies me.

He watches me, his gaze searching, his heart laid bare between us. He's raw and vulnerable, offering me something rare and precious. My pulse races, and I know there's no avoiding this moment. The truth has always been there, waiting for me to acknowledge it, to give it life.

I take a shaky breath. "I love you too."

The words carry every unspoken feeling I've kept inside, every hope and every doubt.

For a moment, the silence between us feels almost sacred, heavy with the power of what we've shared. His eyes soften, his expression a blend of relief and something deeper—something unshakable.

"Don't go. Stay with me. I want more with you. Let's build something real, something lasting. We don't have to say goodbye."

His words surround me, warm and full of promise. For a fleeting moment, I let myself imagine it—staying here, being part of his world, making this love our reality. The vision feels so vivid, so right, that my heart swells with longing.

But the doubts creep in like shadows, pressing against the edges of my thoughts. My life back home—my friends, my independence, everything I've poured myself into—all of it tugs at me, demanding recognition. The thought of giving it up feels like losing a part of myself I'm not ready to let go of.

I draw a shaky breath, my chest tightening as I meet his gaze. The hopeful light in his eyes falters, replaced by a shadow of uncertainty as he senses my hesitation. I love him—deeply, fiercely—but the fear of surrendering everything I've fought so hard to protect refuses to release me.

Unable to bear the intensity of his stare, I glance away, knowing the pain my words will cause. My voice trembles, each word a battle to push out. "I'm not ready, Alex. Not for marriage, not for a future I can't fully see. I love you—truly—but giving up everything I've built back home is terrifying."

The rawness of my confession settles between us, and I see the hurt in his eyes. He doesn't flinch, doesn't look away, even as my words begin to sink in.

My hand finds his, trembling as I try to explain. "You deserve someone who's ready to build that life with you. Someone who can give you everything you want. I don't want to hold you back."

He shakes his head, his grip tightening. "You're not holding me back. You're everything I want. I don't need a perfect plan or promises about the future. I just want you."

I close my eyes, overwhelmed by the depth of his words, my emotions spiraling out of control. "I don't know when—or if—I'll ever be ready for something like marriage. I can't promise what I'm not certain I can give."

He's quiet for a moment, his expression a mixture of sadness and understanding. Then he gently squeezes my hand. "It's okay, Magnolia. We don't have to figure everything out tonight."

There's a warmth in his words that soothes the sharp edges of my fear, and for a fleeting moment, I almost let myself believe we could find a way. But reality presses down, heavy and unrelenting. Guilt twists in my chest, sharp and undeniable, as I summon the courage to say what I know I must.

"Alex." My voice trembles. "I love you more than I can put into words. But I might never be able to give you the life you want and deserve. I can't lead you on, hoping I'll change and suddenly be ready for everything you want. It wouldn't be fair to you."

Tears blur my vision, but I blink them away, forcing myself to press on. "It's going to break my heart to leave you, but it's what I have to do. You deserve someone who's ready to build a life with you without hesitation. I love you too much to hold you back from that."

His jaw tightens, his brow furrowing as my words settle over him. He releases a heavy sigh, his gaze falling to the floor. The pain in his eyes is unmistakable, but there's also a quiet, reluctant acceptance in the way his shoulders drop.

For a long moment, we sit in silence, the unspoken truth hanging heavy between us: we love each other, but love alone isn't always enough.

I sit in the quiet aftermath, aching but resolute. My heart feels impossibly heavy, knowing this week will be our last. Through quiet tears, I reach for his hand, my voice unsteady. "I don't want this to ruin the rest of our time together."

Alex's gaze lifts, the sadness in his eyes tempered by something softer. His fingers curl firmly around mine, his voice steady with quiet resolve. "Then we won't let it. We still have a week together. Let's make every moment count."

Alex's hand rests on the small of my back, his touch firm yet achingly gentle as he draws me closer. Our bodies align naturally, the warmth of him steadying me in the moment. When our lips meet, the kiss is tender and slow, filled with the quiet intensity of everything we feel but can't put into words.

We move with deliberate care, like a delicate dance meant only for us. Each caress feels like a silent vow, each kiss an expression of longing that speaks louder than any declaration. My fingertips trace the sharp lines of his jaw, savoring every familiar contour, while his hands explore me with a reverence that steals my breath.

Alex's lips trail down my neck in a deliberate, tantalizing path, his warm breath sending a cascade of shivers over my skin. When he gently tugs at the strap of my gown, a spark ignites deep within me, growing into an undeniable flame.

Our eyes lock, an unspoken exchange passing between us— vulnerability, passion, and something even deeper.

Piece by piece, we shed the barriers between us, each article of clothing removed with deliberate slowness, savoring the anticipation of what comes next. The brush of bare skin against fingertips feels electric, each caress filled with tenderness.

Alex guides me gently onto the bed, his movements unhurried, his touch steady. His warmth surrounds me as he positions himself between my legs, bracing himself with his strong forearms on either side of my head. Our gazes never waver as our bodies unite in a passionate embrace, becoming one in both heart and soul.

Our bodies entwine, moving in a synchronized rhythm of pure bliss. Every touch ignites a fire within me. As he penetrates deeper, I wrap my legs around him, drawing him nearer. Our breaths become one as our motions intensify, lost in the overwhelming euphoria of lovemaking.

My throat constricts, and a hot flood of tears threatens to spill from my eyes. I tightly shut them, desperately trying to hold back the overwhelming emotions that threaten to engulf me. The heaviness of the moment presses on my chest, making it difficult to even breathe. Despite my efforts, tears escape from the corners of my closed eyes, streaming down and dampening my hair as they fall.

My heart swells with love for Alex. I reach out and cup his face, drawing him close to me. Our eyes connect in a powerful gaze. "I never knew love could be so painful... yet so breathtakingly beautiful," I whisper, pouring my love into him with every word.

"I don't know how to let you go," Alex says, placing a kiss against my lips.

Our bodies intertwine, reveling in the deep connection as he moves in and out of me with an indulgent pace. We savor every touch, every movement, every kiss. Our bodies dance together in flawless harmony, my hips eagerly meeting his as waves of pleasure begin, guided by our all-encompassing love for each other.

A tidal wave of sensation builds, cresting higher and higher until it bursts, radiating through me in waves of tingling warmth. My breath catches, and the words spill out unbidden. "Oh God, I'm coming."

My release unravels him. With a deep, guttural moan, Alex tightens his grip on my hips, his movements becoming more urgent, more raw. One, two, three more thrusts and he finds his release inside of me.

When the storm finally subsides, we collapse into each other, our bodies still tangled, our breaths mingling in the quiet intimacy of the moment. No words are needed; the depth of what we've shared speaks louder than anything we could say. For a moment, time feels frozen though the relentless pull of its march forward haunts the edges of my mind.

A wistful smile tugs at Alex's lips as he pulls me closer, his arms wrapping around me in a way that feels both protective and soothing. The intimacy of this moment, the quiet connection between us, eases the ache of what we both know is coming.

We savor every fleeting second as though it might be our last. A silent understanding passes between us, a shared promise to treasure this love, to hold it close even as the world demands we let go.

As the quiet settles, melancholy remains, but it's softened by something stronger.

Our love.

Chapter 34

Magnolia Steel

THE OFFICE IS UNUSUALLY QUIET, THE TYPICAL HUM OF VOICES and ringing phones replaced by a calming midday stillness. As I sink into my chair, the rare solitude feels like a reprieve—a chance to breathe.

But quiet moments like this come with a cost: they leave room for the thoughts I've been trying to outrun all morning. Only two days remain in Sydney, and the time I've shared with Alex feels like grains of sand slipping through my fingers—no matter how tightly I try to hold on, it's slipping away too quickly. The thought of leaving, of returning to Charleston and pretending this never happened, is a truth I can't bring myself to face.

I need clarity—someone who truly knows me, someone who can help me sort through the mess of emotions I can't seem to untangle on my own.

I pick up my phone, scrolling to Violet's name. Each ring stretches longer than the last, fraying the edges of my resolve. Just as I'm about to hang up, her familiar voice cuts through the line.

"Mags!" Violet's unmistakable Southern drawl wraps around me like a hug. "You caught me just in time—I was about to head out and meet a guy I matched with." Her laugh bubbles through the phone, light and teasing. "Lord help me if he's anything like the last one."

I laugh despite myself, shaking my head. "Meeting up with a stranger? Bold move. Don't you remember how the last time ended?"

Violet's laugh is carefree, brimming with her usual confidence. "Oh please. Like you've got any room to talk, *Miss Charleston-Dating-Julius-Caesar.*"

I can't stop the grin that pulls at my lips. "Touché. But, for the record, my guy's not much of a mystery anymore."

She hums, her amusement clear even through the line. "All right, fair enough. Now spill it, darlin'. What's goin' on with Mr. Bazillionaire?"

I take a deep breath, letting the words tumble out in a rush. "I love Alex so much it scares me. I didn't expect any of this, and now the thought of leaving him feels impossible. I've never felt this way about anyone. He sees me—truly sees me—in ways no other man ever has. But he wants more than I think I'm ready to give. What if I never feel this way again, Vi? What if he's the one, and I walk away?"

"Oh, honey. It sounds like this man has shaken your whole world. And yeah, that's terrifying, but love like that is so rare. It doesn't happen every day." She pauses, her words deliberate. "So let me ask you this, Mags. Are you letting fear run the show? Because it feels like you could be holding back to protect yourself."

Damn if she doesn't know me to my core.

"If this is real—and it sure sounds like it could be—you owe it to yourself to see where it leads."

I swallow hard, Violet's words striking a chord. "But Vi, he wants a life here in Australia— marriage, a family, roots. And I don't know if I'm ready for all of that."

"Magnolia Steel, if anyone can find a way to be both wild *and* rooted, it's you. Just because he's ready for all that doesn't mean he's expecting it from you tomorrow."

"But it wouldn't be fair to lead him on when I don't know if I can ever get there."

"How are you going to know if you don't try?"

"That's going to be hard to pull off with nearly 10,000 miles between us." Talk about redefining long-distance relationships.

"You sound like you've already got one foot out the door, but from where I'm sitting, your heart hasn't budged an inch."

"And my heart won't budge. It'll always be with him wherever he is, no matter the distance between us."

"Come on, Mags. You can't let something this good slip through your fingers because it doesn't fit the picture you painted. If he's worth it—and it sure sounds like he is—you'll figure it out."

A shaky laugh slips out, the tension in my chest easing—just a little. . "I swear, you're too good to me, Vi. I don't know how I'd survive without you."

"Lucky for you, you'll never have to find out. And don't you dare let fear make your choices for you. This is your life, Mags. Make it one you'll look back on with no regrets."

I manage a soft laugh, even as my throat constricts. "Thank you, Violet. Truly. I needed to hear that."

And now I've got a lot to figure out.

"Just don't forget, if you end up miserable because you played it safe and didn't even try, I'll be right here to say, 'I told you so.' But also, I'll be armed with a tub of rocky road ice cream."

A genuine smile tugs at my lips, her words easing some of the ache inside me. "I'd be disappointed if you didn't."

We exchange goodbyes, and as I tuck my phone into my bag, a strange blend of comfort and unease settles over me. Violet's words echo in my mind, simultaneously steadying me and stirring up the storm of emotions I can't escape.

Oh, Alexander Björn Sebring III.

What are you doing to me—making me question everything I thought I knew? My plans, my rules, the neat little boxes I put my life in... you've gone and turned them all upside down, and worse? I don't even know if I want to put them back in their places.

I exhale, shaky and uncertain, and then... movement catches my eye. My stomach drops like a stone.

Celeste is standing there, her expression an enigma, her sharp gaze trained directly on me. Her smile, poison wrapped in politeness, sharpens. "Unfortunate, isn't it? My overhearing your little heart-to-heart about Alex. I'd apologize for eavesdropping, but we both know I'm not sorry."

I lock eyes with her, forcing my nerves to steady. "Your lack of remorse isn't exactly surprising."

Her gaze hardens, and her smug smile deepens, gleaming with satisfaction. "Still, you might want to be more cautious about spilling your heart. You never know who's paying attention."

A prickling unease rises under my skin, the feeling of exposure tightening like a vise around my chest.

Her expression sharpens, her words laced with venom. "What you're doing with Alex? That's called crossing lines. Sleeping with a client is unprofessional and unethical. Honestly, it's disgraceful—taking advantage of him like that."

I know how this game works—there's only one rule: deny everything.

My pulse thunders in my ears, but I inhale deeply, drawing strength from the quiet resolve inside me. Raising my chin, I meet her gaze with a calmness I don't entirely feel. "You're grasping at straws, Celeste. You have no idea what you're talking about."

Her sharp laugh pierces the air, cold and cutting, while her smile drips with triumph. "Oh, but I do. Your little arrangement with Alex? Crossing professional lines, indulging your whims? It's reckless. And it's all about to come crashing down."

Her words dangle in the air, bait disguised as certainty, and my thoughts spiral into overdrive. Celeste is ruthless—she doesn't just play the game; she rewrites the rules to suit her. If there's one thing she excels at, it's exploiting weakness. For all I know, she's recording this, her claws ready to seize on any slip, any word she can distort into a weapon.

The idea knots my stomach, but I force an outward calm. My muscles tense as a sobering truth crystallizes: Celeste isn't fishing for information—she already knows too much. Far more than she should. But how has she pieced this together? And, more importantly, what's her next move?

I maintain a composed facade, forcing calm even as every nerve in my body buzzes with the need to proceed carefully. This isn't just a conversation. It's a high-stakes game, and Celeste is playing for keeps.

A flash of an idea takes hold, and I decide to shift gears, probing for any cracks in her armor. My tone lightens, turning casual, as though the conversation is nothing more than idle banter. "If Alex were a client here—and I'm not saying he was—how exactly would you know? Soul Sync's entire business hinges on discretion. Privacy is the whole point."

My eyes are fixed on her for any sign of a reaction. For the briefest moment, something glimmers in her expression—a slip so fleeting it might've gone unnoticed if I weren't looking for it. Her mask snaps back into place almost instantly, and she arches a brow with an air of calculated indifference. "Maybe I just pay attention. Something you might want to consider doing more often."

Her voice carries the sharp edge of a veiled insult, but I focus on the crack I saw, however brief. It was there—a sign that my words hit closer to home than she intended to let on. She's hiding something, and her deflection only confirms it. Celeste is playing her game well, but now I know where to aim.

Her features smooth into a mask of cold composure, her lips curling into a tight, thin smile. Without a word, she turns and strides away, the sharp click of her heels echoing against the tile with practiced precision.

Shit.

I'm frozen with unanswered questions bouncing around in my head. Lots of them.

Celeste knows something—too much—and the silence she leaves

behind feels deliberate, almost weaponized. The entire exchange only heightens my unease, the tension sharpening every unanswered thought.

Familiar voices echo from the hallway, breaking through the tension like a sudden wake-up call in the dead of night, jolting me back to reality. Sophie, Whitney, and Elijah return from lunch, their laughter spilling into the quiet, disrupting the unease Celeste left behind.

I straighten my posture, willing my expression into something calm, unaffected.

Sophie's smile falters as her gaze sharpens, zeroing in on me. "Hey, you good? You look a little rattled."

I force a half smile. "Oh yeah. I'm fine."

Whitney arches a curious brow. "Maybe you should've joined us for lunch. Looks like you got stuck dealing with Cleopatra this time."

The words make my pulse stutter. "*Cleopatra?*"

Sophie nods, her expression half amused, half exasperated as she gestures toward the lobby. "Yeah, we saw her out front. Not gonna lie, I caught a glimpse and immediately hid behind a plant."

Whitney laughs. "Was she here to stir up more drama because Julius Caesar dumped her?"

The world tilts, their words slamming into me with brutal force, leaving my breath caught in my throat.

Celeste is Cleopatra.

The realization crashes over me like a tidal wave, leaving me reeling. My breath catches as I try to piece together this new reality. Celeste isn't only a jilted ex or a meddler sniffing around for drama—she's Alex's assigned match. The one Soul Sync paired him with. The one who was supposed to capture his attention, his heart.

But how? None of this feels like a coincidence.

She must have orchestrated it. Somehow, she's manipulated the system to her advantage.

A sickening clarity settles over me as the pieces align, each one worse than the last. Celeste's calculated disdain, her veiled threats, her unshakable confidence—it all clicks into place now. She has more than a personal grudge; she's playing a game with the stakes stacked entirely in her favor. And with her insider knowledge of Soul Sync, she's more dangerous than I ever could have anticipated.

Sophie's and Whitney's laughter hums distantly in the background, their casual chatter completely eclipsed by the storm in my mind. How much does Celeste truly know? Has she been plotting all along, or is she simply biding her time, waiting to strike?

And the most terrifying thought... what will this mean for Alex and me?

Chapter 35

Alex Sebring

THE CLOCK ON MY COMPUTER TICKS PAST FIVE, AND I REALIZE I've spent the day shuffling papers, my focus nowhere near my work.

Magnolia and I have only two nights left, and the thought twists painfully in my chest. Each moment feels more fragile than the last, slipping away too fast. But tonight, I'm determined to create a memory she'll carry with her—a night that's ours beyond the ticking clock.

I grab my jacket, taking a deep breath as anticipation mingles with the ache in my chest. The plan is set: tickets to Sydney Opera House. Glamorous, unforgettable—the kind of night I hope she'll think about long after she's gone.

When I get home, she's already there, waiting for me in the living room, a vision of beauty. Her dress fits perfectly, understated yet breathtaking, and her hair cascades over her shoulders in soft waves. The sight of her steals my breath, the ache of how little time we have left sharpening as I take her in.

"Favorite" —a grin tugs at my lips— "you make Sydney look downright ordinary."

Her laugh is light and warm, but her eyes hold a quietness that tugs at me, an unspoken heaviness she hasn't shared. Her smile doesn't quite reach her eyes tonight, and while I chalk it up to our looming goodbye, the feeling clings to me. There's something more beneath the surface.

I press a kiss to her temple, letting my lips linger long enough to savor the warmth of her skin. "I just need a minute to change."

"Take your time. I'll try to remember how to breathe when you come back looking like James Bond."

I chuckle and head to the bedroom, only to find she's already laid out a suit for me—one that perfectly coordinates with her dress.

I'm going to miss that.

Sliding into the jacket, I take a moment to adjust the crisp tie and smooth the lapels, appreciating the sharp lines and perfect fit. It's simple, classic—exactly what tonight needs. A quick glance in the mirror confirms it: I'm ready to make this evening unforgettable with my girl.

When I return, her gaze lifts to meet mine, her eyes sweeping over me with obvious appreciation. "Look at you. Sharp suit, perfect tie—you're definitely giving off Bond vibes."

I offer my arm. "Well then, my lady, shall we?"

She loops her arm through mine. "Lead the way, 007."

"If I'm Bond, does that make you Pussy Galore?"

She smirks, eyes flicking over my suit before meeting my gaze. "I am... and I have a thing for well-dressed men." She steps in closer, her voice dropping slightly. "Though I like them better undressed."

"You're quite a girl, Pussy."

The low rumble of the engine fills the quiet as we ease down the long driveway, the countryside giving way to the twinkle of distant city lights. As we drive toward the opera house, I keep the conversation light, hoping to draw her out of the thoughts that seem to weigh her down.

I cast her a sidelong glance. "You know, there's still time to ditch this plan and head to the Rabbit Hole."

She rolls her eyes, a smirk tugging at her lips. "I can handle a little culture, big guy."

For a moment, the Magnolia I know reemerges—sharp-witted, warm, charming. But as the cityscape comes into view, her gaze shifts to the window, her brow faintly furrowed.

I debate asking her what's on her mind, the question on the tip of my tongue. But I hold back, guessing she's already consumed by thoughts of what's coming—leaving Sydney.

Leaving me.

Still, unease gnaws at the edges of my thoughts. There's more to it than that. I can feel it. I just wish I knew what it was.

The moment we step into the theater, we're enveloped in an ambience that feels timeless and electric. The space is a blend of grandeur and innovation—ornate carvings adorning the walls stand alongside sleek, modern accents, a marriage of old-world elegance and contemporary flair.

Magnolia's eyes roam the theater, studying the intricate details. There's a light in her gaze—a quiet appreciation that makes the moment feel even more special. I nudge her gently, leaning close enough to catch her attention. "I couldn't let you leave without experiencing this at least once."

She turns to me, a playful glint in her eyes. "So, this is part of my grand farewell?"

"Had to prove I'm not all G-Wagons and managing hotel spreadsheets." I lean a little closer. "But don't expect me to translate the opera for you."

Her laugh spills out, soft and unguarded. For a fleeting moment, the rest of the world falls away—it's just her, us, caught in a rare and perfect stillness.

As her laughter fades, something falters in her expression, a tension beneath the surface. It's subtle, but it pulls at me, a quiet reminder that tonight isn't just another evening out—it's one of our last.

As the lights dim further, I lean closer, keeping my voice low. "You've been a little quiet tonight."

Her gaze drops, a thread of hesitation pulling at her composure before she nods. "We'll talk about it later."

There's something unspoken in her words, something she's not ready to unpack, and though I feel the urge to press, I hold back. Instead, I reach for her hand, giving it a reassuring squeeze as the performance begins, letting the moment speak louder than words.

As the lights dim and the first notes of the performance swell through the theater, my focus strays from the stage to Magnolia. Her hand rests lightly on my arm, her fingers tightening enough to tether me to her as the story begins to unfold. I glance at her, catching the wonder in her eyes as she's drawn into the performance, her expression shifting with the rise and fall of the music.

I watch her, captivated by the way her reactions bring the night to life. Her smiles, her gasps, even the subtle lean forward as she's swept deeper into the tale—it all pulls at me. This woman will be gone from my life in two days. The thought pierces through the magic of the moment, a bittersweet ache that refuses to be ignored.

I make a half-hearted attempt to focus on the stage, to let the story pull me in, but my attention keeps drifting back to her. She's all I see, all I feel, a gravity I can't resist.

And then it hits me so sharply it nearly steals my breath.

I love her so much it aches.

The realization is a storm, equal parts exhilarating and terrifying. She's become entwined with every part of me, as vital as the air I breathe, and the enormity of it is both overwhelming and undeniable.

As the final notes fade and the applause swells, the curtains close on a performance that's been nothing short of stunning. My eyes drift back to Magnolia and her expression—soft, awestruck—clutches at something deep inside me.

I'll miss this.

I'll miss her.

We stay in our seats as the crowd begins to thin, reluctant to shatter the fragile spell the evening has cast. When we finally get up and make our way through the grand foyer, the buzz of people talking around us feels distant, inconsequential. It's just the two of us, moving through a world that, for now, belongs only to us.

The crisp night air greets us as we step outside, Sydney sparkling like a postcard come to life. The lights reflect off the water, a kaleidoscope of color and motion, but my attention doesn't focus on the view. Without hesitation, I reach for her hand, and our fingers lace together naturally as if they were always meant to.

The sounds of the city fade into a distant hum as we walk side by side. The cool breeze brushes against us, but the warmth of her presence is all I notice. Every step feels delicate, the moment too precious to disturb, and all I can think about is how to make it last.

I steal a glance at her, catching a hint of something in her expression—a hesitation, a shadow of a thought she doesn't mention. But when our eyes meet, she offers me a soft smile, a quiet shield that hides whatever is churning beneath the surface. "It's a beautiful night."

I give her hand a gentle squeeze, the warmth of her fingers steadying me even as I wish I could unravel the secrets she keeps locked away. "Sydney's pulling out all the stops for you."

Her gaze drifts back to the water, the shimmering lights mirrored on its surface.

"It's still early. Want to hit the Rabbit Hole? For old times' sake?"

Her lips twitch, a small smirk breaking through her pensive mood. "That sounds fun... but I wouldn't mind calling it a night." As the words leave her mouth, she trails her fingers along my arm, her touch light but deliberate, sending a clear signal.

My pulse quickens and every nerve in my body sharpens, attuned to her—her touch, her tone, the unspoken promise in her eyes. It's not just desire; it's the connection between us, magnetic and undeniable.

I nod, keeping her hand firmly in mine as we turn back. It's a silence that speaks volumes, filled with the things neither of us seems ready to put into words.

I give her hand a squeeze. "Stay at my place tonight?"

She looks up, her eyes warming with a playful gleam that momentarily eases the tension between us. "I'd like to see you try and stop me."

Back at the house, we slip into the rhythm that's become second nature. She kicks off her shoes with a soft sigh, and I pour us each a glass of wine. We settle on the couch, the quiet of the room wrapping around us.

Magnolia's fingers trail absently along the stem of her glass, her gaze distant, lost in thoughts she hasn't shared. I wait, giving her the space she seems to need.

"Hey." I reach out and cover her hand with mine. "What's on your mind?"

Her eyes lift to meet mine, a storm of emotions swirling beneath the surface. "There's something I need to tell you. I didn't want to ruin our night, but you need to know."

My chest tightens. "It's okay. You can tell me anything. Whatever it is, we'll handle it together."

She takes a deep breath, the words seeming to cost her as they leave her lips. "Celeste came to Soul Sync again today. It was during lunch, and I stayed back, so I was alone in the office."

The protectiveness surges instantly, my hand tightening around hers. "What did she do?"

"She accused me of crossing lines with a client. She even threw around phrases like *sleeping with a client* and *being unprofessional*. It was as if she knew everything."

My jaw clenches, the anger simmering beneath the surface. "She just walked in during work hours and started making accusations?"

Magnolia nods, her gaze lifting to meet mine, worry in her eyes. "She knew things."

A surge of protectiveness rises within me, unshakable. "What kind of things?"

She hesitates, her breath shaky, her voice trembling enough to cut through me. "Celeste knows you were a client at Soul Sync."

"No... she couldn't know."

"She does, Alex. My coworkers told me she's Cleopatra."

What?

Disbelief and realization collide as I draw my brows together. "Cleopatra?" I echo, the name almost foreign in this new context. "The match Soul Sync set up for me?"

Magnolia nods, her expression mirroring the shock twisting in my chest. "Apparently, yes. Celeste was on the other side of the wall the whole time."

The memories resurface with unsettling clarity as I recall my first meeting with Cleopatra—the cold, detached way she spoke, treating the process more like a strategy session than a genuine search for connection. I remember the clipped tone of her voice, her disinterest in anything personal, and the distinct feeling that I was facing someone entirely unsuited to me, someone who didn't belong in my world.

Something about her voice had nagged at me—familiar yet off, like an echo from a past I couldn't quite place. It lacked warmth and carried a calculated precision as if every word was weighed before it left her lips.

And now it all makes sense—the manipulation, the forced interactions. I'd thought the lack of chemistry was the issue. But no, it was Celeste's nature, her relentless need to control and maneuver everything to her advantage.

Frustration simmers beneath the surface as the pieces refuse to align. "She somehow manipulated the system to match with me."

Magnolia nods, her brow creased in concentration. "How would she even know you applied to Soul Sync? The whole service is built on privacy—clients are anonymous even to most of the staff."

"Exactly." Unease claws at my chest. "Plus, there's no way she could afford the service on her own. Soul Sync charges a fortune. She does well as an influencer, sure, but this is on another level entirely."

Magnolia's lips press into a thin line. "There's more to this. It doesn't feel right."

Whatever Celeste is scheming, it's more than petty jealousy. Her moves are deliberate, calculated, driven by ambition rather than emotion. She doesn't act out of love or simple envy; she thrives on control and manipulating the game to ensure she's always one step ahead.

This isn't about me or Magnolia—it's about power. For Celeste, it's about pulling the strings, watching people dance to her tune. And that makes her not only unpredictable but also dangerous.

Magnolia squeezes my hand, her quiet strength shining through the worry in her eyes. "I didn't want to ruin our night by bringing Celeste into it, but you needed to know."

I draw her close. "You didn't ruin anything, Magnolia. If anyone should be apologizing, it's me. My past shouldn't be coming back to haunt you like this. I hate that she's dragging you into it."

Her shoulders lift with a deep, shaky breath as her gaze drops to our joined hands. "This could turn into a really big problem for me. What if she exposes us to Soul Sync? She knows too much already, and if she's capable of all this—matching with you under false pretenses, stalking us—what's stopping her from going even further?"

Her words are a reminder of how calculated Celeste's moves have been. Anger flares in my chest, a sharp, protective instinct rising. "I'll handle this. Whatever Celeste thinks she's planning, I won't let her jeopardize your job or anything else you've worked so hard for. You have my word."

Her lips press together, the tension in her expression unwavering. "I don't want to lose everything I've worked so hard to build. I've put so much into this."

I reach up, my fingers brushing lightly against her cheek. "You won't lose anything. I promise—I won't let her hurt you or take anything away from you."

My words are more than mere reassurance—they're a quiet vow.

She leans into me, her head finding its place on my shoulder, and

I wrap my arm around her, holding her close. As her warmth rests against me, a quiet certainty takes hold: no matter what Celeste does, no matter how far she goes, I'll protect Magnolia—always.

While I hold her, my mind churns through possibilities, strategies to counter whatever leverage Celeste thinks she has. If she's intent on stirring up trouble, she'll find out I'm not someone to be underestimated.

I close my eyes, anchoring myself in this moment with Magnolia. Her scent, the feel of her resting against me, the quiet reassurance of her trust—it's enough to block out the storm, if only for a little while.

She lifts her head, her gaze meeting mine with soft determination. "Let's go to bed."

No hesitation. I take her hand, the connection between us fierce as she leads me toward the bedroom. There, the unspoken replaces words, every touch a promise, every glance a quiet declaration of what we mean to one another.

As I draw her into my arms, I feel it as clearly as the steady beat of my heart: this love, unwavering and boundless, is worth fighting for.

Chapter 36

Magnolia Steel

THE STILLNESS IS HEAVIER THAN USUAL AS I STIR FROM SLEEP. Reaching out, my hand grazes the cool, empty sheets where Alex should be. The absence of his warmth hits harder than I expect—a sharp, undeniable reminder of what lies ahead. Tomorrow, I'll be an ocean away, and this room, this bed, this life we've built together over these fleeting weeks will slip into the realm of memory.

Where is he?

I sit up slowly, letting the sheet pool around me. My gaze falls on his button-down, draped over the foot of the bed—a soft, rumpled remnant of last night, left behind without a second thought. Reaching for it, I press it to my face. The familiar scent of cedar and something uniquely Alex washes over me, tugging at the edges of my heart.

I slip the shirt on, its oversized fabric engulfing me. The sleeves hang well past my hands, and with each step I take, the soft material brushes against my skin like a whisper of him wrapped around me.

My hand drifts to my chest, pressing lightly against the fluttering ache there. How did it come to this? How did I let him slip past the walls I swore would protect me? This was supposed to be simple—a fleeting escape. But somewhere between his laughter and quiet strength, it became so much more. Now, the thought of leaving feels like tearing away a part of myself.

Light glows faintly under the door, and a low murmur reaches my ears—Alex's voice coming from down the hall.

My steps are quiet as I follow the sound, unease winding through me. Rounding the corner, I hear another voice—that of a woman. Confusion prickles at me, and I pause, straining to make out their words.

"Alex, you're making a mistake."

"Keep it down," he says, frustration tightening his words. "She's asleep, and I don't want her to know you're here."

My breath catches.

Celeste.

My stomach twists in knots, the remnants of sleep chased away by the sharp jolt of unease. Why is she here, in his home, at this time of night? Pressing myself against the wall, I strain to hear, my heart pounding as fragments of their conversation drift toward me.

"Alex." Celeste's voice simmers with intensity as if she's barely holding back. "You're ignoring everything we have, everything that's been right in front of you this whole time. Soul Sync matched us because we belong together. Why can't you see that?"

"You and I are in the past." His response is calm but icy, every word clipped and controlled.

She doesn't let up. "Your relationship with the American is fleeting. What we have is real, Alex. How else would we have been matched?"

Her words spill out, desperate and full of conviction as if she genuinely believes every syllable. And maybe she does.

"Enough," he shouts, his frustration finally breaking through. "What we had ended with that fake pregnancy stunt. No, actually, it was over before that. I'd already decided to end things with you."

There's a pause, the silence heavy, and then her voice cuts through, tight with hurt. "I didn't make the video to hurt you. The positive pregnancy test was to give you a glimpse of how you'd feel if you thought we were going to have a baby together. I did it because I loved you, Alex. I wanted to marry you. I still do. I thought the extra push would help you see that we belong together."

"*Loved me?* You manipulated me at every opportunity. Lied to me. Used me. That's not love."

Her words take on a defensive edge, laced with a plea. "You know I'm not good at expressing emotions and love."

He lets out a bitter laugh, the sound cold and sharp. "That's your excuse? Emotional incompetence doesn't justify manipulation. You don't get to rewrite what happened to suit your narrative."

"People make mistakes." Her trembling words barely hold steady. "I can be what you need if you'll give me another chance."

Alex lets out a low, humorless laugh that slices through the tension like a blade. "That's never going to happen." His words are final, unyielding, leaving no room for any other interpretation.

"You're caught up in a fling with her, but she'll be gone soon. And then you'll have no one but me."

"What I have with Magnolia is not a fling. I love her deeply—more than I've ever loved anyone. She's changed everything for me, Celeste. And even if it were only a fling, it's none of your concern. You need to let this go."

"You'll regret this." Her words are laced with an icy warning. "You'll see."

"I have a lot of regrets, Celeste, but Magnolia will never be one of them."

Her footsteps pause, and for a moment, I think she's leaving. But then she starts in again, shifting to something smug, dripping with venom.

"You know... I wonder how Soul Sync would feel if they knew about your relationship. They might frown upon such unprofessional conduct. Fraternizing with a client isn't very ethical, is it?"

Alex's words come out cold and controlled, each syllable edged with tension. "What are you trying to say?"

"Don't play dumb with me, Alex." Her smugness hardens into

something more cutting. "Imagine the scandal—a staff member breaks up one of their matches and then becomes involved with the client. And not just any client—a rich-as-sin, high-profile one. Soul Sync wouldn't be able to recover from the scandal."

She lets out a quiet laugh, barbed with cruelty. "But even if they did, I would make sure your little girlfriend never works in this industry again. My following is large enough to ensure that if I wanted to, I could ruin her with a few carefully placed words."

"Just go on and say it. What do you want, Celeste?"

She laughs softly, a sound that sends a chill through me. "You're in luck. I'm feeling generous. Two million dollars should be enough to keep my lips sealed. And let's be honest—we both know I could ask for far more, given what you're worth."

My heart sinks. This is it. There's no way Alex would hand over that kind of money for me—not that I'd even want him to. And why should he? This problem is mine.

I swallow hard, the cold wave of reality crashing over me. My career at Soul Sync is over. Celeste will destroy me, dragging my name through the mud until there's nothing left to salvage.

A deep sigh escapes Alex. "Fine. You'll get the money, but only after you sign a legally binding agreement. No reaching out to Soul Sync about Magnolia. No exceptions."

Shock ripples through me, my breath catching. He's going to pay her? I don't want him paying anything because of me—especially to her.

Her laughter cuts through the air, sharp and cruel. "I thought you might at least ask how I knew you were a client. Surely that's a question worth asking, don't you think?"

"I was getting to that. The process is highly confidential. So tell me—how did you find out?"

"Oh... poor... slow... Alex. You really should learn to read your own emails. You never know who might be bought off."

Why would he have someone else reading his emails?

"This is just like you. Taking something personal, something I can't control, and twisting it to your advantage. Manipulation has always been your specialty."

What she's referring to is something Alex hasn't shared with me. And the realization stings—a sharp pang of hurt mixed with disbelief. Why hasn't he trusted me with this?

"I know we weren't truly matched, so tell me—who did you pay off at Soul Sync? How did you manipulate the system? And better yet, how did you afford the service?"

Celeste's laugh returns, cold and soulless. "It wasn't as hard as you might imagine. But I think I'll keep that little secret to myself."

My stomach churns. Whatever she's done, she's woven her way into places she had no right to be. Her smugness, her confidence—it all makes sense now. She's had control over this situation from the start.

My stomach turns as the thought sinks in. *Two million dollars.* The lengths he's willing to go to protect me, to shield me from Celeste's cruelty, are overwhelming. It's too much.

A part of me wants to rush out there, to stop him, to tell him I can't let him make that kind of sacrifice. But I stay rooted to the spot, paralyzed. Guilt and disbelief churn in my mind, leaving me frozen.

Finally, I peel myself away from the wall, each step back to the bedroom feeling heavier than the last. Slipping under the covers, I draw them close, curling into their warmth. This isn't how I wanted this night to feel—tainted by Celeste.

I lie there, clutching his shirt, as if holding on to it might steady the storm inside me. The house falls silent again, save for the faint creak of the floorboards as Alex's footsteps draw closer.

The bed dips slightly as he climbs in beside me, his arm slipping around my waist to pull me close. His warmth seeps into me as he nuzzles into the curve of my neck. "What's this? You know you're supposed to be naked in my bed."

I turn to face him, his features softened by the faint moonlight filtering through the window. My heart stutters, caught between the overwhelming need to cling to this moment and the painful truth of what I overheard.

I take a shaky breath. "Alex... I heard everything."

His eyes widen briefly, but a faint smirk tugs at his lips. "Eavesdropping, are we? You know what they say—nothing good ever comes from eavesdropping."

"You can't pay her. It's too much. I won't let you bear that kind of burden."

His gaze locks on to mine. "I'm doing it to protect you. I have more than enough. No amount is too much if it means keeping you safe."

I swallow hard, his words settling heavily over me, wrapping around my heart like a shield. Yet, a part of me resists, bristling at the idea. "I don't like it when other people try to solve my problems for me. I'm used to standing on my own."

He's silent for a beat, then gently reaches out, taking my face in his hands and brushing his thumb along my cheek. "This isn't *your* problem. It's *our* problem." His words settle over me. "You've carried so much on your own for so long. But you don't have to anymore—not with me."

His words chip away at the defenses I've held on to for years, exposing the cracks I've tried so hard to ignore. I let out a shaky breath, my resolve faltering. "But *two million dollars*, Alex... that's not *help*—it's—"

"I could refuse to give Celeste a cent, let her go through with her threat, let her cost you your job. Then I could give *you* the two million dollars instead, so you wouldn't have to worry about finances. But I know you, Magnolia. You wouldn't take it. You'd never accept that kind of money from me."

"No, I absolutely wouldn't."

"This isn't only about stopping Celeste—it's about protecting what matters. And in case you haven't realized it yet, that's you. It's about honoring who you are and everything you stand for."

I blink back the sting of tears, his words stirring something deep inside me. "I don't want you spending your money on me, Alex. It's two million dollars. It's too much."

He shakes his head, his gaze steady, unyielding. "The cost doesn't matter. I'll pay whatever it takes because I can't stand the thought of you being hurt by someone like her—someone you're dealing with because of me." His hand tilts my chin, his eyes locking on to mine with a quiet intensity that steals my breath. "I love you. And when you love someone, you do whatever it takes to keep them safe."

His words settle over me like a promise, both steady and overwhelming. I reach up, my fingers brushing his cheek. "I don't know how to repay you for this. For any of it. You're doing so much, Alex, and I don't even know if it's right to let you."

The reality of everything he's done—everything he's willing to do—settles over me, bittersweet and overwhelming.

He catches my hand, pressing it gently to his lips, his eyes soft yet unrelenting. "There's nothing to repay. This isn't a transaction, favorite. This is love. This is what it means to stand by someone, no matter what. You don't have to do anything except let me love you."

I swallow the lump forming in my throat, a bittersweet ache blooming in my chest. His unwavering certainty pulls me back from the grip of guilt and doubt. "No one has ever fought for me."

His gaze softens even more, the corner of his mouth lifting in a faint, tender smile. "Maybe that's because no one has ever loved you the way I do."

Tears well in my eyes, blurring my vision as I lean forward, resting my forehead against his. The warmth of his presence, the steady rhythm of his breathing, grounds me amidst my overwhelming emotions. "I love you. I love you so much, Alex."

He pulls me into his arms without hesitation, his hold firm and unyielding, as though he never intends to let me go. I sink against him, feeling the strength and warmth of his embrace, and for a fleeting moment, everything else fades. It's just us—woven together by love, trust, and the raw vulnerability we've finally allowed ourselves to share.

His arms tighten around me, his steady presence enveloping me as I rest my head against his chest. In his embrace, the world feels smaller, safer, as though together we can face anything. His hand glides through my hair in slow, soothing strokes—a silent promise that he's here, that I'm not alone.

I close my eyes, breathing him in, letting his quiet strength seep into the spaces where fear and doubt once lived. The love between us feels both delicate and unbreakable. Yet even as I cling to this moment, a bittersweet ache takes root in my chest—a quiet reminder that soon I'll have to let go.

But not yet.

For now, I stay in his arms, letting his quiet reassurance fill the empty places inside me. We hold each other in the stillness, and as sleep begins to pull me under, gratitude and love settle in my heart, mingling with the ache of our fated goodbye.

Chapter 37

Alex Sebring

THE EARLY MORNING LIGHT FILTERS THROUGH THE DRAPES, casting golden rays over the room. Beside me, Magnolia sleeps peacefully, her breathing slow and steady. I stay still, watching her as if I can capture this moment and keep it forever. The way her hair spills over her shoulder in a messy tumble, the delicate curve of her lashes resting against her cheek—it's a vision I want to hold on to even as the day threatens to take it away.

I wish we could've spent our last night at my place, wrapped up in the comfort of my bed, my space, my world—where I could pretend, even for a little while longer, that she wasn't about to leave. But she needed to stay in the hotel, close to her coworkers, so she could meet them in the lobby when the airport transportation arrives.

Her mostly packed bags sit by the door, a silent reminder of what today means. My chest tightens at the sight.

My steel beauty. That's what she is—strong, resilient, unyielding. But beneath all that strength lies a softness, a quiet warmth she shares sparingly. It's that duality that has completely undone me.

She stirs, her lashes fluttering open, and her gaze meets mine, hazy with the softness of sleep. A drowsy smile tugs at her lips, and my heart clenches. How am I supposed to let her go?

"Good morning." Her voice is still dazed by sleep.

"Morning, my love." My voice is soft, but the emotion behind it feels immense. I brush a strand of hair from her face, needing to touch her, even in the smallest way. "Did you sleep well?"

"Not really." Her hand slips into mine. "Too much on my mind."

I nod, a sigh escaping as I look down at our grasping hands. "I didn't sleep well either. Kept thinking about today... and all the things I should say to make you stay."

Her smile wavers, her gaze dipping briefly before meeting mine again. "Alex—"

We lie there in the stillness, the ache of the day looming between us. Neither of us speaks as if acknowledging what's to come will make it all too real.

Finally, I break the quiet, trying to lighten the mood. "Want breakfast in bed?"

She shakes her head, a faint, bittersweet smile curving her lips. "I'd love that, but I don't have time." Her eyes flick toward the clock on the nightstand. "I need to get up soon to get ready."

Her words are like a chime marking the passing of the last moments we have together. They pull us closer to the goodbye I've been dreading since the day we met.

Magnolia shifts slightly, and looks at me with a quiet sadness I feel down to my bones. "I'm going to miss this—mornings... waking up next to you. I'm going to miss everything."

Her laugh is quiet, shaky, as if trying to mask the emotion behind her words. "I didn't think it would be this hard to leave."

I reach out, my fingers brushing against her skin. "This doesn't have to be goodbye. We can make this work. It could just be a... see you later."

Her smile falters, her gaze dropping to the space between us. "You'll eventually move forward with Soul Sync. The new

Australian crew will find your match... *your wife*, Alex. Staying in touch would only make that harder for both of us."

Her words hit me like a blow, sharp and final. I don't have an answer for her—not one that will make this any easier. All I know is that the thought of her walking out that door today feels unbearable.

My chest is tight. I can't breathe.

"I don't know how to let you go. It's worse than I imagined... so much worse."

Her eyes glisten with unshed tears, and for a moment, she doesn't speak. Then, slowly, she shifts closer, wrapping her arms around me. Her body trembles slightly against mine, and I realize she's crying—silent, shuddering breaths that break through the stillness. I pull her tighter, my bare skin against hers, desperate to hold her together even as I feel like I'm coming apart.

Her forehead presses to mine, her breath warm and uneven. Neither of us speaks, as though words would only ruin this fragile connection. Her fingers clutch at my shoulders, her grip firm and unyielding like she's holding on to something she knows is slipping away.

Finally, she pulls back enough to meet my eyes. "I have to get up." Her words tremble as much as her hands. Maybe more. "The shuttle will be here soon."

I nod, the ache in my chest almost unbearable, but I force myself to let her go. She slips out of bed, her movements slow and deliberate, like every step toward the inevitable is heavier than the last.

I follow her into the bathroom, leaning against the counter as she gets ready. My eyes never leave her, trying to commit every detail to memory. Pulling on my jeans and shirt, I glance at her, wondering how to make the most of these fleeting minutes.

The sharp ring of the phone cuts through the quiet. She glances at me, her eyes filled with sorrow, before turning back to zip her bag.

I answer the call, forcing a calm I don't quite feel. "Yes, hello."

"This is guest services. We'll be up shortly to collect your luggage."

"Thank you."

I set the phone down, the ache in my chest growing heavier.

Magnolia's gaze meets mine, her sadness matching my own. We're running out of time, and it feels like the universe is mocking us, pushing us closer to what we can't avoid.

Lightly coughing, I try to clear the lump in my throat. "I have something for you."

I cross to where my jacket hangs over the chair. From the inside pocket, I pull out a small velvet box. Her brows knit with curiosity, her gaze drops from my face to the box in my hand. She doesn't speak, her eyes searching mine as I step closer and hold it out to her. With a slightly trembling hand, she takes it, her fingers brushing against mine briefly before she opens the lid.

Her lips part, a soft gasp escaping as her eyes land on the delicate necklace inside. Three diamonds glimmer in the light, their placement both simple and striking.

"Each diamond represents one of the months we've had together. The smallest is for the first month, when we were getting to know each other. The second, a little larger, is for the second month, when I was falling in love with you. And the third, the largest—" I pause, meeting her gaze, "is for this last month. Because that's when I knew I loved you."

Her fingers graze the necklace, her touch reverent, as though she's afraid it might vanish if she isn't careful. She looks up at me, her eyes shimmering. "Alex... it's beautiful," she whispers, her voice trembling. "Will you put it on me?"

I nod, taking the necklace from the box. The soft brush of my fingers against her skin as I fasten the clasp sends a jolt of something bittersweet through me. The pendant settles against her collarbone, catching the light just right, looking like it was made especially for her.

Because it was.

She turns toward the mirror, her fingers reaching up to touch the necklace lightly. Her reflection meets mine, her expression full of gratitude and something deeper—something that feels like a promise. "I'll never take it off."

When she turns back to me, her hand still resting over the diamonds, her lips curve into a trembling smile. "Thank you. This means more than I can say."

I cup her face, my thumbs brushing over her cheeks as I hold her gaze. For a moment, we stand there, the world outside fading away. It feels like a piece of me will stay with her, no matter where she goes.

Magnolia wipes at a tear sliding down her cheek, her gaze drifting to the far side of the room. A small, bittersweet smile curves her lips, soft and fleeting. "I have something for you too."

She crosses the room and fetches a neatly wrapped package, its edges precise, the paper smooth. Picking it up, she walks back and places it in my hands, a small laugh escaping her lips. "Don't get too excited—it's not gold or diamonds."

I shift the gift in my hands, its weight solid, as I meet her eyes. "Whatever it is, I'll treasure it because it's from you."

Her smile falters slightly, turning almost shy as she looks down. "Just... promise me you won't open it until after I've gone."

The words twist something deep inside me, but I nod, squeezing her hand gently. "If that's what you want, I'll wait."

The silence stretches between us, heavy with the unspoken. Then she steps closer, wrapping her arms around me, her warmth pressing into the ache already building inside. I pull her in tightly, my arms holding her as though I could shield us both from the inevitability of what's to come.

"I don't know if I can do this. I'm not ready."

Her forehead presses into my chest, her breaths unsteady. "I don't want to go." The tremor in her words lay bare the truth.

"Then don't," I plead, the desperation breaking through, clinging to the hope that maybe she'll stay. "Don't get on that plane. Please."

Her silence fills the space between us, an answer louder than words.

A knock at the door fractures the fragile stillness between us, and

Magnolia's grip tightens, her fingers clutching at my shoulders as though she could hold time itself in place.

I draw in a shaky breath, the ache in my chest growing sharper, heavier. I hold her closer, pressing my forehead gently to hers, desperate to carve out one last moment, one last breath of togetherness.

The knock comes again, more insistent this time—a cruel reminder that the world won't wait for us. A reluctant sigh escapes my lips as I pull back, reluctant to let her go, even though I must.

Summoning every ounce of strength, I force myself to step away and open the door.

"Good morning... *Mr. Sebring?*" The bellhop's polite smile falters slightly when he sees me.

"Come in."

The young man moves with practiced efficiency, collecting bags with a quiet focus. Each bag he lifts feels like a piece of my life being dismantled.

Magnolia stands a breath away, her fingers brushing against mine in a fleeting touch that sends a jolt through me. I glance at her, but her gaze is fixed on the bellhop, her expression calm yet betraying the sadness pooling in her eyes, the unshed tears she's fighting to keep at bay.

I look down at her, searching desperately for the right words—anything to make this easier. My hand trembles as I reach out, brushing a tear from her cheek. "Remember. This isn't goodbye. It's just see you later."

Her gaze meets mine, her eyes shimmering with unshed tears. A fragile smile trembles on her lips. "See you later," she whispers, the words delicate yet unwavering. They hang between us, a thread to cling to as the distance begins to stretch.

She turns to leave, her steps hesitant, then pauses, glancing back over her shoulder. Her eyes meet mine again, the storm of emotions within her spilling into the space between us. "I'm not good at telling people how I feel. There's something in me that's broken when it

comes to that. Or maybe I'm too stubborn to let myself be that open."
She swallows hard, her gaze faltering before lifting again. "But I hope
my gift shows you what I haven't been able to say."

Her words strike deep, raw and honest, each syllable settling
heavily in my chest. She gives me one last look, her eyes pleading for
me to understand everything she can't say. Then, the door closes
behind her with a soft, hollow thud, the sound reverberating like the
final note of a song lingering long after the music fades.

I stand there, frozen, staring at the spot she occupied only
moments ago as though some piece of her still remains in the air. The
silence presses in, thick and unrelenting, amplifying the ache in my
chest until it feels unbearable.

My gaze drifts to the small, neatly wrapped package she left
behind on the table. Trembling, I reach for it, brushing my fingers
over the paper as though touching it might tether me to her. Slowly, I
peel it open, deliberate and careful.

Inside is a journal, soft and weathered. My fingers trace the cover
before I open it, my breath catching at what I find inside. The pages
are filled with her handwriting—small, intimate notes scrawled in the
margins, whimsical doodles, and playlists she'd titled for moments I
hadn't realized she'd marked as special.

Tucked between the pages are photographs—prints of moments
she'd captured on her phone. Her laughter frozen in time, my smile
mirroring hers, snapshots from places we visited, even candid scenes
I'd forgotten. Each page feels like a window into her mind, her heart,
her memories—preserving the life we built together in ways I never
knew she was holding on to.

I flip through slowly, finding entries that begin on her first day in
Sydney before we met, tracing her journey up until now. My thumb
skims the edges of the pages, each one a bittersweet piece of her, a
memory preserved. The deeper I go, the sharper the ache of her
absence, yet the love she's left behind is undeniable, woven into every
detail.

I pause on a page where her handwriting curves softly in the margin, my chest tightening as I struggle to read the words.

Last night at the wedding, when Alex and Tyson had words, I saw something in him I hadn't fully understood before. It wasn't just anger—it was pain, raw and real. When he walked away, I could feel the heaviness of it, like it had settled into my own bones. I wanted to take him into my arms, pull him close, and tell him he didn't have to carry it alone.

That's when I knew. This isn't a passing connection or a fleeting attraction. I love Alex. I love him in a way that makes his pain feel like my own, in a way that makes me want to fight his battles if it means he doesn't have to face them alone.

Reading this journal feels like scaling a mountain, each page a step closer to truly understanding her. I want to know her thoughts, to hold on to the pieces of herself she's entrusted to me. This journal isn't just a gift—it's a part of her. And I vow to read every word, savoring them like threads that connect me to her.

As I close the journal, my fingers caress its cover as though I can still feel her through it. The room feels both achingly full and heartbreakingly empty—alive with echoes of her laughter and the memories she's left, yet hollow without her warmth, her voice, her presence.

The dark skyline stretches endlessly beyond the window, city lights glittering like distant stars. But all I can feel is the space growing between us. My hands clench, resolve hardening within me. This isn't where our story ends—I can feel it in my bones. No distance can erase what we've built, what we've shared.

I set the journal down and take a steadying breath, my gaze fixed on the horizon as if it might offer a glimpse of her. The words leave me quietly, almost a whisper, but they're filled with conviction, steadying me against her absence.

"This isn't goodbye, my steel beauty." My heartache is softened by determination. "It's just see you later."

Magnolia loves me. I feel it in every word she's left unspoken and every moment we've shared. I believe, with all my heart, that the distance will only make her realize how deeply our love goes.

And that's why I can let her go—for now.

Alex and Magnolia's story continues in
American Beauty
Alex and Magnolia Book 2
(The Beauty Series Book 5)

About the Author

Georgia Cates is a New York Times, USA Today, and Wall Street Journal bestselling author—and a former labor and delivery nurse who now delivers swoony love stories instead of babies. A lifelong reader and proud cat wrangler of three, she writes romance with heart, heat, and a dash of Southern charm. Originally from rural Mississippi, she's married to her best friend and is the proud mom of two amazing daughters.

Sign-up for Georgia's newsletter.
Get the latest news, first look at teasers,
and giveaways just for subscribers.

Stay connected with Georgia at:
Facebook, Instagram, and Goodreads

Also by GEORGIA CATES

THE BEAUTY SERIES

Beauty from Pain

Beauty from Surrender

Beauty from Love

The Beauty Series Bundle

Steel Beauty

American Beauty

Beloved Beauty

STANDALONE NOVELS

Waiting for My Queen

Dear Agony

Indulge

Sweet Torment

Standalone Novel Collection Bundle

THE BEACON SERIES

The Soul Always Remembers

The Soul Never Forgets

SOUTHERN GIRLS SERIES

Bohemian Girl

Neighbor Girl

Intern Girl

Southern Girl Series Bundle

BEAUTIFUL ILLUSIONS DUET

Eighty-One Nights

Beautiful Ever After

Beautiful Illusions Duet Bundle

THE SIN TRILOGY

A Necessary Sin

The Next Sin

One Last Sin

The Sin Trilogy Bundle

SIN SERIES STANDALONE NOVELS

Endurance

Unintended

Redemption

Sin Series Standalone Novels Bundle

The Complete Sin Series Bundle

GOING UNDER SERIES

Going Under

Shallow

Going Under Complete Duo Bundle

THE VAMPIRE AGAPE SERIES

Blood of Anteros

Blood Jewel

Blood Doll

The Complete Vampire Agape Series Bundle